DEATH COME QUICKLY

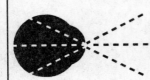

DEATH COME QUICKLY

SUSAN WITTIG ALBERT

THORNDIKE PRESS
A part of Gale, Cengage Learning

 GALE
CENGAGE Learning·

Farmington Hills, Mich • San Francisco • New York • Waterville, Maine
Meriden, Conn • Mason, Ohio • Chicago

GALE
CENGAGE Learning®

LIBRARY OF CONGRESS CATALOGING-IN-PUBLICATION DATA

Albert, Susan Wittig.
    Death come quickly / by Susan Wittig Albert. — Large print edition.
       pages ; cm. — (A China Bayles mystery) (Thorndike Press large print mystery)
    ISBN 978-1-4104-6698-3 (hardcover) — ISBN 1-4104-6698-1 (hardcover)
    1. Women detectives—Fiction. 2. Murder—Investigation—Fiction. 3. Large type books. I. Title.
    PS3551.L2637D44 2014b
    813'.54—dc23   2014005973

Published in 2014 by arrangement with The Berkley Publishing Group, a member of Penguin Group (USA) LLC, a Penguin Random House Company

For Lucia Ferrara Bettler,
always an inspiration

TO THE READER

In our modern day and time, we often think of the plants in our gardens as living things that we admire and tend for our use and for our delight. They feed us, they please us, they enrich our lives and beautify our landscapes. In our worldview, plants are, more or less, creatures that we humans design and manage, on a large or small scale, for our own personal benefit.

But in early human history, when the universe was populated by pantheons of powerful gods and the stars were believed to have a shaping influence on human life, plants were viewed differently. They existed in their own right, separate from humans, and played an active role in an animated, spirit-filled world where everything had meaning and significance. Some plants were of great benefit to humans: they produced food, medicine, fiber, building materials, and more. Some plants offered no apparent

7

benefit: they were distasteful; they were toxic; they had sharp thorns or sticky sap or smelled bad. On a different, more mystical level, each plant had its own particular magic, its own mystical associations. Put simply, as far as humans were concerned, some plants brought good luck; some plants brought bad.

There are plenty of enduring examples of plants that were thought to signify good luck. In China, bamboo (*Bambuseae*) and the jade plant (*Crassula ovata*) both brought good fortune — no household would ever be without one or both. In Hindu cultures, holy basil or tulsi (*Ocimum tenuiflorum*) was a fortunate plant. In Ireland and America, find a four-leaved clover (*Trifolium*) and you'll have good luck.

People in all cultures also feared, and avoided, plants that seemed to bring bad luck: plants that warned of illness, death, or misfortune to come, or plants that actually conveyed misfortune if they weren't used according to the "rules" or with proper respect. The mandrake (*Mandragora officinarum*) is a notorious, and enduring, example. The ancient Jewish historian Josephus (c. 37–c. 100 CE) gives the following instructions for harvesting the magical root:

8

A furrow must be dug around the root until its lower part is exposed, then a dog is tied to it, after which the person tying the dog must get away. The dog then endeavors to follow him, and so easily pulls up the root, but dies suddenly instead of his master. After this the root can be handled without fear.

If you're not willing to sacrifice your dog, forget the mandrake.

While these magical meanings were widely understood and passed down in the oral traditions of their cultures, the botanists who collected "scientific" information about plants in early print books often disregarded information about the magical meanings of plants as mere superstitions, not worth recording. (Mandrake, which caught the attention of magicians and alchemists, is a notable exception.) As cultures were modernized or assimilated, this folk information was often lost.

But not forever. In the middle of the twentieth century, when folklore studies had become an established academic discipline, the study of traditional plant lore became "respectable." Folklorists and ethnobotanists began tramping the woods and fields, collecting old names and old uses for plants and asking local folk what they (and their grandparents and great-grandparents) knew about them. Much of what is now understood about earlier people's interactions with the plant-world in which they lived has been pieced together by passionate amateur and professional botanists, often using the plants' folk names as important clues. These plant detectives have produced important resources, reconnecting us with a time when a comprehensive knowledge of plants, and a firm belief in their relationship with humans, was the best hope for a sustaining harvest and a life well lived. In this book, I've incorporated some of that folk information in the chapter headnotes. I hope it will take you further into a study of these fascinating plants.

An important caution. In every book in the China Bayles series, you will read descriptions of the modern and historic medicinal uses of plants. China and I expect you to consult informed, reliable sources before you use any of these herbs to treat whatever ails you. Many herbs have potent side effects, especially when combined with other herbs or with over-the-counter and prescription drugs. Do your homework. Never use medicines, plant based or otherwise, except with careful, mindful attention.

China and I would not like to lose any of our readers — especially you.

I owe some special debts of thanks. To my friends in the online Story Circle LifeWriters Group, who are infinitely encouraging and helpful. To Peggy Moody, whose patience and skill never fail to amaze me. To Julie Paprock, the winner of the Story Circle cameo character raffle, who took over the reception desk at the Pecan Springs Hospital for an afternoon during the course of China's investigation. To Gianna Martelli, who helped with the Spanish translation. To Natalee Rosenstein and Robin Barletta, at Berkley Prime Crime, always a joy to work with. And to Bill, of course, for everything, always. Thank you all.

Susan Wittig Albert
Bertram, TX

PROLOGUE

The shopping mall was originally built in the 1970s, when Pecan Springs was still hardly more than a small town on the lip of the Balcones Escarpment, at the eastern edge of the Texas Hill Country. But because of its location — on I-35, halfway between Austin and San Antonio — the town hasn't stayed small.

The Hill Country Mall hasn't, either. It has grown, incrementally, until it is now a sprawling regional shopping center with nearly fifteen acres of retail space surrounded by an asphalt parking lot that is surrounded in turn by the hundreds of acres of housing development that have devoured the native prairie. The mall itself is all very contemporary and up-to-date — except for the parking lot lighting system. The mall's customers park their cars in a glittering lake of bright light, of course, whether they are shopping at 10:00 a.m. or 10:00 p.m. The lights promise security and safety, a place where shoppers can come and go with their packages without being afraid, whatever the time of day.

But on the east side of the mall, where the employees are required to park, it's a different story. The initial installation employed sodium lighting that degraded quickly, so that the lights lost 75 percent of their brightness in the first 25 percent of their life cycle. It hasn't been upgraded and is so poorly maintained that at any time, a third of the lights are out of service.

The woman doesn't know that. All she knows is that when she drives into the lot, the whole area is very dark and there are only a few small puddles of pale blue light soaking into the wet asphalt. She parks the car and turns off the engine, then turns it on again, realizing that killing the engine kills the air conditioner. July is just plain hot, even at ten o'clock at night. It rained earlier in the evening and the air is thick and muggy. She makes sure that the doors are locked, then glances around at the scattered cars, wishing she had thought to suggest meeting in the customer parking lot, where there is plenty of light and shoppers coming and going. Or Starbucks or Gino's or one of the crowded campus coffeehouses.

It isn't that she is afraid — she trusts the person she's meeting. As Sharyn said, if there's anybody who knows how to understand the problem and can show them the way out, he's the one. Still, she is just a little nervous about being out here all by herself at this hour of the night. And she wishes she hadn't lied to Felicity in order to get out of the house alone.

But of course this is a very bad business, with many almost frightening implications. She understands the need to talk — to plan, to discuss what to do — without being interrupted or overheard. She understands the urgency, too. The matter has to be settled and the sooner they get out ahead of the situation, the better, especially since it's likely that the documentary is going to rekindle an interest in the Morris collection. Most of her students' work doesn't go beyond the thesis level, but this one — once it has been edited and put together — has a decent chance at national distribution. Which could mean that people will begin looking more critically at the collection, their interest fueled by the sensational facts of Christine Morris' murder.

But the museum board members can't just sit around, twiddling their thumbs and waiting for that to happen. In her opinion, it would be better if they all got together as soon as possible to assess the extent of the damage and the impact on their plans for opening the collection to the public. So far, all she knows is that one piece is compromised and likely others, and that once the truth gets out, there's going to be some serious fallout. The museum was small and private, yes, but it had a great deal of promise, especially with the new exhibitions program they were planning. And it had always enjoyed an excellent reputation. That was at stake now, as were the reputations of the people who'd helped Morris assemble her collection, like the person she's meeting tonight. Yes, they really ought to sit down together, all of them, and hash it out. One-on-one discussion with individual board members would just slow the process. She makes a noise like a chuckle, low in her throat. And this cloak-and-dagger business — meeting in a dimly lit parking lot at ten o'clock at night — well, it's overkill, that's what it is.

She fiddles with the radio dial, tunes it to KMFA in Austin, which plays classical music around the clock. Playing now: a Telemann concerto for oboes and violins. She sits back in the car seat, listening, and thinks again, with sharp and painful regret, about the Izquierdo painting, *Muerte llega pronto,* her favorite of what she had believed — what *everyone* believed — to be an excellent collection, a unique collection, entirely beyond reproach. That painting, with its stark and bloody allegory, had reached into her heart and touched her in a way she simply couldn't describe. It had been painted at a time when Izquierdo herself had actively courted death, after being jilted by her artist-lover, Rufino Tamayo.

It is raining a little harder now. She is vaguely aware of a car driving off and another one pulling up not far away, but she doesn't pay attention. She is leaning back in the seat, listening to Telemann, to the somber, statuesque oboes, and thinking of *Muerte llega pronto,* which always seemed to her to portray the very essence of rejection, the truth of love's betrayal. And now to learn that the painting itself —

Her thoughts are abruptly interrupted by a light rap on the driver's-side window. At first she thinks it's the person she's to meet, but when she turns her head, she is blinded by a beam of blazing light. After a couple of seconds, the light slants down toward the pavement. She blinks, and when her vision returns, she sees a man standing beside the car, wearing a dark raincoat and billed cap,

17

his face obscured in the shadows cast by the flashlight. He has put his right hand on the roof of her car and is bending over to peer through the window at her, no doubt wondering what kind of suspicious activity she is involved in at this hour of the night. A drug deal, maybe? An illicit affair? A terrorist plot, or something equally illegal? He gestures to her to turn off the ignition and get out of the car.

Impatient, she jabs the button and rolls the window down a few inches. "I'm waiting for somebody, Officer." She makes a show of looking at her watch. "He's already late. I'm sure he'll be along in a minute."

"No problem, ma'am." She can't see the man's face, but there's a smile in his voice, friendly, polite. He casts a quick look over his shoulder, then lifts his thumb to point in the direction of the retail buildings. "But we've got a little bit of trouble over there. I need you to get out of your car."

"Trouble?" She frowns. "Well, then, why don't I move the car? I can just as easily park on the other side —"

"I said, get out," the guard repeats, still polite but firm now and not quite so friendly. "No argument, please."

"Oh, all right." With a resigned sigh, she turns off the motor, cutting off Telemann and the air conditioner. She opens the door and gets out. She turns and bends over to get her purse and her umbrella from the seat when, out of the corner of her eye, she sees the man raise his heavy flashlight over his head and bring it down sharply, all of his burly weight behind the blow. She doesn't have time to raise her arm to fend off the attack.

That's all she sees, just the single blow, not the many that follow. All she will ever see, ever know, ever again.

Death does not come quickly. When it finally comes, she is already gone.

CHAPTER ONE

Among plants of ill omen that may be mentioned are the bluebell (*Campanula rotundifolia*), which in certain parts of Scotland was called "The aul' man's bell," and was regarded with a sort of dread, and commonly left unpulled.

In Cumberland, about Cockermouth, the red campion (*Lychnis diurna*) is called "mother-die," and young people believe that if plucked some misfortune will happen to their parents.

The Folk-Lore of Plants, 1889
Thomas F. Thiselton-Dyer

In European folk medicine, *Geranium robertianum* (also known as Herb Robert, death come quickly, stinky Bob, and cranesbill) was used as a remedy for nosebleeds and toothache. The odor of freshly picked, crushed leaves resembles

21

burning rubber and is said to repel mosquitoes. The flower buds were thought to resemble a stork's bill, and this analogical association suggested that the plant might enhance fertility. It was said to bring good luck, but only if it was not carried indoors. To do so invited death.

China Bayles
"Herbs of Good and Ill Omen"
Pecan Springs Enterprise

"Karen Prior was *mugged*?" Startled, I turned away from the front door of my herb shop, where I had just hung up the Closed sign. "Oh, Ruby, that's awful, just awful! When did it happen? Where?"

Ruby stood in the open doorway between our two shops, a deeply troubled look on her freckled face. "Last night, a few minutes after ten, in the parking lot at the mall. She was getting into her car when somebody hit her on the head with something heavy and hard — a tire iron, maybe, or a crowbar. I just heard it from Felicity. She called to tell me why she wouldn't be at our class this evening. She's with her mother at the hospital."

"Sounds like very bad luck," I said. "Wrong place, wrong time. What do the doctors say?" I went around the counter and began closing out the cash register. "Karen will be all right, won't she?"

Karen Prior is a faculty member in the radio-television-film department at Central Texas State University. We met through my husband, Mike McQuaid, who is also on the CTSU faculty, and we've been good friends for several years. Karen is a dedicated teacher and a talented documentary filmmaker whose recent film, *Fakery: The Truth about Art Fraud,* was part of a PBS series. She is an active supporter of the art community in Pecan Springs and served with me on the planning committee for last year's Children's Art-in-the-Park Festival. Her twenty-something daughter, Felicity, is a student in one of Ruby's classes at the Crystal Cave and a part-time garden helper at Thyme and Seasons, my herb shop.

I looked up at Ruby, who hadn't answered. "Karen *will* be all right, won't she?" I repeated. Karen wasn't just a friend. She had volunteered to help Ruby and me build the video-recording setup we now use for our workshops and classes, and she showed us how to create DVDs from the video files so our workshop attendees can view them at home — for which I will be forever grateful. It's not something I could ever do by myself.

"Felicity says she will." Ruby bit her lip. "But you know Felicity, always looking on the bright side. If you ask me, China, the situation sounds pretty grim. There's a brain hemorrhage, apparently. They've done surgery to stop the bleeding, but Karen is in a coma. What makes it so hard is that Felicity offered to go shopping with her last night — it was late, and raining. But Karen said no. She was getting Felicity's birthday present." She shook her head. "Instead, she got attacked."

"I hope the cops get that son of a —" I muttered angrily, pulling the checks and currency out of the register.

If we haven't met already, I suppose I'd better tell you that I'm China Bayles and that Ruby is Ruby Wilcox, the owner of the Crystal Cave, which occupies the other half of my building on Crockett Street in Pecan Springs. In another life (that is, before I cashed in my retirement and bought Thyme and Seasons Herb Shop) I was a criminal defense attorney, white-collar crime, mostly. The large Houston firm I worked with defended big bad guys with lots of money and political connections. We didn't often sully ourselves with common criminals. But when the public defender's office got hit with a budget whammy, some of us in the firm volunteered for pro bono work. I had dealt with people like Karen's attacker — dopers, drifters, desperate for any cash they could beg, borrow, or steal. I have a certain tolerance, even a sympathy for them, since I'm naturally inclined to people who are trying to survive outside the system.

But there's a limit. My stomach knotted as I thought of Karen, energetic, intelligent, dedicated to her students and her work, now in the hospital, in a coma. Between gritted teeth, I added, "When they get the creep, I hope they sock it to him." Aggravated robbery, aggravated assault — first- and second-degree felonies, five to life on the first, two to twenty on the second, and a $10,000 fine on both. And there would likely be additional charges, since muggers were usually on parole or on the lam, with outstanding warrants from a half-dozen jurisdictions. I hoped they would hit the creep with everything in the book.

Ruby leaned against the doorjamb, twisting a curl of carrot-orange hair between her fingers. "Funny thing, though. Well, not *funny,* of course. Odd, I mean. Weird. The guy didn't grab her purse, which was on the seat of her car, in plain sight. Felicity said it looks like he just hit her and took off. Hit her more than once, too."

Well, attempted robbery, then. He probably got interrupted before he could grab her purse and run.

"Witnesses?" I took out my Deposit Only stamp and began stamping the checks, fiercely, as if I were stamping the mugger's face and could disfigure him with one hard whack. "How about surveillance video?" The mall is on I-35, on the east side of Pecan Springs. There had been trouble in that same parking lot a couple of weeks before, and I had read in the *Enterprise* that the mall management was planning to install additional video cameras.

"Felicity didn't say anything about witnesses. Or video." Ruby looked up as the bell over the front door tinkled and the door opened. In my surprise at the news about Karen, I had neglected to lock it. "But we could ask Sheila."

"Ask me what?"

The woman who came into the shop was wearing a trim, sharply creased navy blue cop uniform, a neat navy tie, and a duty belt loaded with a gun, a radio, a flashlight, a baton, and an assortment of additional cop-shop gear. How Sheila Dawson can run with all that stuff slung around her hips is beyond me, but she can definitely do it. I've seen her sprint fifty yards, vault a waist-high stone wall, and bring down a two-hundred-pounder with a flying tackle. She is one tough gal, even when — or maybe *especially* when — she's loaded down with cop gear.

Still, despite her obvious professional qualifications, the first couple of years after she was named chief of the Pecan Springs Police Department were pretty rough. Some of the good old boys had a hard time adjusting to the idea that a woman was in command. But she did what she had to do, the guys got over it (most of them, anyway — there are still a few holdouts), and things are easier now. Not easy, of course. Just easier.

"Ask me what?" Sheila repeated, taking off her cop cap and smoothing back her sleek blond hair. "What could I possibly know that you two don't?"

Next to Sheila I always feel rumpled, disheveled, and dumpy, especially when it's the middle of July, I skipped this morning's shampoo, and I'm wearing jeans and my old green Thyme and Seasons T-shirt. Smart Cookie — Ruby's and my nickname for Sheila — has the impeccably groomed good looks of a Dallas debutante. If you haven't seen her doing her job, you might think she was a candidate for Miss Texas.

Mrs. Texas, rather. Sheila and Blackie

Blackwell, the former sheriff of Adams County, got married last year, after long, uncertain months of back-and-forth, yes and no, then yes and maybe until they finally got to *yes* and *I do.* It wasn't that they didn't love each other. It was the question of whether two cops in the family might be one cop too many. They finally solved it with a coin toss, and Blackie retired from his sheriff's job — gracefully, because he's that kind of guy. A cop's cop. Everybody likes Blackie, although some still aren't too sure about Sheila.

"Ask you whether there were any witnesses to Karen Prior's mugging," I said. "Last night. In the parking lot at the mall."

Pecan Springs isn't a big town, but we're on the I-35 corridor, with Austin forty miles to the north and San Antonio the same distance to the south. The spillover of big-city crime seems to accelerate steadily, as does the drug traffic coming up from Mexico. We don't have that many muggings, but I wasn't sure that the chief would know which case I was talking about. She did.

"No witnesses," Sheila replied, "although a couple of women came along after it happened and called 9-1-1. No surveillance cameras in that part of the lot, either."

"What part of the lot?" I asked.

"She was parked on the east side, where the employees park."

"That's odd," I said. "The employees' lot? Why would she park that far away from —"

At that moment, Khat woke up and jumped down from the windowsill where he had been taking his afternoon nap and began to rub against Sheila's trouser leg, rumbling a deep-throated purr. Khat's full name — Khat K'o Kung — was bestowed upon him by Ruby, who is a great fan of Koko, the talented sleuth of the Cat Who mysteries. Like many Siamese, Khat is arrogant, conceited, and obnoxiously imperial, a cat who is easy to admire but hard to love. Khat, on the other hand, absolutely adores Sheila. When she drops in, he forgets that he is Top Cat, drops his dignity, and behaves like a smitten kitten.

"How *is* Karen?" Ruby put in anxiously. "I just talked to her daughter on the phone, but I'm not sure I got the whole story."

"She's on life support," Sheila replied, bending over to pick up Khat. "The prognosis isn't very good, I'm sorry to say." She rubbed her cheek against his tawny fur, looking from Ruby to me. "Prior is a friend of yours, I take it."

"Yes," I said emphatically, and Ruby added, "Her daughter is one of my astrology students."

Ruby teaches classes in astrology and divination. If that sounds a bit weird — well, that's Ruby Wilcox. A little bit weird, but splendidly so. Today, she was wearing a gauzy orange-and-brown paisley-print Indian-style tunic, orange leggings, and funky orange suede open-toed clogs with three-inch heels. (It's a good thing she's not afraid of heights, since she's already over six feet tall.) Of course, her customers and students don't consider her weird — after all, Ruby's Crystal Cave is a New Age shop, the only one in Pecan Springs. If its proprietor wasn't a little, um, unusual, they would be disappointed.

"I hope you get the creep who attacked her." I spoke fervently. "Any leads?"

"Not yet." Sheila put Khat down on the floor. "We'll do everything we can, of course, but these random muggings are tough. Our best bet is the Crime Hot Line, probably. Prior's ex-husband has already offered a sizable reward, so we're hoping for a tip."

"Ex-husband," Ruby mused. "I don't think I know him."

"Nate Prior," I said. "He lives in Austin, works at the Texas Health Department. He and Karen are still on friendly terms."

Sheila nodded. "The daughter called him early this morning, and he immediately offered to put up the reward. He says he'll go higher if that helps."

I began sorting the credit card slips by the size of the purchase. For a Thursday, sales had been pretty good. "Ruby said the mugger didn't get Karen's purse," I said. "That's strange. You'd think he'd want her credit cards, at least."

"Sounds like an amateur," Ruby remarked. "He whacked her, then looked up and saw somebody coming and got scared and ran off."

"He might have gotten scared," Sheila replied, "but he didn't just whack her once. According to the medical team, he hit her repeatedly, very hard. And he didn't run off — he *drove* off. The employees who called 9-1-1 came along just as he was jumping into his car, obviously in a hurry. But they didn't get the license plate."

Hit her repeatedly. I shivered. "I don't suppose they could ID the car, either."

"Not very specifically, no," Sheila said. "A dark, late-model four-door was the best they could do."

"Late-model four-door?" Ruby asked, wrinkling her nose. "It doesn't sound like the kind of car your everyday, garden-variety mugger would drive."

"My thought, too," Sheila said. "And there's something else, for what it's worth. Prior's daughter told the investigator that her mother received a phone call not long before she left to go to the mall. Felicity got the impression that the call had something to do with a film project that some of her mother's students are working on."

Ruby raised both eyebrows. "Karen went to the mall to *meet* somebody? I thought Felicity said she was shopping for a birthday present."

"That's what she told her daughter," Sheila said. "But Felicity remembered the phone call and thought there might be a connection. We're looking into it from that angle, since — as you say — this doesn't sound like your everyday mugging."

I finished tallying the checks and paper-clipped the calculator tape to the deposit slip. "If you want to know anything about that film Karen's students have been working on," I said, "you can ask Ruby. She's in it."

"No kidding?" Sheila asked in surprise, turning to Ruby. "What role do you play?"

"Myself," Ruby said modestly.

"It's a documentary," I explained. "Ruby is one of the talking heads. She knows the whole brutal story, beginning to end."

"I am an interview subject," Ruby put in quickly. "Talking heads are on TV."

"Whatever." I pulled a blue bank deposit bag out from under the counter.

"Brutal?" Sheila asked. "Brutal, how?"

"It's a documentary about an old crime," Ruby said. "One of my neighbors in the San Jacinto neighborhood was murdered, thirteen or fourteen years ago." She shivered. "She was beaten to death. With a golf club."

"A golf club." Sheila pursed her lips. "What was the victim's name?"

"Christine Morris. Maybe you've heard about her."

"Oh, yes, the Morris case," Sheila said. "We're carrying it in the cold case files, although Bubba swears they charged the right man — somebody named Borden, I think. He was acquitted." Bubba Harris was Sheila's predecessor. He had been chief since Pecan Springs was just a bump on the Texas map, and not a very big one at that. "Of course, it wasn't Bubba's fault," Sheila added with a touch of irony. "He insists that the jury was bamboozled by some slick, highfalutin defense attorney from out of town." She grinned at me. She never misses an opportunity to rub my nose in my former profession. "In any event, Borden walked."

"Bowen, not Borden," Ruby corrected her. "Dick Bowen. He lived next door to Christine. After he was acquitted, he moved to Houston. He's dead now — died a couple of years ago."

"And that slick big-city defense attorney," I put in, "would be Johnnie Carlson." I bent over to hide the fifty dollars in bills and ten dollars in change that I keep overnight under a stack of bags. I always leave the register open. I'd much rather a burglar get away with the cash than destroy the cash register looking for it. "Johnnie's dead, too," I added. "Died several years ago, of a heart attack."

"Bowen's attorney was quite a character," Ruby remarked with interest. "You actually *knew* that guy?"

"For a while, we both worked for the same law firm," I replied. "He and another attorney — both of them renegades — bailed out of the firm a year or two before I did, and opened their own practice. They asked me to go with them, but at the time, I wasn't ready to leave."

Another attorney. That would be Aaron. Aaron Brooks. The thought of him made me smile. I picked up a dust cloth (made by soaking a microfiber cloth in a solution of equal parts vinegar and water, with a dollop of olive oil and a few drops of lemon essential oil) and began wiping the counter, which is the last thing I do every night before I leave. "Johnnie and his partner and I were drinking together one evening, some time after the Bowen trial. He told us the story."

I remember telling Aaron that I wished I'd been at the trial, so I could have watched Johnnie put on his defense. He had mentored me when I tried my first cases and I always learned from him. In the Bowen case, he used the same strategy that the O.J. Simpson dream team had used to squeeze the Juice out of a double murder conviction: basically, convincing the jury that the cops hadn't played by the rules. Unfortunately, that happens all too often. And in the Bowen case, Johnnie claimed that his client was innocent of the murder.

Aaron and I had laughed. "Yeah, Johnnie," I teased, "innocent as a baby, so pure he floats."

Of course, all three of us knew better than that. Sure, there are clients who claim to be totally innocent. But most are totally guilty — and if they're not guilty of the crime they're charged with, they're guilty of something else. (As in, "I did actually cheat on my husband, but I didn't stab the jerk in the heart with my sewing scissors while he was asleep.")

Johnnie answered with a straight — and unusually serious — face, "Not exactly pure, no, which is another part of the story. I had a viable alternative suspect, but I couldn't proceed. The evidence was admissible, but the judge ruled the usual: marginal relevancy, unfair prejudice, confusion of the issues, danger of misleading the jury." He turned down his mouth. "Somebody told me later that the judge and the prosecutor always played poker on Friday nights."

"That's too bad," I said regretfully. "But it's no great surprise."

Regardless of what you might have guessed from watching legal dramas on television, a defense attorney cannot save his client in the courtroom by pulling the real murderer out of his hat at the last moment. Texas, like most other states, operates according to Rule 403 of the Federal Rules of Evidence: "The court may exclude relevant evidence if its probative value is substantially outweighed by a danger of one or more of the following: unfair prejudice, confusing the issues, misleading the jury, undue delay, wasting time, or needlessly presenting cumulative evidence."

Translation: if the defense intends to argue

36

that somebody else committed the crime, the attorney has to present the evidence to the judge before the jury is allowed to hear it. He doesn't have to demonstrate a bulletproof link between the alternative suspect and the crime, but he does have to convince the judge that he is not just guessing, wasting the court's time, gumming up the works, or leading the jury into the wilderness. The attorney can't simply haul witnesses into court and fire questions at them willy-nilly, with the hope of coming up with some clever bit of information that will magically convert speculation into fact, like the miracle of changing water into wine.

And the trial judge has the last word on the matter — until appeal, anyway. He's supposed to recuse himself if he feels that his friendship with one of the opposing counsel (or the royal flush dealt to him by the prosecutor the previous Saturday night) might prejudice his opinion. But most of the time judges don't. They like to think of themselves as impartial as Solomon, which is a pile of horsefeathers, of course. Any defense attorney will tell you that a judge is just a lawyer who's been promoted (via election or appointment) to the bench — and that most trial judges like to be seen as coming down like a ton of bricks on criminals.

Ergo, they tend to favor the prosecution.

"Yeah, too damn bad," Johnnie replied with a shrug. "But I knew we weren't in trouble. The investigating officer was in a hurry to pick on somebody — for his own reasons, of course. And Bowen made the mistake of living right next door. The cops targeted him as their perp without bothering to consider anybody else. But there *was* another suspect, a viable one. Someday I'll show you the notes on my argument in chambers, China, and you'll see why I say that."

"Too bad you didn't pull a Perry Mason," Aaron had said lazily.

I laughed. "Yeah. You could've scored a few extra points for justice."

Johnnie grunted. "Who gives a damn about justice? I didn't need to go to the trouble. The cops zeroed in on the wrong guy when they picked Bowen. He was Pecan Springs' favorite son, a stalwart in the community. He had given money and time to every worthy cause in town. The jury was in his corner start to finish, and the investigators' mistakes gave the jurors more than enough cause for reasonable doubt. I knew Bowen was going to walk, and he did. To hell with justice."

That may sound callous, but it's not.

Finding the real murderer wasn't in John-nie's job description. All he had to do was get his client off. Justice was not his problem.

He downed his drink in one gulp. "But as I say, China, I'll be glad to show you my alternative suspect notes. Maybe someday they'll be relevant. To something or other."

"Hey." Sheila turned back to Ruby. "I'm lost. What's all this about? And what does it have to do with Karen Prior?"

"Karen is a faculty member in Radio-TV-Film at CTSU," Ruby explained. "She's supervising the filming of a documentary about Christine Morris' murder. It's a thesis project for a couple of her graduate students — just about finished now, I understand. And yes, it *was* brutal — the Christine Morris murder, I mean. I was still married to Wade then, and we lived down the street." Wade Wilcox and Ruby have been divorced for as long as I've known her. "I saw the place where she was killed," Ruby added, "and the puddle of dried blood. It didn't get cleaned up for days and days." She shuddered. "The thing about Christine, though —" She stopped.

Sheila waited a moment, then asked, "What about her?"

Ruby sighed. "I hate to speak ill of the

dead. But the truth is that *everybody* spoke ill of her, and while she was still very much alive. She was an out-of-towner — a 'foreigner' from River Oaks — who had an inflated idea of her own importance." River Oaks, deep in the heart of Houston, is one of the wealthiest neighborhoods in Texas. "She came to Pecan Springs and made a career out of making enemies. I'm sure that documentary will be very interesting." She shook her head, frowning. "Gosh. With Karen in the hospital, I wonder what's going to happen to the film. The girls — Kitt and Gretchen — have already put a ton of work into it. I hope they'll be able to finish it."

Sheila started to say something, but her cell phone dinged. She spoke briefly into it, then snapped it shut. "I think I might need to know more about that documentary," she said. She pulled out her notebook. "Kitt and Gretchen? Last names?"

"Kitt Bradley, Gretchen Keene. Kitt is a friend of my daughter, Amy. Both Kitt and Gretchen are grad students in the RTF department. You can reach them there."

"Gretchen Keene?" I repeated, surprised. "I know her. She's Jake's sister." Jake is my son Brian's longtime girlfriend. Gretchen, who was a student in a couple of McQuaid's undergraduate criminology classes, had

40

been to our house several times, either with Jake or with McQuaid's class. I hadn't known she was interested in film.

Sheila wrote down the names and flipped her notebook shut. "I have to get back to the office. How about if I drop in tomorrow and get you to tell me what you know about the situation behind the documentary? It may turn out to have something to do with the attack on Prior. And regardless of what Bubba says, the Morris case is still an open cold case. It might just give us a lead."

"Of course," Ruby said. "I'll be glad to."

"Make it around noon." I put the currency, the checks, the credit card slips, and the calculator tape into the bank deposit bag. "Cass has come up with a couple of new items for the tearoom menu, using roses. You can give us your opinion."

A few years ago, Ruby and I remodeled the back of the building, adding a small but fully equipped and state-licensed commercial kitchen and a tearoom, Thyme for Tea. Cass Wilde does the cooking and Ruby and I and a couple of helpers manage the serving. Cass also does the cooking for our catering service, Party Thyme, and the three of us work together to staff the events — small parties and large. (If you're interested, you'll find brochures on the counters in our

41

shops and on the tables in the tearoom.) Obviously, we are a busy bunch. But you can't have a successful business without keeping busy. It takes a lot of sweat to grow a healthy bottom line.

"Roses? You said roses?" Sheila wrinkled her nose. "Roses are for pretty, not for eating."

"Wrong," I said. "Prepare to be surprised."

"Well, if you're sure." Sheila paused, with a mysterious look. "But I came here with a question and some news, so before I go, I want to tell you. You have to promise to keep it a secret, though."

"Tell us what?" Ruby asked, leaning forward. Her eyes were sparkling. Ruby likes nothing more than having a secret, although she's not very good at keeping them.

"Hey, wait." Sheila lifted a cautioning hand. "First you have to promise not to breathe a word — to anybody."

I zipped the deposit bag shut. "I hope your secret isn't another job, Smart Cookie, because that would mean you'd be moving out of town." I paused, frowning. "But if that were the case, I'm sure I'd know about it already. Blackie would have told McQuaid."

Sheila and I are more than just friends.

42

Her husband and my husband are in business together: McQuaid, Blackwell, and Associates, Private Investigators. Blackie Blackwell and Mike McQuaid. I got used to calling my husband — a former Houston homicide detective — by his last name when we met on a domestic violence case, with both of us on the same side, for a change. Yes, I know. It's dicey to fall for a cop because most of them spell trouble. And because the only thing shared by most female defense lawyers and most male cops is a permanent and reciprocal antagonism. But while I still keep my bar membership current, I am no longer a practicing attorney and McQuaid — although he's still in the investigating business — is no longer a cop. He's a part-time faculty member in the CTSU Criminal Justice Department and a private investigator. And since Blackie signed on last year, their caseload has tripled. They're a good team. They have all the work they can handle, and then some.

"It's not another job," Sheila said. "Well, I suppose it is, but not in the way you're thinking." There was that mysterious look again. "But I won't tell you unless you promise."

"Hey, I know!" Ruby snapped her fingers. "You've decided to buy the house!"

Sheila and Blackie live in an older two-bedroom, two-bath rental home on Hickory Street, on the other side of the alley and just a couple doors down from Ruby's house on Pecan Street. Everyone in the neighborhood likes them and Ruby is hoping that they'll buy the house and stay put.

"Or you're moving out to the country?" I guessed.

Blackie owns a big house with a barn and thirty-five acres not far from where McQuaid and I live. That would be ideal for them. But it's a half-hour drive from town and Sheila's job means that she's on call twenty-four/seven. So Blackie is renting the country house to a friend and keeping the barn and pastures for his horses. He and Sheila drive out there whenever they can get away from their jobs. Sheila has learned to ride, and Rambo — Smart Cookie's Rottweiler, a sworn K-9 officer with his own police badge and bulletproof vest — loves having plenty of open space to run.

"It's not the house," Sheila said. "We're still thinking about buying it, but we think we might need a little more room." Her eyes twinkled. "That's a hint."

"More room, more room." Casting her eyes toward the ceiling, Ruby tapped an orange-painted fingernail against her teeth.

"It's not the job; it's not the house. How about a new hobby? Something that takes up a lot of space. Photography, maybe? Or quilting? But when would you have time for —" She stopped. "Help me out here, China."

Now, this was more than a little funny, because Ruby is a highly intuitive person who — when she puts her mind to it — can read other people's minds. In fact, she could go into the fortune-telling business and very likely make a fortune for herself. She inherited this gift from her grandmother, but she has learned how to dial it down, and she leaves it in the off position whenever possible. I admire her restraint. It's one thing to do birth chart readings and teach classes in the I Ching and runes and other methods of looking into the future. It's quite another to invade a friend's privacy by reading her thoughts, as if she were an open book. I'm glad Ruby keeps that gift of hers under wraps most of the time — like right now.

"I hate guessing games," I grumbled, getting my shoulder bag out from under the counter. "If somebody thinks I need to know something, she should just come straight out and tell me." I reached for the wildest, wackiest thing I could think of. "But okay, I'll bite. How about you're

45

pregnant? Is that it?"

Sheila stared at me. "How did you guess, China? Do I . . ." She looked down at her trim waist. "I can't be showing yet." Her usually calm voice rose — and broke. "Don't tell me I'm . . . *showing*!"

CHAPTER TWO

Purslane (*Portulaca oleracea*) is a small annual succulent with smooth, flat leaves and yellow flowers. In the United States, it's considered a weed, but elsewhere in the world, it is eaten as a salad or leafy vegetable. Purslane is high in omega-3 fatty acids and rich in vitamins and minerals. It may be stir-fried, braised, steamed, or served raw. In Mexico, it is called *verdalagos* and is often used as an ingredient in salsas and taco fillings.

In ancient Greece, purslane was thought to attract good fortune. If you found a patch of it, you would be happy. As a medicinal, it was taken internally to treat colds, stomachaches, and fevers, and used topically to treat hemorrhoids and wounds. It can cause uterine contractions, however, and was once used as an early-term abortifacient. Pregnant women should avoid it.

China Bayles
"Herbs of Good and Ill Omen"
Pecan Springs Enterprise

"Pregnant?" Ruby gasped. "Sheila, you're . . . *pregnant?*" And then, arms windmilling, she rushed to engulf Sheila in a huge hug.

"Hey, careful!" I cried as Sheila took a step backward, falling against a rack of handmade cards and other paper items. "Watch it!"

But it was too late. Papers were flying everywhere. The rack went over. As it fell, it knocked down a wooden shelf that held a display of dried herb and flower arrangements, sending them in all directions. Behind the shelf, on the wall, a dried-flower wreath swung from side to side, then slid down to the floor with a thump.

There was a silence, then a long, angry yowl. Khat crawled out of the rubble, streaked across the floor, and disappeared into Ruby's shop.

"Oh, dear," Ruby said, aghast. "Did . . . did I do all that?"

"Yes," I said.

"No." Sheila was sitting on the floor, a half-dozen dried sunflowers in her lap. She

48

picked a leaf out of her mouth. "I did."

"Oh, Sheila!" Ruby cried. "I'm sorry! I'm such a klutz!" She bent over, brushing bits of dried stems and flowers off of Sheila's shoulders. "I didn't . . . I didn't *hurt* you, did I? Oh, Sheila, forgive me! Please forgive me! The baby —"

"No, you didn't hurt me," Sheila said, scrambling to her feet. "Or the baby. But we've made a mess of China's beautiful displays." She bent over and started to pick up cards. "We're going to need a broom. There are dried twigs all over the floor."

"You are *pregnant!*" I cried. "Stop that, Smart Cookie! Ruby, take those cards away from her." I pushed the stool around from behind the counter. "Sit down, Sheila. *Now!*"

Ruby took the cards out of Sheila's hands. "Is there anything I can say besides I'm sorry?" she asked plaintively. "I am really, really, really sorry."

"You can say you won't do it again," I said. "Sheila, sit *down.*"

"I don't need to sit down," Sheila protested, laughing. "Stop fussing, China. I am not some little Victorian lady. Rambo and I ran three miles this morning, and then I did fifty push-ups."

"Fifty push-ups." I rolled my eyes. "*Fifty*

push-ups. Your kid is going to be an Olympic champion."

"Wouldn't hurt my feelings," Sheila said. "Blackie's, either." She set the card rack on its feet again. "Anyway, you can stop trying to baby me. I am perfectly healthy. I'm just a little pregnant, that's all. Happens to lots of women."

"There is no such thing as a *little* pregnant," Ruby said severely. "You either are or you're not."

"Ruby's right," I said. "It's all or nothing. No in-between."

"How would *you* know, China?" Sheila asked, and I subsided. Yes, I am a mother. And yes, I have two kids, two wonderful kids. But no, I've never been pregnant.

"Well, *I* know," Ruby said. "Been there, done that. Twice. And you are not 'lots' of women, Smart Cookie. You are a female police chief." She frowned down at Sheila's belted trousers, trim as always. "How far along are you, anyway? Three weeks? Four?"

"Eight or nine," Sheila replied. She picked up the wreath and hung it back on the wall.

"Eight or nine? Why, that's two months!" Ruby cried. "It's July now. Two months means that we'll have a baby by —" She began counting on her fingers. "By February! By Valentine's Day!"

"Sounds about right," Sheila agreed. She eyed me. "But I do have a question for you, China."

"Ask *me*," Ruby said. "China's never been pregnant. What does she know?"

"She knows about herbs," Sheila retorted. She turned to me. "What can I use for morning sickness?"

"Oh, poor you!" Ruby exclaimed. "That's misery."

"Bad, huh?" I asked sympathetically.

"It's not good. But the really bad thing is that it's a giveaway." Sheila made a face. "I don't want the boys at the PSPD figuring out that I'm pregnant. Not until I've broken the news to the mayor and the city council. I really want to keep my job, you know."

"You do?" Ruby asked doubtfully. "You mean, you still intend to —"

"Of course I do," Sheila said, frowning. "Why wouldn't I?" She turned back to me. "Do you have any suggestions?"

"Ginger," I said promptly. "Go over to Cavette's Market and ask Mr. Cavette for three or four pieces — hands, they're called — of fresh gingerroot. They're in the produce section. Slice off five or six thin slices, and boil them in a couple of cups of water for about ten minutes. You can add some lime, if you like, and honey. And for emer-

51

gencies —" I stepped to a nearby shelf and took down a couple of small bottles. "Here are some capsules. Keep these in your purse." From another shelf, I took a box of tea bags. "Peppermint tea is good, too. You can brew it in your regular mug and sip it at your desk and nobody will be the wiser." I put the bottles and the box in a paper bag and handed it to her. "On the house. Just for our favorite preggie police chief. Run out of these and I'll fix you up with more."

"Thanks, China," Sheila said gratefully. "I knew I could count on you." She glanced at both of us. "And you promised, remember? You're not going to tell a soul."

"Did we promise?" I gave Ruby an innocent look. "I remember something being said about a promise, but I don't actually remember uttering that word myself. I —"

"Shut up, China," Ruby said firmly. "Yes, we promise. Of course we promise. Every woman has a right to keep her pregnancy to herself. If something goes wrong, then she doesn't have to make explanations. But nothing is going to go wrong," she added hastily. She paused, frowning. "Blackie knows, doesn't he?"

"I told him last week," Sheila said.

"He must be thrilled," Ruby said. "When will we know whether it's a boy or a girl?"

52

"In another few weeks," Sheila said. "And of course Blackie's thrilled. We both are. But . . ." Her voice trailed off and she bit her lip.

"Yes," I said, understanding. *"But."*

Ruby frowned, puzzled. "But what?"

"Just . . . but." I looked at Sheila. "It wasn't planned?"

"Well . . ." Sheila gave a little shrug. "Not exactly. Of course we've talked about it. Both of us have always said we wanted kids someday." She hesitated. "It's just that . . . right now, well, it's tricky."

"So what are you going to do?" I asked.

"Do?" Ruby repeated indignantly. "Why, she's going to have a baby. That's what makes the world go 'round, you know. People fall in love and have sex and then they get pregnant and then they —"

"And then they have to fit the baby into their lives," I said. "How's that going to work for you, Smart Cookie?"

Of course, both Sheila and I know that there's no law that says you can't be a cop and a mom-to-be at the same time. In fact, under the federal Pregnancy Discrimination Act (Title VII of the 1964 Civil Rights Act), employers are required to treat pregnancy in the same way that they treat other health conditions that affect employees' ability to work. The PDA was designed to ensure that women can participate equally in the workforce, without denying them the right to a full family life. It requires employers to treat pregnant women as well — or as poorly — as it treats other employees with health-related issues. But being Top Cop in Pecan Springs and being a mom might be a whole lot harder than Sheila thinks.

"We'll figure it out," Sheila replied, raising her chin with a determined look. "Blackie's telling McQuaid this afternoon. It may have an impact on their situation, too."

May have an impact? Of course it would have an impact. I had to smile at the thought of Blackie doing surveillance with a year-old child buckled into the car seat, or researching online while he gave his baby a bottle. We could give him a new title. Mr. Mom, Private Detective.

Ruby stamped one orange-suede clog. "I do *not* understand this, girls. We are going to have a baby, and all you can talk about are details, details, *details.*"

"Ruby," I said patiently, "Sheila is the chief of a small-town police department in the middle of Texas. If there have been other pregnant police chiefs in this state, I haven't met them. Or heard of them. Or read about them. We are sailing in uncharted waters here."

"Exactly." Sheila picked her cop hat up off the floor. "There's my pregnancy and my job. After the baby is born, there'll be our baby, my job, and Blackie's job, which sometimes requires him to be out of town for a week or more at a time. I'm sure we'll work it out." She sighed. "But first, I've got to review the police department's policy on pregnancy. And the municipal policy, as well."

"Which — I'm guessing — is not too liberal," I said. Pecan Springs is a nice little town and I love living here. But this is Texas, after all, and the city council has never been celebrated for its progressive leadership.

"You got it." Sheila made a face. "I meant to do it earlier — before this happened to one of my female officers. Now that I'm the one who is having a baby, it's awkward. And it's not like there are a couple dozen pregnant female police chiefs I can call up and ask for advice."

"Oh. Oh, yes, I see." Ruby cleared her throat. "Well," she ventured, "there's Frances McDormand. In *Fargo*."

"Yeah, right, Ruby," I said ironically. "A pregnant chief of police — in the *movies*. Somehow I don't think a fictional character could offer Smart Cookie a lot of advice."

Sheila nodded. "I'm very happy about it, actually, when I'm not throwing up. We didn't plan this baby, but now that it's on the way, I'm glad. Most of the time." Her smile was crooked. "Not when I think about the chief's job, though. And not when I remember that Blackie left his job so I could keep mine."

That was the deal they'd made. Given the high divorce rate among police officers, not to mention the double risk of disability and death, they had decided to be a one-cop couple. Blackie gave up the job that had been in his family for decades, while Sheila kept hers. Now, confronted with the impending reality of motherhood, Sheila might be forgiven for wishing the decision had gone the other way.

I felt a twinge — envy, was it? Or even, just possibly, jealousy. Or (if I was being honest) just plain wistfulness. One of my two best friends in the world was having a baby. I wasn't. I had decided long ago that I was not cut out for motherhood, but that was before McQuaid came into my life, bringing his son, Brian, as well. And then Caitlin, my brother's daughter. I now had two of the best children in the world, and I was a mother — but not really.

Sheila's pager began to chirp. She took it off her belt, looked at it, and put it back, suddenly all cop, all business. "I really *have* to get back to the office." She glanced around at the wreckage. "I'm sorry about this mess. You won't mind if I leave you with it?"

"Not in the slightest," Ruby said. "We'll take care of it." She raised her voice as Sheila put on her hat and went out the door, carrying the bag of emergency anti–morning sickness supplies I had given her. "See you tomorrow for lunch."

"Got it," Sheila said without turning around. "But tell Cass that she can forget the roses, as far as I'm concerned."

"Caitlin," I called. I put the big yellow Fiesta ware serving dish in the middle of the kitchen table.

Thursday nights, we usually have a skillet supper. Tonight we were having zucchini out of the garden (where there is much too much of it), with chicken, rotini, and roasted garlic, mozzarella, and Parmesan cheese. "Time to set the table for supper."

Upstairs, Caitlin stopped in the middle of her third rendition of "Clair de lune," her summer violin recital piece. A moment later, light footsteps clattered on the stairs.

Twelve-year-old Caitlin joined our family two years ago. Biologically speaking, she's my niece, my brother Miles' daughter — my half brother, actually, but that's a whole other story. Tragically, she lost both of her parents before she was eleven. She's my daughter, now, and McQuaid's.

Caitie is small for her age and fragile looking, with pixie-cut dark hair and large dark eyes, not as sad as they used to be, I'm glad to say. That's partly because McQuaid, Brian, and I have taken her into our hearts, helping her to feel loved and secure. But it's also due to her violin, her chickens (known familiarly as "the girls"), and her scruffy orange alley cat, Pumpkin.

My mother, Leatha, gave Caitlin the violin I scorned when I was her age, and she immediately fell in love with it. She's studying with Sandra Trevor, who teaches strings at CTSU and says that Caitie has a fine talent. "I'm not sure I'd call her a prodigy," Sandra told McQuaid and me when she suggested that Caitlin enter the Young Classical Artists Competition sponsored by the university. "But she is certainly exceptional. I'm sure she'll do well."

She did, placing at the top of her age group. McQuaid and I do what we can to encourage our daughter's remarkable musical talent — and to make sure that she leads a normal life, in spite of it. Which is where the cat and the chickens come in.

"Hey, Mom." Caitie bounced into the kitchen, followed by Pumpkin, who had already squandered eight of his nine lives in riotous living before he showed up on our doorstep and announced that he had arrived and would someone please warm up a saucer of milk because he had come a long way and he hadn't happened on anything much to eat in the last hundred miles or so. Oh, and a bed would be rather nice, too, thank you very much.

"How about a sweet, fluffy kitty instead?" I'd asked, when Caitie begged to adopt him. But the scruffy, down-at-the-heels tomcat had already clawed his way into her heart.

"He's just like me when I first came to live here," she'd said, clutching him in her arms. "He doesn't have any family. He needs somebody to adopt him. He needs *me*." The cat, knowing a very good deal when it bumped into him, had powered up his pussycat purr, unpacked his bags, and moved right in.

Pumpkin and Caitlin's girls are the only resident creatures at our house these days, except for a few of Brian's fugitive lizards, the ones who were absent on safari under the refrigerator or in the laundry hamper and hence could not be located when he decided to release their friends and relations back into the wild. I don't miss the lizards and I cheered (under my breath, of course) when Brian sold his tarantula, Ivanova, to another arachnid collector.

"I'm sorry, but I can't take you to college with me," he'd explained to Ivanova as he packed her up, with her terrarium habitat and hides and toys. "And if I asked Dad and Mom to take care of you, they might let you get loose." I shuddered at the thought.

But all of us do miss dear old Howard Cosell, McQuaid's ancient basset. Howard went to the happy hunting grounds a few months ago, after a brief illness. He was well loved and deeply mourned. But he'd had a long life and a happy one, especially since we moved to the country. True to his inner basset, he loved chasing rabbits and squirrels. He never caught one, of course: they were much too speedy for him. But he once managed to corner an armadillo against the stone fence and took a bite. McQuaid and I still laugh when we remember Howard's surprise and disgust when he actually got a taste of the creature. There's probably another dog in our future, but we miss dear

Howard too much to think about that just yet.

Caitlin went to the table, leaned over to peer into the casserole dish, then looked up at me in pretended alarm. "Mom, that's not —"

"No, of course it isn't," I said, going to the fridge. "You don't think I would do such a thing, do you?"

"Just checking," Caitlin said cheerfully and threw me a dimpled grin. Her girls — three white hens and three red hens — live in the palatial plywood edifice that McQuaid and Brian erected in the backyard. The girls proved to be astonishingly productive, once they got the hang of it. They deliver an average of five eggs a day, seven days a week, forty-plus weeks of the year. Caitie (who bought her chickens out of her babysitting money) sells some of her eggs to us and the rest to our neighbors, bringing in enough to cover the cost of chicken feed and retire the debt they accrued in the months before they started laying. She says she is thinking of doubling her flock in the fall, with the idea of using the money for a new full-size violin. Leatha has offered to buy the violin for her, but Caitie, who is an entrepreneur at heart, wants to earn the money herself.

I pulled the salad fixings out of the fridge:

purslane from the sunny corner of the backyard; and from the garden, some Malabar spinach, a few green onions, a handful of cherry tomatoes, and two cucumbers. I feel virtuous when I feed the family at least one dish that we grow ourselves. And even more virtuous when one of the greens is a weed. (That is, a plant with a bad reputation.)

"Jake's coming for supper," I told Caitlin. "Her parents aren't back from their field trip yet. So set the table for five, please."

Jake is Jacqueline Keene, Brian's girlfriend and — coincidentally — the sister of one of the documentary filmmakers that Ruby had mentioned to Sheila. Dr. Keene, the girls' father, is on the anthropology faculty at CTSU. He and their mother, Annie, a high school teacher, were supervising a group of students doing a dig in the remote jungles of Belize and wouldn't be back for another week or so. Jake is a great kid, and she and Brian have been going together so long, and so comfortably, that McQuaid and I view her almost as a member of the family. There's a certain danger in this, I suppose, but all we can do is trust to the good judgment and common sense of both kids. McQuaid has made sure that Brian knows and respects the facts of life, and Annie tells me that she's had the Conversation with Jake. Teen sex is not a subject that any of us take lightly.

Things will change in a big way at the end of the summer, though. Brian has been accepted at the University of Texas at Austin. Jake, who decided that she would rather attend a smaller, more familiar school, will be at CTSU. Both their worlds will widen out to include new ideas, new places, new people. By this time next year, they may find themselves going in very different directions.

Caitie got the silverware out of the drawer. "Guess what," she said.

I hate "guess what," which always strikes me as a not-so-subtle one-up. When an adult pulls it on me, I never bite. But this was Caitie, and she's special. I played along, frowning, pretending to think.

"Well, how about this? Pumpkin chased a desperately hungry coyote away from your chicken coop, while the girls cowered in the corner, quaking with fear." Pumpkin is perfectly capable of this. He is one fierce cat. And we do have coyotes — not to mention bobcats, and mountain lions.

"A good guess but wrong." Caitie giggled. "Guess again."

I pressed a forefinger against my forehead,

frowning, pretending to think very hard. "You won four gold Reading Circle stars at the library, which is twice as much as anybody else." Actually, I knew this for a fact, because Jenni Long, the children's librarian, had stopped at the shop to tell me. The kids get a gold star for every five books they read this summer. At twenty and counting, Caitlin was far ahead of the pack.

"How did you know that?" Caitie exclaimed.

"A fairy whispered it in my ear," I said. "She also said, 'Tell Caitie that's quite an achievement.' "

Caitie giggled, that sweet little-girl giggle that always goes straight to my heart. "Thank you. But it wasn't what I was thinking. You have to *guess.*"

I gave her a quick hug. "That's for the gold stars. But that's it for me, I'm afraid. I've totally run out of ideas. What is it I'm supposed to guess?"

"Mrs. Banner is going to have a baby." She began laying out the silverware on the table. "She said so when I took her my eggs."

"That is totally wonderful," I said enthusiastically, reaching for the salad bowl, which lives on the second shelf in the cupboard. The Banners are our neighbors up the lane.

Sylvia raises sheep and sells their fleece, online, to spinners and weavers. Tom does oil and gas consulting and builds birdhouses for a hobby. They're a nice couple, in their late thirties and married only a couple of years. This will be a first child for both. "A boy or girl or do they know yet?"

"A boy. They're going to name him Thomas, after his daddy. Mrs. Banner says I can come and help her take care of him, but he will be too little for me to babysit — at least for quite a while." There was a brief silence. "Mrs. Banner is kind of old for babies, isn't she?" Caitie asked. "I mean, she's got gray hair. Not as much as you have," she added thoughtfully, eyeing the gray streak in my brown hair. "But some."

"Gray doesn't mean ancient," I said defensively. "And older women do have babies." Was this a teachable moment? "In fact," I added, "you can conceive a baby right up to the time your periods stop." We had discussed periods several times recently, and while Caitlin is still maybe a year away from the big day, her supplies are already stashed in her bottom dresser drawer. I believe in being prepared.

"I read about that in a book I got at the library," Caitlin informed me. She put her head on one side, her dark eyes serious and intent. "Have *your* periods stopped, Mom? Could *we* have a baby?"

Talk about teachable moments. I was considering how best to reply to this when the screen door banged and I was saved from saying anything at all. Brian barged into the kitchen, followed by Jake. Brian — dark haired, blue eyed, remarkably like his dad — towers over me now. When he comes into the room, it feels crowded. Jake is tall, too, thin and cute and lively, with steady gray eyes and a bouncy blond ponytail. She isn't quite as tall as Brian, but almost. And they're both athletic: Brian lettered in baseball, and Jake played basketball and trombone in the Panthers marching band. All-American kids. There are moments when I would like to stop the clock and tear up the calendar and keep them both — and Caitie, too — just as they are, forever young, sweet, and innocent, before sex and all that jazz. Thank goodness that's not in my power.

"Ah, chicken for supper," Brian said, with an approving glance into the casserole on the table. His voice is past the squeaky stage now, and reliably deep. "Hey, Cait. Have you counted your girls lately? I was out there a few minutes ago, and I only saw five. Three white ones and two —"

"You lie!" Caitlin shrilled furiously. But she banged down the silverware on the table and sprinted through the door, nearly smacking into McQuaid, coming up the back steps.

"Whoa, there," McQuaid cautioned. "Watch it, kid, or you'll end up on your nose."

"I gotta go count my girls!" Caitie cried and rushed down the steps.

Jake smacked Brian on the arm. "Brian McQuaid, that was *so* mean. You go out there right now and apologize to your sister."

"Ditto that, Brian," I said sternly, tearing the Malabar spinach into the large bowl that already held the washed purslane leaves. Teachable moment or not, I was glad to be off the hook, at least for now. "You know how Caitie feels about those chickens."

Jake picked up the silverware and began to arrange it beside the plates. "Go, Brian," she commanded.

"You're ganging up on me," Brian protested, scowling.

"You got it!" Jake and I said together, and Brian went.

"We need to keep this girl around," McQuaid said to me, slipping an arm around my waist as I stood at the counter, mixing the greens. "She manages that boy better than we do." He kissed the back of my neck, then headed for the fridge.

I shivered. McQuaid is a big man, six feet, one-ninety-plus, with the broad, muscled shoulders of an ex–college quarterback who is still in very good shape. Even after years of sleeping with him, some of them blessed by matrimony, my body is still very much aware of his body. It's an awareness that often feels almost electrical, as though the voltage just got tweaked up a notch or two.

McQuaid opened the refrigerator door. "Jake, how much would you charge to keep Brian in line?"

"Sometimes the magic works; sometimes it doesn't." Jake gave a little shrug. "I know he *hears* me, but he doesn't always listen."

"I've had the same experience," I said dryly. "The napkins are in the drawer by the dishwasher, Jake — let's use the red ones. You kids can have milk or tea, which-ever you want." To McQuaid, I added, "Pour a glass of that for me, would you?" He was getting the white wine out of the refrigerator.

"Done," he said and put my wineglass beside my plate. He bent over the casserole dish. "Hey, chicken." He frowned at it. "That isn't —"

68

"No." The timer buzzed and I went to the stove. "A thousand times no." I took the rolls out of the oven. "Why is everybody so concerned about the source of that chicken? You don't really think I would —"

"I'll go see what Brian and Caitlin are up to," Jake offered diplomatically and headed for the door.

McQuaid lounged against the counter. He was wearing jeans and my favorite blue plaid shirt, the same color as his eyes, and his dark hair was rumpled, as usual, where he'd been running his fingers through it. He has a jagged scar across his forehead — a knife-fight trophy from his days as a Houston detective — and his nose has been broken more than once. His features are too rugged to be called handsome, but he's certainly tall, dark, and sexy, every inch an alpha male. After he left the police force, he served for several months as Pecan Springs' acting police chief; on another occasion, he took an undercover assignment with the Texas Rangers. He got badly shot up on that case, though, and I don't mind telling you that I was nervous when he hung out his shingle as a private detective. But most of his cases have been of the seek-and-find variety, more of an intellectual challenge than a physical one — at least so far. I'm not as uneasy about his work as I used to be, especially since Blackie came on board. Blackie Blackwell is the quintessential lawman's lawman, smart, cool, and utterly dependable. I worry less, knowing he has McQuaid's back.

McQuaid sipped his wine. "How was your day?"

"The usual," I said. "Until Ruby told me that Karen Prior was mugged last night."

"Mugged!" That caught his attention and he straightened up. "Karen? Where? Is she going to be okay?"

"Yes, mugged. At the mall. And no, not okay. The docs repaired a brain hemorrhage, but it doesn't sound good. She's in a coma, on life support — or she was, late this afternoon."

"Aw, hell." McQuaid groaned. "Life support. Did they get the s.o.b. who did it?"

"Not yet. A couple of girls spotted the getaway vehicle. A late-model four-door."

"Say *what*?" McQuaid pulled his dark brows together. "Since when are muggers driving late-model cars?" He paused, frowning. "Is there more to this than a simple mugging?"

I began chopping a cucumber. "There might be. Sheila told Ruby and me that Felicity — she's Karen's daughter — reported that her mother got a phone call before she went to the mall last night. Felicity had the impression that the call might have had something to do with a documentary that a couple of Karen's students are working on. Coincidentally, one of the girls happens to be Jake's sister."

"Oh, yeah? Gretchen? Good student. She took a couple of courses from me — Enforcement Systems and Practices and Criminal Investigations, as I remember. Got an A in both. She's thinking about a career in law enforcement. Or at least she was."

I nodded. "Felicity seems to think that her mom might have been planning to meet the caller. Which doesn't necessarily have anything to do with the assault, of course." In fact, when the phone call was checked out, the caller would probably turn out to be one of the students working on the film.

"Nevertheless." McQuaid swirled the wine in his glass. "The cops are looking into it with that in mind, I suppose." He pushed his lips in and out. "You talked to Sheila today, huh? Did she mention . . . ?" He eyed me quizzically, leaving the sentence hanging.

"Yes and yes." I finished chopping the second cucumber and added it to the purslane and Malabar spinach in the salad

71

bowl. "Sheila said Blackie was planning to talk to you. I hope he's pleased."

"*Dazed* is more like it," McQuaid said with a chuckle. "His boys are grown and he could be a grandfather. Now *this.*" Blackie has two sons from an earlier marriage, one in Dallas, another in the air force. "A baby is going to be a big change for him."

"In more ways than one," I said, thinking that babies were entering into the day's conversations a little more frequently than I was accustomed to. I began dicing the tomatoes. "Sheila is going to have to juggle her workload. And Blackie might not be so willing to take cases that involve travel." I put the tomatoes into the salad. "I hope they know what they're getting into."

"Does anybody?" McQuaid asked thoughtfully. "I mean, you can look only so far ahead. The rest . . ." He shrugged. "But that's life. You just have to take it on faith." He held up his wineglass, studying it. "But they must have wanted a baby. Otherwise —" He didn't finish the sentence.

"Mistakes happen," I said. I chopped the green onions, dumped them into the bowl, and found the salad tongs in the drawer.

"Mistakes don't happen to Blackie and Sheila," McQuaid said with a confident chuckle. "They're careful. And deliberate."

"Also maybe passionate," I said, amused. "Just a little." He was watching me speculatively, one dark eyebrow quirked. I frowned, thinking of Sheila. And Sylvia Banner. "You don't . . . I mean, you're not wishing that we . . ." I got the dish of beans — canned pork and beans with some added garlic and chopped onions — out of the microwave. "That it was happening to us?"

"Nooo," he said slowly, drawing out the word. "The thought did cross my mind a while back. That it might be nice for us to have a child of our own. But that was before Caitie came along. She'll be with us for at least six more years, and by that time —"

"And by that time Brian may have given us a grandchild," I said with a little laugh.

He pulled his dark brows together. "Brian? You've got to be kidding, China. He's . . . he's just a kid! He —"

"I'm willing to bet that the kid has the right equipment," I said equably. "And that it's in excellent operating order. Let's just hope his head overrules the rest of him — and whatever might be going on between him and Jake."

McQuaid scowled. "I'd better have another talk with the boy. Make sure he understands the ground rules." He finished off his wine. "Oh, by the way, we picked up

73

a new case this week."

"That's good, isn't it?" The "Associates" part of the agency name is wishful thinking. There are just the two of them, McQuaid and Blackwell. Sometimes they're stretched, and sometimes they get cases that have to be worked when the only people on the streets are the law and the outlaw. They can end up working twenty-four/seven. I couldn't begin to imagine what Blackie was going to do when there was a baby in the house. He and Sheila would have to have live-in help, wouldn't they? No wonder they were thinking of getting a bigger house.

"Definitely good," McQuaid replied. "And definitely better than the alternative. But Blackie still has his hands full with that situation in San Antonio, so this one is mine."

I eyed him. "Care to tell me about it?" Sometimes he will; mostly he won't.

"It's a bee in Charlie Lipman's bonnet." He shrugged. "He doesn't have a client — it's something he wants to look into for his own reasons. It's personal."

Ah, *personal.* Which meant that McQuaid wasn't going to give me any of the grisly details, at least not right away. Charlie Lipman, Pecan Springs' most popular lawyer, has been a close friend for as long as both of us have been in Pecan Springs. McQuaid handles most of Charlie's investigations. And since Charlie's clients are usually prominent local citizens, McQuaid often finds himself digging up dirt on prominent local folk. It's a good thing he doesn't tell me everything he knows. I might not be able to function around some of these people.

"Judging from what Charlie has told me so far, though," he added, "it's a thin case. A very thin, very old cold case. If I can dig up any leads at all, it's likely to involve some forensic accounting."

"Well, if you're looking for accounting help, you won't do better than Kate," I remarked. Kate Rodriguez is Amy's partner: Amy, the wild child, Ruby's daughter and the mother of Baby Grace, Ruby's grand-daughter. Amy and Kate have been living together for several years now. Kate owns her own accounting firm and does the books and the tax accounting for Ruby's and my shops and our tearoom.

"No problem there," McQuaid replied. "Kate is the first one I thought of, too. The big problem is getting my hands on the records. That's going to take some out-of-the-box thinking."

"I'm sure you'll come up with something creative." I put the dish of beans on the table. "Supper's ready. You'd better go out and see what's keeping the kids."

McQuaid set his empty glass down and pulled me against him. "Yeah," he said. "But all this talk about babies reminds me of sex." He tipped my head back and gave me a lascivious grin. "Maybe we could make a date, you and me. Like, tonight?"

"Sounds good to me," I said and kissed him on the chin. "But no babies. You hear?"

"Aww," he said, drawing the word out. "You are such a spoilsport, China."

But he was grinning when he said it.

CHAPTER THREE

In England, red roses must be pruned carefully, for bad luck will follow if the petals fall from the blossom as it is cut. In Italy, in the last century, you weren't supposed to give a fully opened rose to someone as a gift. If you did, a close relative of the recipient would surely die.

China Bayles
"Herbs of Good and Ill Omen"
Pecan Springs Enterprise

When Jake comes for supper, she and Brian usually take over the kitchen cleanup. This evening, though, McQuaid wanted Brian's help with a project out in the barn, and the two of them disappeared. Caitie had done the dishes the night before, so I gave her a break and volunteered to work with Jake. Anyway, I wanted to talk to her.

"I understand that Gretchen is working on her thesis project with Dr. Prior," I said as we cleared the table. "I wonder — did you hear what happened?"

If Jake were an ordinary teen, I wouldn't have gone into it with her. But she demonstrated just how adult she is when she and Brian were involved in a tragic — and deadly — situation with one of the coaches at the high school a couple of years ago. She has her head on straight.

"Gretchen told me that Dr. Prior was mugged in the parking lot at the mall." Jake carried the casserole dish to the kitchen counter. "Actually, Dr. Prior is a friend of Mom's, as well as Gretchen's supervisor. She's been to our house for dinner a couple of times." She shook her head gravely. "Sounds pretty awful."

"I'm afraid it is," I replied. "I just heard about it this afternoon. I wonder — did Gretchen know any of the details?"

"I don't think so," Jake said. "She and Kitt — Kitt Bradley is Gretchen's partner on the documentary — wanted to go straight over to the hospital to see her. But when they heard that she's on life support, they thought they would probably be in the way. They decided to send flowers instead." She turned around. "What should I put this leftover chicken into?"

I got a dish out of the cupboard. "Here —

this one's about the right size." I paused. "I understand that Felicity — Dr. Prior's daughter — thought her mother got a phone call from somebody before she went to the mall. About the documentary, I mean."

Jake scraped the chicken into the dish. "That's what Kitt told Gretchen. They were wondering who it could be."

"It wasn't one of them? Kitt or Gretchen?"

"Nope." She looked up at me, her blue eyes troubled. "In fact, Gretchen got a call herself."

I turned on the water to rinse the plates. "About the documentary, you mean?"

"Yeah." Jake put the dish in the fridge. "Some guy. Gretchen asked who it was, but he wouldn't give his name. He was, like . . . warning her. He said it wasn't a good idea to go around stirring up hard feelings about something that was over and done with. She should stop doing it and make sure her film never came out. And then he hung up." She paused. "Gretchen said it was kind of creepy."

"I'll bet." I began putting the plates into the dishwasher. "When did this happen? Did she tell Dr. Prior about it?"

"Last week sometime. I don't remember when. And no, she didn't tell Dr. Prior, at

79

least not right away. She and Kitt talked and decided it wasn't important enough to bother her with it." She paused. "But a couple of days later, Kitt got a call, too, so they changed their minds." She gave me a sideways glance. "Kitt recorded it. The call, I mean, on her cell phone. She wasn't sure it was legal to do that, though. So please don't tell anybody."

"She doesn't have to worry." I rinsed the silver and began dropping it into the dishwasher bin. "Texas has a one-party-consent wiretapping law. Kitt can record any call she's on without telling the other party." I paused. "We're assuming, of course, that the other party to the call is in Texas. If he — it was a guy?"

Jake nodded.

"If he was calling from a state that requires two-party consent, it would be illegal. But it was somebody who knew about the documentary, so we're safe in assuming that he's from Pecan Springs." I paused. "And that he might be the same guy who called Gretchen."

Jake nodded again.

"Do you know what he said?"

"It was pretty much the same message that Gretchen got. A warning. She should stop filming because the documentary was stirring up old bad feelings. Stuff like that."

"She still has the recording?"

"Well, she did — I guess she still does. She came over to our house and played it for Gretchen. It sounded . . . well, it was a little scary. That's when she and Gretchen decided they should tell Dr. Prior."

"When was that?"

"The call? A couple of days ago. They told Dr. Prior right away." Jake looked worried. "Do you think those calls had anything to do with the mugging?"

"Maybe. But Gretchen and Kitt really ought to talk to the police, Jake. There's obviously something going on here."

"They don't want to get involved," Jake replied. "They've mostly finished filming and they're ready to start editing. Their deadline is coming up in a few weeks."

"I understand about not getting involved," I said. "And that was pretty much okay — until Dr. Prior was assaulted. Now that's happened, the girls need to come forward with what they know, so the cops can put all the information together."

As I spoke, I thought of something else, and my skin prickled. Karen had been attacked — *savagely* attacked — and the evidence was mounting that the assault wasn't random, that it had something to do with the documentary she was supervising. If that was true, Gretchen and Kitt could be in danger, as well.

But I didn't say this to Jake. And I wasn't going to trust the girls to decide to share what they knew with the police. I said, "Tell you what, Jake. Chief Dawson is a good friend of mine. I'm going to call her tonight and tell her about these phone calls. Please let the girls know that somebody from the police will be in touch with them, and that it's perfectly okay to tell the investigator about Kitt's recording. In fact, if she still has it on her phone, they'll be glad to have it. It may turn out to be important."

"Sure," Jake said gratefully. She gave me a quick glance. "Thanks, China. I'm glad I talked to you. I was beginning to worry a little bit. Now I know that everything will be okay."

"I'm sure it will," I said. But I wasn't quite as confident as I sounded.

As soon as Jake and I finished tidying up the kitchen, I went into the living room, sat down in my favorite chair, and called Sheila at home. I gave her a quick rundown on the phone calls that Gretchen and Kitt had received, and mentioned that Kitt had recorded hers.

"Smart move," Sheila said approvingly.

"Very smart. That recording could give us something to work on, China. Thanks for letting me know."

I hesitated. "I don't want to jump into the middle of this, but I'm concerned about the girls' safety. They're making a film about a murder that's still officially unsolved, and it sounds like somebody seriously wants them to stop what they're doing. We know of two warning phone calls for sure, and maybe a third — the one to Karen. And there's the attack."

"I'll have the investigating officer call both students and make arrangements to talk to them," Sheila said. Then she paused, thought for a moment, and said, "No, I'll handle this myself. I need to get out of the office. I feel like I'm drowning in paperwork." She sighed. "Or maybe I just want to put off dealing with the department's pregnancy policy. I've been sitting here, reading what we have, and I can see how much work it needs. I feel like I'm about to stir up a hornet's nest. And since I'm the one who's pregnant, I'm the one who'll get stung."

"I'm sorry about that," I said sympathetically. "But I agree that it's a good idea for you to get away from the paperwork. I think the girls will be more comfortable talking to you, anyway." As chief, Sheila doesn't have the time to do much fieldwork, even though she's very good at it. "Oh, and don't forget about tomorrow," I added. "Lunch is on us."

"Just don't ask me to eat the daisies," she said.

"Roses," I corrected her. "We'll be eating roses."

There was a silence. Then Sheila said, tentatively, "You sure I shouldn't bring a sandwich?"

Pecan Springs was settled in the 1840s by German immigrants who arrived by ship in Galveston and trekked westward across the coastal prairie to the Balcones Escarpment. There, they settled a little village they called New Braunfels, which is now primarily known for its waterpark — the Schlitter-bahn — and its Wurstfest, where last year, over 100,000 hungry people chowed down on bratwurst-on-a-stick, kartoffelpuffer (potato pancakes), fried sauerkraut, fried dill pickles, German potato salad, and drechter kuche (funnel cake). But many hardy souls didn't tarry in New Braunfels. Still on the lookout for good places to live and grow gardens and raise livestock and children, they headed west to Fredericksburg and Mason and Hondo and north to Pecan Springs and San Marcos, along the western edge of what is now known as Texas' "German belt."

That early German settlement accounts for the "German vernacular" architecture you see when you drive up and down our streets in Pecan Springs. My building on Crockett Street — the two-story limestone structure that houses Thyme and Seasons, the Crystal Cave, and Thyme for Tea — was built by a German master mason who cut all the pieces of stone so perfectly that they still fit snug and true, well over a century later. The building sits about ten yards back from the street on an attractive, sunny lot, which I've filled with theme gardens, both for display and for harvesting. At the back, on the alley, there's Thyme Cottage, the name I've given to the lovely old stone stable that the previous owner-architect remodeled as his living quarters. It has a fully equipped kitchen and spacious main room with a fireplace and plenty of comfortable seating, which makes it ideal for classes and workshops. I also rent it as a bed-and-breakfast and list it in the *Pecan Springs B&B Guide* and online. This week, it is rented to a couple from Chicago who are planning a move to Pecan Springs and are looking for a house in the area.

One of my favorite mystery authors, a guy named John D. MacDonald, once wrote that the early bird who gets the worm usually works for somebody who comes in late and owns the worm farm. But I am the early bird and I own the worm farm, so to speak, and it's definitely not to my advantage to come in late. There's too much to do to keep the worm farm operating. And besides, in the summer, the worm farm gets very hot, very quickly, so I try to get out there as early as I can, while it's still cool.

On this particular Friday morning, the roses in several of the gardens needed to be deadheaded. I was working in the apothecary garden, which is planted with many different healing herbs: echinacea, garlic, peppermint, lemon balm, horehound, yarrow, and lavender, as well as dill, rosemary, thyme, and pots of aloe vera. But its centerpiece is a large, lovely *Rosa gallica,* the ancient apothecary's rose.

These days, most of us grow roses for their beauty and their fragrance and don't realize that many cultures have considered them to be a valuable medicine. In the first century CE, the Roman naturalist Pliny the Elder documented the use of roses in the treatment of thirty-two different health conditions. The petals were used as a poultice to control bleeding, brewed as a tea to treat stomach ailments, made into a tonic to treat depression and lethargy, steeped in wine to cure headaches and hangovers, dried and powdered as a digestive aid, and made into a conserve as a treatment for colds and sore throat.

But roses have their culinary uses, as well. Our tearoom doesn't offer a large menu, but our lunches (soups, mini-croissant sandwiches, quiches, pastas, salads, and fresh fruit) are a welcome alternative to the Tex-Mex cookery and fast-food burgers that are standard Pecan Springs lunch fare. This summer, Cass Wilde has been developing several dishes for our tearoom, using roses from the gardens around the shops, which is ideal, because there are a great many roses and we never use any chemical sprays. We grow only antique roses, like *Rosa gallica* and *Rosa rugosa.* They require less care, have more fragrance, and seem to taste sweeter than other roses. The rose dishes Cass has been working on include a pasta dish made with capellini (pasta that's just a little thicker than angel hair), shrimp, and rose petals; rose petal salad and sandwiches; a chilled strawberry-and-rose-petal soup; and a deliciously spicy cookie made with rose water and cardamom, cinnamon, and coriander. But before these items go on the menu, they have to pass the taste test. So we offer them to select customers — people we can trust to tell us what they think. Today it was Sheila's turn. She'd be trying out Cass' new capellini with shrimp and rose petals.

The tearoom is an exceptionally attractive place, with hunter green wainscoting partway up the old square-cut limestone walls, green-painted tables and chairs with floral chintz napkins, and deep-set windows that look out onto the gardens. There are hanging pots of ferns and a small crystal vase of fresh flowers and herbs at each table. We also have several tables on the outside deck, in the expansive shade of a large live oak tree.

Sheila was on time, which was unusual. "Let's eat on the deck," she said when she finally arrived. "Okay?"

"It's a little warm," I cautioned. I knew this, having already spent a couple of hours in the garden that morning. "You sure? It's much cooler inside."

"But there's less chance of being interrupted or overheard," Sheila said. "I have some questions to ask, and I'd just as soon

88

not share them with the rest of your customers."

I got it. Pecan Springs is a small town, and people aren't above listening in on other people's table conversations, then retailing the news to the next friend they happen to meet. What's more, the good old boys in town may be a little slow in lining up behind our first female chief of police, but the women admire Sheila and always want to chat with her. They'd be less likely to keep interrupting us if we sat outdoors.

The thermometer was nudging 90, but a haze of high cirrus clouds filtered the July sun and a breeze rustled the live oak leaves. I led Sheila out to a table on the corner of the deck and we sat down.

"You feeling okay, Smart Cookie?" I asked. "Not still throwing up, I hope."

"I bought some fresh ginger on the way home yesterday," Sheila said. "I made some tea this morning and felt a lot better after I drank it." She patted her shoulder bag. "I have an emergency supply of your ginger capsules and peppermint tea, just in case."

"That's great," I said. "If those don't work, let me know and we'll try something else." Chamomile, slippery elm, and red raspberry leaf tea were other options. We would find something that helped.

"Oh, *here* you are," Ruby said, coming out on the deck and closing the door behind her. "Why don't we sit inside? It's a lot cooler."

"We can get used to it," I said. "Smart Cookie doesn't want people listening in on our cop talk."

"Oh," Ruby said. "Well, okay. I just got off the phone with Felicity," she added, brushing the leaves off a chair before she sat down. "Her mother is in emergency surgery. There's some new bleeding in her brain, and the doctors aren't very optimistic." She tried to smile. "Of course, where there's life . . ."

Her voice trailed off as Becky Conway brought glasses of iced hibiscus tea, plates of garden salad, and a basket of rosemary and garlic breadsticks. Becky is a sprightly college student with short blond hair who helps out in the tearoom and the shops.

"Yes, I heard," Sheila said gravely. "The update came into the office just before I left. I'm afraid it doesn't sound good."

Emergency surgery. Thinking of Karen, lively, intelligent, committed, I felt a twisting pain inside — and a rising anger at the person, a man, presumably, who had put her there. Not quite trusting my voice, I said to Sheila, "Anything on the assailant's

90

vehicle?"

"Nada." Sheila shook her head. "We're looking, of course. But no. Nothing yet."

We sat for a moment in silence, each of us dealing with this unhappy news in her own way. At last Ruby sighed and spoke.

"I guess that's no surprise. About the vehicle, I mean. There must be quite a few like it in Pecan Springs."

"A late-night assault with no witnesses," I said thinly. "Could be hopeless." I glanced at Sheila. "How about the phone call Felicity mentioned to you? The one her mother got before she went to the mall. Any leads there?"

Ruby passed the bread sticks and Sheila took one. "The call came on the landline. The carrier is checking and we might have something tomorrow." She made a face. "Or the next day, or the day after that. I don't know why the phone companies can't respond any faster. But maybe we'll have better luck with the call Kitt taped." She began munching on the bread stick. "This is good." She peered at it. "What are these little green bits? Rose leaves?"

"No," I said. "Rosemary and thyme." Smart Cookie can be forgiven for failing to learn the fine points of cooking. She has her hands full with the police department.

"The call to Kitt" — Ruby sipped her iced tea — "have you listened to it yet?"

I had told Ruby about the previous night's conversation with Jake, and Amy's friendship with Kitt gave her an extra interest. As if she needed one. In her dreams, Ruby is a Girl Detective, a cross between Nancy Drew and Kinsey Millhone.

"I had a couple of emergencies this morning, but I've made arrangements to meet Kitt as soon as I leave here." Sheila picked up her fork and began on her salad. "Before I talk to her and Gretchen, though, I want to know more about this documentary they're filming. What's the story?"

"Karen usually has several master's students under her supervision," I said. "As their thesis project, they film a documentary, which is shown to the public. This summer she's supervising Gretchen and Kitt, as well as three or four other teams."

"Both Gretchen and Kitt are smart young women," Ruby put in. "Talented and dedicated. I was impressed by the way they handled their equipment, the cameras and mikes and lights and stuff like that. They've got an interesting project — interesting locally, anyway. And they know what they're doing."

Sheila took out a notebook and a pen,

flipped to a new page, and dated it. "What *are* they doing, exactly? I'll get the story from them, too. But I'd rather you clue me in first."

Ruby nodded. "They're filming a human-interest documentary about the murder of Christine Morris and the trial of the guy who was accused of killing her — Dick Bowen. It'll also be about Pecan Springs, something like the episodes of *City Confidential*. Have you seen that TV show?"

"Yes. True crime, usually a murder, with a focus on the setting where the crime took place."

"Right," Ruby said. "So the film will start with a segment about the town — its history and so forth. Then there'll be a segment about Christine Morris and the way people saw her — neighbors and people who knew her. A segment about the murderer, too, and people's opinions about him, good and bad." Ruby raised her fork, about to dig into her salad. "The *accused* murderer, that is. In this case, the jury decided he wasn't guilty. So we don't know — officially, that is — who killed Christine Morris."

Sheila finished writing, put her notebook beside her plate, and went back to her salad. "You haven't seen any of the footage?"

Ruby shook her head. "Kitt said they were planning to get the rough cut done in a few days. Their deadline is the end of the month."

"Yesterday," Sheila said, "you implied that people didn't much like Christine Morris — and that it was her fault. You said something like, 'She made a career out of making enemies.' Can you tell me more about that?"

Ruby picked at her salad. "Well, I guess you could say that Christine was the kind of person everyone loves to hate. She was an outsider to Pecan Springs, so her criticisms — and there were lots of them — rubbed people the wrong way. She was always feuding with her neighbors, fighting with the zoning and planning people, badgering the city council. She was beautiful, thin, platinum blond, always dressed fit to kill. But as far as most people were concerned, she was a royal pain in the neck."

Sheila made another note. "I went back and read the Morris case file. Unfortunately, the police work on the case seems to have been a little sloppy."

"A *little* sloppy?" I raised my eyebrows. "I don't know the details, but according to Johnnie Carlson, the police work was downright criminal."

Of course, that's what the defense always says — or tries to. I've said it more than once or twice myself. In fact, the surest way to win an acquittal is to introduce reasonable doubt by pointing out some carelessness — accidental or deliberate — in the cops' handling of evidence or witnesses or warrants. If the carelessness involves a search warrant, or the lack of one, the fruits of the search, no matter how damning, can be tossed out. And cops are exactly as human as the rest of us. It's only in cop fiction that they do everything right, every time.

Sheila looked at me. "Carlson didn't happen to show you his trial notes, I don't suppose."

"Nope. No reason to." I hesitated. The jury had acquitted and the attorney and his client were both dead. Privilege was a moot issue. "They're probably still around somewhere, though," I said cautiously, thinking of what Johnnie had said about having evidence of an alternative suspect that was excluded by the trial judge. "Why? Something you need to know?"

"Maybe. Probably nothing I can't get from the transcript, though." Sheila gave me a frowning glance. "Skimming the file quickly, it looked to me like Bubba and his boys made the right call, although they screwed up when it came to the physical evidence." She paused. "Based on what you've said, though, Ruby, I wonder if Dick Bowen was acquitted because the jury decided that Morris deserved what she got. The . . . um . . . careless police work merely gave them a convenient excuse to acquit."

"It's possible." Ruby tilted her head. "Personally, I always thought the jury acquitted him because —"

"Here we go, ladies." Ruby was interrupted by Becky, who appeared with a tray and three attractive luncheon plates. In the center of each was a mound of thin pasta in a light creamy sauce flecked with orange-pink rose petals, and a half-dozen pretty, pink cooked shrimp. Each plate was decorated with a tiny bouquet of rosemary, parsley, and a single pink rosebud. Sheila looked down at it dubiously.

"Taste it before you say a word," Ruby cautioned. "It's delicious."

It was. And even Sheila had to admit it. "Never in my wildest dreams," she murmured, "did I imagine I would be eating pasta and shrimp with roses — and loving it. Forgive me for doubting."

"Forgiven," I said, and there was a brief silence while all three of us indulged ourselves. At last, Ruby put down her fork. "I think it might benefit from a little more Parmesan," she said thoughtfully.

"I think it's perfect," Sheila said.

"We could put Parmesan on the table," I suggested. I looked down at the pasta. "I was wondering about adding just a bit of snipped chives."

"Or minced fresh rosemary," Ruby said.

"Oh, that's a good idea," I replied appreciatively. "Or how about just a tiny bit of —"

"I really, really think it's fine just as it is," Sheila put in. She looked at Ruby. "You were saying? About Richard Bowen, I mean, and why he was acquitted."

"The defense was aggressive and the police made mistakes," Ruby said, "but I always thought that Bowen got off because the jury basically liked him. He was a really nice guy who devoted a lot of time to the community. He wasn't married, and he didn't have a family — brothers, sisters, parents, I mean. He gave a lot of money to charity, and he was always helping people who got into financial trouble. He was on the board of the Friends of the Library and coordinated the fund drive, which you know he couldn't do unless he was a big donor himself. He sang in the choir at the Presbyterian church. He volunteered at the Humane Society one weekend a month, and he worked at the food pantry during the holidays. He liked to wear a Santa suit there, when he was handing out packages of food."

"Did he have time to work?" I asked. "What did he do for a living?"

Ruby frowned at me. "Don't be cynical, China. Of course he worked — in the town planning department. I don't remember exactly what he did. But everybody knew him as a *volunteer,* you see. He was always getting his picture in the newspaper, maybe partly because he was best buddies with the editor, Frank Donnelly. That was long before Hark took over the paper." Hark Hibler is the current editor and publisher of the *Pecan Springs Enterprise* and my boss. That is, I edit the Home and Garden page that comes out once a week, in return for free newspaper advertising for the shop, the tearoom, and Party Thyme, our catering service. It's a good deal all around. Hark is also Ruby's current flame.

Sheila's eyebrows went up. "Bowen was Donnelly's *buddy*?" Her emphasis made the meaning clear.

"Oh, I don't know about *that,*" Ruby replied hurriedly. She frowned. "I mean, I heard some rumors, but I didn't really believe them. This was over a decade ago, remember? I'm sure it was different in Austin or San Antonio or Houston, but here in Pecan Springs, we were pretty naive about that sort of thing. We just assumed that everybody was . . . well, you know. Straight."

"Yeah," I said, still cynical. "It's amazing how simple life used to be." Of course, it never was simple. It just seems that way, looking back.

"Anyway," Ruby said, "for whatever reason, Frank Donnelly didn't much like Christine. Every time she showed up and harangued the city council, he would print her tirade in the *Enterprise,* along with the most unflattering photo he could find. He was obviously trying to make her look . . . well, like a shrill, angry woman with a big chip on her shoulder."

"What did she harangue the city council about?" Sheila asked.

Ruby wrinkled her forehead. "It was a while ago, and I've forgotten the details. But as I remember it, she had a beef with the planning and zoning people. She wanted to open an art gallery on the first floor of her house, to sell paintings from her collection. She had bought the vacant lot across the alley behind the house, for parking. But the property was zoned single-family residential. The neighbors were opposed to any changes and the zoning office turned down her request. She took the fight to the council and started trying to dig up dirt on the people in the zoning office. Every meeting, she would jump up and start making accusations. There were a lot of harsh words, back and forth."

"Bottom line, the jury didn't like the victim and was more than happy to exonerate the man charged with her murder," Sheila said flatly.

"Hey, wait," I protested ironically. "I thought it was that slick Houston defense attorney who got Bowen off the hook."

"Well, that, too," Sheila conceded. "And I suppose the DA might have done a better job with jury selection. The defense challenged a couple of people, but the state's voir dire was exceedingly skimpy. Unusual for a murder case."

"Who was the prosecutor?" I asked.

"Henry Bell," Sheila replied.

I rolled my eyes. "Why am I not surprised that the state lost?"

Henry "Ring-a-Ding" Bell was a twenty-year veteran of the Adams County prosecutor's office, a good old boy who had a reputation for cozying up to as many of the other good old boys as necessary to ensure his reelection. Ring-a-Ding was still in office when I first arrived in Pecan Springs, and I had observed him in action a time or two. He may have been a good prosecutor in his salad days, but those were long since behind him and he was well into dessert. Fortunately, Pecan Springs, back then, didn't require the services of a real legal eagle, and Ring-a-Ding kept on keeping on for much longer than he would have, say, in Austin or San Antonio, where there's much more competition. Fortunately, he has been admitted to practice before the bar in that great courtroom in the sky. He's probably losing his cases there, too.

"Let's get back to the victim," Sheila said. "What can you tell me about her, Ruby? She wasn't originally from Pecan Springs, I understand."

"Oh, no *way,*" Ruby said emphatically. "Christine started her career as an anchorwoman for a Houston television station. Then she married an ob-gyn with a ton of money, gave up her television career, and became a River Oaks socialite. Then she got into art collecting. She especially admired twentieth-century Mexican art, and she bought quite a lot of it. She was widowed when her husband died of an early heart attack a few years later. But she never lost her taste for the limelight. She was attractive, slim, and always very well dressed. She liked to be the center of attention."

Sheila was making rapid notes. "How did she get from Houston to Pecan Springs?"

"Her cousin Sharyn — her only living family member — grew up here. Sharyn Tillotson. We went to high school together. She and Christine were on good terms at the time. Christine was looking for a place where she could be active in local organizations and . . . well, *belong.* But she wanted a starring role, too, which is hard to manage in Pecan Springs — unless you're born here. If you're not, you'll be an outsider all your life. No matter how hard she tried, Christine would always be an outsider."

"I know something about that," I said ruefully. It was true. I've been here long enough to think of myself as a native, but the real natives still view me as a foreigner — and they always will. This isn't necessarily bad, of course. Being an inside outsider has a certain advantage. You can understand more about the town and its people *because* you have a double viewpoint. You're likely to see things the natives never notice.

Ruby nodded. "But Christine made things worse for herself by making a special point of *criticizing* everybody. People didn't like that. And they didn't like her — even after she married Doug Clark."

"She was married to Douglas Clark?" I asked in surprise.

Doug Clark is Pecan Springs' most prominent developer and builder. He got his start some twenty-five years ago, when CTSU lifted its campus residency requirements and the student rental market began to blossom. He took advantage of the situation in a big way, building dozens of cheaply constructed duplexes and shoddy apartment complexes around the campus perimeter, then branching out into strip malls and retail buildings. Then, as Austin spilled south along the I-35 corridor and San Antonio crept north, he became a major player in Pecan Springs' development and construction market and the Clark operation went upscale, graduating from cheap construction to something much more impressive. A couple of years ago, he put together the package for the Hill Country Villa, an exclusive singles complex on Sam Houston Drive. Rumor has it that he's working on a project that's even bigger and more elegant.

"Ruby's right," Sheila put in dryly. "It was a short marriage. According to the trial transcript, Christine Morris filed for divorce three years after they were married. On grounds of adultery."

Adultery. In one way, I wasn't surprised. Doug Clark has a long-standing reputation as a womanizer — the more the merrier is his mantra. In another way, I *was* surprised. Texas is a no-fault state: to get a divorce, you simply claim incompatibility, and both spouses are off the hook. But there are strategic reasons to claim adultery — and where divorce is concerned, it's always all about strategy. One of the reasons is revenge: "I'll get that miserable jerk for cheating on me. I'll rake his name through the mud — and hers, too." The other reason has to do with . . . yes, you guessed it: money. The wronged spouse can sometimes get a bigger piece of the community property pie, the wronger, the bigger. As I said, it's always all about strategy.

"It was a messy divorce," Ruby remarked, "and Pecan Springs loved every tasteless, tawdry moment of it."

"Adultery usually boils down to money," I said thoughtfully. "And Douglas Clark is a great big fish. Christine must have reeled in a very nice property settlement."

"Charlie Lipman would know the details," Ruby said. "He was Christine's lawyer. All I know is that she got the house, which was huge. And the paintings they bought while they were married — or, rather, that *she* bought while they were married. By that time, she had developed an arrangement with a couple of New York galleries, where paintings from her collection of Mexican artists were displayed and sold."

"Ah," I said. "She was setting herself up as an art dealer. That can be a lucrative business."

"The house," Sheila said. "That would be the house where she was killed?"

"Yes. It's now the Morris Museum of Mexican Art, at the end of San Jacinto."

"I know the place," I said. "It's striking. Very modern. Architectural." I'd never been inside, but from a distance, it looked like stark white windowless cubes arranged in geometric stacks, with a second floor cantilevered out over a paved plaza and a sculptural roof that curved upward, like the rim of a saucer. A flying saucer.

"If you think it's modern now," Ruby said with a wry chuckle, "you should have heard what the neighbors said about it back then. They hated the place, partly because Doug tore down a perfectly lovely Victorian in order to build on the property. He hired a famous architect from Dallas and gave the house to Christine as a wedding present.

She loved it, I heard. It had acres of wall space where she could hang her paintings. She told everybody that she was going to use the first floor as an art gallery."

I was surprised again, but the pieces were beginning to fall into place. "The museum that exists now is an expanded version of her gallery, then?"

"Something like that," Ruby said. "Christine had already set up a foundation for her art. In her will, the foundation got the house and a substantial sum of money to maintain her collection — basically, a private art museum."

"A *private* art museum?" Sheila asked. "What's that?"

Ruby frowned. "I'm not sure, exactly, except that it's privately funded and open only by appointment, mostly to groups — schoolkids, ladies' clubs, things like that. Anyway, once the foundation took over the house, it pushed through the zoning change. Christine would've been proud. Before she died, she was making a career out of her interest in art." She chuckled. "That, and seriously annoying the neighbors along San Jacinto."

San Jacinto Avenue was a neighborhood of gracious older homes built in the early part of the twentieth century. I could see why, when the Clark-Morris house was first built, it would have seemed terribly incongruous, an intrusion of modern architecture, like a rude thumb in the eye of the neighbors. And I could see why Gretchen and Kitt had decided that this particular story might make an interesting documentary.

"San Jacinto Avenue," Sheila mused. "I was looking at the crime scene photos, and I saw that when the murder occurred there was a six-foot-high chain-link fence around the property. It was ugly and very much out of place in that neighborhood. The fence isn't there now. Was it Morris' idea? Why?"

"The fence?" Ruby laughed. "Oh, you bet it was her idea." She sat back as Becky came to refill our iced tea glasses and collect our empty plates. "Are we ready for dessert?" she asked.

"Not for me, thank you," Sheila replied. "I'm full."

"No is not an option," Ruby said cheerfully. "We're having the pudding, Becky." To Sheila, she added, "It's cool and very light. The perfect dessert for a hot July day."

"If you say so." Sheila went back to her question. "So why did Morris put up the fence?"

"It was the dogs, mostly," Ruby said. "If I remember right, most of the time she lived in that house, she had three: a couple of German shepherds and a Doberman. Her husband hated them — they were one of the reasons for the divorce, Sharyn told me. They were always barking, day and night. You could hear them for blocks. The neighbors were constantly complaining."

"Sharyn?" I asked. And then, "Oh, yes. The cousin."

"Right. Sharyn Tillotson. She was the one who introduced Christine and Doug and always took credit for their marriage. I don't know the details, but apparently she and Christine had a major falling-out over the terms of some family member's estate. Christine was the executrix, and Sharyn felt that she didn't distribute the proceeds according to the will, or something like that. Supposedly, they weren't on speaking terms when Christine was killed. Sharyn said she didn't get a nickel out of Christine's estate." She frowned. "I guess she had a change of heart, though. She manages the Morris Foundation."

Sheila cleared her throat. "The *fence,*" she said firmly.

"Before the fence went up," Ruby replied, "Christine's dogs kept getting loose. They scared the neighborhood kids and dug up people's landscaping. Dick Bowen — he lived on one side of her — called Animal Control and they came out and picked them up. Christine gave up the two German shepherds, but she paid to get the Doberman back and she built that ugly fence — mostly to spite Dick, we thought, since he was the one who called the animal cops. Of course," she added, "she would have had to take down the fence if she got the zoning variance she wanted. People don't want to visit an art gallery that's surrounded by a six-foot chain-link fence."

"So Morris never got the variance for her gallery?" Sheila asked.

Ruby shook her head. "She blamed Dick Bowen for that, too, since he worked in the planning office. But the fence wasn't just a spite thing. Sharyn told me that Christine was absolutely paranoid about theft. She was convinced that somebody was trying to break into her house and steal her paintings. She installed an expensive alarm system, too."

"Was her collection all that valuable?" I asked curiously.

"Apparently it was," Ruby said. "I don't remember the exact figure, but when her estate was probated, it was valued in the millions, including the house and its contents. Anyway, she was always complaining to the city council that the police didn't do enough to patrol the San Jacinto neighborhood. And I think there might have been at least one attempted break-in that was foiled by the alarm system."

"I wonder if the defense looked into that," I said, mostly to myself. But Sheila heard me and gave me a curious look.

"You're thinking . . . what?" she asked.

I shrugged. "Just thinking. Go on, Ruby. You were saying —"

"That Christine was paranoid," Ruby said. "That was why she had those dogs. And why she installed those two giant yard lights, front and back. They burned dusk to dawn, every night. The darn things lit up the neighborhood like a football field. We didn't think of it as light pollution back then, but that's what it was. Pecan Springs has rules against that now."

Becky arrived with the pudding, in three elegant glass dishes, garnished with sprigs of mint. Sheila put in a spoon and tasted it.

"Oh, my," she whispered. "What *is* it?"

"Muhallabiyeh," Ruby said comfortably. She said it again, slowly, giving more stress to the second syllable. "Moo-HEL-lu-bee-ya. It's a Middle Eastern pudding made with rose water."

"I take back everything I said about

roses," Sheila said. "This is delightful."

"Those yard lights." I picked up my spoon. "I'll bet they went over well with the neighbors."

"Everybody hated them," Ruby replied. "Some people even speculated that she was killed over those lights. Dick Bowen objected to them more than anyone, since the front light shone right into his living room and bedroom. A few weeks before she died, Bowen tried to get the city council to pass an ordinance against those lights. But by that time, some of the council members were scared of Christine, and he struck out." She shook her head. "Everybody was relieved when the house was taken over by the foundation and the fence and the lights came down. By that time, the neighbors were reconciled to the idea of a museum, I guess — especially since it's private and doesn't attract a gazillion visitors. When the foundation asked for a zoning change a couple of years later, it went through without any fuss. So I guess Christine won on that score, in the end. Even if she wasn't around to enjoy her triumph."

"The council was *afraid* of her?" Sheila asked curiously. "Why? I didn't find anything like that in the case notes or the transcript."

Ruby was about to answer, but Cass came up to the table just then, wearing her yellow and green Thymely Gourmet apron over a white T-shirt and white pants. Cass — pretty and blond, with blue eyes and a lovely complexion — has always been oversize, partly because she is (as she says) "just built big" and partly because she's a top-flight cook and enjoys her own cooking. But for the past five or six months, she has been on a personal weight-loss campaign, counting calories, walking in the evening, and going to the gym every morning. She's lost about twenty-five pounds, with another twenty to go. But it's for the sake of her health, she says, not because skinny is beautiful. "I believe in curves," she says flatly. "Thin just doesn't do it for me."

And there's another reason for this weight loss. Many of the clients in Cass' Thymely Gourmet meal-delivery service are upscale singles who commute to Austin or San Antonio, aren't crazy about cooking, but want to eat right and keep their weight down. So she has developed a line of low-calorie, heart-healthy, home-delivered gourmet vegetarian meals. "I figured I'd better lose a few pounds to market the new line," Cass says with a frank grin. She's a good advertisement. Customers who knew her "before" can see the "after" difference and imagine themselves minus a few extra pounds.

Cass walked around the table. "What did you think about the shrimp pasta?" she asked. "Did you like it?"

Ruby and I looked expectantly at Sheila, who was frowning thoughtfully. "Well, actually, I'm not sure," she said at last. "I'd like to think about it some more. Are there any leftovers? I could take some home and give it another test."

Ruby and I laughed. "I don't think restaurant critics do doggie bags," Cass said.

"I'm not a restaurant critic," Sheila replied with dignity. "I am the chief of police. And doggies have nothing to do with it."

"I didn't think so," Cass said with a grin, "although I'll bet Rambo would gobble it down and woof for more." She turned to Ruby and me. "How was the muhallabiyeh?"

"Delicious!" we exclaimed in chorus.

"Was it difficult to make?" Ruby asked.

"Nah," Cass said. "I recommend a double boiler, though." She paused. "That could be one of the recipes we put on the table for take-home."

"Great idea," Ruby said enthusiastically. "Audience participation," she said to Sheila.

"We try to put a recipe for one of our dishes on every table. When people make the dish themselves, they'll think of us."

"And in this case, buy their rose water and orange blossom water from us," I said. "Specialty items."

"Oh, so that's it," Sheila said with a laugh. "The take-home recipes are made with ingredients that *you* have for sale."

"Our mamas didn't raise no dummies," Ruby said smugly.

There was a low vibrating buzz, and Sheila took her cell phone out of her uniform pocket and looked at it. "Excuse me," she said and got up from the table. Phone to her ear, she walked down the steps from the deck and into the garden.

"You liked the shrimp pasta?" Cass asked again.

"More Parmesan," Ruby said.

"On the table," I put in. "We could put it in a shaker."

"And maybe some snipped chives," Ruby added. "Oh, and don't let Sheila fool you. She loved it. We all did."

"Parmesan — I don't think so," Cass said. "And if you put it on the table, people will be tempted to use too much. But I'll take the chives under consideration." She turned to Ruby. "Oh, drat. I forgot. I was supposed to tell you that somebody named Kitt called. She wants you to call her. As soon as you can."

To her credit, Ruby didn't say *Well, why didn't you tell me earlier?* She put down her napkin and got up. "Back in a flash," she said.

But a "flash" lengthened into several flashes, and rather than wait by myself at the table, I decided to head back to the shop. The tearoom was nearly empty, but there were a couple of people I knew, just finishing their lunches, and I stopped to say hello. I was going into the shop when Sheila caught up with me, looking grim.

"Bad news?" I asked.

"Terrible news," she replied. "I'm sorry to have to tell you, China, but —"

At that moment, Ruby came through the door from her shop, carrying her phone. She looked distraught.

"I'm afraid I have bad news," she said. "Kitt says —"

"Wait, Ruby." I held up my hand. "Smart Cookie got here first. Go, Sheila."

Ruby and I both turned to Sheila. The muscles around her mouth had tightened and her eyes had a flat, hard look, a cop look.

"Karen Prior died a little while ago, in

surgery. We're not dealing with simple assault now. This is a murder investigation."

CHAPTER FOUR

In the traditional folklore of plants, some have a reputation for being unlucky when picked. One of these is Herb Robert (*Geranium robertianum*), a low-growing wild geranium with reddish-pink blooms, red stems, and leaves that turn red late in the growing season. Throughout England, the plant is said to belong to Robin Goodfellow, or Puck, a rascally house goblin or nature sprite who makes it his business to cause trouble. (The name *Robin* is a familiar form of Robert.)

In the north of England, Herb Robert is known as "death come quickly" and was thought to be a certain harbinger of death. In the county of Somerset, children were warned, "If you pick Herb Robert, the

China Bayles
"Herbs of Good and Ill Omen"
Pecan Springs Enterprise

Karen was . . . dead? My stomach muscles knotted. "Oh, no!" I exclaimed.

"Oh, God," Ruby whispered. "That's *terrible*! Oh, poor Felicity! She was close to her mother — losing her will be so hard!"

There was a long silence while all three of us tried to deal with the news. I don't know about the others' feelings, but I was coping with a jumble of fury, grief, and an almost physical pain.

"I'm sorry," Sheila muttered. "I am . . . so sorry."

I understood. Every good cop I have ever known has hated the senseless loss of a life. I wouldn't be surprised if she was blaming herself for Karen's death. It might be unreasonable, but good cops do that, too.

Trying to steady my voice, I turned to Ruby. "Was Kitt calling to tell you about Karen?"

Ruby shook her head. "No. I don't think . . ." She paused, gulped once, started again. "I don't think she knows about Karen yet. She was calling to ask if I'd seen Gretchen today. The two of them were supposed to get together this morning in the media lab, to work on editing their film. They were going to meet Sheila later this afternoon. But Gretchen never showed up. Kitt's been calling her cell, but there's no answer. She's called friends, too. Nobody's seen her."

Sheila and I exchanged glances, and Sheila's mouth tightened. "Has Kitt turned in a report to the police?"

"I asked her, but she said she thought there was some sort of waiting period on missing persons — twenty-four hours or something. I told her you were here and that I'd find out and call her right back."

"There's no waiting period," Sheila replied shortly. "And given Gretchen's connection to Dr. Prior, I think we need to open a search as soon as possible. I suppose Kitt has checked with Gretchen's parents?"

"I asked," Ruby replied, "but Kitt said there's no point in trying. They're out of town and almost impossible to reach."

"The Keenes are doing anthropological fieldwork," I put in. "Both of them. They're in Belize, in the jungle, and won't be back for another two weeks. But Jake — Gretchen's younger sister — is here in Pecan Springs. She had supper with us last night. She's the one who told me about the phone call Kitt recorded."

I remembered that the two Keene daughters, Gretchen and Jake, were staying by themselves, with a next-door neighbor to look in on them. Which was certainly okay, since both girls were responsible young people, old enough to manage by themselves, in ordinary circumstances. This particular circumstance did not sound at all ordinary. Maybe I should —

"Let's not panic," Sheila cautioned. "The girl probably just forgot about meeting her friend."

"But she doesn't answer her cell," Ruby reminded her.

"Yes, there's that." Sheila glanced at me. "You don't happen to have the younger sister's cell phone number, do you?"

"No, but Brian does," I replied promptly. "I'll get it."

I reached in my pocket for my phone as Sheila said to Ruby, "Under the circumstances, we'll make this a priority. Call Kitt back and —" She stopped. "No. Give me her number, Ruby, and I'll call her myself. If she'll come down to the station, we can get the information into the system faster."

I had turned off my phone while we were having lunch, and when I turned it on, I saw that there were a couple of missed calls from McQuaid. But I had to talk to Brian first. We had hired him to paint our house this summer — a big job, since the house itself is big: a two-story, five-bedroom Victorian with a turret and a porch that wraps around three sides. For the past month, Brian has been working on it steadily, with a little help from Caitie on the trim around the windows. (We solved two problems at the same time, as it turned out. While he's painting, he's also keeping an eye on Caitlin.)

It was several rings before Brian picked up, and I pictured him on a ladder, a paintbrush in one hand. "I need Jake's cell number," I said, reaching over the counter for a pencil and a scrap of paper.

"Hang on a sec," he said. "I've got it on my speed dial, and I never remember it." A moment later, he read it off to me and I wrote it down. "How come you're asking, Mom? Is there a problem?"

I didn't want to spook him. "Not really," I said in an offhand tone. "Ruby is looking for Gretchen, and I thought Jake might know where she is." I paused. "You haven't seen her, have you? Gretchen, I mean."

"Are you kidding?" He laughed. "The only thing I've seen is the business end of this paintbrush. Oh, and Dad called. He was trying to get in touch with you. He said he left a couple of messages on your phone."

"I had it turned off. Anything urgent?"

"Nope. He just wanted to tell you that he has to go to Austin this afternoon — some research he's doing for Mr. Lipman. He probably won't make it home in time for supper. He said he'd pick something up for himself and we should just go ahead."

"Okay," I said. "In that case, how about if I stop at Gino's and get a pizza?" Gino's Italian Pizza Kitchen served up Pecan Springs' very first pizza in the late 1950s, at a time when most folks around here had never tasted one. Texans tend to go for burgers or fried chicken, and pizza was slow to catch on with the townies. But the kids at CTSU — which was a small teachers' college back then — loved it. They made Gino's an enduring success. Gino Senior is gone now, but Gino Junior carries on, and his pizza is still the best in town.

"Great by me," Brian replied enthusiastically. "Bring home a super-size and I'll ask Jake to come over."

"I'll ask her myself," I replied, thanked him, and clicked the connection off. "I've got Jake's cell number," I said to Sheila. "How about if I call her?"

"Please," Sheila said. "You know her."

But a call to Jake didn't net us any information. She had last seen Gretchen at breakfast and didn't expect her home until late evening. I didn't want to alarm her, so I didn't say why I was asking.

"She left at nine to meet Kitt at the media lab," she added. "They're working on the rough cut today. Here, let me give you Gretchen's cell number."

I took it down. "We're having pizza tonight," I said. "How about coming over and eating with us?" I paused and added, "Brian would have asked you, but he's got his hands full with a paintbrush."

"Sure," she said enthusiastically. "If Brian can pick me up. Gretchen and I are sharing Mom's car, but she drove it to the media lab. She's planning to work with Kitt this evening, so I'm on my own. I'd love to come for pizza."

I hadn't thought of transportation. Between the kids and their friends, I sometimes feel like I'm running a taxi service. "We can save Brian a trip into town if I pick you up on my way home from the shop," I said. "Okay?"

"Sure. That'll be great," Jake said. "Thanks!"

I said good-bye and hung up quickly, before she could ask if there was any news from the hospital. I didn't want to tell her that Dr. Prior was dead — not over the phone. She was going to be very upset.

"Jake thinks her sister is working with Kitt at the lab all day," I told Sheila. "No help there. But she did say that Gretchen is driving their mother's car."

"Right," Sheila said, sounding resigned. "Kitt can give me a description of Gretchen, and I can pull the mother's vehicle registration. But I'll have to phone the sister and get a number where I can reach the parents."

I copied Jake's cell number and gave it to her. "But could you hold off on contacting her?" I asked, still concerned about frightening Jake. "She's coming to my house for pizza this evening. If Gretchen hasn't turned up by that time, I'll tell her what's going on and get the Keenes' contact information for you. There probably aren't that many cell towers in the jungles of Belize, anyway — and there's nothing the parents can do right away."

Sheila put the number into her notebook. "Works for me." She turned toward the door. "I'll call Kitt and meet her at the station."

I stopped her. "Don't you think it would be a good idea if you sent a uniform to pick her up at CTSU? We don't know what's happened to Gretchen. It might not be smart for Kitt to go wandering around —"

"Good idea." Sheila opened the door. "I'll just pick Kitt up myself. The campus isn't that far out of my way."

People often tell me that they'd love to quit their jobs and enjoy the "freedom" of owning their own business. They seem to have the idea that as a shop owner, I can come and go whenever the spirit moves me. Of course, it is true that I can get one of my helpers to take care of customers while I run an errand or spend a couple of hours in the garden. It's also true that we are closed every Monday, which is my day to get caught up with the rest of my life — except, of course, when there's something at the shop that I desperately need to do. But Tuesday through Saturday, ten through five, I'm on the job. Even when I'd rather be somewhere else.

Like this Friday afternoon, when I would rather have been out looking for Gretchen. Unfortunately, I didn't know her well enough to know where to start looking or even to suggest where other people might look. But I definitely felt I should be doing *something*, since Gretchen's parents were friends and her sister was my son's girl-friend, almost a member of the family. The feeling was unsettling.

Luckily for me, though, the foot traffic in the shop was heavy, with the phone ringing frequently and customers in and out most of the afternoon. I was almost too busy finding plants, looking for books, answering questions, checking in a new shipment of bulk dried herbs, and managing the cash register to think about the death of Karen Prior or worry about what might have happened to Gretchen.

Almost, but not quite. Karen was a dark shadow at the back of my mind and Gretchen was an ominous knot of apprehension in the pit of my stomach, and the minute I closed the shop and finished clearing the register, they jostled their way into my full awareness. Karen was dead and I could only mourn her, try to think of a way to comfort her daughter, and hope that her killer would be caught and convicted and imprisoned for as long as the law allowed.

But Gretchen was — Gretchen was *where*? What had happened to her? What did Gretchen's disappearance, if that was what it was, have to do with Karen's murder? Was there any connection? And what did Karen's murder have to do with her students' documentary, if anything?

Ruby was scheduled to teach a class that afternoon, and I hadn't seen her. When I finished the end-of-the-day chores, I locked the outside doors in the tearoom and the shop, turned off the lights (except for the one I leave burning behind the counter), and went into the Crystal Cave to see if there had been any news.

If you've ever been in Ruby's shop, you'll remember it as an extraordinary experience. When you come in, you're struck by the fragrance of Ruby's handcrafted sandalwood and clove incense; the sweet, delicate music of the Celtic harp DVDs she likes to play; and the dragons and faerie figures hanging from the ceiling. You can shop shelves stocked with rune stones, crystals, and candles; tarot cards and New Age CDs and goddess T-shirts and colorful scarves; ritual supplies and altar materials and fantastic jewelry. You can browse books on spirituality and astrology and the mind-body connection and healing herbs. There are a couple of comfortable chairs; nobody will make you get up if you'd like to sit down and read for a while. And if you peek around the corner into the small classroom, you might see a dozen women on zafus and meditation benches, quietly meditating; or find Ruby with a circle of tarot students seated on the carpeted floor, cards spread out in front of them. Or you might spot her with her projector and screen and Power-Point, discussing a birth chart with an astrology class.

Today, her students — from their serene expressions and their quiet, gentle good-byes, I guessed it was a meditation class — were just leaving the shop. I could hear Becky running the vacuum in the classroom. Ruby, still wearing the gold silk chiffon kimono jacket she puts on when she teaches meditation, was perched on a stool behind her counter, clearing out her register. She looked up when I came in.

"Any word from Sheila?" she asked quickly. "Have they located Gretchen yet?"

"That's what I was about to ask you," I said. "Kitt would have called here if Gretchen had shown up, wouldn't she?"

"I don't know," Ruby said, pulling a long face. "She might not have thought of it." She closed the register drawer and reached for her cell. "It won't hurt to check. I'll call her." But a moment later, she was shaking her head. "The call went to her voice-mail box. She must have turned off her phone."

"I suppose there's nothing else we can do." I glanced at my watch. I had to get to the bank before the drive-up window closed. "McQuaid went to Austin and won't be home for supper, so the kids and I are doing a pizza from Gino's and a salad. Jake is coming, too. Want to join us? Caitlin would love it."

Ruby and Caitlin are special friends. They bonded when Caitlin first arrived, through a mutual love of the color pink and all things faerie. (It's a long story: I'll have to tell you some other time.)

"Thanks," Ruby said. "I appreciate the offer, but Hark is bringing a couple of steaks to throw on the grill." She shrugged out of her kimono and hung it on a hook.

"How's that going?" I asked curiously.

I knew she was seeing Hark again — how seriously, I could only guess from Hark's frequent smiles and general geniality. He's had a crush on Ruby for several years, but in her heart of hearts, she's been stuck on Colin Fowler. Their fatally flawed affair ended when Colin was murdered two years ago. Ruby's survivor guilt was enhanced when she learned that she was the beneficiary of his substantial life insurance, now safely tucked away for Baby Grace's college education. But her heart-to-heart connection with Colin changed when she went to visit a friend who had just inherited a haunted house built by a widow whose grief for her lost loved ones had imprisoned her for a lifetime — and even beyond. Ruby came back from that visit feeling a great deal better about a great many things in her life.

"How's that going?" Ruby repeated. She put her head on one side, as if she were trying to decide how to answer. "Well, if you're hoping that I'll say I've fallen madly in love with Hark, you'll be disappointed."

I suppose I was, a little. Ruby in love is a sight for sore eyes. But then again, not so much. For Ruby, love has always been marked by excitement, passion, futile longing, and the expectation of heartbreak. If it's none of these things, it isn't love. Hark is not at all exciting, and although I can't personally speak to his potential for physical passion, it's hard to imagine him inspiring either futile longing or heartbreak. He's a big man who makes me think of Garrison Keillor — slow talking, slow moving, with a heavy, bearlike build, sloping shoulders, and dark hair that's always rumpled because he's always running his fingers through it. He is quiet and intelligent, with a gentle and generous spirit. He cares for Ruby and can provide the kind of stability she needs — even though she doesn't know she needs it.

In other words, he is definitely not Ruby's type.

And then she surprised me.

"Not *madly* in love, anyway," she said.

"Oh, yeah?" Now I really was curious. "What's that supposed to mean?"

"That I like him a lot?" It was a question. Pensive, she tapped the end of her pencil against the tip of her nose and added, "That I like him a lot — and love him a little, maybe?"

"Well, good for you," I said heartily. Ever since I've known her, I've thought that Ruby's problem with love is loving too much. Liking a lot and loving a little strikes me as a substantial improvement. "How does Hark feel about this development?"

I didn't have to ask, however. Patience is one of Hark's signature virtues, along with sturdiness, reliability, et cetera. I imagined that he was pleased. Delighted, probably. Overjoyed.

Ruby didn't get to answer. Her cell phone dinged briskly. She reached for it, spoke, listened, and then said, "That's great news, Kitt! Where?" To me, she mouthed, *They found Gretchen.*

"Wonderful!" I said and waited for the details.

Her eyes widened as she listened. "Well,

131

things can be replaced. They're positive she's going to be okay?" A long exhale, more listening. "Of course," she said finally. "It's good that they're keeping her overnight. You never can tell about concussions. Thanks for letting me know." She closed her phone with a snap. "That's a relief," she said to me.

"Where in the world *was* she?" I asked urgently.

"In the janitors' closet in the basement of the communications building on campus. The door was locked from the outside. One of the custodians heard her banging on the wall and let her out. A good thing, too." She shivered. "It might have been Monday before she was found."

"The *basement*?" I was startled. "What in the world was she doing down there?"

"It's the quickest way to get from the parking lot to the elevator," Ruby said. "I know, because Kitt wanted to show me around the media lab a couple of weeks ago, and that's the route we took. Since it's summer, there are a lot more parking spaces around the back of the building. Kitt and Gretchen have been parking back there and using the basement door. It's a little spooky, but there was no reason to think it wasn't safe."

"Yeah, right," I said dryly. "Nothing is ever not safe, until it isn't."

Ruby nodded. "Well, it wasn't safe this time, obviously. Gretchen was waiting for the elevator when it happened. She's got a mild concussion, and of course she was plenty scared, especially when she began to think she might not get out for a while. But otherwise, she's going to be okay. The guy who hit her snatched her camera — her purse, too."

"*Hit* her?" I asked, thinking immediately of Karen. And then, "Took her camera?"

Ruby nodded. "Her camcorder. It's one of the digital cameras the girls are using to record their documentary — a really nice one. Apparently somebody saw her go in, knew that the basement was likely to be deserted, and wanted a camera. This one was just too tempting to pass up, so he grabbed it."

"Her purse." I narrowed my eyes. "What about her purse?"

"Kitt said the janitor found it in a trash can just outside the basement door. Empty, of course. The only thing in it was her car keys. I guess he didn't want to be charged with auto theft."

Her camcorder. One of the cameras the girls were using to record their documentary. My skin prickled. Something was going on here — something besides the opportunistic theft of an expensive camera and the contents of a purse.

"They're keeping her overnight at the hospital?" I asked.

"Uh-huh." Ruby frowned. "You said her parents are in Belize. What about her sister? Will she be okay by herself?" She paused, concerned. "I wonder if anybody has thought to let her know what's happened."

I hoisted my bag over my shoulder. "As it happens, I'm on my way to pick up her sister. She's having supper with us tonight. I'll tell her about Gretchen — if she doesn't already know — and ask if she'd like to stay at our house overnight." I gave Ruby a knowing grin. "You and Hark have a wonderful time. Don't do anything you wouldn't want to see on the front page of the *Enterprise.*"

"That leaves it pretty open," Ruby said.

I was halfway to the door when I thought of something else. I turned. "This other girl, Kitt. She's a friend of Amy's, I understand."

"Right," Ruby replied. "In fact, they're neighbors. I met her at one of Amy and Kate's get-togethers."

"What's her living situation? I mean, does she live alone? With a girlfriend?"

"She's married," Ruby replied. "Her husband is also a grad student, in engineering, I believe." She looked at me. "Why are you asking?"

"No reason," I said. "Just curious."

But it was more than that, of course. The bits and pieces were beginning to add up. And I didn't like what I saw on the bottom line.

That pizza had to wait for a while. Five minutes before I got to the Keenes' house, someone from the police department called Jake to tell her that her sister had been in an accident. She was frantic to go to the hospital and make sure that Gretchen was really okay, so that was where we headed. But the Adams County Hospital is only a short drive from the Keene house, and I managed to stall Jake's questions about what had happened to her sister.

"I don't have the details," I said. "Let's save all that until we see Gretchen. She can tell us." Jake — upset enough already — complied.

Julie Paprock, whom I met when she helped out with Caitie's Girl Scout troop, was on duty at the hospital reception desk. She's a platinum blonde with a trim figure and plenty of bounce — which she needs to

135

keep up with all of her volunteer work in the Pecan Springs art community. I introduced Jake and explained who we wanted to see.

Julie gave Jake a sympathetic look. "Your sister is feeling much better. I know she'll be glad to see you." To me, she added, "Gretchen's friend Kitt just went to the cafeteria to get some supper, so both of you can go in." She gave us the room number. "But when Kitt comes back, one of you will have to leave. Okay?"

We thanked her and went down the hall to the room.

At twenty-three, Gretchen is a grown-up version of Jake, not quite as athletic, a little more well-rounded, a little less blond, and very pretty. But not at the moment. Her head was bandaged; there were abrasions on her arms, her cheeks, and her forehead; and she was going to have one heck of a shiner in the morning. Jake burst into tears when she saw her, and I was startled at the damage. From the abrasions, I guessed that after she was knocked unconscious, she was dragged facedown across the cement basement floor and into the closet.

"I'm okay, guys," Gretchen said weakly. "Really I am." She reached for Jake's hand, managing a chuckle. "Or I will be tomorrow, when they let me go home." She closed her eyes. "Right now I've got one humongous headache. It just won't quit."

"But what *happened*?" Jake burst out. "All the cop said was that you were in an accident, and I was scared to death. Is the car okay? Where is it?" To me, she added, "It's our mother's car. She told us we could use it as much as we wanted while she and Dad were gone."

Gretchen opened her eyes and glanced at me. I shook my head just a little, letting her know that I hadn't told her sister what had happened.

"It wasn't that kind of accident, Jake," Gretchen said. "The car is perfectly okay. Kitt says it's right where I've been parking it this summer. Behind the communications building."

Jake let out her breath. "Well, *that's* good." She paused, trying to figure this out. "But if it wasn't the car, what kind of accident was it?"

Gretchen sighed. "I was waiting for the elevator in the basement of the communications building. Somebody conked me over the head and snatched my camcorder and my purse."

"Oh, no!" Jake exclaimed, horrified. "Oh, Gretchen, poor you!"

"Afraid so. I woke up in a cleaning closet, but the jerk who hit me had bolted the door on the outside. I was in there for hours and hours. Somebody finally heard me banging a bucket against the wall and let me out." She grinned crookedly. "The only serious damage is to my head. And that's not permanent, so there's no need to alarm Mom and Dad. The news will keep until they get home. There's nothing they can do, anyway."

"Did you get a glimpse of your assailant?" I asked.

"I wish." Gretchen sighed. "As I told the cops, Ms. Bayles, I didn't hear a thing. I have no idea what he hit me with — or even whether it was a he or a she."

"So you've already been questioned?" I asked.

"Yes. Twice. By a policeman and then by the chief." She managed a smile. "I feel important."

"I can think of less painful ways to be important." I frowned. "The video that you and Kitt were working on — had you deleted the files from your camera?"

"No," Gretchen said. "They were all still there, although of course I've backed everything up on my laptop. The camera has a thirty-two-gigabyte memory card, about four hours of recording. There were two other cards in my purse, with more of the footage. Kitt and I were going to download everything — her files and mine — to the computer in the media lab this morning. We need to start editing if we're going to get finished by the end of the term."

"I see," I said. "Did you get your purse back?"

"Yes, and I'm glad. It's my favorite purse. Why?"

"Just an idea," I said. "If you'll tell me where it is, I'll check for those memory cards."

"In the drawer here beside the bed." Her head must hurt, because she gestured with her eyes, careful not to move. "They're in the side pocket, in a plastic sleeve."

I took out the purse and explored the side pocket with my fingers. "I can't find them," I said. "You look, Jake." I handed the purse to her, but Jake couldn't find them, either.

"Damn," Gretchen exclaimed, disgusted. "The jerk took my camera *and* the memory cards. And my credit card. But at least he left the car keys."

"And as long as the files are backed up, you still have everything," I said.

"Yes, but —" Gretchen stopped, frowning. "The camera. Those memory cards. You don't suppose —"

She was silent for a moment, and I wondered where she was going with this. When I heard her next question, I knew she had made the same connection I had.

"Ms. Bayles, how is Dr. Prior? I asked a couple of nurses, but nobody on this floor seems to know. That seemed a little odd to me, but . . ." Frowning, intent, she searched my face.

That was when I had to tell the girls that Karen had died. The next few moments were difficult for all three of us. We wept, talked, and wept some more. By the time we had dried our tears, Kitt — a short, wiry, high-energy young woman with pink-streaked brown hair spiked in a punk cut — had returned from the cafeteria, with a milk shake for Gretchen. I had never met her, so I introduced myself, then turned to Jake, remembering what Julie had said about one of us having to leave.

"Brian and Caitie will be wondering what's happened to supper. I'd better go pick up that pizza." I paused. "You can stay here with Gretchen or come with me — and stay overnight, if you want. The guest room is always ready." That's the thing about living in a house that's big enough for a B&B. There's plenty of room for a guest or two.

Jake was indecisive. "If I hang out here, I guess Kitt can take me home."

"No, Jake," Gretchen said firmly. "I want you to go with Ms. Bayles — and spend the night at their house, too. I'll feel better if I know you're there."

"But I think I should stay with you," Jake protested.

"It's an order from your big sis," Gretchen said, taking the sting out with a smile. "I'm in good hands. And Kitt and I have some talking to do."

I understood. Gretchen had to tell Kitt about Karen's death. But I also wanted them to talk about the other business, the camera. To nudge them toward that, I said, "Maybe you could discuss those missing memory cards." I added, casually, "Gretchen, how about if Jake and I stopped at your house and picked up your laptop — just to be on the safe side? We could take it to my house."

"The safe side . . ." Gretchen pulled her brows together. "Do you really think —" She stopped, considered, and came up with the right answer. "Sure," she said. "Good idea. Okay, Jake?"

"I don't see why," Jake said with a shrug. "But it's fine with me. Listen, Gretch, is it okay if Ms. Bayles and I swing past the com-

munications building so I can pick up
Mom's car?" She patted her purse. "I have
my keys."

"Another good idea," Gretchen said approvingly. She looked at me. "Let's talk
tomorrow morning. Could you call me?"

"Sure thing," I said. "You rest now. Get a
good night's sleep."

"Sleep?" Kitt grinned. "Are you kidding?
There are some really hunky docs out there.
I'm gonna load this girl into a wheelchair.
We're goin' cruisin'."

"Hey, Kitt," I said, "I thought Ruby told
me you were married."

"I am," she said. "And I love my guy. But
a little eye candy never hurt — and it
doesn't even have any calories."

Jake and I laughed. Gretchen sighed.

"Kitt," she said, "I don't think I'm up to
cruising. Not tonight, anyway."

On the way out of the hospital, I stopped
at Julie's reception desk. "Keep an eye on
Gretchen and Kitt," I said with a grin. "Kitt
is threatening to take Gretchen cruising,
looking for hunky docs. But the hunky docs
just might come looking for them."

Julie is a mother and grandmother who
likes to be involved in her kids' lives, so I
knew she would understand. "Oh, to be
young again," she said with a twinkle.

■ ■ ■ ■

It was after eight when McQuaid got back from Austin. Brian and Jake were playing a video game, in Brian's room with the door open, standard operating procedure at our house when we have kid guests. Caitlin was putting her girls to bed in their coop, a ritual that involves saying a personal good night to each chicken, with congratulations and thanks for the egg laid that day. I had finished folding two loads of laundry and was curled up in my reading chair with the latest issue of *The Herbarist* (the annual journal of the Herb Society of America) and a glass of wine. McQuaid came into the room with a Lone Star beer and a bowl of stick pretzels and sat down in his recliner.

"Whew," he said. "Friday night traffic in Austin is a bitch, pure and simple." He crunched a pretzel. "Make that 'any night traffic in Austin,'" he said. "That city has gone from bad to worse, traffic-wise."

"Did you have any supper?" I closed the journal. "If not, you'll have to forage. We finished the pizza, but there's some bean salad left, and plenty of sandwich fixings."

"Thanks. I picked something up on the way home." He paused. "Have you heard from the hospital today? How's Karen Prior doing?"

I took off my reading glasses and gave him the bad news. McQuaid had known Karen longer than I had and had worked with her on several faculty committees. He was as shocked and saddened — and angered — by the news as I had been. And when I related what had happened to Gretchen, his eyes grew even darker.

"Son of a bitch," he muttered. He chewed on the information for a while, adding it up. He came to the same conclusion I had. "You say you've got Gretchen's laptop?"

"Yes. Upstairs, in my bottom bureau drawer. I felt a little awkward about asking, but Gretchen seemed to get the point."

McQuaid put his beer down. "Let's see if I have this right," he said, in his cop voice. "Karen Prior was supervising the filming of a student documentary about a murder that took place thirteen or fourteen years ago here in Pecan Springs. She was attacked in the mall parking lot, but her purse wasn't taken — doesn't look like a robbery, and the circumstances suggest a prearranged meeting, maybe having to do with the documentary. One of the students was attacked two days later. Her camera and its memory cards were stolen." He frowned.

"So tell me about this cold case the students are filming."

"Here's what I know." I began to relate Ruby's story about Christine Morris' murder. I didn't get very far.

"Whoa." He held up a pretzel like a baton. "Christine Morris."

"Yes. She was married to —"

"Douglas Clark. The developer."

"That's right." I eyed him curiously. "What do you know about the marriage?"

"Nada. But I might know something about the divorce." McQuaid nipped off the end of the pretzel. "In fact, my trip to Austin . . ." He paused, gave it a second thought, then said, "Okay. Go on with your story." He popped the rest of the pretzel in his mouth.

"You're not going to tell me, huh?"

I was not being snarky. Sometimes McQuaid discusses his cases with me; sometimes he doesn't. When he first hung out his shingle, I promised myself I wouldn't nag him for details, no matter how tantalizing the case might be or how much I might like to sink my lawyerly teeth into it. I've kept my word.

"Maybe later," he said, taking another swig of beer. "Go on."

I gave him the story at length and in

detail, and not omitting my tangential connection to the case via my Houston ex–law firm buddy Johnnie Carlson, attorney for the defense, now deceased. And Johnnie's theory of an alternative suspect, which the judge had kept from the jury. But which had turned out not to be necessary, because the jury had acquitted.

McQuaid listened and worked on his beer. When I was finished, he said, "I need to let Charlie know about this. It might have some bearing on his reason for sending me to Austin today. Any problem with that?"

"Of course not." I added wryly, "But you might just ask Charlie if there's any problem with your sharing your trip to Austin with me. Not that I'm curious, of course."

"What? You curious? Never." McQuaid picked up his empty and heaved himself out of his chair. "I'll talk to him right now. If he's sober, that is."

"Good luck," I said, putting on my reading glasses and picking up the journal again. Charlie is one of my favorite people, but he's developed a serious drinking problem, especially on weekends. His weekend usually starts on Thursday night and ends, oh, around Tuesday, sometimes Wednesday. The drinking may be affecting his legal practice, but his clients are mostly local folks who have known him a long time and like him enough to take his failings in stride. At least they know what they're getting into.

Fifteen minutes later, McQuaid was back in his chair, this time with a glass of iced tea and a couple of Cass' lavender cookies.

"Was he sober?" I asked.

"Almost." McQuaid shook his head. "Dunno how that guy functions, the amount of booze he puts away."

I put *The Herbarist* down again and peered over the top of my glasses. "You going to tell me what that trip to Austin was about?" Not nagging, honest.

"Yeah. Charlie says it's okay." He munched on a cookie. "Actually, what he said was, 'Tell China to figure it out and tell us what's going on.' "

I frowned. "Was he being sarcastic? He was really PO'd with me when I got involved in that business with George Timms." Timms was a local big shot who recently got into trouble over breaking and entering and suspicion of murder — then had a fatal encounter with an authentic Texas mountain lion. Charlie came close to accusing me of siccing the cat on his client.

"Sarcastic? Not on your life, kid." McQuaid chuckled. "Lipman's got a crush on you. If I hadn't married you, he would've been first in line."

"Oh, yeah? Well, I'm complimented," I said ironically. "The next time he gives me hell for sticking my nose into one of his cases I'll just think of it as a big smoochy kiss. So what was up with your trip to Austin?" Not nagging, no.

McQuaid stretched out in his chair. "Charlie asked me to look into the details of a major property deal — a mall development on I-35 south of Austin, about twenty years ago."

I considered this for a moment. "Help me out here. Is this supposed to be related to what we've been talking about?"

McQuaid shrugged. "Maybe, maybe not. We'll see what it looks like after I have a chance to dig into the financing details. But Charlie has the notion — could be a cocka-mamie idea, of course — that the development package was part of a hidden assets scheme." He gave me a significant look. "Doug Clark was the developer — one of the developers," he corrected himself. "It was a big project, and there was quite a bit of local money in it, one way or the other."

"Ah, so," I said thoughtfully. *A hidden assets scheme.* Now, that was interesting. In fact, it was downright intriguing. I sipped my wine, imagining the possibilities, which were legion. "According to Ruby, Charlie handled Christine Morris' divorce. She sued on grounds of adultery, and Charlie brokered a substantial property settlement. Christine got the house, the artwork they'd acquired while they were married, and a big chunk of change — exactly how big, nobody knows, of course." I paused. "But from what you've just said, I get the idea that Charlie is now thinking that not all of the marital property was declared at the time of the divorce."

"What?" McQuaid raised both eyebrows, pretending enormous astonishment. "You're suggesting that somebody *cheated*?"

Maybe you won't be shocked to learn that one spouse can (and sometimes does) attempt to conceal money and property from the other spouse, during the marriage — and during the divorce. If so, you won't be surprised when I say that, given the will and the way, those assets may be so cleverly hidden that they can never be traced and properly divided. If you're planning to get a divorce and you suspect that your spouse intends to tiptoe away in the dark of night with some of the community property hidden under his coat, you need to hire a lawyer who specializes in preventing (or discovering) this sort of shenanigan. Don't hire Charlie Lipman. He's a good guy, a good lawyer, and he talks a good game — when he's sober. But he might not be careful enough when it comes to getting an accurate valuation of your marital property and community assets. I would hate for you to get gypped.

"So the bottom line is that Charlie suspects that Doug Clark got away with a chunk of change," I said. "And if it was a mall deal, it might have been a *big* chunk."

"It's possible," McQuaid acknowledged, putting words to what was going through my mind. "Charlie handles a lot of run-of-the-mill divorces, but he isn't a specialist. At the time, he might not have asked the right questions or dug deep enough to find everything."

"And there's the alcohol," I said. Charlie was drinking now. He might have been drinking back then.

"Yes, there's that," McQuaid agreed.

I chewed on my lip. "But let's say that Doug Clark hid some of the marital assets and defrauded his wife out of some of her share of the community property. The Clark-Morris divorce was a long time ago. And besides, the wench is dead. Over a decade dead. Not to be callous, but the issue seems moot to me."

"Moot to me, too," McQuaid conceded. "But let's just say that, at some point after the divorce was final, Christine herself began to suspect that the divvy had been based on an incomplete accounting, and decided she wanted more."

My turn to raise an eyebrow. "Is that what happened? If so, I wonder when."

It wasn't an idle question. In Texas, the court divides the community property when the decree is granted. If one spouse discovers hidden assets after that time, she (or he) can file a motion to overturn the divorce agreement and reallocate the assets. There are exceptions, but in general, this should be done within two years after the final decree. After that, the injured spouse — ex-spouse, that is — has to sue the other for marital fraud in civil court. There is no statute of limitations on fraud.

And then the issue began to seem a little less moot. Yes, the wench was dead, which was the point. Was she dead *because* she was prepared to charge her ex-husband with marital fraud? Was Doug Clark the alternative suspect Johnnie had been prepared to name?

"I have no idea when," McQuaid replied, "or even *if.* Charlie didn't get into that kind of detail. He just gave me the general picture, pointed in the direction of the assets — that is, where he thought the assets might have been hidden — and told me to start digging." He finished one cookie and picked up a second. "That's what I was doing this afternoon."

"Did you have any luck?"

"Not yet. But I talked to a guy who was involved in the deal and came up with a couple of leads. I don't know if they'll pan out, but they're worth following up. I can't do anything more until Monday, when the Williamson County tax assessor's office is open and I can look at the property records."

I nodded. McQuaid is a top-flight investigator, competent, thorough, and dogged. It's what he liked best about police work — what he likes best about being a PI. If the information was out there, he would find it.

But a bigger question had come to me. "Doesn't all this seem a little . . . um, coincidental? Gretchen and Kitt are currently making a documentary about the Christine Morris case. Karen and Gretchen are attacked, and Gretchen's files are stolen. And here's Charlie, almost two decades after the fact, hiring an investigator to look into Doug Clark's financial holdings."

"Yeah," McQuaid said.

"Not to mention that private investigators don't come cheap," I said. "Even those who are friends of the lawyers who hire them and might be inclined to give them a break."

"Hey." McQuaid gave me a wounded look. "I bill Charlie at the same rate I bill every other lawyer." He finished the cookie and licked his fingers. "Well, maybe a little less. But not much."

I went on. "I have known Charlie Lipman a long time, and while I wouldn't exactly call him a skinflint, I've never known him to put down so much as a nickel of his own money on a case. So who the heck is picking up the tab? It certainly isn't the possibly defrauded spouse, who has gone on to glory. But who else would have an interest in this matter?"

"I have no clue." McQuaid sat there, his eyes narrowed, going over the situation in his mind. "But it's something I'd like to know." He looked at me. "What's on your agenda tomorrow, China?"

"It's Saturday," I reminded him. "You know what that means."

He nodded. "Farmers' market. Right? And then you'll be at the shop the rest of the day?"

"That's the plan." This is the second year for the Pecan Springs Farmers' Market,

153

which has turned into a popular community tradition. "Caitie will be helping, as usual. When we're done, she's going to play with one of her friends. I'm picking her up after I close the shop. I assume that Brian will finish painting the porch. What about you?"

"Not sure yet," he said. "But if Charlie's available — and sober — I'd like to talk to him."

"One more thing," I said. "On the way out of the hospital this evening, I stopped to chat with Helen Berger, the charge nurse. She said that the doctor will likely release Gretchen tomorrow, probably after lunch. I'm thinking it would be good if she stayed here for a few days, instead of going home. Just to be on the safe side. Jake could stay, as well. The guest room has two beds."

McQuaid cocked his head. "And this is because . . ."

"This is because some unknown assailant killed Karen," I said patiently, "and conked Gretchen over the head. Because if Gretchen were my daughter, and I was in the jungles of Belize on a research trip, I would want a friend to keep a close eye on her. Because —"

"Probably the smart thing to do," McQuaid interrupted. He stood up and stretched. "Hey, it's a pretty night out there.

How about if we go sit on the porch swing for a little while?" He held out his hand enticingly. "Looks like a thunderstorm might be coming in from the west. We can listen to the tree frogs and watch the lightning flicker, and . . . well, neck."

Tree frogs, flickers of lightning, maybe even a roll of thunder or two. Around our house, there is never a dull moment.

But necking . . . now, that's another matter entirely. You never know where something like that might lead.

CHAPTER FIVE

The plant we call Queen Anne's lace (*Daucus carota*) was said to be associated with the devil, perhaps because of its similarity to the deadly poison hemlock. The flower is named for Anne, wife of James I of England and an avid lace maker. The tiny reddish-purple flower in the center was said to represent a drop of the queen's blood, caused when she pricked her finger. Children were warned not to pick it and bring it into the house, because bad luck would certainly follow.

In traditional medicine, a tea made from the root of *Daucus carota* was prescribed as a diuretic to prevent and treat kidney stones. Hippocrates reported that the seeds of the plant were used as a popular contraceptive and abortifacient.

Other folk names for the plant: mother-die,

devil's plague.

China Bayles
"Herbs of Good and Ill Omen"
Pecan Springs Enterprise

Friday night's thunderstorm was gone by midnight and the morning sun rose in a brilliant blue sky, on what promised to be a very hot July Saturday. It was a perfect day for loading up the kids and a big picnic cooler and the tubes and heading for the Guadalupe River or driving to Austin to go swimming in Barton Springs, which averages a chilly 68 degrees year-round, even when it's 102 in the shade.

But summer Saturdays are market days. Caitie and I were up early and out in the garden to pick and bundle up bunches of fresh basil, rosemary, dill, parsley, sage, and cilantro (not my favorite herb, but lots of people like it). Usually, I like to do the picking after the morning dew has dried, but we were pushed. By the time the raindrops and dew had dried, our market stall would be set up and the cooler of fresh herbs would be half-empty. By noon, when the market closed, every bunch of herbs would be gone and I'd be wishing we'd picked more.

This is the farmers' market's second summer, and both the vendors and the shoppers are thrilled with its success. The location is especially convenient to Thyme and Seasons: across the street from the shop, in the parking lot of Dos Amigas restaurant. This morning, two of our local farms (CSAs, or community-supported agricultural enterprises) had set up double booths and were displaying an artful arrangement of organically grown summer vegetables. Donna Fletcher's Mistletoe Creek Farm booth was especially attractive, with baskets of tomatoes, tomatillos, green beans, and red and yellow and green bell peppers; stacks of sweet-corn ears; pyramids of cantaloupes and melons; and trays of eggplant, okra, cucumbers, and summer squash. A couple of Fredericksburg peach growers were having trouble keeping up with the traffic at their booths, while other booths featured home-baked artisan breads, as well as cheese from Hill Country goats, honey from hardworking Adams County bees, and even locally brewed beers. The idea, of course, is to encourage people to develop a taste for locally grown vegetables and fruits, instead of lettuce imported from California or cheese from Wisconsin or apples from New Zealand. It's an idea that seems to be catching on.

Caitie and I do this every Saturday morning between May and October, so it doesn't take us long to be ready for the early-bird customers. Leaving Becky in charge of the shop for the morning, I set up the blue plastic canopy (the Texas sun would be brutal without it), put up the shelves at the back of the stall, and covered our two tables with red-checked oil-cloth. On the shelves, Caitie arranged packages of dried herbs and potpourri, handcrafted soaps and lotions, homemade herbal jellies, boxes of herbal teas, and books on growing and cooking with herbs. From the canopy, I hung several chili ristras, onions, and rosemary wreaths and swags. On the table: trays of two- and four-inch pots of herb plants: parsley, thyme, sage, bay, lamb's ears, and artemisia — as well as a stack of copies of my own book, *The China Bayles Book of Days,* which always sells well at market, especially since I'm there to autograph it.

As soon as we got set up, I phoned Gretchen at the hospital to find out how she was feeling and ask if she would agree to come and stay with us for a few days. She was better, she said, although she still had a headache.

"And a beautiful green and purple eye," she added ruefully. She was hesitant to accept my invitation. But when I said that Jake could stay, too, and that McQuaid and I thought her parents would say it was a good idea, she agreed.

"Did you talk to Kitt about the situation?" I asked.

"Yes." There was a pause, and then she said, "Kitt and I have been thinking about this, Ms. Bayles. We're afraid that our documentary has stirred up trouble. We can't imagine what or why, since both of the people involved are already dead — Christine Morris and the guy who was acquitted — not to mention the prosecutor and the defense attorney. And now Dr. Prior —" Her voice trembled, then broke. "Anyway, Kitt and I have decided to drop it. We feel just terrible, like we're to blame for what happened. And without Dr. Prior, we can't go on."

"I understand why you feel that way," I said sympathetically. "But you're *not* to blame, Gretchen."

"But we must've done *something*." Gretchen's voice was full of pain. "Otherwise, Dr. Prior would still be alive." She sniffled. "If we could only figure out what it was that we did that started all this!"

"Maybe we can," I said. "Let's talk about this tonight and see what we can come up with. I'm working today, but Jake has your mom's car. How about if I call her and ask her to pick you up when the doctor releases you?"

Her answer was unhesitating. "Sure, it would be great if Jake could pick me up. And would it be okay if I ask Kitt to come over for the evening? Her husband had to drive up to Dallas — his mom's in the hospital — so she's all by herself tonight."

"Of course," I replied. "We're planning a backyard barbecue this evening. Please invite her to stay for the night if she wants to. We can put a futon mattress on the guest room floor. It'll be an all-girls sleepover."

"Thanks, Ms. Bayles. I'll tell her." Gretchen sounded relieved. I thought I knew why.

I was digging out the last bundle of basil for a customer when somebody said, "Good morning, China." I turned to see Charlie Lipman, looking like Rush Limbaugh after a hard night on the town. His shoulders sagged, the pouches under his eyes sagged onto his mottled cheeks, and his belly sagged over his belt. Charlie is no older than I am, but to look at him, you'd swear he'd already crossed over to the south side of sixty. When he occasionally remembers to smile, you can glimpse the man he used to be, before life's disappointments turned him sour.

I took the money for the basil, thanked the customer, and said, "Hey, Charlie. What's up?"

He took the unlit cigar out of his mouth. "Jes' saw Mike," he drawled. "He says you mebbe know somethin' 'bout this here doc-u-ment'ry them girls're doin' over at the college."

Charlie was born to upper-class parents in a Dallas suburb, graduated at the top of his university class, and spent a year at Oxford. He speaks a polished and lawyerly English when he's before the bar. Fishing, hunting, or hanging out at the farmers' market, he likes to talk Texan.

"I know a little," I said, "but not as much as you'd like. If you want to get the story straight from the horse's mouth, go across the street to the Crystal Cave and ask Ruby Wilcox. She was interviewed for the film." I paused, then added, "When your client was murdered, Ruby lived down the street."

Charlie chewed on his cigar for a moment. "Might do that," he acknowledged.

I should have kept my mouth shut, but my curiosity was getting the better of me. "This hidden assets business you asked McQuaid to look into. Do you think it could have had anything to do with Morris' murder?"

If my question bothered him, he didn't show it. He took the cigar out of his mouth, admired it briefly, and put it back. "Dunno," he said. "But myself, I never thought Bowen did it. Bubba and his boys did their usual slipshod work with the evidence, or worse. And Ring-a-Ding —" He shrugged and lapsed into pure Texan. "Fella couldn't pour piss out of a boot if the directions was written on the heel."

" 'Or worse'?" I asked, even more curious and not at all surprised. Defense lawyers, even ex–defense lawyers, are never surprised when they hear of police indiscretions. They've seen their share. And when they don't see it, they pretend to.

Charlie gave me a knowing look. "Warrantless search. That's how they found that broken-off golf club handle in Bowen's backyard, wiped clean of prints. And the rest of the matching golf clubs in the golf bag in Bowen's garage. And the bloody shoes in the garbage can — which, by the way, was *not* in the alley, but on Bowen's property, inside his back gate. One of Bowen's neighbors confirmed the location."

I hadn't heard about the shoes, but Ruby had mentioned the golf club — the murder weapon. I knew the right question to ask. I knew the answer, too, but I asked it anyway.

"Why didn't Johnnie Carlson get the club and the shoes excluded?"

Warrantless searches — searches and seizures that are conducted without a search warrant — are restricted under the Fourth Amendment, which every defense attorney has by heart. "The right of the people to be secure . . . against unreasonable searches and seizures, shall not be violated, and no Warrants shall issue, but upon probable cause, supported by Oath or affirmation, and particularly describing the place to be searched, and the persons or things to be seized." Evidence obtained when the police enter your property without a warrant is supposed to be excluded at trial, and it's the defense's job to make that happen. But there are exceptions. Among them, "exigent circumstances," which includes "hot pursuit." That is, a cop can come into your yard if he claims he's chasing a criminal.

"Carlson objected," Charlie said sourly. "But you know the drill. Barry Rogers was the lead investigating officer. He testified that while he was at the crime scene, he heard a noise like somebody banging a garbage can lid and thought he'd better go look."

Barry Rogers. He'd left the force when McQuaid was acting chief of the PSPD, under some kind of cloud, although I'd never known the details. I did know that Rogers had carved out a successful second career as a real estate broker, though — successful, that is, judging from the house where he and his wife Janine lived, next door to the eighteenth fairway out at the country club.

Charlie gave a wry chuckle. "On cross, it developed that Detective Rogers only *thought* it was a garbage can lid he heard and he only *thought* he heard it. When he went to look, he found the bloody shoes in Bowen's garbage can, in the alley. Which was a lie, according to a neighbor who testified as a defense witness. Like everybody else on that route, Bowen kept his can inside his yard, because the garbage truck had a bad habit of running over it if it was left in the alley. Rogers further claimed that the gate into Bowen's yard was open and he had reason to believe that the killer was on the premises. He went in hot pursuit, of course, and that's when he spotted the broken-off golf club handle, lying in a flower bed next to the fence. His hot pursuit took him into the garage and lo and behold, there were the rest of the clubs, a matching set, in a golf bag in a corner. And when they were checked for prints, they had Bowen's all over them. Except for the club that was used as a murder weapon. That was wiped clean."

"A veritable trail of clues," I remarked ironically. "A cop would have to be an idiot not to follow it. Even without a warrant."

"Exactly. The other two cops on the scene backed up Rogers' testimony, of course, and the judge — the Honorable Roy Lee Sparks — let it all in." He made an impolite noise. "The blue wall of silence."

"The blue wall of silence" is no mystery. It's the unwritten code that keeps police officers from reporting another officer's mistakes, intentional or otherwise. In the judicial system, there's even a word — *testilying* — for the perjured testimony that an officer gives in court when he's covering up for his own or another officer's misconduct during an investigation. Police, prosecutors, defense lawyers, judges — they all know about this kind of behavior. And every single study of police perjury that's been made has concluded that the practice is widespread and condoned in police departments across the United States, large and small, urban and rural. There was no reason to believe that the Pecan Springs Police Department was exempt.

"I get it," I said quietly.

"I'll bet you do," Charlie remarked and patted me on the arm.

"I suppose the jurors got it, too," I said. The most famous case of a jury that "got it" was the jury that acquitted O.J. Simpson. The jurors believed that some (if not all) of the evidence was corrupted; that Detectives Mark Fuhrman and Philip Vannatter were lying; and that their perjury was supported by the other police officers who testified. The defense was successful in arguing that they couldn't convict a man when there was that much reasonable doubt, which in our legal system translates to "not guilty."

"You bet they got it. They acquitted, didn't they?" Charlie laughed, then sobered. "But what I want to know is what this has to do with the documentary those students are making. And Karen Prior's death, damn it." His eyes narrowed, and he muttered, as if to himself, "Or what Douglas Clark may or may not have done with community property during the divorce proceedings."

"Sorry, Charlie," I said regretfully. "I can't help you with any of that." I hesitated. I was guessing that McQuaid had told him about Karen, and that Charlie had known her — which was no surprise. Pecan Springs is a small town. I wanted to ask who he might be working for on the investigation of those hidden assets — who his client was. But that wasn't a question he, or any lawyer, would answer. "Do keep me posted, though, will you?" I added.

"Yeah," Charlie said. "And if you get any information about —"

A woman thrust a package of chamomile tea at me. "Says on this box that this stuff will make me sleepy," she said impatiently. "Is that true?"

"Hang on a moment," I told her. "Any information about what, Charlie?"

"Forget it," Charlie said and stepped back. "I've bothered you enough for one morning. I'll go see if I can find Ms. Wilcox." He raised his hand and disappeared into the crowd.

"Sorry," I said to the customer. "Now, how can I help you?"

The farmers' market may look like a lot of fun, but — in terms of the work involved — it's no picnic, especially on a hot July day. Any vendor will tell you that. I was glad when noon rolled around and Caitie and I could take down the booth and head for the air-conditioned shop, where I mopped the sweat off my face and neck and swigged down a large glass of iced tea. Caitie and I shared a chicken salad sandwich and some cookies from the tearoom, and I paid her twenty dollars for helping with the market. She put it in my purse for safekeeping and then skipped off down the alley to spend the afternoon with her friend Robin. I went to work.

Summer Saturday mornings are busy because of the market, but the afternoons are iffy, sometimes good, sometimes slow. The locals are mostly at the river or out on the lakes or cooling off in the shade with a frosty margarita, or even doing some minor garden work, although it's really too hot.

But the heat doesn't seem to daunt the tourists who come to Central Texas to visit the Bullock Texas State History Museum in Austin or the Sophienburg Museum in New Braunfels, take photos of the dolphins at San Antonio's SeaWorld, cruise around in the glass-bottom boats at Aquarena Springs in San Marcos, chill out underground in the Cascade Caverns near Boerne, or tour the justly famous Painted Churches of Schulenberg. And there are the wine lovers who pour into Gruene's Grapevine tasting room to sample an array of Texas' best wines, and the fans of Gary P. Nunn and Emmylou Harris who flock to Gruene Hall for country-western music. Plenty of them end up in Pecan Springs on a Saturday afternoon, and some of them make it a point to drop in at Thyme and Seasons, to see what's new in the shop or to walk through the gardens. If you're in the vicinity, please consider this an invitation. I'd a lot rather be talking to you than dusting the shelves or sweeping the floor.

The shop was middling busy that afternoon, with foot traffic and telephone calls. One of the calls was from Kitt, accepting the invitation to supper and a sleepover, and offering to bring potato salad and deviled eggs for our picnic. Another was from Sheila, who wanted to know if I knew where Gretchen was.

"I asked the officer assigned to that incident to keep track of her," she said, sounding frustrated. "But she checked out of the hospital and apparently didn't go home."

"That's because she went to my house," I said. "Jake picked her up. Both she and Jake are staying with us until their folks get back from Belize. Sorry — I should have asked her to let you know where she would be."

I cradled the receiver against my shoulder and smiled at the customer who was purchasing a glass jar of herbal bath salts, made with calendula and chamomile, lavender, ylang-ylang, and geranium.

"I find this very soothing," I said to the customer, a woman about my age with a look of strained weariness on her face. It was true: I had a jar of it at home and used it when things really got to me.

"Soothing?" Sheila asked doubtfully. "Well, I agree that it's a good idea for Gretchen to stay with you, but I wouldn't call it —"

"Not you, Smart Cookie," I said into the phone. "Hang on a minute."

I put down the receiver and rang up the sale. When the woman had gone, I picked it up again. "Soothing bath salts," I said and added, "Oh, by the way, I have Gretchen's laptop at the house, too. I picked it up last night. Under the circumstances —"

"Smart," Sheila said, approving. "What about the other girl?"

"Kitt. She's coming tonight. It's a sleep-over." I chuckled. "Just us girls. Want to join us?"

I pictured Sheila's eyes rolling. "Not," she said firmly. "Blackie and I are going riding at his place this evening. We're planning to stay overnight. I need to get away from this place for a few hours." Blackie keeps an RV parked beside a pretty creek that runs through his property, so he and Sheila and

Rambo can stay out there in comfort.

"Just don't fall off your horse," I said sweetly. "It wouldn't be good for the baby." Before she could respond to that jab, I added, more seriously, "Anything on Karen Prior's assailant?"

"I wish," Sheila said with a sigh. "No, nothing so far. But I would definitely like to talk to Gretchen and Kitt. Since they'll both be at your place, why don't I stop there on my way back to town tomorrow morning? Maybe about nine?"

"Make it ten," I said. "I'll try to get them out of bed and coffeed by that time, but I can't promise."

"Do your best," Sheila said sternly. "Remind them that this is a murder investigation."

I sighed. "Speaking of which, do you know when Karen's funeral is scheduled? And what about Felicity? Is anybody staying with her?"

"I talked to Felicity again today," Sheila said. "We're still trying to get a fix on the phone call her mother got before she left for the mall. She said that her grandmother — her mother's mother — drove down from Oklahoma City. No date yet for the funeral. There are relatives on both coasts, apparently."

Two anguished women, I thought. A mother grieving a murdered daughter, a daughter grieving a murdered mother. I could only hope for their consolation, knowing that they would find none.

Whether death comes quickly or slowly, it is utterly, completely final. It shadows everyone it touches.

It took an effort to shed that darkness. But by the time I closed the shop, picked Caitie up at Robin's house, and drove home, I was ready for a picnic. As it turned out, my family — bless them — had already done most of the work. The temperature was still in the low 90s, so I changed into shorts and sandals and poured myself a tall gin and tonic with plenty of ice and a twist of lime, feeling a special gratitude for our family evening together. Felicity and her grandmother didn't have that privilege.

Supper was in experienced hands. McQuaid had put a brisket (liberally rubbed with kosher salt, coarsely cracked black pepper, garlic powder, and cayenne) into the smoker early that morning and left it there all day, basting with his secret high-test barbecue sauce whenever he thought of it. At five thirty, he put on some links of smoked venison sausage, and when I got home at five forty-five, he was sharpening his slicing knife. I went out to the back deck to join him.

"Did you talk to Charlie today?" I asked, resting my head against his arm. I can't explain it, but there is something very sexy about a man who is slicing a barbecued brisket, especially one he has cooked himself, start to finish.

"I did." He tested the knife's edge with a quick cut and held out the slice on the tip of the blade. "What do you think?"

I tasted, chewed, and rolled my eyes. "You are *sooo* good," I cooed. "A gourmet cook. And a stud, too. What more could a girl want?"

"That's me," McQuaid said comfortably and began to slice. "All around good guy. Especially in bed."

"Mmm," I said, agreeing. "So what did Charlie say?"

"A lot of things." He kept on slicing.

I stole a slice of brisket and nibbled on it. "I talked to him myself this morning, at the market. He claimed that there was police misconduct in the Morris murder investigation. A warrantless search." I licked my fingers. "But the evidence was allowed in anyway."

McQuaid shrugged. "Wouldn't be the first

time. Won't be the last, either."

"So you talked to Charlie," I persisted. "He didn't happen to give you a hint about who his client is on that hidden assets investigation, did he?"

McQuaid forked a bite of brisket, chewed thoughtfully, and said, "Next time, I think I'll use more garlic. Not everyone would agree, I suppose, but in my opinion, you can never have too much garlic."

I poked him in the ribs. *Charlie,* I said. "Hidden assets. His client."

"Okay, okay." McQuaid gave an exaggerated sigh, humoring me. "I dropped in at his office early this morning and asked him about the coincidences. My assignment, Prior's death, the documentary. He knew about the documentary, but not about Karen. He was acquainted with her. He was jolted to hear that she's dead."

"Weren't we all," I said soberly. "How did he find out about the documentary?"

"One of the student filmmakers interviewed him a couple of weeks ago. She knew he'd handled Christine Morris' divorce and asked him to talk about her — what kind of person Morris was, her run-ins with the city council, that kind of thing. He said he gave the girl about five minutes, nothing specific, nothing she couldn't have found out from reading the newspaper."

I nodded. Of course, Charlie was free to speak generally about his client, although he would be careful not to violate privilege. In 1998, the entire legal profession breathed a collective sigh of relief when the Supreme Court ruled, 6–3, that the attorney-client privilege survives the client's death, thereby taking lawyers all over the country off the hook. Christine Morris might be dead, but as far as Charlie was concerned, she was still his client and their communications were still privileged.

"But after the interview, he got to reflecting on some things that had happened, and started thinking about this and that and wondering." McQuaid sliced off three more pieces, then paused. "Charlie doesn't have a client." Another two slices. "He's acting for himself."

For himself? "But why?" I asked, frowning. "Charlie Lipman isn't exactly the type to lay out cold hard cash on an investigation just out of intellectual curiosity."

McQuaid hesitated. "Of course, I'm only guessing. But I think maybe he feels that he didn't do all he might have when —"

"Hey, Dad!" It was Brian, standing at the back door. He and Jake had been shucking the sweet corn for supper. "We finished the corn and the water's boiling. Want us to dump it in?"

"Yeah, we're about ready out here," McQuaid replied. He added, "Hey, Brian, slice up a couple of those yellow onions, too, will you?" To me, he said, "There's more. Let's get into it later."

Jake had already put a bowl of fresh tomatoes and cucumbers on the cloth-covered picnic table. Kitt (who was delighted to join us and happy about the idea of staying all night) had brought potato salad and a dozen deviled eggs. I did nothing that required much mental or physical exertion, except to pull a peach cobbler out of the freezer and pop it in the oven. Caitlin made a pitcher of lemonade. Then she and Gretchen (who was under orders to take things easy for a day or two) set the picnic table under the live oak trees in the backyard with our favorite red plastic picnic plates and yellow paper napkins, with a Mason jar in the center full of bright yellow sunflowers, orange butterfly weed, and lacy wild carrot. It was all very Norman Rockwellian and very pretty.

Supper was on the picnic table at six and by six forty-five it was history. By seven, the kids were cleaning up the kitchen and putting the dishes in the dishwasher, and

McQuaid and I had taken our glasses of wine out to the front porch, where we each settled in a white-painted wicker rocking chair to appreciate the quiet green landscape.

Chapter Six

According to an entry tagged "malicious magic" in Daniel Moerman's *Native American Ethnobotany,* the Iroquois used a prickly, vining plant called smilax (*Smilax hispida*) to bring about bad luck or accidents. They also used the plant to construct a crude doll, like a voodoo doll, with the aim of killing a woman who was causing trouble.

China Bayles
"Herbs of Good and Ill Omen"
Pecan Springs Enterprise

Our house is located in the Hill Country west of Pecan Springs, a half mile off Limekiln Road. Over the years we have lived here, we've added another twenty acres to the original three that came with the house, so it's easy to feel that we're alone out here, on the edge of a wilderness that stretches all the way to the western horizon.

That isn't true, of course. Over the past decade, the Hill Country has been filling up fast, with gated communities swallowing up the woods and prairies and small towns pushing out their boundaries farther and faster every year. But drought is a constant threat and water has become a major problem. Even the grow-baby-grow crowd has to admit that there are limits. Most counties are tightening their building and well-drilling restrictions and putting the brakes on development.

But this house has been here for a long time, and the land around it has stayed wild. Our nearest neighbors, the Banners, are well out of sight, and Limekiln Road is far enough away, and buffered by trees, so that we rarely hear a vehicle. From our porch, McQuaid and I can look out onto an expanse of grass and an old stone wall overgrown with greenbrier, our native Texas species, *Smilax bona-nox*. (If you have ever tangled with this thorny vine, you will appreciate two of its common names: cat's claw and blaspheme-vine.) Beyond the wall is a wide meadow, rimmed with juniper, live oak, and mesquite trees. Tonight, in the shadows under the distant trees, a doe and two fawns, still wearing their baby spots, were cropping grass. Low in the west, the sun was about to duck behind the hills. The high-pitched song of the cicadas filled the air, and the honeysuckle at the near end of the porch scented the slight breeze. It was a lovely summer evening, almost too hot to sit outdoors, but not quite. When you live in Texas, where there's too much air-conditioning too much of the time, you learn to go outside whenever you can, even if it is a little too hot.

I picked up our before-supper conversation where we left off. "You said there's more to tell about Charlie."

"Yeah." McQuaid leaned back in the rocker and propped his sandaled feet on the porch railing. "Turns out that he and Christine Morris were . . . involved." He gave me an oblique glance. "Romantically involved, that is."

I stared at him. "Are you kidding? I understood that she sued for divorce on grounds of adultery. And that Charlie was her attorney."

"Nope. Not kidding." McQuaid shrugged. "Wouldn't be a first, you know. Happens all the time."

"Well, maybe," I muttered. But while love affairs between lawyers and their clients may make for stimulating television drama, they are a very bad idea — in spite of the fact that the State Bar of Texas has never quite managed to bring itself to specifically prohibit them. I found it hard to believe that Charlie would be stupid enough to get himself into that kind of situation.

And there was something else. From everything I'd heard about Christine Morris, she was a consummate fashion plate — clothing, hair, jewelry all flawless, a beautiful woman. But in the decade or more that I've known Charlie Lipman, he's looked like the quintessential Texas country lawyer, given to wrinkled suits and coffee-stained white shirts. He is not what anybody would call a hunk. And definitely not a suitable escort for a fashion queen.

"You're surprised?" McQuaid asked, eyeing me. "Hey, sex happens, China. Love, too, sometimes — although maybe less frequently than sex. And Charlie didn't always look and dress the way he does now." He paused thoughtfully. "He didn't drink, either. At least, not so much."

"How would you know?" I challenged. "You've only known him for as long as I have. And all that time, he's been . . . well, just the way he is now. Just Charlie."

"Blackie told me," McQuaid said. "Charlie used to be the sharpest tool in the box. But something happened in his personal life

— Blackie isn't sure what. After that, he started going downhill. Of course, as a lawyer, he's still plenty good. He's just . . ." His voice trailed off. "He's just Charlie."

I sighed. "So Charlie told you that he and Christine Morris were involved. I assume that this went on while he was representing her in her divorce action."

"He didn't say when. It could have been after the divorce was granted, for all I know."

I went back to the point. "So how does this . . . romantic involvement play into the current situation?"

"Don't ask me," McQuaid said. "But if I had to guess, I'd say that he thought of something in the course of his interview for the documentary — something he had forgotten about or maybe decided not to pursue. He thought more about it and concluded it was something he wanted to investigate, because of his involvement with Christine. So he called me and asked me to look into it for him."

"*It* being the possibility that Doug Clark hid some — or a substantial portion — of his assets during the property settlement." I shook my head. "If Charlie was sleeping with Christine, maybe even wanted to marry her after the dust settled, I would have thought that he would have dug for those assets with every spade and shovel he could find. And if he didn't do it then, why bother now?"

"Dunno." McQuaid shrugged. "But they weren't sleeping together when this happened, apparently. According to Charlie, some time after Christine got her divorce, the two of them ended their relationship and she began seeing someone else."

"Anybody I know?" I asked curiously.

"A guy named Roberto Soto," McQuaid said.

"No kidding." I was mildly surprised. Soto was an art dealer based in San Antonio. Some years before, he had been indicted by the feds for wire fraud, conspiracy, and the sale of a forged painting. I couldn't remember the artist at the moment, but it was a name I recognized at the time.

"Yeah," McQuaid said with a chuckle. "*That* Roberto Soto. The one your friend Justine took to the cleaners."

I knew about Soto because Justine Wyzinski, a San Antonio attorney in private practice, had represented one of his customers in a civil suit against him. Soto hadn't admitted guilt in the federal case, but he pled to a lesser charge in return for a fine. And he paid court costs and restitution in the civil case Justine had brought. Interesting, but ancient history by now, and most people had probably forgotten it. Still . . .

"Ruby told me that Christine was collecting Mexican art, in a big way." I paused. "I wonder if she bought any of her stuff from Soto."

McQuaid shrugged. "Maybe. But I'm not sure Charlie knew very much about that part of it. Christine was still his client, even if they were no longer otherwise involved. Shortly before she was killed, she came to Charlie with the claim that her ex-husband had hidden some of ~~~ arital property in a complicate~ ~~~ ~~~rangement. She wante~ ~~~ Depending on ~~~ get the divorce ~~~ a civil fraud ~~~ the investi- ~~~ dropped it." ~~~ ~~~ed it. And

~~~ ~~~ that his ex-wife wa~ ~~~ business affairs?"

"~~~ ~~~ have been smart to let him in on t~~ secret." McQuaid frowned at me. "What are you thinking?"

I shrugged. "Oh, nothing. Except that this is shaping up to be a more complicated matter than it seemed at first." Doug Clark and hidden assets, Roberto Soto and Mexican art. Briefly, I made a mental note to ask Justine — a friend from law school — if she knew what Soto was doing with himself these days.

McQuaid gave me a curious look. "I thought the neighbor killed her. What's his name — Bowman?"

"Dick Bowen." I *tsk-tsk*ed. "Don't forget. The jury found him not guilty."

"Which doesn't mean that he *didn't* do it," McQuaid pointed out. "As you very well know, China, juries acquit for all sorts of reasons. They might have believed he was guilty as sin but let him walk anyway."

He was right, of course. The jury's "not guilty" didn't necessarily mean that Bowen was innocent. But judging from what I'd heard from Charlie that morning, I'd say that the smart money was on somebody else — on Johnnie's alternative suspect, maybe. That trail of clues sounded like it was laid down for the benefit of the investigators, who had followed it obediently — without a warrant.

"After Christine was killed," I said, "did Charlie go to the police with what he knew about those assets?"

"He didn't *know* anything," McQuaid said. "All he had was Christine's suspicions. And at the time she asked him to look into

186

it, Charlie says, she was pretty unbalanced. This was when she was causing a lot of trouble, haranguing the city council and making wild claims all over the place. He didn't quite believe her."

"But he does now? I wonder why he's changed his mind." I leaned forward, itching to get into this. "Listen, McQuaid. Charlie told me some interesting things about the Morris murder investigation. Turns out that the lead investigating officer was —" I was interrupted by a light rap on the door into the living room.

"May we join you?" Gretchen asked, and a moment later, she and Kitt were seated on the porch swing.

Kitt wore a pair of narrow, hip-looking glasses, and her pink-streaked brown hair gave her the look of an untidy child. "Thanks for inviting me to sleep over tonight," she said, pulling her knees up under her chin and wrapping her arms around her legs. "Jerry will be home tomorrow night, which is good. After everything that's happened, I don't mind telling you that I'm just not real crazy about staying by myself."

Gretchen's eye was several colors of purple and green, and the abrasions on her arms were bandaged. "Kitt and I have been talking about the documentary." She pushed the swing with the toe of her sneaker, setting it swaying. "We really do feel responsible for what happened to Dr. Prior."

McQuaid cleared his throat. "I didn't get all the details about your film," he said in a kindly voice. "Maybe you could fill me in on what you're up to. Words of one syllable, please. I don't know the first thing about moviemaking."

Gretchen and Kitt exchanged glances, and Gretchen spoke. "A documentary is a requirement of the master's degree in the film program. We do the whole thing ourselves, start to finish. We're supposed to choose a topic, do the research, create a storyboard, shoot the interviews and other scenes, dig up the archival footage we want to use, do a rough cut and the final edit."

Kitt picked up the story. "Then we have to screen it for a critique team, go back and rework wherever necessary, and do a final screening for the public. We get graded on all the steps along the way." She stopped, chewed on her lip, then added, "We actually thought we had a good shot at a national distribution for this project. My uncle works with a company that distributes independent films, both home video and broadcast. He's seen some of our footage. He's been encouraging us."

Ah, I thought. If somebody knew about a potentially wider distribution of the film, that person might be nervous enough to make a threatening call to the filmmakers. But why would he — or she — attack Karen? She was only the filmmakers' supervisor. It didn't make sense.

A mockingbird flew to the top of the small yaupon holly at the far end of the porch and began to chirp in a bossy tone, as if he were lecturing us for sitting on *his* porch. The sun was gone now, but the western sky was tinted with pastel lemon and pink. The meadow was empty. The doe and her fawns had melted into the purple shadows of the trees.

"I'm curious about the topic," McQuaid said. "What made you decide to choose the Morris murder for your documentary?"

Gretchen spoke up. "I was in your class one day — Criminal Investigations, I think it was — when you lectured about cold cases and the reasons why some crimes are never solved. I thought that was really interesting. When Kitt and I started talking about the documentary, I went to the newspaper morgue and glanced through old copies of the *Enterprise.* That's when I stumbled over Christine Morris' murder. I was still a girl when it happened, so I didn't remember anything about it. But when I told Kitt, she liked the idea because Ms. Morris collected Mexican art, paintings, mostly, but other stuff, too. Which gave it a really interesting angle. Some of the paintings in the museum are spectacular, and since it's private, people don't know much about it."

"I have an undergraduate major in art history," Kitt put in. "And Dr. Prior was interested in the concept because it involved the museum. She was on the board of directors."

"She was?" I asked, surprised. Ruby hadn't mentioned that — or maybe Ruby hadn't known.

Kitt nodded. "Just for the last six months or so, I think. And she had done a documentary of her own on art fraud, a couple of years ago. It was shown on PBS and got quite a lot of attention."

McQuaid nodded. "Now I get the connection."

"But basically," Kitt said, "we liked the idea of making a film about this quiet, sleepy little town, not at all the kind of place where you'd expect a murder — especially a sensational murder. There were plenty of newspaper photos we could use, and people who remembered it and might be willing to talk about it. Apparently, the victim was quite a character, a troublemaker, according to some people. And the fact that the killer got off —"

"The *accused* killer," I corrected gently.

"Oh, yeah, right." Kitt nodded. "The accused killer was acquitted, which we thought was a curious kind of twist. Everybody said it was because Ms. Morris was such a bitch and the killer — excuse me, the *accused* — was a really nice guy who did a lot of volunteer work around town. The jury liked him, even though he killed —" She stopped and glanced at me. "Even though he was *accused* of killing this woman. It seemed like a good story."

"And it's set right here in Pecan Springs," Gretchen put in, "which cut down our travel time and saved us money. Of course, the victim and the . . . the —"

"Defendant," I offered, for the sake of variety.

"Thank you. Anyway, the victim and the defendant are both dead, and so are the prosecutor and the defense attorney. So we wouldn't have to worry about defaming them. Not that we'd do that, of course," Gretchen added hastily. "At least, not on purpose. But sometimes documentary filmmakers get into trouble for that."

They certainly do, I thought. Even Michael Moore gets sued for defamation every now and again. And while truth is an absolute defense, it is sometimes difficult to prove. Not everybody agrees on what is true and what isn't. Ms. Morris would probably not have used the word *bitch* to describe herself.

"Bowen is dead?" McQuaid sounded surprised.

Gretchen nodded. "After the trial, he quit his job, sold his house, and moved to Houston. He committed suicide three or four years ago."

"He sat in his car in his garage with the motor running," Kitt said. "Carbon monoxide poisoning." She looked regretful. "We couldn't interview him, but we shot some video of the house where he lived, and we got some archival material on his death from one of the Houston television stations."

Suicide, I thought, after he was acquitted of murder. That was ironic. Remorse? Guilt? Did that mean he was really guilty? Or it could have been something else. Maybe he'd been sick, or he hadn't been able to find another job. Maybe —

"So where are you on this documentary?" McQuaid asked.

"We've done most of the research," Kitt said. "Dr. Prior approved our storyboard, and we've shot a lot of interview footage — not all, though. There are still several people we wanted to talk to. But we've got shots of the newspaper coverage and some really good archival footage from a couple of the Austin television stations. The next big step is the editing. *Was* the editing," she corrected herself and pulled down her mouth. "As Gretchen said, we've decided that we just can't go on with the film. It . . . it just doesn't feel right."

"It's more than that, actually." Gretchen's voice was tight. "It feels dangerous. Dr. Prior is dead. I was attacked and my camera and memory cards were stolen. Next time, it could be Kitt. And one of us could end up —" She shivered.

"End up *dead,*" Kitt said, throwing up her hands dramatically. "Like Dr. Prior."

I wanted to dispute her assertion, but I couldn't. She was right.

McQuaid stood up. "The reason it's dangerous is because somebody apparently feels threatened," he said, leaning against the porch railing. "Somebody has something to hide. He — or she — is afraid you'll uncover it. Or that you already have."

Finally, Gretchen spoke. "I just don't get

it, Ms. Bayles. In his interview, Chief Harris laid out all the evidence the police collected, piece by piece. Bloody shoes, the broken golf club, the matching clubs in Mr. Bowen's garage, even blood on the garage door and a bloody rag on the floor. It all pointed to Mr. Bowen, every bit of it. The jury let him off, yes. But in his interview, the chief —"

"The former chief," Kitt amended.

"Right. The former chief said that he got off because of a smart defense attorney and a sympathetic jury who liked Mr. Bowen too much to convict him. But that he was guilty, just the same."

"The cops can be wrong, Kitt," I put in firmly. "That happens, you know." Worse than that, the police can lie on the witness stand, plant incriminating evidence, and deliberately overlook exonerating evidence. They can, and they do — although of course *nobody* would ever want to say that this could happen in Pecan Springs, where everybody always does the right thing, every time, in every circumstance. And if they happen to do the wrong thing, it's because . . . well, because they just weren't paying attention, or they had a momentary moral lapse. Or something.

"And if Bowen didn't kill her," I went on,

"somebody else did. It's possible that the killer is still here in Pecan Springs and is terrified of being found out." The words hung like an ill omen in the quiet air.

"But it was such a long time ago," Gretchen protested. "It's ancient history. Surely —"

"There is no statute of limitations on murder," I said.

There was another silence. "Uh-oh," Kitt said softly.

"Yeah," Gretchen said. She looked from me to McQuaid, her eyes wide, now, and frightened. "Do you really think . . . ?" Her voice trailed off.

"I don't know about the cops making mistakes or a killer running around," McQuaid said slowly. "I'm not ready to go there just yet. But I do think it's possible that your documentary has scared somebody. Which is why Dr. Prior was attacked and you" — he looked at Gretchen — "spent a day in the janitor's closet and a night in the hospital."

There was a silence. At the back of the house, the screen door slammed and Brian called out to Jake. From upstairs came the sound of Caitlin's violin, the clear, sweet melody of "Clair de lune." Ordinary family sounds, in an ordinary house, on an ordinary night. And we were talking about murder. Two murders, over a decade apart. I thought about Bowen's death and shivered. Two murders and a suicide.

"The people you've interviewed," McQuaid said. "Do you have a list?"

"Well, of course we do." Gretchen sounded frightened. "We told you. We have a storyboard."

"Which is what, exactly?" McQuaid asked.

"Which is, like, a series of sketches that tell the story of the film," Kitt said. "All the interviewees are listed there. You could look at that."

"Or you could look at the interviews themselves," Gretchen added. "I have my laptop here. I've downloaded all the video files to it."

"And I have mine," Kitt added. "We could look at the video on your TV."

"We've done some editing already," Gretchen said, "but it's still a rough cut, and most of the interviews are raw footage. So there's a lot of stopping and starting and hemming and hawing, and some of our questions are audible. It'll be a lot cleaner and smoother when we finish." She stopped. "Anyway, that was the plan. I guess we won't be doing it now." She looked at Kitt, frowning. "Maybe we should find out the date of the last day to drop the course. I don't want an incomplete."

Kitt nodded, agreeing. "I don't want to finish it with another instructor, either."

"Dr. Prior's students won't be penalized," McQuaid said. "On Monday, check with somebody in the dean's office. They'll tell you what to do."

"How much time would it take to see the whole video?" I asked.

The girls exchanged glances, shrugs, head shakes. "The rough cut is maybe five or six hours," Gretchen said.

"Or more," Kitt said. "We could look at some of it tonight, if you want. It'll give you an idea of what we have."

"Sounds right," McQuaid said, pushing away from the porch rail.

Gretchen got out of the swing. "I'll go set it up," she offered.

"Oh, one other thing," I said. "Chief Dawson says that she'd like to talk to the two of you. I told her that you were staying here overnight, and she said she'd stop by around ten in the morning. So let's don't stay up until all hours — okay?"

"Whoa." Kitt looked alarmed. "The chief? Why does she want to talk to *us*?"

"Can't you guess, Kitt?" Gretchen looked

at me, her eyes dark. "We really have caused a lot of trouble, haven't we?"

CHAPTER SEVEN

In Malay mythology, the banana plant (*Musa acuminata*) was believed to be the home of spirits called *pontianak*s, the ghosts of women who have died in child-birth. *Pontianak*s were said to attack pregnant women, attempting to snatch their babies out of the womb. Their presence was announced by the fragrance of plumeria or jasmine, then by a horrible stench.

In Hawaii, it was bad luck for a woman to plant a banana in her garden. The planting had to be done by a male who was a close friend but not a blood relative.

China Bayles
"Herbs of Good and Ill Omen"
Pecan Springs Enterprise

For his birthday last year, McQuaid — a fervent football fan who never misses a televised University of Texas game if he can help it — got a big flat-screen television. After much discussion, we installed it on one wall of our living room. Then, for *my* birthday, we built bookcases around it. Just one of the many little compromises that keep a marriage going.

While McQuaid and I got comfortable on the sofa that faced the screen, Gretchen and Kitt, who seemed to know exactly what they were doing, plugged in a cable, turned on Gretchen's laptop, logged on, and brought up the file. A moment later, on the large TV screen, we saw a series of full-color video images of Pecan Springs. The first was the imposing pink granite courthouse and the retail businesses around the courthouse square: Pete's Barbershop, the dime store, the old Grande Theater and Opera House (newly remodeled), and the Sophie Briggs Historical Museum, where you can see Sophie Briggs' collection of ceramic frogs and a fancy dollhouse that once belonged to Lila Trumm, Miss Pecan Springs of 1936. That sequence was followed by footage of the park beside the picturesque Pecan River and the old Springs Hotel, then the gate to the CTSU campus and its turreted, towered Old Main building, a Victorian Gothic built in the early 1900s. Following that, there were video images of tree-lined streets and houses in the older part of town, taken from a moving car.

"We decided to start with different views of Pecan Springs," Gretchen said, fast-forwarding through the rest of the town's images. "To set the scene, so to speak. We were going to have a voice-over narration through all of this part, telling about the town, when it was founded, something about its history, that sort of stuff."

"An ordinary, pretty little Texas town," Kitt chimed in, "that looks like a place where only good things happen. Where you wouldn't expect a murder."

Gretchen stopped fast-forwarding as a video of a modernistic white house came onto the screen. It was the house at the end of San Jacinto Avenue, which Doug Clark had built for his bride as a wedding present. In front was a tasteful sign, announcing that this was the Morris Museum of Mexican Art, open by appointment only.

To McQuaid, I said, "That's where Christine Morris was killed."

"But it didn't look like that back then," Kitt said. "It looked like —"

And there it was: a black-and-white still photo of the place as it was when Christine lived in it. The house was surrounded by a six-foot chain-link fence with a large sign, *Beware: Bad Dog.* A tall utility pole dominated the front yard, one of the two giant security lights, I guessed.

"Ruby says that Christine was paranoid about somebody breaking in and stealing some of her valuable paintings," I said. "That's why she had those yard lights installed. She left them on all night. She had a Doberman, too."

"I'll bet the neighbors loved those lights," McQuaid remarked dryly. He shook his head. "Living alone in that big house with a lot of valuable art — I'm not surprised she was paranoid. She was a magnet for thieves."

"Here she is," Gretchen said.

A series of color and black-and-white photos appeared on the screen, beginning with a glamour shot of a beautiful woman, with skin so youthfully taut that it suggested cosmetic surgery and a blond coiffure so artfully styled that it looked like a wig. This was followed by photos of a skinny little girl in a Brownie uniform, a pimply teenager in a sweater with a Peter Pan collar, and a pretty twenty-something wearing an academic gown and mortarboard — images of a much younger Christine Morris. Then a sequence showed her in front of the television camera, in her earlier incarnation as a Houston television anchorwoman; as a smiling bride in an elaborate white wedding dress and veil on the arm of a tall, dark, and handsome man who must have been her rich ob-gyn husband; and in evening clothes as a River Oaks socialite.

After that, there were photographs and even some video footage of her life in Pecan Springs: showing off an important Frida Kahlo painting she had acquired; posing beside a Cadillac with her husband, Doug Clark; with Clark at a prestigious gala; posed alone in front of her house. And — in several distinctly unflattering newspaper photos — addressing the city council, her fist clenched, her mouth open, her eyes squinting, anger written across her face. And a montage of stark newspaper headlines: *Morris Bawls Out Mayor Perkins; Morris Accuses Zoning Committee of Malfeasance; Morris Attacks Bowen for Incompetence; Morris Feuds with Neighbors over Dogs, Fence, Lights; Morris Slams City Officials.*

"Yeah," McQuaid said. "I get the picture."

I got the picture, too. Gretchen and Kitt had done an excellent job of putting together a vivid, compelling portrayal of Christine Morris' life, from childhood to adulthood. They had covered so much territory that I almost felt I knew the woman. Almost.

But I had been in the business of representing defendants, telling their stories in front of juries. I understood how, with a half-dozen clever tweaks — leaving a few things out, putting a few things in — a man or woman could be made to seem one thing, or something entirely different. Christine Morris couldn't be as superficial as the photographs made her seem, or as angry as Frank Donnelly's newspaper headlines suggested.

As if in answer to my questions, the next scenes documented Christine's art collection. The girls had taken their camera inside the museum, showing dozens of artfully displayed paintings on the walls, along with pottery, sculpture, tiles, baskets, and weaving. A woman of late middle age accompanied the camera, pointing out and commenting on individual objects. She was tall and solidly built, nicely dressed in a brown slack suit, cream-colored blouse, and medium heels. A caption identified her as Sharyn Tillotson, the president of the Morris Foundation and chair of the museum board.

"I'm impressed," I said. "I had no idea we had something like this, right here in Pecan

204

Springs. They must keep a pretty low profile."

"It's a private museum," Gretchen said. "It's open only on a very limited basis, which seems like a shame to me. All that wonderful art, in that great space, and very few people get to appreciate it."

Then, as close-ups of individual paintings appeared, Gretchen said, "Ms. Morris had been collecting twentieth-century Mexican paintings for nearly twenty years. These are among the best — and the most valuable. There are a couple by Diego Rivera and three by Frida Kahlo."

I don't know much about art, but even I could see that these paintings were quite striking in their bright colors, bold forms, and folk art motifs. And I had recently seen a Diego Rivera painting on *Antiques Roadshow,* valued at a million dollars. Titled *El Albañil* and painted in 1904, the painting had been in the owner's family here in Texas since the 1920s. They thought it was a copy — or a fake — and hung it behind a door.

Gretchen went on. "Dr. Prior told us that Ms. Morris sold a number of pieces to galleries in New York, for tens of thousands of dollars. When she died, there were paintings all over the house, hung on the walls, stacked in the closets and corners, piled in a storeroom. Until they did an inventory, they had no idea of what was involved. The most valuable paintings were the Riveras and the Kahlos, and another by . . ." She frowned. "I forget."

"Gerardo Murillo," Kitt put in. "He signed his work 'Dr. Atl.' I read that one of his paintings recently sold at auction for one point six million dollars."

McQuaid whistled between his teeth. "A million six?" he muttered incredulously.

Dr. Atl. Now I remembered. That was the painter whose forged painting Roberto Soto had admitted to selling — although he continued to maintain, as I recalled, that he had no idea that the work was a fake when he sold it. The prosecutor had decided he didn't have enough evidence to go to trial and settled for a plea to a lesser charge.

Another painting came on the screen and the camera moved in for a close-up. "This one isn't as valuable as the others," Kitt said. "But it's my favorite. The artist is María Izquierdo. The image is so full of anguish, as if she had lost all heart. She painted it in the 1930s, after her lover had left her for a young student. Dr. Prior said it was her favorite, too. Of all the paintings in the collection, she liked that one best."

The painting occupied a wall by itself, at

the foot of a glass-enclosed stair with glass treads that seemed to float in space. It was dark and moody, with the look of an allegorical narrative: a nude woman, gaunt and angular with long, dark hair framing her face, and dark eyes and a theatrical red mouth. She was staring into a mirror that offered no reflection, only a sinister blackness. Against her breast, she held a flower with five vivid pink petals and fernlike green leaves. The leaves were veined and tipped in red blood, dripping blood onto her flesh. I recognized the plant immediately: Herb Robert. The painting was titled *Muerte llega pronto* — Death Come Quickly.

I shivered. The artist had perfectly caught the sense of ominous foreboding that Herb Robert was traditionally thought to convey. It was a plant that should never be picked, it was said, for it brought certain death. At the back of my mind rose the dark shadow of an unwelcome thought: it was Karen Prior's favorite painting, and now Karen was dead.

"Gruesome," McQuaid muttered. "Don't think I'd want that bloody thing hanging on my wall."

"Me, either," Gretchen admitted with a shudder. "I prefer cheerful stuff myself."

"Frida Kahlo always gets all the attention," Kitt said, "but what people don't know is that Izquierdo was the first woman Mexican artist to exhibit outside of Mexico. That was in 1930, at Manhattan's Art Center. So she really is quite important."

Gretchen hit the play button and the video moved to the final act in Christine's life. I pulled in my breath as the next photos appeared on the screen, more black-and-white stills, probably police photos. The first was the body of the murdered woman, dressed in a filmy pastel negligee and feather-trimmed robe, sprawled facedown at the foot of a short flight of wide stone steps leading up to the paved plaza under the cantilevered section of the house. One foot still wore a satin mule; the other was bare. One arm was folded under her, the other flung loose, above her head, the fingers curled as if she were clutching at the last precious moments of life. And then a close-up, the back of her head split wide open, her hair a thick, bloody mat, blood pooled under her face. Christine wasn't beautiful now, no. Not beautiful, ever again.

"Dr. Prior told us we should delete this photo," Kitt said. "She thought it was too . . . grisly." It was. Murder is ugly, ugly, ugly.

"We thought we'd replace it with this

photo," Gretchen said.

The next shot showed the body covered with a sheet, almost covered but not quite. The hand was still visible, still reaching, still clutching, and one bare foot. In this view, I could see the murder weapon — the metal head of a golf club, attached to a broken-off eight-inch section of wooden shaft — lying on the step beside the body. Beside it was the bloody print of what looked like a tennis shoe with a gridded sole. *The bloody shoe,* I thought. The killer must have bent over his victim and stepped in her blood. I shivered, feeling sick.

McQuaid leaned forward and asked a cop question. "Fingerprints on that golf club? And what about DNA?"

"As far as DNA is concerned," Kitt said, "we never heard it mentioned. I guess they weren't looking for it."

I wasn't surprised. Bubba Harris, the Pecan Springs police chief at the time of Christine Morris' murder, was an old-school fundamentalist as far as detective work was involved. He put a high priority on shoe-leather police work. He would have seen DNA as something akin to hocus-pocus. Anyway, the Texas Department of Public Safety's crime lab didn't begin testing DNA until 1994, and the lab operated on a limited basis for five or six years after that.

"Fingerprints," Gretchen said, pausing the video. "The police said there weren't any, either on the head or the shaft. But the club was part of an antique set that belonged to Mr. Bowen. The police found the top part of the broken shaft in his backyard. It matched the rest of the clubs in a golf bag in his garage."

"Does that seem odd to you?" I asked McQuaid. "No prints on the murder weapon that so obviously belonged to Bowen. If he went to the trouble of wiping off his prints, you'd think he'd be smart enough to dispose of the murder weapon somewhere other than his backyard."

"Or choose a less distinctive weapon in the first place," McQuaid agreed. "Unless, of course, it was a crime of passion and he grabbed the first thing at hand."

"But if it was a crime of passion and he was angry enough to grab the first thing at hand, would he wipe the weapon — *his* golf club — clean, and then drop it where it could be found? Doesn't make a lot of sense."

McQuaid lifted his shoulders, agreeing. "Doesn't make a lot of sense to me, either, babe."

Gretchen resumed the video, showing a black-and-white photo of a pair of tennis shoes. "They found blood-spattered shoes that matched the shoe print beside the body. They were in Bowen's garbage can in the alley."

"Hold that shot, please," I said to Gretchen. To McQuaid, I said, "Charlie told me that a neighbor testified for the defense that Bowen kept his garbage can *inside* his yard, not in the alley."

"Ah." McQuaid's lips quirked. "No warrant, I suppose."

"You got it. According to Charlie, the lead investigator — Barry Rogers — testified that while he was at the crime scene, he heard a noise like somebody banging a garbage can lid. So he hotfooted it out to the alley behind the house to check. That's when he found the bloody shoes. In Bowen's garbage can. In the alley."

"Barry Rogers," McQuaid said, sounding disgusted. "That guy couldn't investigate his way out of a paper bag. Or worse: he might try to plant the paper bag, *then* investigate it. Without a warrant. When I was acting chief, I fired the jerk. For cause."

"What kind of cause?" Now I was definitely curious.

"Shaking down a drug dealer and framing

211

— attempting to frame, that is — an innocent man. Rogers was a bad actor for most of his career, but Bubba Harris looked out for him. When I came on the job, Rogers' partner figured I might take a serious look at the situation and blew the whistle." He shook his head. "The way Bubba ran the department, it was too easy for cops like Rogers to get by with stuff. I wasn't going to let that kind of business go down on my watch." He turned back to Gretchen and asked another cop question. "What time did the murder take place?"

"Between nine p.m. and two a.m., according to the autopsy. The police thought she was attacked when she went outside to get her cat."

"And when was the body discovered?" I asked.

"Not until shortly after noon the next day," Kitt said. "The lawn mowing service came to mow the grass. One of the employees saw her and called the police."

McQuaid and I exchanged glances. He spoke first. "So Rogers claimed he heard that garbage can lid banging sometime after noon, huh?" His voice was edged with sarcasm. "I guess he figured that the perp was just hanging around until the police showed up before he bothered to dispose of those bloody shoes."

"In his own personal garbage can," I said with amusement. "In the alley."

McQuaid snorted. "And then Rogers dashes off in hot pursuit — twelve hours after the murder — to search Bowen's property. Without a warrant."

"I'd like to have heard what the defense did with that," I said. "No wonder the jury acquitted." I added, to Gretchen, "Those were really Bowen's shoes?"

Gretchen paused on the next image, a pair of shoes, one turned over to reveal the bloody grid on the sole. "Bowen said they were his gardening shoes. He always took them off and left them in the garage, beside the door into the house."

"And he usually left the garage unlocked, I suppose," McQuaid said thoughtfully, and Gretchen nodded.

"Huh," I grunted. "I'll bet Johnnie Carlson argued that his client was either not guilty by reason of insanity — or he was framed. No killer in his right mind would choose one of a set of his own golf clubs as the murder weapon, then drop the broken club in his own backyard and put his bloody shoes in his own garbage can." I rolled my eyes. "I've seen some pretty clueless criminals, but nobody could be that dumb."

"The defense attorney argued that there was some sort of frame-up," Gretchen said. "I read it in the transcript."

This was getting interesting. "You wouldn't happen to have a copy of that transcript, would you?" I asked.

And there was something else — an idea forming in the back of my mind. Johnnie had mentioned notes on his arguments for an alternative suspect, and I thought I knew where they were. He and Aaron Brooks had been in practice together, after they both left the firm where we'd worked. Gorgeous, hunky Aaron, with whom I had had a wild and rather wonderful fling back in the days when I was young and foolish. Together, Johnnie and Aaron had been Brooks and Carlson, with an office on University Boulevard, a few blocks from the Rice University campus in Houston. Johnnie was dead and buried, but that didn't mean that his notes were, too. I was suddenly curious. And after all, he had offered to let me read them. The last time I had seen Aaron had been a couple of years ago, at the wedding of a mutual friend, an attorney we had both worked with. Afterward, we had slipped out for a drink, to catch up on our lives. Maybe I could persuade him to let me —

"The transcript?" Gretchen slid me a

sideways glance. "I borrowed a copy. I'll be glad to loan it to you, if you want. It's kind of . . . well, long." Her tone suggested that she couldn't imagine why I would be interested in reading such a boring document. She pressed the play button and the film resumed. "Mr. Bowen — the defendant — lived here. This is how it looks now."

The house Dick Bowen had lived in wasn't as strikingly conspicuous as its ultramodern neighbor, but it was very attractive — a 1960s one-story brick and frame ranch with an attached garage, neatly trimmed landscape shrubs, and a carefully manicured front lawn. The curbside mailbox featured a large rosemary bush and a bright planting of marigolds and zinnias.

The color video of the contemporary house was replaced by a black-and-white still photo. "We got this photograph from the newspaper," Kitt said. "It was taken around the time Mr. Bowen was arraigned." The house hadn't changed, except that when Bowen lived there, a large live oak tree dominated the front yard. Pecan Springs has never paid its city employees very well, and a fleeting thought crossed my mind. How had Bowen been able to afford such a nice house in the San Jacinto neighborhood?

McQuaid might have been thinking the same thing. "Bowen was married?" he asked.

Gretchen wrinkled her nose. "Nope. He was a longtime bachelor. He lived alone — and very quietly, according to the people we talked to."

"That was one of his problems," Kitt put in. "The murder took place on a Tuesday night. He swore he was in bed asleep, but there was nobody to corroborate his claim. The people in his office testified that he came to work Wednesday morning at the usual time and behaved the way he always did. They didn't notice anything strange about him. Of course," she added regretfully, "we couldn't get any video of that testimony. Trials weren't being televised back then."

I could have told her that it was a little more complicated than that, and that the decision was made before she was born. In the famous 1965 case of *Estes v. Texas* — involving Lyndon Johnson's crony Billie Sol Estes, convicted on multiple counts of fertilizer and mortgage fraud — the U.S. Supreme Court held that the way in which television cameras were used in the courtroom deprived Estes of his Fourteenth Amendment rights. Television cameras weren't allowed back into Texas courtrooms until 1991, and then only in civil trials. Now, cameras are permitted in some criminal proceedings in some counties, at the discretion of the trial judge.

But instead of going into this camera-in-the-courtroom explanation, I changed the subject. "The Doberman," I said. "What was the watchdog doing while his mistress was being beaten to death with a golf club?"

"The prosecution brought that up," Kitt said. "It turned out that the dog had been at the vet's. He'd had problems with dysplasia and was getting a new hip. He wasn't due to be released until Thursday. The woman who came in twice a week to do Ms. Morris' cleaning testified that she told Bowen that the dog was gone and when he'd be back. So he knew that the coast was clear."

"Who else knew that the dog wasn't there?" I asked, more sharply than I intended. "Sorry," I muttered, before McQuaid could remind me that we weren't in a courtroom and that Kitt wasn't a witness.

But Kitt didn't seem offended. "Actually, it seems like everybody in the neighborhood knew that the Dobie was gone. The people we interviewed said he wasn't a very good watchdog because he barked at *everything,* constantly, day and night. They all figured he must be out of commission because they hadn't heard him for a day or two. The woman who did Ms. Morris' cleaning also worked for some of the other neighbors, so word got around that the dog was getting his hip fixed." She grinned. "Several of the neighbors remembered wishing that he was getting his *bark* fixed."

Ah, yes. The dog that didn't bark in the night, not because the dog knew the killer but because the dog wasn't there and the killer knew it. I wondered whether Johnnie Carlson had remarked on that neat little Holmesian barking-dog trick. But I refrained from asking. I could check it out in the trial transcript.

And that thought prodded me into the startled realization that, yes, I really *had* decided to read the transcript, however boring it might be. Not only that, but I was planning, posthumously, to take Johnnie up on his offer to read his trial notes on the alternative suspect — that is, if I could coax Aaron to let me have a look.

Why? Because I wanted to decide for myself whether the jury had done an admirable service to the causes of justice and jurisprudence by acquitting Dick Bowen?

No. I already understood and appreciated

the jury's willingness to poke a hole in the blue wall big enough to let some version of the truth escape. But *somebody* had murdered Christine Morris. Somebody had attacked and killed Karen Prior; somebody had attacked Gretchen Keene and stolen her camera. Were these somebodies the same person or different people? What were the motives? The transcript and Johnnie's notes might give me a place to start.

"And this," Gretchen said, "is Mr. Bowen."

And there he was, a short, seriously overweight man of forty-five or fifty, wearing a white shirt and tie and rimless glasses, seated behind a desk littered with papers. His brown hair was thinning; his face was soft and round; his smile was friendly, almost ingratiating. He might have been a schoolteacher — chemistry, maybe, or history — but the plaque on his desk announced that he was Richard Bowen, Building Inspections, Zoning. That photo was followed by several newspaper stills. One of them showed Bowen in front of the city council. The caption read: *Zoning Committee Denies Morris Request.*

"I noticed the headlines in the earlier shot," McQuaid said. "*Morris Accuses Zoning Committee of Malfeasance. Morris Slams*

219

City Officials. What was all that about?"

"Ms. Morris was having a feud with the planning and zoning people," Kitt replied. "It had to do with getting a variance or something."

"The section of San Jacinto where she lived was zoned single-family residential," I said to McQuaid. "She wanted to open an art gallery on the first floor of her house. But the neighbors opposed any zoning change, and she got turned down. After that, Ruby said she launched a campaign against the zoning office. She would go to city council meetings and complain. It sounds like she was pretty universally hated, except in the art community."

"Well, even there . . ." Gretchen let her voice trail off.

"What?" I asked curiously.

Kitt cleared her throat. "We talked to another man who was on the museum board until very recently. Dr. Cameron."

"That would be Paul Cameron," McQuaid said to me. "He retired at the end of the fall semester." He leaned toward me and lowered his voice. "He's getting old and a little . . . slow."

That, I thought, was an understatement. I was acquainted with the man, who had taught art history at CTSU for decades and

— while he was just sixty-five — was obviously suffering from some form of dementia. CTSU did away with age-based mandatory retirement a few years ago, so a faculty member can go on teaching until he decides to quit. For the past couple of years, Cameron's lectures had become increasingly garbled and his colleagues had been pleading with the dean to "encourage" his retirement. They must be glad it had finally happened and they could hire a younger, more productive art historian to take his place.

I wasn't sure that his wife, Irene, would be glad, however. The Camerons had had problems, I'd heard — serious financial problems caused by Paul's erratic and unwise investments in the stock market over the years. He had always earned a solid faculty salary with good retirement benefits, but rumor had it that they had been on the verge of losing their house to the bank more than once. I could only hope that his faculty benefits would cover his care, when he needed it.

It made sense, though, that Paul would have been asked to serve on the museum board. He'd been a strong supporter of the arts in Pecan Springs for decades and knew everyone who was involved in art activity.

"It was a little . . . um, difficult to talk to

Dr. Cameron," Kitt said tactfully. "He has a tendency to wander off the subject. We went ahead and filmed him because we were there. There might be a few sound bites we could use, but his footage would take a huge amount of editing. He was more than willing to talk to us, though."

"I'll bet he was," McQuaid muttered. "The problem is getting Paul to *stop* talking."

Kitt giggled, agreeing. "Anyway, we gathered that he had some strong opinions about Ms. Morris' expertise as a collector of Mexican art. He doesn't like Ms. Tillotson very much, either." She ducked her head. "In fact, he said that both of them were 'as ignorant as dirt' when it came to real art."

"He said that was Shakespeare," Gretchen put in, "so I looked it up. It's in *Othello.*"

"And he especially didn't like the man Ms. Morris bought some of her paintings from," Kitt added. "An art dealer from San Antonio. 'Wily as a fox,' he said."

Ah, yes. "Soto?" I asked, and Kitt nodded. "What didn't Dr. Cameron like about Soto?"

Gretchen frowned uncertainly. "He didn't say, exactly. Or rather, he said, but it was hard to figure out just *what* he was saying.

It had something to do with one of Ms. Morris' paintings."

"Did you tape that part of the interview?" I asked.

Kitt sighed. "We pretended to tape it, but I shut the camera off. By that time, he was getting really garbled. There wasn't going to be anything worth the time it would take to edit."

I added "See Paul Cameron" to my mental list of things to do and wondered when I was going to do them all. Johnnie's trial notes might be in Aaron's office — I had his home phone number, which he had given me with the invitation to call him if I was ever in town. The shop was closed on Monday, so if I decided to go, I could drive there and back that day. Tomorrow was Sunday. Maybe I ought to see Paul and —

"Besides Dr. Cameron," McQuaid asked, "who else have you talked to?"

"Well, there was Mr. Lipman, Ms. Morris' attorney," Kitt said. "And Mr. Davidson, another neighbor on San Jacinto. He told us that all the neighbors were mad at her about those yard lights and that barking dog, and that he thought he might have seen somebody looking into Mr. Bowen's garage."

"We talked to the jury foreman, Mr. Peters," Gretchen chimed in. "He said that the jury didn't convict Mr. Bowen because they agreed with the defense attorney. They thought the police did some things they shouldn't have done and that there was a reasonable doubt that Mr. Bowen was guilty. He gave us some other names of jurors to talk to, but we haven't done that yet." She sighed. "I guess we won't, now."

"We also talked to several people who worked with Mr. Bowen," Kitt said. "In fact, I think one of them is next on the tape." She grinned. "Actually, it's kind of a comic segment. Want to see it?"

"Sure," McQuaid said. "I'm ready for a laugh."

An image filled the screen — a large woman in her sixties, with tightly curled blue-white hair and saggy jowls, her cheeks rouged, her lips fire-engine red, the lipstick bleeding into the age wrinkles around her mouth. She wore a bright green dress and gold hoop earrings as big as bangle bracelets that dragged down her fleshy earlobes a good inch. She sat, posing self-consciously, on a living room sofa, surrounded by a heap of crocheted pillows. In her lap, she held a small Pekinese, who wore a matching green bow in her topknot.

"Why, it's Florabelle Gibson," I said in

surprise. "And Mimi." I hadn't seen Florabelle in a while, but for a time, she was a regular customer in my shop, usually with her dog. That Pekinese was the most foul-tempered animal I had ever seen. "Why is she in your film?"

Gretchen pushed the pause button, and Florabelle Gibson was caught with her eyes half-shut and her mouth wide open. "She testified on behalf of Mr. Bowen. She was a secretary in his office, but she's retired now."

"Which office was that, exactly?" Mc-Quaid asked.

"The Pecan Springs planning department," Gretchen replied. "Mr. Bowen was a building inspector, and also zoning. Ms. Gibson managed the paperwork, so she knew him pretty well."

She hit the play button and Florabelle trilled, in an exaggerated East Texas twang. "Well, naturally, I never thought for one single minute that Mr. Bowen could've done what the prosecutor said he did." She fluffed up Mimi's ears, and the dog bared its teeth. "He was the nicest, kindliest man anybody ever wanted to know, always happy when he came to work in the morning, always glad to see folks, even those hard-boiled, crusty old contractors he had to work with as an inspector. And generous? Why, that man gave money to every good cause in this community. He was an angel, is what he was."

The screen went black for a moment, then Florabelle's image reappeared. "What exactly did he do in the department?" she asked, as if she was repeating a question. "He was in charge of all the building inspections in Pecan Springs, that's what he did. He was really good at it, too, believe you me. Oh, and he was on the zoning committee, too. As I said, he was a good man to work with, always so helpful to everybody."

She pulled down her mouth. "Ms. Morris, on the other hand, was a genuine pain in the patootie." She pursed her lips and said it again, emphatically. "A genuine pain in the pa-*too*-tie."

On the film, from behind the camera, I heard Kitt ask, "Ms. Morris was a pain? What makes you say that?"

"Why, because." Florabelle seemed to be surprised that her questioner didn't already know the answer. "She was always bad-mouthin' folks, always diggin' up dirt on this one or that one. Nobody likes somebody like that."

"What kind of dirt?" Kitt prompted.

Florabelle tossed her head. Her earlobes flapped and her hoop earrings danced.

"Well, just take for instance that zoning variance she was trying to get so she could sell those gawd-awful paintings she set so much store by. Mrs. Rohde was the one in the office who turned down her paperwork, on account of she didn't fill it out right. Then lo and *be*-hold, two, three days later, Mr. Hanson — he was the big boss at the time, Jimmie Lee Hanson, you know him? — he called Mrs. Rohde into his office and gave her you-know-what for being rude to Ms. Morris, who had complained about it in a letter to him." She harrumphed. "Which was a lie, pure and simple, 'cause my desk was right next to Mrs. Rohde's and I couldn't help but hear every little thing that was said, and there was not one single word that came out of Mrs. Rohde's mouth that was anything but polite. All the rude was on Ms. Morris' end, and there was plenty of it."

"No wonder people didn't like her," Kitt said mildly.

"Yes, and I'll tell you, young lady, there was plenty of other folks who would have done that woman in, if they'd had half a chance." Florabelle raised her hand and pointed, and I saw that there were rings on every fat finger. "And that's egg-*zact*-ly what I told Chief Bubba Harris, when he

227

came into the office and started asking questions about Mr. Bowen. I said to him, 'Mr. Bowen did not do this, no way, José! He's no angel, definitely not. But if you want to turn up rocks to look under for a killer, there's plenty of them lyin' around right under your feet, every last one of them with something slimy on the bottom side.'"

Florabelle laughed sarcastically, showing coffee-stained teeth. "But did he listen to me? He did not. He already had it in his head that Mr. Bowen was guilty. The way I look at it, though, there was somebody *wanting* Mr. Bowen to look guilty, to get him outta the way. It was the same person as wanted to shut Ms. Morris up. And I had me a pretty good idea who that was." The screen went black.

Gretchen hit the pause button. "That's all there is of that footage," she said. "Her dog got sick and threw up all over the couch so we had to quit."

At that moment, the telephone rang in McQuaid's study. "Excuse me," he said and went to answer it.

"Could you play that last bit back?" I asked.

Gretchen hit the back button and replayed Florabelle's last statement: "The way I look at it, there was somebody wanting Mr.

Bowen to look guilty, to get him outta the way. It was the same person as wanted to shut Ms. Morris up. And I had me a pretty good idea who that was."

I leaned forward. "Did Ms. Gibson tell you who she thought that person might be?"

Kitt frowned. "No, she didn't. And I didn't think to ask her." She gave a little shrug. "To tell the honest truth, Ms. Bayles, I didn't take her very seriously. But I could go back to her and ask her to explain."

"Absolutely not," I said quickly. "We are talking *murder* here. You two don't want to get any more involved than you already are." But if Florabelle had another possibility in mind for the murder of Christine Morris, I personally wanted to hear it. I added her to my mental list of people to talk to. And to the girls, I said, apologetically, "Sorry. I don't mean to snap at you."

"It's okay," Gretchen said with a rueful smile. "We realize we've stirred something up — something pretty bad. We just don't know what it is. Or what we can do about it."

"Well, let me ask you this," I said. "Aside from Florabelle Gibson, did any of your other interviewees voice similar suspicions? Did anybody else give you the idea that they suspected somebody — somebody in particular — of killing Christine Morris and framing Dick Bowen?"

Kitt and Gretchen exchanged uneasy glances. "Not really," Kitt said.

"I see." I turned to Gretchen. There was something else I needed to confirm. "The camera that was stolen — and the memory cards. All of what we've been looking at was on either the camera or the cards?"

"Some of it was in the camera," Gretchen replied promptly, "but it was all in the memory cards. I used them to back everything up." She glanced at Kitt. "Kitt's stuff, too. The people she filmed."

So whoever took those memory cards could be looking at this video right now. "And how much of your film had Dr. Prior seen?" I asked.

Kitt frowned. "We gave her a copy of everything last week. She must have glanced through it, at least, because she told us that she'd flagged a few things to talk over with us before we finished the editing and added the voice-over narration. She said she'd give us her list and we could discuss the changes she wanted made."

"Did she give you the list?" I was thinking that Karen might have identified something in the video that gave her a reason for concern. If so, I wanted to know what it was.

Both girls shook their heads. "It might be in her campus office," Kitt offered tentatively. "Or in her office at home."

"Or in her briefcase," Gretchen suggested, and then added, "Actually, we don't *know* that she made the list. She just said she was going to. But it seemed important to her."

I nodded. "Thanks. When you talk to Chief Dawson in the morning, you might suggest that she look for it. Also, she'll probably want to look at your video. I think it might be helpful if you two sat down right now, while you're thinking about it, and made a list of all your interviewees, in the order in which they appear in the film. Oh, and include the names of the people you wanted to interview but didn't — and the reason why. It would also be good to make notes of any segment that you think might interest Chief Dawson particularly — like the Gibson bit. Can you do all that?"

"Sure," Kitt said. "We can tell her where in the footage she should look, too. That way, she can skip through the irrelevant material." She made a face. "Some of it's pretty boring. Of course, it wouldn't be, if we'd had a chance to edit it."

McQuaid came back into the room. He

was looking troubled. "That was . . . my partner," he said in a guarded tone. "He's at the hospital with . . ." He glanced at the girls, not wanting to spill Sheila's secret. "With his wife." He added, quietly, "Threatened miscarriage."

"Uh-oh," I said softly. "Oh, dear. Oh, *dear*. That's really . . . that's too bad." I thought of Sheila's excitement about her pregnancy, in spite of the morning sickness and the uncertainty about managing work and family, and my heart turned over. Losing the baby would be a terrible disappointment, for both her and Blackie. I took a breath. "But if it's only a threat, let's hope the doctors can stabilize her."

He nodded. "Yeah. Blackie sounds optimistic. They're keeping her overnight, maybe over Sunday night, too. When she goes home, she'll have to stay off her feet for a few days."

I got to my feet, fighting off a sudden leaden weariness. Sheila's secret was likely to be public knowledge before she wanted it to be. However her pregnancy turned out, the next few days were going to be hugely difficult for her — and for Blackie. How would they handle that? How could I help?

The girls were watching us curiously, but I followed McQuaid's lead. We hadn't mentioned any names they would recognize, and we weren't going to. In the morning, I would tell them that something urgent came up and Chief Dawson couldn't meet with them after all. She'd make arrangements to talk with them later. In the meantime —

"Hey," I said, taking a deep breath and lifting my arms through the weariness and overhead, into a yoga stretch. "I've just about had all the excitement I can handle for one evening. I'm having a glass of milk and some cookies before I turn in for the night. Anybody want to join me?"

CHAPTER EIGHT

Some plants are symbolic of both bad luck and good fortune. In Italy, to present a chrysanthemum to someone is considered to be very bad luck, for it is a funeral flower. In Korea, white chrysanthemums represent grief for the loss of a loved one, and in Japan, the flowers are used only on altars and at funerals: anywhere else means bad luck. In China, however, chrysanthemum wreaths are placed on doors and windows to "get rid of the bad luck and bring in the good." And in the United States, the flowers represent cheerfulness and good times.

Lemon verbena (*Aloysia citrodora*) is not only essential to any well-managed herb garden, but it has the power to change bad luck to good. Basil given as a gift is said to bring good luck to a new home, but it has long been associated with dying and may foretell an early death. In the west of England, if you grew a crop of parsley, you shouldn't give any of it away, because you would be giving your good luck along with it.

China Bayles
"Herbs of Good and Ill Omen"
Pecan Springs Enterprise

Don't tell me it's my imagination. Gardeners know that climate change is here and that our planet is heating up. We've seen temperatures getting warmer every year, to the point where residents of the Texas Hill Country are experiencing long, unbroken strings of hundred-degree days. One year recently, Austin was on the grill for a blistering record of ninety days with a temperature of 100 degrees or higher and twenty-seven hundred-degree days in a row. And here in Pecan Springs, our average July daytime high now hovers around 95 degrees, nighttime lows around 75. Bottom line, it's hot and getting hotter.

This week, we were working on the upper end of the average, and the Weather Channel was forecasting a 3:00 p.m. high of 103. It was a mild but humid 78 when I got up before the sun rose and went out to the veggie garden to get a couple of the raised beds ready for the fall planting, which in our neck of the woods begins around the end of July. When I'd finished moving compost from the pile into the raised beds and mixed it in, the crystalline blue sky had turned cloudy and the wind had swung into the south, bringing up moisture from the Gulf. The temperature had cranked up to 82 and the discomfort index was in the nineties and nudging higher. I was glad to head for the kitchen to begin making pancakes for the breakfast gang.

Sunday breakfast at our house usually occurs in shifts, because everybody has things to do. I made a tall stack of pancakes and left them on the counter with a big plate of scrambled eggs (compliments of Caitie's girls) and bacon, to be reheated in the microwave whenever people wandered in. I set out a small pitcher of ginger syrup for the pancakes and a larger pitcher of orange juice, with glasses.

While I was working, I cast a quick glance at the empty spot beside the stove where Howard Cosell's basket used to sit and — with a sharp pang — remembered that he wasn't with us any longer. When I was in the kitchen, Howard was always there, gazing up at me soulfully (no breed of dog is quite so soulful as a basset), begging for a handout. It was hard to believe that he wasn't under the table, licking up crumbs off the floor; or out in the yard, trying futilely to catch a grasshopper; or stretched out on the back steps, waiting for somebody to trip and fall over him. I suppose that we're never the most reliable judges of what is meaningful and true in our lives, or what will matter the most when it isn't there any longer. I don't think I fully appreciated Howard until he was gone and I could see the basset-sized hole he left in all our hearts.

Breakfast set out, buffet-style, I went into McQuaid's study and made several phone calls: one to Karen Prior's daughter, Felicity; one to Florabelle Gibson; and one to Dr. Cameron's house, where I spoke with Paul's wife, Irene. In all three cases, I explained what I had in mind and asked what would be a good time to drop in.

Felicity suggested that I come as soon as I could, since she and her grandmother had been invited to brunch by the next-door neighbor.

Florabelle, who was surprised to hear from me and delighted at the prospect of having company, said that any old time would be perfectly fine with her, since she never went anywhere, now that her feet were swelling so much she could hardly get her shoes on. "Just me and Mimi, all by our lonesomes," she said. "So do come on, China, dear."

Irene Cameron, whom I knew through our university connections, was amenable to my dropping in, but a little more cautious. I didn't tell her why I wanted to see her husband.

"I'm not sure Paul is feeling up to it today, China," she said. "He has his good days and his bad days. But stop in for a few moments this afternoon and we'll see what happens."

"What time would be good for you?" I asked.

"Could you make it around three or three thirty? He'll be up from his nap by that time. He's usually at his best then. But it's hard to predict how . . . rational he's going to be."

"Of course," I said sympathetically. I felt sorry for Irene. She had once enjoyed what seemed to be a promising career as a painter. I had seen some of her earlier work — still lifes, florals, and landscapes, mostly — and liked it very much. And I wasn't the only one. She had exhibited in national competitions and won prizes for her paintings. She had even had a one-woman show at one of the galleries in San Antonio, and I'd heard that collectors had picked up almost all of her work. I hoped she was still painting, but I knew that, these days, she had to spend a great deal of her time with Paul.

Before I went to bed the previous night, I had phoned Ruby to tell her about Smart Cookie. She had been as concerned as I. Now I phoned Blackie for an update. He sounded tired and discouraged, unlike his usual upbeat and optimistic self. Sheila would be coming home later that day but would have to stay flat on her back for some time — how long, it wasn't clear.

"We don't know yet whether she'll be able to keep the baby," he added. "Right now, it's touch-and-go. And when she'll get back to work is anybody's guess. She's anxious about that, of course," he added. "She's got good backup in the department, but you know Sheila. She shows up for every play. She hates being benched."

I debated telling him what I was going to do but decided against it — at least at the moment. I could always tell him later, after the fact. "Tell her we love her," I said. "We're thinking of both of you."

McQuaid, who is a longtime gun collector, had disappeared into his shop, where he was working on an M1903 Springfield rifle, an early one he'd just acquired from one of his collector buddies. Since their date with the police chief had been canceled, Gretchen and Kitt offered to take Brian, Jake, and Caitlin to Barton Springs for the day. Dipping into that chilly water would cool everybody off, and then they could toast themselves in the sun, on the grassy slopes above the pool. Before the girls left, I made a copy of the list of interviewees that they had compiled the night before and folded it into my purse. I'd have time to study it later.

After the gang was out of the house, I showered and buttoned myself into a cool white sleeveless blouse, stepped into a denim wraparound skirt, and strapped leather sandals on my bare feet. I don't wear stockings unless it's a command performance, and definitely not today. I ran a comb through my brown hair, noting that the gray streak down one side seemed to have gotten a bit wider, and decided against makeup. The thermometer outside the kitchen window announced that it was already 92. Since it wasn't ten o'clock yet, I suspected that the Weather Channel might miss its prediction by a couple of degrees: 105 wasn't out of the question. Some women may be able to wear eye shadow and mascara when they go out on hot days. I am not one of them.

McQuaid came in from outside. "Looks like we'll have a crowd for supper again tonight," he said. "What are we having?"

"I was about to ask you the same thing," I said, unplugging my cell phone from its charger. When he's home on weekends, McQuaid does a lot of the cooking. It's one of the things I love about him.

He pondered that for a moment. "Okay — so how about brisket sandwiches, with the rest of the brisket from last night? Everybody can make their own. I'll cook up some baked beans in the slow cooker — that'll keep the house cooler."

"Sounds right," I said. "I'll mix up a bowl of potato salad when I get home — there's some mashed potatoes left from Friday. And there's the rest of that cabbage, for coleslaw. And some deviled eggs from last night." There might be a few other things in the fridge, once I had a chance to look. For Sunday suppers, we try to use up the leftovers, in order to get a fresh start on the coming week. Otherwise, things get shoved to the back of the shelf, and you know what happens after that.

"Watermelon for dessert," McQuaid said with satisfaction. "I saw a ripe one out in the garden that's about the right size. I'll put it in the fridge to get cold." It suddenly dawned on him that I wasn't dressed in my usual shorts and T-shirt and that my hair was actually combed. He raised both eyebrows. "You're going somewhere special?"

"I asked Felicity Prior if I could drop in for a few minutes this morning," I said carelessly. McQuaid is not in favor of my doing investigative things on my own. "And maybe a couple of other stops. You know, just —"

"China." McQuaid was stern.

"What?" I asked, innocently.

"I don't suppose it would do any good to suggest that you leave the investigating to Sheila. She gets paid for stuff like that."

"Sheila has one or two little problems of her own," I said and picked up my purse. "By the time she gets back on her feet, her in-box will be overflowing and she'll be up to her chin in departmental paperwork. Karen's death is a priority with her, but there's only so much one woman can do. I'm giving her a hand, that's all."

That was true, as far as it went. But there was something else, and McQuaid knows what it is. He feels it, too, maybe even more than I do. In our professional lives, both of us developed the habit of getting involved in other people's problems, he as a cop, I as an advocate. We may operate from different sides of the street, but we both work in the same neighborhood: we can't help getting involved.

McQuaid rolled his eyes. "You keep your nose clean, woman. I don't want to have to bail you out of jail. Or worse."

"Yes, sir, Officer McQuaid, sir," I said. "I'll do my best to stay out of trouble."

In two strides, he was across the kitchen, folding me into the safety of his arms. "Hey," he murmured, his lips against my hair, "I only love you, you know. And you do have a tendency to get yourself into jams."

He was thinking of the jam I'd gotten into just a few weeks before. I had driven down into Fayette County to talk to Ruby about a situation that couldn't wait and got stuck in the middle of a serious tropical storm, in a haunted house, with a pair of murdering bank robbers on the loose. McQuaid had to call on one of his helicopter-pilot buddies to help him bail Ruby and me out. He hasn't let me forget it.

"I know," I said contritely. "But I'm just doing a few drop-in calls today, nothing at all challenging. And definitely nothing for you to worry about."

I didn't tell him what I had planned for tomorrow because it wasn't actually scheduled yet, although with any luck, it would be. If I told him, he would definitely be worried.

He'd be jealous, too.

Karen Prior's house on Steven F. Austin Drive wore a large black bow on the front door, and some thoughtful person had left a pot of white chrysanthemums and a card on the front steps. I picked them up and when Felicity came to the door, I handed them to her.

"One of your friends left these for you," I said soberly. "Felicity, I am so very sorry about your mother."

Felicity was pale and vulnerable looking, her ash-blond hair pinned on top of her head, the straggling ends curling damply around her slender neck. Barefoot, in white shorts and a ragged green T-shirt and no makeup, she looked as if she were about twelve years old.

"Thank you," she said and held the flowers up to her face. "People have been giving us so much. Food, flowers, everything." She gestured toward the living room, which was banked with bouquets. "You should see the kitchen. The refrigerator is totally full. Gramma and I will never be able to eat it all."

"I hope your grandmother is okay," I said quietly. I had met Karen's mother a couple of summers ago, when she'd visited Pecan Springs. Karen had been her only daughter.

Felicity let out a long, jerky breath and the words tumbled out with it. "She's not okay, not really. How can she be okay? How can either of us *ever* be okay?"

There wasn't anything I could say to that, but there wasn't time to say it, anyway. Felicity was rushing on.

"The only way I can explain it to myself is that Mom's luck just ran out. She was in the wrong place at the wrong time, and something random and horrible happened to her. Maybe the person who attacked her didn't mean to kill her." Another breath, this one pulled in, and more words. "But it is what it is. I guess we just have to get used to it, somehow."

I was long past the point of agreeing with her, even for politeness' sake. I had already convinced myself that Karen's death had nothing to do with luck. The person who attacked her might not have intended to kill her, true — although according to Sheila, she'd been hit more than once, and hit hard. And I was sure that their meeting was no accident. Karen had something, or knew something, that her attacker wanted or needed. Or thought he did. But of course, he — or she — could have been wrong. Karen could have been killed for . . . nothing.

Felicity tilted her head, watching me curiously. "You wanted to look for something in Mom's studio? Some notes, I think you said?"

"Yes. She told Gretchen Keene and Kitt Bradley that she was making notes on material she thought they should delete from the documentary they were working on for her class. The notes could be here or in her briefcase or in her office at school."

Felicity looked as if she wanted to ask me why I wanted the notes, but she turned and led the way to a large, windowless room at the end of the hall — her mother's home video studio. Two walls were lined with bookshelves and in the corner between them was a built-in desk, piled high with untidy stacks of what looked like student papers and portfolios. Karen's brown leather briefcase sat open on the desk. A third wall of the room was a solid bank of video equipment, with several monitors and a large soundboard. She used another corner of the room for recording, so there were several cameras, a couple of mikes, and a ceiling rack of directional lighting and lights on tripods. A fourth wall was a green screen, with a couple of chairs.

"Mom did a lot of her work here," Felicity said. "It's just the way she left it." Sudden tears filled her eyes and she blinked rapidly. "Make yourself at home, Ms. Bayles. Would you like something — coffee, tea?"

"No, thanks," I said. "I'm hoping I can find what I'm looking for on the top of one of those stacks, so I won't have to dig for it."

I had to dig. It was in the very bottom of her briefcase, jotted on the back of a used envelope from the personnel office at CTSU and luckily sticking out of her grade book. At the top was written, in Karen's bold hand, *Keene/Bradley: problematic material for discussion.* Under that was written, in a brief list, four items: *Bloody photo, Gibson's suspicions, Irene Cameron — painting, Sharyn.* There was a phone number at the bottom, with a 210 area code — San Antonio. And in the envelope I saw a thumb drive, neatly labeled *Keene/Bradley* — the copy of the raw documentary footage that Gretchen and Kitt had given her for review, I guessed.

As I picked up the grade book, I noticed something under it — a catalog from Sotheby's in New York, which even I, definitely nonliterate in the arts, recognized as a prominent art auction house. The catalog, dated the previous November, advertised an auction that featured Latin American art. On the cover was a painting of orange and red curtains, gracefully knotted and so realistic that I could see every last wrinkle. It was entitled *Angelus,* by Claudia Bravo, and was estimated to sell at auction for a minimum of $900,000.

I suppressed a whistle at the price. Way too rich for my blood, and for Karen's, too, I was sure. What was her interest in this catalog? There was a yellow sticky note on one of the inside pages and, curiously, I opened to it. The photograph on the page looked like the painting I had seen in the girls' documentary, the one Kitt had said was Karen's favorite in the Morris collection. It was María Izquierdo's *Muerte llega pronto.* Death Come Quickly. The flower was Herb Robert, the herb of ill omen. It was estimated to sell for $110,000 to $125,000.

I frowned down at the photograph. How could the painting be hanging in a private collection in Pecan Springs and be on the auction block in New York at the same time? But then, I don't know much about art. Maybe the two paintings weren't quite the same. After all, I'd had only a glance at the one in the documentary. The artist had probably painted several versions of the same scene, either to correct a problem or maybe just to decide which one she liked best. Artists did that sometimes, didn't they? I remembered reading that Edgar Degas painted thirty-some studies of women taking a bath — although maybe he just liked working with nude models.

I copied everything down and left the envelope and the thumb drive where I found it, slipping it into Karen's grade book rather than leaving it sticking out. I also took the precaution of closing the briefcase and putting it on the floor under the desk, out of sight. I would let Sheila know what I had discovered and why I'd been looking for it. She could send someone to pick it up, if she thought it was important. But I slipped the Sotheby's catalog into my purse. I was curious about it. I wanted another, more careful look.

Back in the hallway, I suggested to Felicity that it might be a good idea to lock her mother's studio and put the key in a safe place.

She frowned. "But why —"

I could have told her that someone might come looking for whatever it was he had wanted to find when he attacked her mother. But I didn't.

"Because the police may want to have a look," I said. "I'll let Chief Dawson know I was here. But it would be a good idea not to let anyone else in the room. You might tell your grandmother, too."

Felicity thought about that for a moment, a small frown deepening across her forehead. "You're not thinking that the attack on Mom was . . ."

She looked up at me, her gray eyes widening as she began to get a glimpse of what was behind my suggestion.

"But it *couldn't* be, Ms. Bayles!" Her hand went to her mouth. "My mother has never done anything that somebody might want to kill her for! What possible reason could there be?"

I wondered whether it was easier for Felicity to believe that her mother had been the victim of random bad luck than to think she might have been deliberately targeted.

"You're most likely right," I replied gently. I wanted to say that the reason, if there was one, was locked inside the skull of a killer. But she didn't need to hear that, not right now. "We don't know for certain, though, do we? So let's just play it safe."

She nodded hesitantly. "I guess," she said,

although I wasn't entirely sure she was persuaded.

I left her on the porch, holding a large basket of cake and cookies that had appeared beside the front door. I went out to my car and called Blackie. He was at the hospital, waiting for Sheila to be released. She was doing better, he said, but she'd still have to stay in bed.

I briefly sketched out the situation and suggested that he ask Sheila to send somebody over to the Prior house to put a police seal on the door to Karen's video studio, and a strip of crime scene tape on the front of the house. That would go a long way to deter a possible break-in. And Sheila wouldn't have to get out of bed to do it. A simple phone call would take care of the job.

Blackie agreed but gave me the same line I'd heard from McQuaid. "This is police business, China." He didn't say *Buzz off,* but I heard the warning in his voice.

I have learned that it's useless to argue with cops or ex-cops on this subject. Law enforcement types (and Blackie and McQuaid certainly fit the description) do not like civilians messing around in what they regard as their business. But there's a limit to what the law can do and do well, and the smartest cops (and ex-cops) understand that, somewhere down deep in the recesses of their cop hearts.

So I said, with a smile in *my* voice, "Tell Sheila I'll update her this evening. Okay?"

I hung up before he could tell me I should go home and make lunch for my husband and kids.

Florabelle Gibson and Mimi the foul-tempered Pekinese live in a one-bedroom apartment in a seniors-only complex on Buchanan Drive, on the south side of Pecan Springs, not far from the river. The apartment is on the second floor, with a quilt-sized balcony bright with blooming geraniums, with pots of basil, lemon verbena, and straggly lemon balm, along the railing, where they could catch the sun.

I rang the little brass button beside the door and heard, from inside, Florabelle's quavery voice. "Is that you, China?"

"Yep, it's me," I said pleasantly.

"Well, then, come on in. I'd get up and open the door for you but my feet are killin' me."

The draperies were drawn against the July sunshine and the room was dim. But it was light enough to see that Kitt's camera had been exceedingly kind to Florabelle. She had gained weight since the last time she was in the shop, and in person, she was even heavier than she had appeared in the video. She was sitting on the sofa, surrounded by crocheted pillows. Her face was puffy and sallow, as if she hadn't been sleeping well. Her blue-white hair was covered with a hairnet decorated with colorful ribbon butterflies, and she wore a gaudy red-and-green-print cotton housecoat with red buttons the size of silver dollars. The loose garment did nothing to conceal her enormous bosom and outsize white thighs, unattractively visible because her feet were propped on a hassock in front of her. She wore men's white socks and no shoes. Her swollen ankles were the diameter of small trees. Next to the sofa, within arm's reach, was an aluminum walker. I felt immediate compassion for her.

"China Bayles, honey, you are a sight for sore eyes!" she cried happily, holding out her hand. "So glad you dropped in to see me!"

Mimi the Peke with pique, on the other hand, was not thrilled at the idea of a stranger (more or less) intruding into her private domain. She crouched in a wing chair that obviously belonged to her and told me so in two sharp warning barks, followed by a muttered snarl, just to make sure I got the message.

I opened my shoulder bag and took out the small, ribbon-wrapped package I had picked up on my way out of the house that morning. I handed it to Florabelle. "I remembered that you used to buy this lavender bath oil when you came into the shop."

It wasn't a bribe, exactly. More like a little friendship offering. But I did hope it might make her a little more willing to talk to me.

"Oh, thank you!" she cooed and untied the ribbon. She held up the bottle. "How'd you know I was completely out? I would've come to the shop to buy some, but I'm not getting around as much as I used to. I have to wait for somebody to take me, because I can't drive, with my ankles all swelled the way they are." She nodded toward the small kitchen, separated from the living room by a counter. "After you called, I stirred us up some lemonade — with a little snipped lemon balm in it. It's in the fridge and the glasses are in the cupboard on the right, over the sink. Would you mind getting us a glass apiece?" She grimaced. "It's my bad luck to be stuck on this couch. I can cook my meals and do the housework, what little there is of it, with just me and Mimi. But once my feet are up, the rest of me likes to just sit."

"I feel that way sometimes, too," I said. I went into the kitchen, got out the pitcher of lemonade, and found ice cubes in a tray in the small refrigerator freezer. On the four-burner gas stove, there was a pot of simmering chicken, with some carrots and potatoes peeking out. A head of cabbage and bag of celery were on the counter.

"Want me to put the cabbage and celery in the fridge?" I asked.

"Oh, did I leave them out? I was making some chicken soup for supper. That's something I can eat on for three, four days, once I get a pot of it made. Yes, please do put them away, dear."

Pouring the lemonade, I said, in a conversational tone, "I had a chance to see you on film yesterday. I'm a friend of Kitt Bradley. She showed me the video she made of you and Mimi."

Florabelle's eyes brightened. "Oh, that!" she said, waving her hand. The ribbon butterflies bobbed on her hairnet. "Mimi dearly *loves* being on camera. Did she look pretty?"

"Beautiful," I said, putting the glass on the table beside Florabelle, being careful to stay well outside of Mimi's snapping range.

"Her green bow exactly matched your dress."

"See there, Mimi?" Florabelle said happily. She leaned toward the dog and patted its head gently. "This lady says you looked beautiful." Mimi did not seem terribly impressed.

"Nice that you noticed her hair bow," Florabelle said to me. "Mimi does like to dress up a little, when she's got somebody to admire her. I'm afraid she gets bored, just the two of us here all day, all by our lonesomes, with nothing to do but watch television." She sipped her lemonade, then put down the glass. "That filming session was just real . . . interesting. Made me remember all kinds of stuff." She shook her head. "Poor Mr. Bowen. He sure got the short end of the stick in that situation. Real bad luck." Another head shake. "He's dead now, y'know."

"That's what Ruby Wilcox told me," I said quietly. "Somebody else said it was suicide."

"Ruby." Florabelle smiled. "Now, there's somebody I like and don't see near enough of. Next time you see her, tell her Florabelle would love it if she would drop in for a visit. If she's got the time, she could bring her tarot cards and do a layout for me. I'd really like to get a peek at what's around the next corner. Ruby is so good at that. She —"

"I'll tell her." I cut her off, wondering what was behind the nervous chatter. "Suicide," I repeated. "Was that what you heard, too?"

Florabelle didn't quite meet my glance. "Suicide is what Frank Donnelly put in the paper, because that's what the police said. He put it on the front page, too, even though it happened over there in Houston." She took an uneven breath. "And if you're asking me for my personal opinion, no, I have to say that I didn't believe it happened that way. Frank didn't, either. He told me so. Real upset about it, he was. Can't say I blame him."

"My goodness," I said. I was surprised. "But if it wasn't suicide, then how —"

Now that she had gotten started, she was going on, with a rush. "The thing that made up Frank's mind, y'see, was that Mr. Bowen didn't leave a note for him or let on in any way whatsoever that he was thinking of doing something so serious as killin' himself. Frank just kept saying that, over and over. 'Dick would've cued me in,' he'd say. 'He wouldn't leave like that without saying good-bye to me.' " She looked down at her pudgy fingers, pausing delicately, selecting a neutral phrase. "Frank and Mr. Bowen were . . . best friends, y'see."

"Ah," I said and nodded. "Ah, yes, that's what Ruby said."

She sighed. "Of course, everybody knew what was going on between them. But back then, folks didn't talk about s-e-x the way they do now. Gay marriage and all, right out in the open. Which is good, if you're asking me for my opinion. To each his own is the way I see it." She cast a pious look upward. "Whichever way God made us, that's whichever way we are, and He wouldn't want us trying to change it."

"I heard it was carbon monoxide poisoning," I said. "Mr. Bowen sat in his car in a closed garage with the motor running. But you don't think that's how it happened?"

Florabelle eyed me for a moment, as if she were deciding how much to say. "Well, that's the way they *found* him," she said at last. "Sitting in his car in that garage, stone-cold dead, and his car outta gas, after running for who knows how long, hours probably." She stopped, biting her lip.

"I see," I said encouragingly, and waited for the *but.*

After a moment, she came out with it, in a different, edgier voice. "But that's not to say that he got in that car on purpose, you know. In order to kill himself, I mean. Somebody else could have put him there, couldn't they? Not saying somebody *did*," she added hastily, correcting herself. "Just saying they *could have*. Of course I might be wrong." She picked up her glass and swigged the lemonade. When she put it down, her fingers slipped and it clattered on the tabletop. "But I don't think so."

Well. This was too big to deal with right now. I filed it away to consider later and went on to the issue I had come to discuss.

"When I saw the video, I was struck by something you said at the end of your segment, Florabelle. You said you thought somebody wanted to make Dick Bowen look guilty — the same person who killed Christine Morris. You said you had a pretty good idea who it was."

Florabelle was chewing nervously on her lip. "I guess I'd better learn to watch my big mouth. Not since the trial has anybody asked me what I thought about that killing or how I felt about Mr. Bowen. So when the girl turned on her camera, it was a chance to say what I was thinking, which maybe I shouldn't have."

"The police didn't question you at the time?" No, probably not. They wouldn't have any special reason to talk to Bowen's

259

coworkers, other than to determine his demeanor the morning after the murder. Thanks to the enterprising efforts of Barry Rogers, the cops had already uncovered all the evidence they needed. They wouldn't want to hear anything that might contradict or complicate their theory of the crime.

Florabelle shook her head. "Only to ask me if I'd noticed anything out of the ordinary about Mr. Bowen that morning." She turned to the dog and clucked with her tongue. Mimi got up, stretched, and jumped delicately from her chair to the sofa, settling close to her mistress, who stroked her silky fur. She went on, "After the girl packed up her camera gear and left, I started thinking about how much I said. I was sincerely hoping she'd take that part out. About the killer making Mr. Bowen look guilty." She looked up at me. "Do you think maybe she would, if I asked her?"

"You could try, I suppose," I said cautiously. I wasn't going to tell her that Gretchen and Kitt had decided to scrap their project. I wanted to keep the pressure on.

Florabelle pushed out a gusty sigh. "Well, I sure hope she will. Like I said, me and my big mouth." She picked up her glass again and drank down another gulp of lemonade. "I wouldn't want somebody to get the wrong idea. I mean, I wouldn't want anybody to think I know something when all I do is suspect it." She looked down at Mimi and brushed a piece of fuzz off her ear. "How come you're asking about all this, China?" She picked up a small comb from the table and fluffed the dog's silky tail. "You're not fixing to go back to lawyering, are you?"

"No more lawyering for me." I chuckled. "My shop keeps me pretty busy these days, and I like what I do there. Let's just say that I have a . . . personal concern in this matter."

"A personal concern." She looked up at me, pushing her lips in and out, much more businesslike now. In her voice, I heard something of the professional woman she had once been, perhaps not all that long ago. "I wonder just what kind of personal concern you'd have. Ms. Morris was killed a long time before you came to Pecan Springs."

I decided it was time to tell her the real story. Part of it, anyway. "Karen Prior, the faculty member who was supervising the girls' documentary film, was killed this week — mugged in the mall parking lot. She was a friend of mine."

Florabelle put down the comb. "I saw that

261

on the news. But I didn't know it had anything to do with that video."

"Nobody knows for sure," I said. I added vaguely, "The police seem to think there might be some sort of connection. I thought I might learn something from the film, so I watched it — part of it, anyway. That's how I came to see you and Mimi." I leaned forward and repeated myself. "You said you thought the killer of Christine Morris framed Dick Bowen, and that you knew who that was." I watched her intently. "*Do* you?"

"I don't see how that could have anything to do with a parking lot mugging."

"Neither do I," I confessed.

She was silent for a moment, chewing on my question. "If I tell you," she said finally, "what will you do with the information?"

"I don't know," I replied. "As you say, it was a long time ago." I didn't say that there is no statute of limitations on murder, although I could have.

She thought about it some more, then made up her mind. "Well, I'll tell you, China, although I still don't see what the connection could possibly be. That woman who was killed — Christine Morris — liked nothing better in this world than making folks mad at her. She went around with a string of enemies rattling along behind her, like a dog with a bunch of tin cans tied to his tail. But so far as I know, there was only one person with a serious reason to want her dead. That was her husband, Douglas Clark."

"Why?" I asked. "What reason did he have?"

"Christine was digging around, looking for some money he didn't mention when they were getting divorced — money that should have been declared in the financial settlement and wasn't. She wanted her share, and she was bound, bent, and determined to get it."

I thought of McQuaid's investigation into this same matter. "How did you find out about that?"

Her answer was so simple that I had to try not to smile. "My niece, Jerri Rae, worked in Charlie Lipman's office." She gave me a quizzical look. "I guess you know Mr. Lipman. He was Christine's lawyer during the divorce."

Well, of course. Attorney-client privilege is expected to extend to the paralegals and other office staff, but it often doesn't. Lawyers have a big stake in keeping their mouths shut, and they do, as a general rule. The paid help — especially if they think they're seriously underpaid — have no stake at all. There's no way to keep their tongues from wagging, short of pasting duct tape over their mouths or locking them in the closet at the end of the day. The authorities would frown on that.

"Are we talking about a lot of money?" I asked.

She shrugged. "I never heard any of the details. But it had to do with some kind of big real estate development — multiple millions of dollars, Jerri Rae said. I have no idea how much of that money Clark would've had to hand over. Mr. Lipman told Christine that if they could prove he'd hidden it intentionally, Clark would have to pay a big fine, maybe even go to jail. But then all of a sudden Christine Morris was dead, and her ex was home free." She gave me a sideways glance. "You see the point I'm making?"

"I see," I said. "It sounds like Douglas Clark might have had a million-dollar motive for killing his ex-wife. But I don't get the second part. Why would Clark want to frame Dick Bowen for the murder?" If Bowen himself hadn't killed her, somebody *had* framed him, using his golf club and wearing his shoes — both apparently easy pickings from his unlocked garage.

"Well, because." Florabelle's mouth tightened and she sat up straighter on the sofa. "Because Clark was scared that Mr. Bowen was going to blow the whistle on his building code violations."

I blinked. "Code violations?"

"Yes. That was after the balcony collapse. Which of course wouldn't have happened if Mr. Bowen hadn't taken the money in the first place." She pulled down the corners of her mouth. "Now, I am not for one minute excusing him for what he did. It was wrong, pos-o-*lutely* wrong. But that doesn't alter the fact that he was a wonderful person. He just made a mistake, that's all." A long, heavy sigh. "Unfortunately, after the first one, he made a few others."

"Wait a minute, Florabelle. 'If Mr. Bowen hadn't taken the money'? *What* money?"

She looked at me as if I ought to be smart enough to understand this without having it spelled out for me in so many words. "Mr. Bowen was the city building inspector." She spoke with an exaggerated simplicity, as if she were explaining this to a third-grader. "Douglas Clark was in the building business. He had to get Mr. Bowen's approval on his plans and engineering documents, and on the new construction, once it was built. Everything had to be according to code, start to finish. Pecan Springs was a lot smaller then than it is now, and Mr. Bowen was the only building inspector. He had the final say-so on every project, start to finish. Once he signed off, it was all A-OK."

And then a lightbulb went off in my brain. Duh. Of course. What we had here was your basic shakedown racket. Bribery, subornation, corruption.

"So Dick Bowen was shaking him down — Douglas Clark, I mean." At her frown, I turned it around. "Douglas Clark was paying Dick Bowen to keep him quiet on some infraction of the building code?"

"Yep." Her mouth quirked at the corners. "That's how it was. But make that multiple infractions. Multiple payments. While it was going on — two years, maybe three — it amounted to a lot of money. I don't know how much, but I'd say in the tens of thousands, maybe more. All of it in cash."

I was beginning to put it all together. The house that Dick Bowen lived in, in the best part of town — well above his pay grade as a city employee. The money he donated to charity. The contributions he made to the Friends of the Library, the financial help he offered to people in trouble. Why, the man was a modern-day Robin Hood! He took bribes from Douglas Clark in return for

266

closing his eyes to the code violations in Clark's construction projects — those cheaply built duplexes, substandard apartment complexes, shoddy strip malls — then turned around and gave the money away. Not all of it, of course. He lived in that nice house, in a neighborhood he couldn't afford without the money he took from Clark.

"Were other developers involved in Bowen's bribery scheme?" I asked. "Or was it just Clark?"

Florabelle's response was prompt. "So far as I personally know, the only deals he made were with Clark. If there was anyone else, I never heard about it. And I think I would have."

Yes, she probably would have. Florabelle seemed to know everything about everything else. I pictured her with her ear to a keyhole, or her hand over the receiver while she eavesdropped on a phone call, or sorting through notes on Bowen's desk. With Florabelle in the office and in her prime, there would have been no secrets.

"Did you actually see the cash changing hands?"

"Once or twice. I saw the permits, too." And then, fending off the question she knew was coming, she said, defensively, "And if you're thinking I was in on the payoff, you can forget that. Nobody paid me a cent, not Douglas Clark and not Mr. Bowen, either. I'm just a nosy person, and maybe a little suspicious. I like to know what's going on around me. When I was working in that office, I listened hard. I did a little digging. I learned things I wasn't supposed to know. But I didn't take any money, and that's a fact."

"But you could have blown the whistle," I reminded her, "either when you first saw the payoffs or later. It doesn't bother you that you didn't step up with what you knew?"

She shifted uncomfortably. "Well, yes, it did. Especially after that balcony collapse. That was when Mr. Bowen decided he'd had enough. I overheard him telling that Clark he wasn't taking another dime." Her housecoat had crept up and she twitched it, covering up one white, dimply knee. "But of course I wouldn't have wanted to do anything that might hurt Mr. Bowen. He was doing such good, for so many people. A real role model, as they say."

I frowned. "Balcony collapse?" It was the second time she'd mentioned it.

She looked down at her arthritic fingers, flexing them as though they hurt. "I guess that was before your time. It was one of the student apartments that Doug Clark had built on Pedernales Drive, over near the campus. Some girls were having a party and several of them went out on their third-floor balcony. It pulled away from the building and dumped everybody three stories down onto the concrete parking lot. Luckily, nobody died, but a couple of girls were hurt pretty badly. Their bad luck."

"How awful," I breathed. But of course, it wasn't exactly bad luck. Building codes are designed to prevent events like that. Breach the code, the building suffers. People suffer, too.

"It was. Awful, I mean." She pressed her lips together. "There was an investigation, of course. And lawsuits."

I'll bet. If it could be proved that a building inspector had overlooked (or had been paid to overlook) violations, there would be both criminal and civil penalties. Pecan Springs would have been sued, too, in addition to the owner and the builder. I'd never gotten into premises liability, but I had dated a guy who worked for a firm that specialized in slip-and-fall litigation. He'd once told me that he'd gotten a million-five for a stair collapse.

Florabelle went on. "Clark's lawyers pointed out that there shouldn't have been that many people on the balcony — there were seven or eight, apparently, and they were dancing. The apartment manager had even posted a sign beside the balcony door saying that no more than two people should be on the balcony at any one time. It was also in the lease and the tenants were told to read it before they signed. But you know kids — they don't pay attention."

"What happened to the lawsuits?"

"Clark's insurance company settled out of court. Luckily, Mr. Bowen's role in it didn't come out."

I nodded. "So when the balcony collapsed, Bowen decided he was going to quit doing business with Clark?"

"Right. I heard Mr. Bowen talking to Clark on the telephone the week after it happened. It was weighing on his conscience, really making him miserable. What's more, he was thinking of turning himself in. He didn't come right out and tell Clark that's what he was going to do, but I knew Mr. Bowen pretty well and I had a suspicion that was it. Maybe Douglas Clark had the same suspicion. Maybe that's why —" She gave a little shrug.

I finished the sentence for her. "That's why he decided to frame Bowen for Christine's murder?"

"That was my guess. Ms. Morris was killed a couple of weeks later."

"And what about you?" I challenged. "Didn't you think that you might have prevented the whole thing by telling the authorities about the bribery scheme — *before* that balcony collapsed? Or maybe just telling Bowen's supervisor, and letting him decide what to do?"

She ducked her head with a half-guilty gesture. "I guess I could have. But I didn't, before, because . . . well, because it didn't seem that important. And afterward, there were serious injuries." She lifted her hand, rubbing her pudgy cheek with a nervous gesture. "By that time, *I* was getting scared. I didn't want to see Mr. Bowen hurt, because he was . . . well, he was such a darned good guy. Maybe it doesn't sound that way to you, with me telling you that he took bribes." She gave me an earnest look. "But like I said, he didn't keep that money. Oh, maybe a little for himself, but mostly he used it to help people. Also, for all I knew, maybe Mr. Bowen's boss, Mr. Hanson, was in on it, too. If I went to him and told him the whole story, it would be just my luck to get fired."

That sounded credible to me. I went on. "What about later, after Christine Morris was killed and you suspected that her ex was framing Bowen? Why didn't you go to the police? Or better yet, to Bowen's defense attorney? He might have been able to build your testimony into his defense."

"Well, I did testify for Mr. Bowen," she said. "I testified to the fact that he acted entirely normal in the office the morning after the murder. But by then, I was even more scared." She sighed heavily. "Call me chicken if you want to. But I figured I'd better keep my mouth shut."

I could understand that. I've known witnesses who refused to testify for reasons not nearly as good as hers. After the fact, it's always easy to be all noble and pure of heart and say that somebody should have said or done this thing or that thing — especially when it's somebody else whose future is on the line. People do what they do, or what they feel they have to do. They get caught in one trap or another and they can't see any way out. Who was I to judge?

She sighed. "I suppose, if I'd thought the jury would find Mr. Bowen guilty, I would have gone to the police. But I couldn't believe they'd convict him. And I was really just guessing, you know. About Doug Clark being the murderer, that is. I didn't have any *evidence.* And I was afraid that if I told the police about the bribes, Mr. Bowen might have looked even more guilty when it came to the murder. I mean, he had taken money to let a balcony fall off a building and injure a couple of girls — what would keep him from whacking his pain-in-the-patootie neighbor over the head with his golf club?" She lifted her shoulders and dropped them in a heavy shrug. "So I just kept my mouth shut. When he was acquitted, I felt like a thousand-pound weight was off my shoulders. *I* was free and clear, too, right along with Mr. Bowen."

There wasn't any reply I could make to that. And anyway, she wasn't finished.

Her mouth tightened down to a hard line. "Now that I've told you all that bad stuff, China, I want to be sure you get this straight. What I know about the money Mr. Bowen took for overlooking a few code violations has nothing at all to do with the way I feel about Mr. Bowen the man. He was a good-hearted, solid-gold citizen who cared about this community and the people in it. He volunteered, he worked hard, he gave his time, he contributed money. What he did on the sidelines or under the table was no business of mine."

Except that she had made it her business when she put her ear to the keyhole or listened in on the phone to find out what was going on. Her failure to act on what she knew helped the criminals evade detection, which could make her party to the crime. But chapter 7 of the Texas Penal Code — Criminal Responsibility for the Conduct of Another — is complex. There might be a moral issue here, but there was no point in making a legal issue out of it. And as I said, who am I to judge? I nodded and kept my lawyerly mouth shut.

A smile quirked her lips. "To tell God's honest truth, it tickled me right down to the soles of my feet that the money came out of Douglas Clark's big fat pot of ill-gotten gains and went straight to the Humane Society and the homeless shelter and the food pantry and all the other causes that Mr. Bowen supported. Douglas Clark would never have given them one thin dime."

I nodded. "Just a few more questions, if you don't mind. You said you didn't have any evidence that Douglas Clark killed his wife — other than your suspicions about his motive. Do you have any evidence that he framed Dick Bowen for the murder?"

She shook her head. "Just that it makes sense. But I guess that's not evidence."

It wasn't. "And Bowen's suicide. Do you have any specific reason to suspect that it was . . . something else?"

Another head shake, a regretful one this time. "I wish I did have a reason. I would really like to know what happened to Mr. Bowen — and if somebody killed him, I'd like to see the killer pay." She gave me a long and penetrating look. "If you can come up with anything in what I've told you that helps you find out who mugged your friend, why, you can add a whole lot better than I can. I don't see it, myself."

Mimi, sensing that we had come to the end of the conversation, stood up, stretched, and gave a sharp, commanding bark.

I got Mimi's message. It was time I left.

CHAPTER NINE

In Mexico, marigolds are known as *flor de los muertos,* the flower of the dead. According to legend, they sprang up from soil stained by the blood of the unlucky victims of the early Spanish explorers. Today, Mexican families visit the cemeteries where their loved ones are buried, bringing offerings of marigolds and other flowers, food, and drink. The orange and yellow flowers, like the rays of the sun, are thought to lift the souls of the dead so they can feast on the offerings. Marigolds were said to bring good luck.

China Bayles
"Herbs of Ill and Good Omen"
Pecan Springs Enterprise

When I parked the car in Florabelle's lot, I had cracked the windows and put up one of those folding sunshades that keep the sun out. But while the shade may block the light, it doesn't do much about heat. Getting into my little Toyota was like climbing into a solar oven. I folded the shade and stowed it, rolled down the windows, turned on the engine, and powered up the air conditioner. I'd let it run for a while until the heat buildup in the car had dissipated.

And I'd take a moment to replay my conversation with Florabelle Gibson and consider what I had just heard. When I'd made arrangements to see her, I was on a fishing expedition. In the video, she had intimated that she knew something, but frankly, I had pegged her as somebody who was trying to boost her sense of self-importance by pretending to know more than she did. What I had found was something altogether different. Florabelle might be lonely and in ill health, but she knew more, remembered more, and suspected more than I could possibly have guessed. She had a story to tell and she was pleased to have an audience. But how much of what she had said was reliably informative? How many of her suspicions had any factual foundation?

For starters, I was convinced that she was telling the truth about the bribery. I remembered something Johnnie had said. His client was innocent of the murder, he had insisted, but "not exactly pure, which is another part of the story." Was he talking about the corruption? A careful investigation of the city records from that era might turn up some affirming evidence, if somebody knew the right places to look. But to what end? I didn't see how any of that old business could have any connection to the attack on Karen.

And while Florabelle's claim that Clark had murdered his ex-wife might be credible, it looked, at least from this distance, impossible to prove — unless, of course, Johnnie had offered Clark as his alternative suspect and documented the evidence in his case file. Otherwise, while there might be a motive (the hidden assets, assuming they had existed), there wasn't a single sliver of evidence. All I had was what-ifs and maybes. The police must have immediately considered the ex-husband a prime suspect, especially since there had been a nasty divorce. If they had done even a half-competent job, they would have checked the man's alibi for the night of the murder.

On the other hand, the lead investigator had seriously compromised the existing evidence, so there was plenty of reason to suspect police incompetence. And Clark might have hired somebody to do the killing for him. But that theory was as suppositional as everything else. No facts, no evidence, no proof — unless I could find something in Johnnie's trial notes. And once again, no connection to Karen, as far as I could see.

The same thing was true about Florabelle's idea that Clark had framed Bowen for the killing. Obviously, *someone* had framed him — that is, if Bowen hadn't committed the crime himself. But unless Johnnie had come up with something, there was no evidence that it was Clark who had framed him. No wonder Florabelle hadn't gone to the police. She had nothing at all on which to base any accusation.

And then there was her notion that Bowen hadn't committed suicide, which was as unfounded as anything else. I had to admit that it was intriguing, but —

My cell phone rang. It took a moment to fish it out of my bag and see Ruby's ID. "Hey, Ruby," I said. "What's up?"

In her usual Ruby way, she plunged right into it. "China, I've been thinking about Karen — and about the possible connections between her murder and the documentary. And a lot of other stuff, too."

A lot of other stuff. I picture the interior of Ruby's mind as something like a large crystal ball, with ghostly images forming out of the pearly shadows, taking on luminescent shapes and disappearing, then reappearing in another form. Ruby is an intuitive. She doesn't think logically. Her mind leaps from apples to soccer balls to kids' dirty uniforms to milk and chocolate chip cookies after the game. But she comes up with some startling insights, based on ways of knowing that are entirely unlike any standard linear logic. For Ruby, two plus two can just as easily equal 104 — and more often than not, she's right. I make it a habit to listen to her.

"So I called Sharyn Tillotson," she concluded.

"Sharyn Tillotson?" I asked, drawing a blank. Then, "Oh, Christine Morris' cousin." Ruby had mentioned her earlier, and I had copied her name from the list in Karen Prior's briefcase.

"Right," Ruby said. "Sharyn and I knew one another back in high school. We haven't kept up with each other's lives, but you might call us friendly acquaintances. I think I told you that she manages the Morris Foundation, which operates the museum. She chairs the board of directors."

"Uh-huh." The air conditioner was beginning to cool the car. I chased out an inquisitive bee and rolled up the windows.

"We talked for a bit on the phone. It turns out that Sharyn is our go-to girl for information about the Morris Museum. She seems to know more about it than anyone. And maybe I didn't mention it, but Karen was on the museum board."

"I heard that last night, from Kitt and Gretchen," I said. "Seems to be a connection there."

"I could talk to Sharyn by myself," Ruby went on, "but I really think it would be better if both of us saw her. She's offered to give us a tour of the museum this afternoon, but only if we can get there by twelve thirty or quarter of one. She has something she has to do at three. And she'll be out of town all next week."

The museum. Which also happened to be the place where Christine Morris was killed, next door to Dick Bowen's house.

"Sure," I said. "Let's do it." I was supposed to see Paul Cameron at three or three thirty, so a tour of the museum would fill the empty hours between now and then. I looked at my watch. It was not quite twelve, and I hadn't had anything to eat since breakfast. It would be nice to sit down to a leisurely lunch with Ruby, but there wasn't time. "I'm only about twenty minutes away

281

from the museum. How about if I pick up a quick bite to eat, then meet you there?"

"Super. Oh, and by the way," Ruby added, "I didn't think it would be a good idea to tell Sharyn why we're curious about the place. So I made up a cover story."

"A cover story?"

"You know," she said impatiently. "A reason for the two of us to invite ourselves to the museum this afternoon. I told her that you were generously considering donating your time — and the plants — for an herb garden at the museum. A garden of lovely Mexican herbs. She was ecstatic at the idea, China. After your garden is up and growing, she wants to give a party to celebrate it. She thinks it could be an excellent fund-raiser."

"An herb garden!" I squawked. "Ruby, I don't have time for —"

"Never mind, dear," Ruby said in a soothing voice. "I didn't say you were actually going to do it. I said you were *considering* it. You can consider it and decide not to, can't you? Or you can consider it and suggest it to the herb guild. I'll bet they'd be glad to take it on as a project. I also suggested to Sharyn that we knew of someone who might be interested in donating to the museum. Donating cash, that is."

"Honestly, Ruby —"

"Well, we do."

"Well, who?"

"My sister, that's who. Ramona has scads of money." That was true. Ruby's sister, Ramona, got the best divorce deal in the whole wide world. She's been trying to buy a business, but she hasn't yet figured out which one to buy. Ruby added, "Giving her money to worthy causes makes Ramona feel good about herself. I thought if Sharyn believed we had a possible donor on the hook, she'd be more willing to talk to us. And tell us more."

"Ruby," I said severely, "you are so *wicked*."

"I know," she said in a modest tone. "Sometimes I surprise myself."

The Taco Bell was the nearest fast-food emporium, so I zipped through the drive-up and got a chicken burrito and a medium diet iced tea. I wolfed it down, realizing how hungry I was and thinking that when you're hungry, even fast food is good, particularly Tex-Mex fast food. While I was eating, I thought of something else I needed to do, and now was the right time to do it. I licked the salsa and sour cream off my fingers, pulled Aaron Brooks' business card out of my wallet, and flipped open my cell phone. When he picked up, I said brightly, "Hi, Aaron. It's China. China Bayles. A voice from the past."

His chuckle was just as I remembered it, as warm and rich as a cup of chocolate on a chilly evening. "Yo, China. You sound very present to me. What's up? Are you in town? Will we have a chance to get together? I *hope* so."

Aaron always makes me smile. We have seen each other only sporadically over the years since I left the law, moved to Pecan Springs, and married McQuaid. But on the rare occasions when we've managed to get together, it's as if we haven't been apart for more than, oh, an hour or two. Instant connectivity, its warmth and engagement essentially unchanged from the last time we connected. I have no idea whether Aaron has that kind of relationship with other women. I wouldn't be at all surprised if he does, dozens of them. But that's none of my business. We have it, and I was planning to exploit it, shamelessly.

"I'm not in town yet, Aaron," I said, "but I'm planning to drive over tomorrow — that is, if I can see you. I have a huge favor to ask."

"Hey, wow, tomorrow? That's wonderful,

China!" There was no hesitation at all. "I'm in court first thing in the morning, but I'll be back in the office by ten. Will you be alone, or will Mike be with you? How about lunch?" Then a slight pause, perhaps for breath, but still no uncertainty. "I hope it's a favor I can deliver on."

"I'll be alone," I said. "I'll need to get back to Pecan Springs at a reasonable hour — the kids are at home this summer — but I'd love lunch. Thanks. And yes, I hope you can deliver, too. It's maybe a little dicey, on your end."

I told him what it was. When I finished, he was quiet for a moment, processing. I pictured him raising one blond eyebrow, pursing his lips, frowning. In his midforties now, Aaron is a Robert Redford lookalike — that is, the way Robert Redford looked when he was in his forties, which in my opinion was totally yummy. No wonder Aaron makes a girl's heart pound. Even a married girl. But this was business and I love being married. I told my heart to stop acting as if it belonged to the ingénue in a chick-lit romance.

"Look, Aaron," I said, "if you're nervous about doing this — confidentiality and all that — maybe you should go through Johnnie's notes yourself. He was your partner, after all, so there couldn't be any serious objection. I could tell you more definitively what I'm looking for. If you see something you think might help, you could —"

"Nah." He broke in. "That's not necessary, China. The issue of privilege is moot. You probably don't know this, but Johnnie's client in that case — I forget his name — is dead. He checked out a few months before Johnnie died. The old car-in-the-closed-garage trick. As I recall, there were no surviving relatives."

"Bowen," I said. "Richard Bowen. And yes, I've been told about his death." I paused and added, offhandedly, "I've also been told, by someone who says she knew him pretty well, that suicide was unlikely. Do you have any information about that?"

Information, that was what I was after. Not suspicions or hunches, but facts — although Bowen's death was only tangentially related to my main purpose for making this trip: getting a look at whatever Johnnie Carlson had included in his trial notes about his alternative suspect.

But of course, it might be a wild-goose chase. Johnnie's notes could be incomplete, or his theory wildly off the mark. When the case permits, every defense lawyer will attempt to introduce an alternative suspect in order to create a reasonable doubt, and the attempt is often built on flimsy evidence. Johnnie's evidence, whatever it had been, might not have been relevant to the Morris murder. And there might be no connection at all to Karen's death. In fact, now that I thought about it, I wondered why I imagined that the two were related in the first place. I could be wasting the whole day — except for seeing Aaron again, of course, which would be rather nice. Perhaps you could call it a wild-gander chase.

"Oh, yes, Bowen," Aaron said thoughtfully. "No, I don't have any information about that. He died a couple of weeks before Johnnie, as I remember it. I do know that Johnnie had stayed in touch with him — I think he even helped him locate the house he bought, here in Houston." He paused. "Okay. I'll have the case file out for you so you can get started on it when you arrive. You can read it in the office, or copy and take whatever you like. What time, do you think?"

Houston is two and a half hours from Pecan Springs. If I could get out of the house right after breakfast —

"Maybe I can make it by ten," I hazarded. "Or shortly after, depending on the traffic, of course." You can never predict Houston traffic. I don't know how one stalled car or one minor fender bender can shut down three lanes of a four-lane freeway and back traffic up for miles, but it happens. Frequently. And by the time you finally get to the point of the slowdown, the dramatic event that strangled the flow of traffic has been magically erased. All that's left are the skid marks. You never get to see what happened.

"Super," he said, with evident satisfaction. "Skip breakfast and come hungry. Remember that café you used to like so much? Tiny Boxwood's, at that garden center? Let's go there and grab some quiet time. We've got a lot to talk about."

His voice held the smile — dimpled, just a little on the shy side — that was famous for warming the cockles of the coldest juror's heart.

It certainly warmed mine.

Ruby was waiting when I got there. She was dressed as if for a garden party, in a summery short-sleeved floral print dress and white sandals, with a white stretchy band around her frizzed carrot-orange hair. She eyed me. "You're not wearing your jeans," she said, noting my denim wraparound skirt with approval.

"It's Sunday," I said. "And this is uptown." I looked at the house and whistled. "Definitely uptown."

It's relatively easy to find houses like the Morris house in Austin, especially out in West Lake Hills. Here in Pecan Springs, not so much. It had probably cost close to a million dollars to build back when Doug Clark gave it to his bride. It was likely worth three times that now, or more. The architecture was striking, white windowless boxes stacked next to and on top of boxes, with a second-floor wing cantilevered out to one side, under a flying saucer roof. It dwarfed the nearby houses, making them look tired and anachronistic. It was no surprise that the neighbors were outraged when it was built, although they might have a different idea about it these days, especially now that the landscaping was in place. And the fact that it was now a private museum probably raised the property values across the neighborhood, rather than otherwise.

Sharyn Tillotson, the foundation president and chair of the museum board, met us at the front door, a heavy, carved oak affair that looked as if it had come out of a Mexican cathedral. I recognized her from the documentary: a solid-framed, striking woman, rather tall, neatly dressed in white summer slacks and a silky blouse, with an antique silver Mexican medallion necklace that matched her silver earrings. She wore low white heels and her brown hair was pulled back into a bun at the nape of her neck and skewered with a pin that matched the silver medallions. She had a square jaw, almost masculine, and a firm mouth that looked as if smiling might be a challenge.

But she was smiling now, as she should be, since Ruby had led her to believe that she knew someone who might give the museum some money — and that I was eager to install an herb garden on the museum property. Sharyn especially wanted to let me know that this was a very good idea.

"Let's go around to the plaza," she said, in a voice that was deep for a woman, with almost the resonance of a man's. "I know the perfect place for an herb garden, in a corner next to the rose garden." Over her shoulder, she added, "We've been thinking of converting the plaza into an outdoor dining area. We do occasionally invite our donors to join us for parties and other fundraising events. A garden of Mexican herbs would fit beautifully into what we have in mind."

I had to admit that the corner was lovely.

The big chain-link fence was history now, replaced by a dense yaupon holly hedge that separated the museum from what had once been the Bowen house. It was already too hot for roses, but a few stragglers were still in bloom. I could picture a garden that would include at least a dozen herbs, and probably more, since many herbs that are native to Mexico are native to Texas, as well. A garden would require very little maintenance — far less than those roses, which really didn't belong here in this setting. I rattled off a few of the herbs that came to mind, the familiar ones: marigold, prickly pear cactus, lemon verbena, cumin, Mexican oregano, cilantro, epazote, papaloquelite, Mexican tarragon, basil, peppers, and hoja santa, the Mexican root beer plant.

The garden had been Ruby's idea, and not something I'd been keen on doing, but I got carried away. It's always like that, when I'm talking herbs.

"The plants could be arranged informally, like a cottage garden. Or even arranged in a small, semiformal garden, in keeping with the architecture. It could have walks paved with white rocks or limestone flags, in a four-square design. In the center, you could have either a water feature or a small potted tree — maybe a Mexican lime — or even something very sculptural, a large yucca, for instance. In the summer, marigolds would be nice. They have lots of Mexican symbolism. And you might consider taking out the roses. They require a great deal of upkeep, and I don't think they belong in this setting. You could replace them with low-care natives, like agarita or cenizo or even palmetto, if you wanted some drama."

I stopped. I was talking too much. Lecturing, actually.

But Sharyn didn't seem to think so. "How nice that you're interested in doing this, China. I'll let the board know about your generous offer, and they can decide whether they'd prefer something informal or a little more formal."

"China is *very* generous," Ruby said, bestowing a sweet smile on me. Then she took me off the hook — well, almost. "Actually I was thinking that maybe, if she supplied the plants from her shop, the herb guild would agree to do the planting. They've worked with her on a number of garden projects."

"I could help arrange that," Sharyn said promptly. "The president of the guild is an old friend of mine. China, if you would design the garden and supply the plants, I'll be glad to ask her for volunteers."

"Sounds like a plan," I said, since there was nothing to do but agree. Of course, I could put in a little sign: *Plants donated by Thyme and Seasons Herb Shop.* It would be good advertising — although since the museum was private, nobody but the board, and maybe some donors, would see it.

"Well, then," Sharyn said, very gracious, especially now that the garden question had been settled. "It's awfully warm out here. Why don't we go inside and chat for a few moments over a glass of iced tea. Then, if you like, I'll be glad to give you the grand tour. I'm sure you'll enjoy seeing the collection."

She led us across the plaza to a door that opened into the side of the house. As we went, I glanced around, recognizing this as the place I had seen on the video, where Christine Morris had been killed. Those were the steps where the body had lain. And over there to the left, visible through the yaupon holly hedge that had replaced the chain-link fence, was the Bowen house. It was so close that I could have thrown a rock through one of the windows. I resisted the urge to point this out to Ruby. There was no point in making Sharyn nervous by letting her know that I recognized the spot where her cousin had been murdered.

A moment later, we were entering a light, open room — the lounge, Sharyn called it. She gestured to a seating area with a sofa, chairs, and coffee table on which sat a colorful painted tray, a confetti-glass pitcher of iced tea, and matching confetti-glass goblets. The stark whiteness of the walls was partially relieved by a vivid grouping of paintings of flowers in Mexican folk art style. There were bright marigolds, painted in rich reds and oranges and yellows, and fanciful balloon flowers and others in gorgeous purples and blues and lavender. There was a plaque under the group, and I saw with interest that they had been painted by Irene Cameron, Paul's wife, and that they were for sale. The prices were displayed discreetly on each painting, and all were in the $300 to $500 range — a little pricey for me, but if I could have afforded to buy one, I certainly would have. I studied the paintings, wondering whether Irene might have smaller, lower-priced paintings that I could display in my shop. The marigolds would be especially nice.

"This is the room we're planning to convert to a dining room," Sharyn said. "We're expecting to expand our membership and open the museum to groups — carefully selected, of course — on a rental basis, for parties. We won't prepare the meals on the premises, though. We'll have them catered."

Ever the entrepreneur, Ruby said quickly, "Did you know that China and I have a catering service? I'll drop off a brochure for you to review. Party Thyme — China and I and our friend Cass Wilde — would be glad to bid on the next event you're planning."

I admire Ruby's business sense. She's way ahead of me in that department. I wouldn't have thought of suggesting that.

"Thank you," Sharyn said. "Yes, do give me your brochure, Ruby, and I'll share it with our board. We would rather do business with someone we know than with strangers, of course." She smiled. "Now, would you like to have iced tea? Or there's coffee, if you'd rather."

I accepted the offer of tea. So did Ruby, and we sat down while our hostess easily hefted the heavy pitcher and poured. I noticed her square hands and thought once again that she was a solid and muscular woman. I remembered that Ruby had said that she and her cousin were not on good terms at the time of Christine Morris' death, and the thought crossed my mind that —

"I've put together a packet of material for

you, and another for the possible donor you mentioned," Sharyn said, handing us our glasses. "Your sister, I think you said?"

"Oh, thank you," Ruby replied, picking up the two envelopes on the table and tucking them into her purse. "I'll be sure to pass this on to Ramona. Your card is here, isn't it?" She looked and found it. "Oh, yes. Well, if she has any questions, she can call you and discuss."

Sharyn looked gratified. "Meanwhile," she went on, "I thought you might like to know a little of the history of this unique house." She waved her arm in an expansive gesture. "And something about our fine collection of Mexican art. It's one of the very best in the state, although that fact isn't often recognized. Of course, we're quite small in comparison to the publicly funded museums — we have just a thousand carefully selected pieces, on display and in storage. And we have remained private."

"Private," Ruby mused. "That's a little unusual, isn't it? I thought museums were open to the public."

"Many are," Sharyn said. "But Christine made that stipulation in her will, as well as appointing me to oversee the foundation and the collection itself. She wanted the house maintained as a setting for the collection, but she didn't want a lot of curious gawkers traipsing through it every day, just to have something to do. And while there's enough money to support the house and the collection, there isn't enough to manage it as a museum that's regularly open to the public. To do that, we would need to hire a larger staff, and more security. Some of the works are extremely valuable."

"Maybe you could just fill us in briefly," Ruby suggested. "China didn't grow up here in Pecan Springs the way you and I did. She may want to ask questions." The smiles she and Sharyn exchanged were just slightly pitying, establishing the two of them as native Pecan Springers, birds of a feather. I was the outsider. Which was okay. In fact, it was a wily move on Ruby's part, connecting her and Sharyn.

"Oh, of course," Sharyn replied, launching into what sounded like a practiced spiel. "The Morris collection was initially the work of my cousin, Christine, who began collecting Mexican art, both contemporary and traditional, more than thirty years ago. She had exquisite artistic taste and a very good sense of what would constitute an impressive collection. She made numerous trips to Mexico, building relationships with dealers in Mexico City and bringing back pieces that she enjoyed."

"You said 'initially,' " I broke in. "Does that mean that you have continued to collect, after her death?"

"We have accepted several donated collections," Sharyn replied cautiously. "They are mostly folk art pieces, but there are some quite valuable paintings and a few contemporary sculptures. And the foundation itself has acquired a few items. Now, as I was saying, Christine continued —"

"Excuse me for interrupting," I said, "but I'm curious. Are you able to sell items from the collection?" I smiled toothily. "That is, if I wanted to buy something, could I?"

Sharyn waved toward the paintings on the wall behind us. "We have a few things for sale, like these splendid florals by Irene Cameron." Her voice was a little warmer, now that she sensed that I wasn't just a gardener but a potential customer. "As you can see, Irene is quite an accomplished painter. And some of our donors allow us to sell works that they have contributed. So yes, we might be able to arrange a purchase, if you see something you like."

"Thank you," I said.

She took a breath and went on with her speech. "Christine continued to expand her collection after she came here to Pecan

Springs and married Douglas Clark, a well-known real estate developer, who built this unique home for her. She wanted to fill it with her art and invite the community to share her passion for the artistic achievements of our South-of-the-Border friends. Unfortunately, she died before she was able to realize all her dreams —"

"She was murdered, wasn't she?" I interrupted again. I was an outsider, not a true-blue Pecan Springer. I wasn't expected to have good manners. But I was now a possible customer, which put Sharyn somewhat on the spot.

"Tragically, yes." Sharyn shook her head sadly. "I'm sure you remember it, Ruby. A senseless, brutal act. But Christine had had the wisdom and foresight to establish the Morris Foundation, which had already assumed ownership of her collection. At her death, the foundation took over this house and named a board of local people who shared her passionate love of —"

"I think I heard that the neighbor who was charged with her murder was acquitted," I said.

Now I had her full attention. "Yes, that's true," she replied carefully. "The police were convinced of his guilt, and so were Christine's friends. I know I was — the man was clearly guilty. But the jury believed otherwise." She was frowning now, as if she wondered how her friend Ruby could have such an uncouth acquaintance. "It was a heartbreaking end to a life dedicated to the arts. But thankfully, Christine's collection remains with us, a tribute to her memory. We do our very best to take care of it, just as she would have done if her life had not been so tragically cut short."

Ruby intervened hurriedly, as if she wanted to deter me from making another ill-mannered blunder. "The foundation — how is it managed? The museum has a board, doesn't it? Does the board manage the collections?"

"Those are good questions, Ruby," Sharyn said, relieved to move toward safer ground. "The board employs the resources of the foundation in the management of the collection. I am the president and there are six — no, currently five members." She hesitated, then found it necessary to explain her correction. "We just lost one of our members, I'm sorry to say. We'll be filling her vacant position shortly. Our board is responsible for —"

"Was that Dr. Prior?" I asked. "Karen Prior? She was a member of your board, wasn't she?"

Her eyes widened slightly. "Yes. I'm sorry to say that Dr. Prior . . . died last week." She shook her head, as if in disbelief. "Another enormous tragedy — so senseless."

"Ruby and I both knew Karen," I said. "I'm also acquainted with Paul Cameron. He retired from your board recently, I understand."

"Yes, that's right, he did," she said, now almost defensively. For an outsider, I had more connections in Pecan Springs than she had thought. "Dr. Cameron hasn't been . . . well, lately. We were sorry to lose him, of course. He brought a great deal of experience to our little group."

I wondered briefly about that, since Dr. Cameron had told Kitt that he thought Sharyn was "as ignorant as dirt" about art. But it was likely that he had never shared his opinion with Sharyn herself.

She was going on. "However, I'm glad to say that Dr. Cameron's wife, Irene, will be returning to fill Karen Prior's place. She served several terms on the board in years past and has an extensive interest in twentieth-century Mexican art. In fact, she wrote her master's thesis on Mexican women artists. As you can see, she is quite a gifted painter herself." She gestured toward

301

the floral paintings. "And so helpful." She paused, adding with evident pride, "Our board is a working board, you see. We share curatorial duties — and a great deal of the work that keeps this place going."

Ruby frowned. "I don't know a lot about art museums. But isn't that a little . . . unusual? Don't most museums have curators who manage the collections?"

Sharyn nodded. "Yes, of course. But we are less like everyone's idea of a museum and more like a private collection that offers limited public access, mostly to educators and students. And since we are privately funded, our foundation can manage the museum a little more informally. But we assure our friends and supporters that we oversee the collection with the greatest diligence."

Yes, of course. But there *was* a foundation, which presumably operated as a tax-exempt nonprofit. In fact, my skeptical self was wondering if Christine's motivation for creating the foundation in the first place hadn't been simple greed: she aimed to save herself a bundle on taxes. The initial donation of the art, and the house, would have been tax deductible. The cost of housing, securing, maintaining, and insuring the art — a substantial outlay — could be covered by cash gifts, also deductible. The foundation wouldn't pay sales tax on art it purchased. And if any items from the collection were sold at a profit, the foundation wouldn't pay a cent in capital gains. (A private owner, on the other hand, would fork over at least 28 percent of the gain to Uncle Sam.) Moreover, at Christine's death, there would have been no estate tax. A hefty, IRS-blessed gift all the way around — as long as Christine, or anyone associated with the foundation, did not use it for "self-dealing," tax-speak for manipulating your nonprofit for your own personal benefit. For example, if the IRS discovers that you have listed a painting as the property of your foundation and then hung it on your living room wall, it will revoke its blessing and is inclined to get nasty about it.

Sharyn was going on. "When we first began to work with Christine's collection, we found it to be very disorganized. Some of the paintings weren't framed and many were not yet hung, simply stacked around the walls and tucked into closets and here and there. We invited a knowledgeable gentleman — the man who had helped Christine acquire some of her art — to serve as curator. He saw to the framing and hanging of the art and established the provenance of her works. Luckily, Christine had maintained a skeletal record of her acquisitions, so he had something to go on. He no longer formally curates for us, but he's always available to answer questions and provide guidance."

"Just out of curiosity," I said, "who was he?"

Another uncouth question. Sharyn looked like she wished she could think of a reason not to answer it. "Roberto Soto," she said, with obvious reluctance. I caught her watching me to see if the name registered.

Of course it did, but that was my little secret. I wondered if Soto was still in the art business. I put a tick beside my mental note to give Justine a call and see what she knew about his current activities.

Reassured by my silence, Sharyn went on. "Mr. Soto has an art gallery in San Antonio and was a close friend of the Camerons — Paul was chairman of the museum board at that time."

A close friend? Remembering Kitt's report that Paul thought Soto was as "wily as a fox," I was a little surprised.

"Anyway," Sharyn continued, "Mr. Soto undertook the work for us out of his affection for Christine, whom he had known quite well. He did such a good job that we

304

haven't had to do anything more than update our current acquisitions. And plan and arrange exhibits for our invited guests, of course. We would do far more if we had the funding to hire even one full-time staff person." She squared her shoulders and raised her chin, as if she were admitting to a disability. "But we don't, so we simply go on and do whatever we can, always grateful for the board members' generosity with their time and talents."

"Very commendable," I said and added, "But surely your board doesn't put in night-time duty as security guards."

"No, of course not." She chuckled as if I had made a small joke, a very small joke. "We employ a security service. When Christine lived here in the house, she installed an excellent alarm system. And I live upstairs," she added in an offhand way. "Which means that there is someone on the premises at all times. This is a quiet neighborhood, and we've never had any trouble. I doubt that we ever will."

No trouble — except for a bloody murder, that is. Had anyone inventoried the art to find out whether any of it had disappeared at the time of the murder?

But I was distracted from that question by the thought that the director of the foundation lived upstairs. This small piece of information seemed to throw a different light on the situation. I wondered whether she was paying rent, and whether the IRS might attribute the value of her living quarters to "self-dealing" — which of course was none of my business.

And once more, I remembered that the women had been estranged at the time of Christine's death — so estranged that Christine had left Sharyn nothing in her will. But that situation had obviously changed. Sharyn may not have directly inherited anything from her cousin, but from the looks of things, she might as well have. She was in possession of both the house and the collection, wasn't she? From an outsider's point of view, it appeared that her relationship to the Morris Museum was more that of an heiress than a foundation manager or a board president. I filed the observation under "Think More about This." I had no idea what it might mean, but it was interesting.

"Well." Sharyn put down her glass and stood with a smile. "I know that we're all a little pressed for time this afternoon. Shall we take a look around?"

"I'd love that," Ruby said promptly. "I can't believe that I've lived in Pecan Springs all these years and I've never seen the collection."

The architect had designed the interior of the house to take your breath away, and it certainly took mine. The stark glacier-white walls, some of them curving or set at irregular angles; the gleaming hardwood floors, displaying an occasional rug (carefully cordoned off as a piece of art); the sweep of vaulted ceilings, visually extending the space; the perfectly designed illumination, both track and recessed lighting. There were no windows on the main floor — partly, I supposed, for the sake of security, but also to avoid light spilling onto the art.

And of course, the walls and floors were just the backdrop. Against them was displayed the art: paintings, collages, and textiles on every wall, pedestals displaying ceramics, shelves filled with jewelry, niches filled with sculptures, vases, folk art figures. I couldn't have begun to name the artists or the works, but Sharyn could and did, proudly. A *fumage* by Antonio Muñiz, two of Enrique Chagoya's lithographs, a life-size acrylic painting of a nude female by Jorge Figueroa Acosta, a sculptural metal figure by Byron Gálvez, a series of brightly woven native serapes, a remarkable trio of large painted masks.

"Amazing," I murmured. Even I, with my scant knowledge of art, could see that this was one impressive collection.

Beside me, Ruby's eyes were growing larger and larger. "Astonishing," she whispered.

Sharyn paused with us at the entrances of several smaller rooms, each one painted a different color — dark blue, mahogany, glowing gold — depending on the colors of the paintings displayed on the walls. Then, at the end of the main hall, she led us through a wide doorway into a large alcove and turned on the lights. The walls here were painted a stunning burnished copper color, against which six paintings were displayed.

"These are among our most precious paintings," she said. "We have two by Diego Rivera and three — actually, three! — by Frida Kahlo. And this —" She turned with a theatrical gesture to a lurid landscape of an erupting volcano that occupied one wall. "This is our Dr. Atl." She stood for a moment, letting us take them in. "Aren't they spectacular?"

I let out my breath. "Truly," I said, hardly knowing what to say. Yes, truly, truly spectacular. I turned to look at the painting by Dr. Atl, which pictured fiery lava spouting into the air and spilling over the top of a mountain, reflecting in bloodred flows across the rocky foreground. I let my glance linger on it, wondering —

"Amazing," Ruby squeaked. "My goodness' sakes. I had no idea. Utterly *no* idea." She shook her head. "Why, these must be worth a fortune!"

"They are quite valuable," Sharyn agreed quietly. "And insured, of course. But as I say, they are safe with us."

We stood for a few moments, looking first at one painting, then at another. And then, ready to go, I turned back toward the wide doorway through which we had come into this room. At the end of the hall, against the far wall, was the glass-enclosed stair I had seen in the documentary, the glass treads seeming to float in space, an artwork in its own right.

And there, beside the stair, was the painting I had seen on that wall, simply framed in dark wood. *Muerte llega pronto.* Death Come Quickly. Karen Prior's favorite painting, by María Izquierdo. And in my purse, slung over my shoulder, was the Sotheby's catalog with the photograph of this very same painting — or rather, a painting by this title, perhaps the same, perhaps different. I wanted to whip it out and compare

309

the two, but something told me that this was not the moment for that.

I stepped close, trying to see the painting clearly enough to remember the details. It was an unsettling work and I doubted that I would ever think of it as a favorite. But there was something about it — the authenticity and power of the emotion, perhaps — that drew me into it. It was a painting of betrayal, I thought. Of a terrible loss. Of a wish for death. A wish for a quick death that would put an end to unbearable pain.

Ruby pulled in a ragged breath. "Oh, my," she breathed and put her hand on my arm, leaning against me. "China, I —"

I turned to look at her. "Ruby, are you okay?" I whispered.

"Not really," she murmured. She closed her eyes and opened them again, and her fingers clamped down on my arm, hard, as if she were trying to anchor herself. "I don't think I'm seeing what you're seeing. But please, don't let Sharyn know. She —"

Sharyn was paying no attention to our whispers. She was lost in the painting, gazing at it with a kind of reverence. "It's simply stunning, isn't it? It isn't the most valuable piece in our collection — Izquierdo isn't nearly as well-known as Frida Kahlo or Diego Rivera and her work doesn't command their prices. But the dark, earthy colors, and that astonishing pink flower, and the blood . . ." She took a breath. "This painting was Christine's favorite. And now it is mine."

I turned to look at her, but her gaze was fixed on the painting, and a small smile curved the corner of her mouth. I wondered if she had actually heard those five words as they fell like shards of splintered glass into the fragile silence around us. *And now it is mine.*

And now it is mine.

Outside, on the street, Ruby and I stood beside our cars, in the shade of a massive live oak tree.

"Are you okay, Ruby?" I asked, concerned. "What did you mean when you said that you weren't seeing what I was seeing? What was that about? What were you seeing?"

Ruby's face was pale and her hand, when she put it out to me, was trembling. "Nothing," she said, in a half-choked voice. "I was seeing just . . . nothing."

I frowned. "You mean, you were seeing nothing out of the ordinary?" I prodded. "Just the painting?"

"No," Ruby said faintly. She closed her eyes. "I was seeing *nothing,* China. There was nothing in that frame. It was empty." She opened her eyes wide. "Totally empty."

I stared at her. Ruby is a highly intuitive person, sensitive to things that other people miss. I have known her to see strange things, hear strange noises, feel strange breezes, smell strange smells. I have been with her when she's seen ghosts, and when she's seen dead bodies. But I have never known her to see . . . nothing, especially when there is clearly *something* there. And there was something. I saw it myself.

"Uh-oh," I said. "You're sure? You didn't just . . . you know, space out?"

"No." Ruby sounded irritated. "I did not 'space out.' I turned to look at that painting, just as you did. But all I could see was the empty frame, and behind it, the blank wall."

"Well," I said and stopped. Ruby amazes me sometimes, and when she does, I know it's with good reason. She understands something I'm missing. I need to pay attention. I tried again.

"Well, why?" I managed. "Why do you think you saw . . . nothing? I mean, I was seeing a painting of a woman holding a blossom of Herb Robert — death come quickly — with blood dripping out of the petals and leaves. It's the same painting that's in the video Kitt and Gretchen shot."

"I don't know why I couldn't see the painting." Ruby sounded very tired. "I just have no clue." Her voice rose. "But it means *something*, China. Something serious. And I have the feeling it has to do with Sharyn."

"With Sharyn? In what way?"

"I don't know. There's something about her that's just . . . not right." Ruby shook her head, perplexed.

I shivered as I thought again of Sharyn's hands, and the sound of her voice when she said *And now it is mine.* Then I remembered the Sotheby's catalog. I reached into my purse, pulled it out, and opened it to the page that Karen had marked with the yellow sticky note.

"I found this in Karen's briefcase," I said. "It's a photograph of the painting we're talking about, or of something very similar. Can you see *this* one?"

Ruby blinked. "Sure," she said, looking down at the photograph. "It's a woman, holding a pink flower." She peered more closely. "The flower is bleeding on her. She's sad — no, she's anguished." She put her finger on the painting's title. "*Muerte llega pronto.* That fits, doesn't it? Death Come Quickly."

"Yes, it does," I said. "It fits."

313

Ruby took the catalog from me and looked at the cover. "Sotheby's," she said. "They auction paintings and stuff, don't they?" She flipped back to the marked page. "And they're auctioning *this* one? The one that everybody but me can see? The same painting? How does that work?"

"They've already auctioned it," I said, pointing to the date on the cover. "Last November. They expected to get $110,000 to $125,000 for it. But I'm not sure it's the very same painting. Maybe it's a similar painting, by the same title."

"Something very weird is going on here," Ruby muttered.

"Two weird somethings," I said. "Number one, the painting you can't see, even when it's hanging, big as life, a foot in front of your nose. Number two, the painting that Sotheby's auctioned off, with the same title." I paused, wrinkling my forehead. "No, make that three somethings. The fact that Karen had this auction catalog in her briefcase. Which means that she must have spotted the lookalikes, as well."

Ruby looked perplexed. "You don't suppose this had anything to do with . . . you know. With the mugging."

"I don't know. I've been concentrating on trying to figure out whether there's a connection between Karen's mugging and Christine Morris' murder. But this is something different. I'll have to think about it." I frowned. "Any idea why you couldn't see the painting on the wall, Ruby?"

She was studying the photograph in the catalog. "Because it isn't really there?" she hazarded.

"But it *is* there," I protested. "I saw it; Sharyn saw it. This isn't the emperor's new clothes, Ruby. We were *not* pretending to not notice that it's gone."

"I know," Ruby said slowly. "But maybe . . . maybe —" She closed the catalog and held it up. "Is it okay if I take this home with me? I want to do some research."

"Sure." I leaned over and opened her car door for her. "What are you going to do with it? Show it to your Ouija board?" I smothered a snicker. "Ask the I Ching to give you a clue? Consult your rune stones?"

"Don't be tacky, China." She stuck her lower lip out, scowling. "This is serious stuff."

"I'm sorry," I said, penitent. "You're right. Sometimes my tacky self just can't resist showing off. I know there's a reason you couldn't see that painting — a *serious* reason. I hope you can figure it out. Please use any means you can think of, including the Ouija board."

Ruby folded her long legs into her car. "Actually," she said, "I was thinking of trying something else. Something different." She closed the door, put the key in the ignition, and rolled down her window.

"What's that?" I asked curiously, through the open window. What could be more *different* than Ruby's Ouija board, rune stones, and I Ching?

"Google," she said.

I rolled my eyes. Google. Why hadn't I thought of that?

"I thought I'd check out Sotheby's website," she added. "They might have posted the results of that auction — the price, maybe. I don't know what that would tell us — probably nothing. But it's worth a shot, don't you think? And I could surf around and look for some of Izquierdo's other paintings — get some information about her and her background."

"It certainly is worth a shot," I said. "When you've got everything doped out, Ruby, call me and tell me about it. Okay?"

"Sure thing." She waggled her fingers at me, put her car in gear, and drove off.

CHAPTER TEN

In Devonshire, England, it is considered unlucky to plant lilies of the valley, for these tiny white bells are said to ring forth the death of the one who plants them.

China Bayles
"Herbs of Good and Ill Omen"
Pecan Springs Enterprise

As I got into my car, I looked at my watch. Perfect timing — it was just after three o'clock. Paul and Irene Cameron lived only about six blocks away. I could stop in and see Paul, who should be up from his nap and ready for a chat.

I was ready, definitely. Now that I had seen the collection for myself, I had some questions I wanted to ask him about the Morris Museum and the functioning of the museum board. What was Sharyn Tillotson's role in the management of the collection? Did the board keep on top of what was going on, or did they let Sharyn run things, more or less? What could he tell me about the paintings that were on exhibit, those that had been purchased, and those that had been sold? But Kitt had said that Paul was unfocused and had a tendency to wander off the subject. I hoped he was feeling up to giving me some answers.

The Camerons' house was a large, very nice two-story frame home, surrounded by pecan and live oak trees, not far from the river. I was on my way up the walk when Irene came out on the stoop to greet me, closing the door behind her. She was wearing a painter's smock and there was a streak of paint on one bare arm.

"I'm so sorry, China," she said regretfully. "But it turns out that this isn't a good afternoon for Paul after all. He's tired and awfully grumpy." She sighed and made a little face. "I'm afraid he's not making a lot of sense, either. You wouldn't enjoy your visit. And he'd be terribly frustrated — embarrassed, too. He knows when he's not in full control, but he just can't stop himself."

I was a little surprised that she was telling me this, since we didn't know one another that well. But I knew that she must be relieved to see a friendly face — and embarrassed herself, on behalf of her husband.

"That's too bad," I said, feeling a surge of sympathy for her, as well as for Paul. Someone had told me that she had been his graduate student when they married. She must be twenty years younger than he, and very pretty, with a delicate diamond-shaped face, clear gray eyes, and brown hair that she wore plaited in a thick braid down her back. When he was on the CTSU art faculty, her life had been full of all the usual faculty doings — exhibits, lectures, parties, concerts. It must be a very different life now, and very lonely, if he continued to go downhill. How would she deal with the challenge of his care? I thought again of the rumor that Paul's erratic financial investments had jeopardized their house and wondered how she was managing, financially. It must be a difficult struggle.

"It is the way it is," she said in a practical tone and brushed her flyaway brown hair out of her eyes with the back of a paint-smeared hand. "I'm afraid it won't be long before we'll have to make . . . other arrangements for him."

"I'm so sorry to hear that, Irene," I said. "He's always been such an active, energetic guy."

"Oh, he still has a lot of physical energy,"

she said ruefully. "And he's bigger and stronger than I am, which makes it difficult to manage him, especially when he's being . . . you know, contrary. He can be a handful at times. But I try to save time to do what I enjoy doing, as much as I can. He always encouraged me to do that." She looked down at her splattered smock and managed a tremulous smile. "As you can see, I'm painting. At least, I'm trying to, although I'm a little out of practice. But I would love to sell more of my work, to help out with expenses. I actually have a show coming up in a couple of months, if I can manage to get enough done. One of our friends has promised to set it up for me at his gallery in San Antonio."

"That's wonderful, Irene," I said, with genuine enthusiasm. I could hear the strain in her voice, a little tremble, some hesitancy. Perhaps her art would help to relieve some of the stress of being a full-time caregiver for her husband. "I saw some of your work — the flower paintings — at the Morris Museum earlier this afternoon. They are really quite lovely."

A pleased smile broke across her face. "Oh, thank you! I'm glad you liked them."

"They gave me an idea, actually," I said. "I wondered if you might like to hang a few of your floral pieces in my herb shop. The marigolds are especially wonderful. They would have to be priced quite a lot lower, though, maybe in the forty-to-sixty-dollar range. At that price, I think I could sell several."

She frowned thoughtfully. "Well, perhaps. Actually, I have several paintings of lilies of the valley — they're smaller, and I think I could let them go at that price. As I said, I really need to help out with expenses. Let me think about it and I'll get back to you."

"Of course," I said. "Oh, by the way, when I was at the Morris, Sharyn mentioned that you're returning to the board, to fill Karen Prior's place."

"Yes." Irene gave an awkward little shrug. "I enjoyed my work with the collection and I'm glad to be going back, although I wish it could be under . . . different circumstances." She shook her head bleakly. "That was just terrible about Karen Prior." Her voice broke. "A mugging! I could hardly believe that something like that could happen to her."

"I know," I said. "It was a terrible shock." I paused, then added, "I saw a painting at the museum today that I understand was Karen's favorite. I found it quite striking. I wonder if you could tell me something about the artist. *Muerte llega pronto,* it's called. Death Come Quickly."

Irene shifted uncomfortably. "I don't think I recognize it," she said, after a moment. "It must not have been in the collection when I was on the board. Who painted it?"

"María Izquierdo," I replied. I found it curious that she didn't know the painting, especially since she had written her thesis on Mexican women artists. "I didn't get a chance to ask Sharyn about it," I added. "I'd like to find out more about the painter. She was apparently quite well-known."

Another uneasy hesitation, then she stepped back and put her hand on the doorknob. "I've read about Izquierdo, but I don't know anything about her work." She cocked her head, listening. "Oh, dear, Paul is calling. I'd better go and see what he's up to." She gave a resigned sigh. "It's not a good idea to leave him alone too long, when he's in this mood."

I nodded. "I'll phone you in a day or two. Maybe he'll be feeling better."

"Maybe he will," she said with a sad little smile. "I hope so, anyway. Do call — I'm sure he'd like to see you if he could. And that will give me time to think about those pieces for your shop."

"The lilies of the valley would be especially

nice," I reminded her.

She nodded and closed the door. I heard the latch click firmly.

I got in the car, flicked on the air conditioner, and sat for a moment, thinking about how easily a health problem — mental health as well as physical — can derail even a happy marriage. Irene had every right to look forward to a long life with her husband. And now she was having to deal with the financial fallout of his erratic financial behavior and figure out how she could pay for whatever care he was going to require, which wouldn't come cheaply, I was sure. It was good that she was painting again, of course, but very sad that she had to do it in order to pay the bills.

I turned on the ignition and drove off. Thinking about Paul and Irene — and Felicity and her grandmother — made me sad. Illness and death changed everyone's lives. I suddenly felt very grateful that I could go home to my contented marriage and our more or less financially secure house, where McQuaid and I and the kids, along with Gretchen and Jake, would be sitting down to supper in a couple of hours. We would laugh, tell jokes, mind our manners, tease each other a little, and love each other a lot. We would be a *family.*

At home, in the kitchen, I scrubbed a batch of Yukon Gold potatoes from the spring crop in our garden — we never get many, but they are very good, especially for potato salad. When they were on the stove and the water was coming to a boil, I picked up my phone and dialed Justine Wyzinski. She wasn't there, so I left a message on her answering machine.

I had some questions for her. About Roberto Soto.

I had work to do after supper, so while the kitchen cleanup crew got busy, I went upstairs to our bedroom, stripped and showered, and pulled on the oversize T-shirt I sleep in. Then I flopped on the bed under the ceiling fan with the transcript of Richard Bowen's trial. I read the best parts (Johnnie's cross-examinations and the defense section of the trial) with some attention and skimmed the rest quickly. I also looked for the court record of the closed hearing at which Johnnie had offered up his alternative suspect, which should have been with the transcript but wasn't. Maybe it would be in the case file in Aaron's office.

The transcript made it clear that the case had presented so many challenges for the prosecution that poor old Henry Bell simply didn't stand a chance, even though he was ably aided and abetted from the bench by the Honorable Roy Lee Sparks. His Honor did his friend Ring-a-Ding the favor of allowing in the evidence seized during Barry Rogers' warrantless search, probably because if he hadn't, Bell would have had to drop the charges. The tainted evidence against Bowen was the *only* evidence there was. There wasn't a word about the Morris Foundation, of course, and not much about Christine Morris' art collection, except that there was one and that it was valuable enough to prompt her to install an alarm and a fence. There wasn't much about *her,* either, and her ex-husband's name barely entered into it. The trial was all about Dick Bowen.

From the transcript, I could see that the prosecutor was building his case almost entirely on motive and opportunity. He called three witnesses to testify to Bowen's hatred of the victim, who had accused him at several city council meetings of abusing his power on the zoning committee. Other witnesses testified that he hated her dogs, her chain-link fence, and her annoying security lights. Ring-a-Ding used these to build his simple theory of the crime. According to him, Bowen had come to the end of his rope one dark night, pulled on his gardening shoes, grabbed a club out of his golf bag, then dashed next door to beat the lady to death. Unfortunately, however, the Pecan Springs police had committed so many errors that the case against Bowen — which was based only on the golf club, the gardening shoes, and next-door proximity — was compromised from the get-go.

Johnnie's cross of the lead investigator, Barry Rogers, was a masterpiece of contained and biting sarcasm. He began by eliciting the information that Rogers had entered this case with a recent history of poorly managed investigations, one of them so full of errors that the judge had thrown it out. Johnnie got Rogers to admit that if he didn't bring in a solid case on this one, he was in serious trouble. And then, over the course of one painful morning's testimony, it emerged that Rogers had not properly secured the crime scene; that he had conducted a warrantless search of Bowen's premises, based on the patently bogus assertion of "hot pursuit"; that he had not ordered the victim's hands bagged to preserve any possible evidence; that the crime scene photographs taken by a junior police officer were so flawed as to be essentially worthless for forensic purposes; and that there was (or appeared to be, in the best of the photographs) a print of a different shoe in the pool of blood around the victim's body. The second shoeprint was never investigated.

Regarding the defendant, Rogers conceded that Bowen's garage was widely known to be unlocked and that the main garage door was regularly left open so that the contents were visible from the street. Further, he admitted that he had not ordered a police canvass of the neighborhood in order to determine whether anyone had seen a person entering the unlocked garage (presumably to borrow Bowen's gardening shoes and his golf club) or had noticed any suspicious activity at the Morris house on the night of the murder.

Finally, it emerged that the medical examination of the corpse (performed in Bexar County, since Adams County had no ME at the time) had not determined whether Christine Morris had had recent sexual intercourse. Somehow or other, that essential part of the autopsy had either been overlooked or its results had not been recorded, nobody seemed to know which. I could just imagine Johnnie's incredulous tone as he asked the artfully phrased question, "You mean to tell this court that no one determined whether the murdered woman had had sexual intercourse before she died?"

And the subdued reply: "No, sir."

At which Johnnie must have rolled his eyes, for he requested that the question be read back to the witness, who (by now thoroughly confused) had answered, "Yes, I guess," and then dejectedly, "Oh, hell, I don't know."

I could hear Johnnie's ringing disgust as he said, "This witness is excused," and strode back to his seat.

It was a Bad Day at Black Rock for Ring-a-Ding, who might have remembered a classic line from that film: "You want to register a complaint? To register a complaint, boy, you've got to have evidence. You got evidence?"

Johnnie's strategy was to challenge the credibility of the investigation, the evidence, and the witnesses, and he was off to a good beginning on cross during the prosecution's case. When it came time to open for the defense, he put on a series of witnesses, each of whom reminded the jurors of what they already knew, that Bowen was a Good Samaritan who spent all his spare time contributing to the welfare of the community. Then he put on several witnesses, including Florabelle Gibson and Bowen's boss, Jimmie Lee Hanson, both of whom testified that Bowen had come to work the morning after the murder as cheery as he always was — "not at all like a man who had bludgeoned his neighbor in a fit of rage just a few hours before," as Hanson put it.

Johnnie also called the neighbor across the street, Mr. Davidson, who testified that Mr. Bowen was a "trusting sort" who often left his garage door open and had invited the neighbors to borrow his garden tools, as long as they were returned in good condition. "Kind and considerate," was the way Mr. Davidson put it. "He'd go a mile to help you out."

As his final witness, Johnnie called Detective Barry Rogers. Judge Sparks wouldn't let the defense offer up an alternative suspect, but he gave Johnnie some latitude in using the evidence to suggest that there was one. Under Johnnie's questioning, Rogers testified, reluctantly, that the padlock on the inside of the back gate had been unlocked and the gate left open, presumably by Ms. Morris. That although the house contained a great many valuable paintings and Ms. Morris was concerned about theft, the alarm system in the house had been turned off at the console, presumably by her. And that there was an unopened bottle of champagne in the refrigerator and two crystal flutes on the kitchen counter. Johnnie could have brought out these facts on cross in the prosecution's case, of course, but saving them for the defense made a much greater impact.

All these facts added up, Johnnie said in his closing argument, to the likely presence of someone whom Ms. Morris expected, who had come in through the back gate, carrying the defendant's golf club and wearing his shoes.

"But the police don't have a clue about this person," Johnnie said, with his trademark sarcasm, "because they didn't bother to ask the neighbors what they might have seen or heard. They had already made up their minds that my client was guilty, and that assumption led them to conduct a sloppy, careless, incompetent investigation. Ladies and gentlemen, the unlocked gate, the silenced alarm, the champagne glasses, the possible bloody print of another shoe — they all add up to a reasonable doubt. And when there's doubt, you must acquit."

To which the jury, after deliberating for a very brief two hours and twenty-two minutes, agreed. They found Richard Bowen not guilty of the murder of Christine Morris. And that was that. Time to break out the bubbly.

But who *had* killed her? In the process of reading, I learned that Douglas Clark had a very firm alibi for the night of the murder. Like the dog that didn't bark in the night, he was in the hospital, recovering from an unscheduled emergency appendectomy. As far as the police were concerned, that removed him from the suspect list. They didn't appear to have considered whether he might have hired a hit man to do the dirty work for him.

And they didn't reopen the case, either, after Bowen was acquitted. I'll bet if I knocked on Bubba Harris' door right now and asked him if he thinks they got the right man, he'd say, "You damn betcha we got him! *His* weapon, *his* shoes. It was him, all right."

As for Dick Bowen, he had insisted on testifying in his own defense and had done quite a credible job of it. "I have nothing whatsoever to hide," he insisted — although of course he did, if Florabelle Gibson was to be believed, or if I was to credit Johnnie's remark that his client wasn't exactly pure. Bowen was hiding a big pocketful of bribes, paid to him by Douglas Clark. But of course, none of that was brought up. The transcript shed no light at all on that little caper, which now appeared to me to be completely irrelevant.

Or rather, if there was any relevance, I wasn't seeing it. And when McQuaid came into the room and began to strip for bed, I was happy to lay the transcript aside and get on with . . . um, more immediately relevant and interesting matters.

I was up early the next morning, and dressed in a slim khaki skirt, brown tank top, colored scarf, and low heels for my one-day excursion to Houston. I was putting on my makeup (I was a little out of practice because I don't wear it very often) when McQuaid asked me where I was going. I told him I was planning to drive down to Houston for the day to see Lucia Bettler, who teaches cooking classes and owns and manages an herb shop called Lucia's Garden.

It was true. Lucia is a good friend, and I try to see her whenever I'm in Houston. She's a great fan of the work of the Mexican artist Frida Kahlo, and I thought she might be able to tell me something about María Izquierdo. I had phoned her the evening before, to make sure she'd be in the shop today.

Of course, I was seeing someone else, too. But McQuaid knows Aaron Brooks and doesn't trust him — not because he's jealous, necessarily, although that might be part of it. But they had butted heads in a murder trial when McQuaid was with Houston Homicide, and McQuaid still remembers. I would tell him tonight, after the fact, when he could see that I was home safe and sound — and entirely unmolested.

The sky was a gloomy gray, overcast with low clouds heavy with moisture scudding up from the Gulf. Unfortunately, in Texas, clouds don't necessarily signal rain. They just mean that the day will most likely be a bad hair day, if your hair is inclined to get lank when the weather turns muggy, the way mine does. I wasn't in a very good mood, anyway. I hate the drive to Houston — or rather, I hate the last sixty miles of it, when the traffic picks up and everybody drives as if they are doing laps on the Indianapolis Speedway on Memorial Day.

It's odd, but I don't remember feeling this way when I lived and worked in Houston, when my whole life — every personal and professional moment of it — was spent in the fast lane, actual and metaphorical, pedal to the metal as hard as I could to stay ahead of the competition. I guess I was so habituated to the insane speed at which everybody operated that I simply didn't notice. Maybe all of us were like that, frogs swimming in water that is rapidly coming to a boil, and we didn't notice a thing.

I notice now. Life in Pecan Springs isn't nearly as simple as I had expected it to be. But it is definitely slower and sweeter, and the commute between our house in the country and my herb shop and gardens in town is a cakewalk. If I had to drive on the Houston streets and freeways five days a week, every hair on my head would be gray and my nails would be bitten down to the bloody quick.

Last year, McQuaid (whose watchword is safety first when it comes to cars and guns) bought me one of those hands-free cell phone devices to use when I'm driving. It came in handy today, because there were several calls. The first one was from Brian, who couldn't find his favorite shirt (it was in the dryer, which is totally off his radar). What that boy will do about his laundry when he goes off to college next month is beyond me. Do they teach Washing and Drying 101?

The second call was from Caitlin, who told me with great excitement that Mrs. Banner (the neighbor who is having a baby) has a friend who has a rooster who would love to have some hens for his very own (he lives with another rooster, who is selfishly hogging all the hens for himself). Mrs. Banner's friend hates the thought of having her rooster for Sunday dinner, so she would like to find him a new home. If we adopted him, he and the girls could have s-e-x, couldn't they? And then the girls wouldn't just have eggs, they would have baby chicks, wouldn't they? And she would call him Lucky Boy, because he was lucky to escape being Sunday dinner.

I deferred a ruling on the request until we had a chance to sit down and discuss the pros and cons of giving Lucky Boy his very own harem of hens. But I did remark that if the girls were allowed to have baby chicks, there wouldn't be just one rooster. There would be *more* roosters (the gender distribution of chickens is probably like that of humans, I would guess, approximately fifty-fifty, boys and girls). And more roosters would lead to the same uncomfortable situation in which Mrs. Banner's friend found herself. Are we willing to have roast roosters for Sunday dinner, and if so, who will do the terrible deed? This question was met with a long silence, and then Caitlin made kissy noises and went off to think about it.

The third call was from Ruby, who had returned from her Web-surfing expedition with some interesting information about María Izquierdo.

"She was born in 1902 in a small Mexican village," Ruby read from her notes. "When she was fourteen, she was married off to an army colonel and had three children, one, two, three, just like that. It's probably fair to say that this wasn't her idea. In 1923, her husband moved the family to Mexico City, where she took art classes whenever she could manage to get away. Four years later, she left her husband and children and went to study art full-time."

"Really?" I broke in. "That was *brave.*"

"Oh, you bet," Ruby said. "And there's more. At the Academy of San Carlos, María met Rufino Tamayo. He was an artist, and it wasn't long before they were lovers. She also met Diego Rivera, who took her under his wing. She had her first exhibition in 1929, in Mexico City — and that same year, her work was shown in New York. In fact, she was the very first Mexican woman to have a New York exhibition. Then, in 1936, she had an exhibit in Paris."

"My goodness," I said, checking my rear-view mirror. There was a large truck on my bumper and I sped up. "She sounds *important.*"

"She was, apparently. Her work was praised everywhere. She and Tamayo lived together for four years, but he left her in 1933 for a younger woman. She was distraught, and the breakup led to a depression that affected her painting for several years. A French poet named Artaud wrote that her paintings have the 'color of cold lava, as if in the semidarkness of a volcano.' "

"Ah," I said, remembering the painting on the wall. Betrayal, desolation, loss, unbearable pain, symbolized by the flower. *Muerte llega pronto.*

"In 1945," Ruby went on, "María was invited to paint a mural in Mexico City. But she had made some powerful enemies by speaking out against some of the prevailing trends in Mexican art, and they were able to block the commission." She took a deep breath. "After that, her career suffered. She began having nightmares. She painted one of them — she called it *Sueño y Pensamiento,* Dreaming and Thinking. I've seen a photograph of it, China. She's painted herself holding her own severed head out of a window, while her headless body disappears — literally — into the distance. The year after that, she suffered a debilitating stroke. It more or less ended her artistic life. She died a few years later."

"That's tragic, Ruby." It was, but I was finding it a little hard to concentrate. I was trying to get away from the truck and watching for the turnoff — a left exit — from 290 onto I-610 South.

"And prophetic, too, wouldn't you say?" Ruby asked. "I mean, she paints a severed head, and then she suffers a stroke that virtually incapacitates her. It's as if her dream foretold the future."

I began edging left, sneaking in behind a pickup loaded with cardboard boxes wrapped in plastic. Flags of ripped plastic were peeling off in the wind and flying across the freeway. "Yes, prophetic," I said and moved one more lane to the left, to avoid the flying plastic, which could blanket the windshield and leave me sightless. "Yes."

"But wait, there's more!" Ruby exclaimed, like that voice on the television commercials that wants to sell you two or three of something you don't want even one of. "I found out that Izquierdo's work is really hot right now. That painting I just told you about — *Sueño y Pensamiento?* It sold at Sotheby's recently for a whopping four hundred fifty thousand dollars!"

338

"Wow," I said, slipping between two cars to get into the near left lane. "Nearly half a million! That's a *lot* of money, Ruby."

"Right. And now the Mexican government has declared Izquierdo a national treasure, which means that her paintings can no longer be taken out of the country without the government's approval." Ruby took a deep breath. "That would tend to drive up the prices even more, wouldn't it?"

"I'd think it would make her paintings harder to get," I said.

"Oh, and guess what! That painting you showed me in the Sotheby's catalog, the one Karen marked with the yellow sticky? I checked the Web page for that auction lot. *Muerte llega pronto* went for far more than the estimate. In fact, it sold for twice what they estimated, China. A cool quarter million."

A quarter of a million dollars. I wondered whether it had gone to a museum or disappeared into a private collection, where it wouldn't resurface until it was put up for sale again. I thought of the painting I had seen on the wall of the Morris Museum — and Ruby *hadn't*. How was it related to the painting that somebody had bought at Sotheby's? Why did Karen have the Sotheby's catalog in her briefcase? Did she know something about that painting — those *two* paintings — that might explain her death? And why couldn't Ruby see that painting when it was hanging right in front of her eyes?

"Ruby," I said, "that weird business with the painting yesterday — have you figured out what it means?"

"I've tried," Ruby replied. "I asked the I Ching why I couldn't see the painting. The answer I got is interesting and seems very apt. But I haven't been able to make any sense out of it yet."

"What did you get?" I asked.

The I Ching, the "Book of Changes," is an ancient Chinese oracle. Ruby consults the oracle in the traditional way, by tossing down fifty dried yarrow stalks from the garden and picking them up in a certain pattern. Some people find it easier to use four coins. And easiest of all, you can have your computer make a random choice for you. Any of these methods will result in a figure called a hexagram, a series of six lines stacked one on top of the other, either "changing" lines (broken in the middle) or "unchanging" (straight). There are sixty-four possible hexagrams, each of which has been interpreted by Asian scholars and teachers in a variety of ways.

"I got hexagram 20," Ruby said. "Kuan. Four changing lines topped by two unchanging lines. It has a kind of double meaning — seeing and being seen. Or viewing and being viewed. It suggests contemplation. Perspective. Or maybe setting an example for others to look at and follow."

Typical I Ching. It means so many things that, practically speaking, it means nothing. "Well," I said, trying to be encouraging, "at least the answer is in the right ballpark. I don't know about contemplation or setting an example, but you were certainly having a 'viewing' problem."

"I need to give it some more thought." Ruby paused. "Oh, and I talked to Sheila a little while ago. She's home. *With* the baby."

"Oh, that's good!" I said and breathed a sigh of relief.

"But she has to stay flat for a couple of days," Ruby added. "The doctor wants to be extra sure. Which means that she can't go to work."

"Poor Sheila," I said sympathetically. I was safely off 290 and swinging under the overpass onto 610, heading south. "Having to stay flat will drive her crazy. Knowing her, though, I'm sure she'll find a way to manage the entire police department from her bed."

Of course, she'd have to begin telling people why she was in bed, which would cause a lot of head shaking and tongue wagging. I could just imagine what the good old boys of the Bubba Harris era would have to say about a pregnant police chief.

"Actually, China, she's a little ticked off at you," Ruby said hesitantly. "Somebody told her that you had been at the Prior house yesterday morning, and that you were rummaging through Karen's office. She wanted me to tell you to get out of her case and quit messing up her investigation." She cleared her throat, sounding embarrassed. "She said something about obstructing justice."

"Obstructing justice," I muttered under my breath. I was trying to move right, into a slower lane, to get away from the garbage truck that was still riding on my back bumper. But some jerk in a burnt orange Hummer with University of Texas license plates was threatening to cut me off. Talk about obstructing!

"China? Did you hear me, China? Sheila said to stop fooling around and stay off Karen's case. She said she's sorry, but she really has to insist. You're a civilian and you're not supposed to —"

The Hummer driver had the nerve to

blow his horn at me. It sounded like an eighteen-wheeler's air horn. I used a very rude word.

"I should do *what*?" Ruby asked, startled.

"Not you, sweetie," I said apologetically. "Listen, I gotta go. This traffic is murder. But if you talk to Sheila again, tell her I'm not on Karen's case, and I'm not obstructing justice." At least, I told myself, not so's she'd notice. "I'm in Houston for the day. I'm getting together with Lucia Bettler."

"Oh, good," Ruby said, relieved. "Tell Lucia I said hello. I've been meaning to drive over and visit." She paused then, sounding doubtful. "Are you *sure* this trip doesn't have anything to do with Karen's mugging?"

I laughed. Ruby knows me too well. "Actually, I hope it does," I confessed, "but it's a long shot — a very long shot." It depended on what was in Johnnie's notes, or in the transcript, if there was one, of the closed hearing on the defense's alternative suspect strategy. To tell the truth, I had been enthusiastic about coming to Houston to work on the case, but that was when I was back in Pecan Springs. Now that I was here, the doubts were setting in. There were too many little pieces to this puzzle, and none of them seemed to be connected. I didn't see how this trip was going to turn up anything that would help us learn why Karen had been killed.

A raucous truck horn sounded behind me. I flinched and clutched the steering wheel harder. In fact, I was beginning to wish I hadn't given up my precious day off to play dodgem cars with garbage trucks and Hummers pushing seventy miles an hour in Houston traffic.

Chapter Eleven

Yarrow is one of those herbs that has a contradictory reputation. For centuries, it was carried in battle as a lucky charm and believed to protect the warrior from harm. In China, it was considered one of the luckiest of plants. Where yarrow grew, people said, neither tigers nor wolves could venture and poisonous plants could not be found. In Europe, it was grown beside the door and strewn across the threshold to keep evil from getting into the house.

But in some parts of England, yarrow was known as "devil's nettle" and "bad man's plaything" and associated with witchcraft. In Wales, yarrow went by the name "death flower." Carry it into the house, and death will follow.

China Bayles
"Herbs of Good and Ill Omen"
Pecan Springs Enterprise

345

To reach Aaron's office, I stayed on 610 South across town to the Southwest Freeway, then got off at the Kirby exit, made a right at the light, headed south across Bissonnet, then made another left a few blocks farther on. His law firm still goes by the name Brooks and Carlson, but he has moved from the large concrete-and-glass building where he and Johnnie once had an office to a single-story frame house — green with a tasteful purple trim — in an area of other fixer-upper houses that have been converted to professional offices, thereby raising the property values and the tax base. The building has a small off-street parking area, a couple of trees in the back, and a landscaped front court, bright with clumps of yellow and pink and lavender yarrow, purple coneflowers, sunny black-eyed Susans, orange-and-yellow lantana, and bright red Turk's cap, all heat- and drought-tolerant perennials that need practically no tending.

I parked, got out, and stretched, pulling the kinks out, then shouldered my bag, went up the walk, and rang the buzzer beside the front door. Not so many years ago, clients simply opened the door and walked into law offices right off the street, but no more. There have been too many nutcase shootings, and lawyers are by nature a paranoid lot. From the intercom, a chipper female voice asked my name. I gave it and waited for the click that allowed me to open the door.

Aaron's receptionist, a trim and tidy thirty-something woman named Tiffany Franken, was wreathed in pretty smiles. Her hair is dark, cut short to emphasize its natural curl. She has blue eyes, a fetching sprinkle of freckles, and a snub-nosed .357 Magnum in her desk drawer. I happen to know that she's a crack shot.

"Hello, Ms. Bayles!" she said with pleasure. "We don't get to see you often enough. How's life in the Hill Country?"

"Much slower than life in the city," I said, still feeling that garbage truck breathing down my tailpipe. "And there's a heckuva lot less traffic."

"It's horrible, isn't it? I'm almost afraid to get on the freeway, and the streets aren't a lot better." She smiled warmly. "Mr. Brooks is in the conference room. He has the materials you wanted. Would you like some coffee? A soft drink?"

I thanked her, declined, and headed down the short hallway to the conference room — probably the dining room when this was a real house. Three of the walls were floor-to-ceiling bookcases, filled with legal volumes and reference works. The fourth wall, painted a rich chocolate brown, featured a large bay window dressed with tasteful wooden blinds, filtering the view of a dense yaupon holly hedge. The obligatory polished oak table stood in the center of the room, with the obligatory eight polished chairs with leather seats, all impressively lawyer-like. On the table was a four-inch-thick three-ring binder and a couple of file boxes.

And there he was, my former lover, as blond and good-looking as ever — although I had to admit that he seemed older and more tired than I remembered, and he'd gained some weight. But never mind that. He had always been a natty dresser, and that hadn't changed: he wore a gray Armani vest and pants, a pale lavender pinstripe shirt, and a fuchsia-and-navy paisley tie. My heart was tripping along pitty-pat, pitty-pat, like the unruly heart of that foolish chick-lit ingénue.

I had come on business, however, and my heart, every last unruly ounce of it, belongs to my husband. So I exerted a firm control over the silly pitty-patting, straightened my shoulders, stuck out my hand, and managed a friendly, collegial "Hello, Aaron, nice to see —"

And that was as far as I got before he folded me into his arms, crunching my nose against his tie, which smelled of that delicious vanilla pipe tobacco that I always loved. After a moment, he took a step back, tipped up my chin, smiled down at me, and said pleasantly, "Shut up, China Bayles. I'm going to kiss you."

He did, at length, and effectively. And then he let me go.

"Very good," he said, as I struggled to get my breath and smooth my hair. "Quite remarkable, in fact, and exactly as I remembered it." He gave me an appreciative up-and-down glance. "Now that we've got that out of the way, we can get on with what you came for."

"Wait just a darn minute," I said indignantly. "Why did you do that, Aaron?"

He looked at me, his blue eyes very clear, his dimples showing. "Why, because I wanted to," he said innocently. "I've been wanting to do that ever since you telephoned. Haven't *you*?" He raised one blond eyebrow, teasing. "Come on, now. Fess up. Yes, you have."

"I have not," I said firmly, straightening my tank top and trying to hide my fluster. "Not even a little."

He pulled those eyebrows together in a

frown and folded his arms across his chest in his best courtroom manner.

Give me a break. "Oh, all right. Yes. Maybe a little. But just because I want to do something doesn't mean I have to do it," I added righteously. "Mature people don't act on all their impulses."

The smile lines around his eyes crinkled. "My dearest China, you are just as human as I am, and sometimes humans do what they want to do just because they want to do it. So quit making a big friggin' deal about a little kiss between old friends." He reached out a hand and his fingers brushed my cheek. "Okay?"

"Okay," I growled. I noticed a glint of gray in his blond hair and modified my tone. "You're perfectly right, Aaron. It's no big deal. No big deal at all." Then why did I want to touch that glint of gray? And why was my heart still pitty-patting?

"Good." He dropped his hand.

And that's when I saw it. The plain gold band on his left hand. I did a double take, then reached for his hand, turned it over, and said, "Hey. Looks like you're keeping a secret." Was I annoyed? Well, maybe, just a little. But to tell the truth, I was mostly relieved. It felt as if the playing field had just been somehow leveled.

"A secret?" He grinned. "Not really. I was going to tell you over lunch." He tilted his head. "Sorry I didn't invite you to the wedding. It was kind of . . . impulsive. We took a weekend and flew to Vegas to get married."

"Do I know her?"

"Maybe. Paula Hemming. She's an assistant DA with the Harris County district attorney's office."

I pulled my eyebrows together. "Tall, stunning brunette? Glasses? Mega-smart? Formidable in the courtroom?" And on the home front, too, I'd bet.

"That's her," Aaron said jauntily. "Just celebrated our first anniversary yesterday. And guess what!"

He knows how I feel about guessing games. I rolled my eyes, remembered Sheila and Mrs. Banner, and said, "Okay, I'll bite. The two of you are pregnant."

He stared at me. "How'd you know? We just found out last week and neither of us have told anybody. We don't even know yet whether it's a boy or a girl."

"I'm clairvoyant," I said with a crooked grin. "Congratulations, Counselor."

And there was that twinge again. One of my best friends was having a baby. One of my old flames was having a baby. I felt . . .

well, left out.

"Yeah," he said. "It's great. Wonderful. Peachy. Of course, Paula is the kind of woman who wants to have it all. A great job *and* a couple of kids." His voice dropped a notch. "I don't know if she realizes what kind of change it's going to mean, though. We're in the habit of keeping long hours — sometimes we only see one another on weekends. Not even that, if one of us has a big case."

I knew all about that. It was the kind of relationship Aaron and I had had when we were together. Brutal schedules, nerves like bare electrical wires, ready to short out and flare up. And always the uneasy feeling that we were ships passing in the night, bound for different home ports. I could have reminded him of that, but I took the safer route.

"I'm sure you'll work it out," I said. "Good luck."

"Yeah, right." He didn't sound all that confident. He gestured toward the binder and file boxes. "Anyway, there's the Bowen casebook. You know Johnnie — he was a sloppy note-taker, he wasn't systematic about documentation, and his trial work was more or less seat-of-the-pants. And Bowen was before laptops, of course. Now we scan everything in and keep the files on flash drives."

I sighed. The notebook looked formidable. I had the feeling that I wouldn't be able to find what I needed — even if it was there, which it probably wasn't.

Aaron was going on. "However, I was glad to see that Johnnie's trial assistant — a young attorney named Stan Simpson — kept the Bowen materials pretty well organized. Looks like it's all there: the witness interviews and depositions, pretrial motions, briefs, jury information, witness lists, exhibits, notes for opening and closing statements. And the yellow tablets Johnnie scribbled on during testimony — mostly illegible, I'm afraid. The trial transcript is in the green box. I was late getting out of court this morning, so I didn't have time to do more than look through it. Anyway, I wasn't sure what you were looking for, exactly."

"I'm not either, exactly," I said. "It falls into the I'll-know-it-when-I-see-it category."

He nodded and glanced at his watch. "And as it turns out, one of my clients has gotten himself into a little trouble and I have to see what I can do to help him get out of it. He's down in Pearland, which means I need to cancel our lunch." His voice changed, and he turned down his mouth. "I mean it when I say I'm sorry, darlin'. I was looking forward to catching up with your life."

"I'm sorry, too," I said and wasn't surprised when I realized that this was true. "I'll let you know the next time I'm in Houston. And in the meantime —" I was gesturing toward the table, about to remark that I had certainly enough to keep me busy, when I was interrupted.

"In the meantime," he said, pulling me toward him, "let's have one for the road."

I couldn't have resisted if I'd wanted to, which I didn't, actually. It was a nice kiss, sweet and lingering, just the right combination of sexy and friendly and nostalgic, reminding us both that we had shared some very lovely moments together, a very long time ago, when the earth was young and we were different people.

And then he picked up his suit jacket from the chair where it was draped, slung it over his shoulder, and strode toward the door.

"Stan Simpson has his own practice now, but if you have questions about anything relating to that trial, I can arrange for him to give you a call. If you want copies, let Tiffany know. She'll take care of you."

"Thanks," I said, with a little smile. "Safe

travel. Stay clear of Hummers and garbage trucks."

"Say again?" he asked, puzzled.

"Never mind," I said. "Go." He went.

I watched the door close behind him, thinking that it was like a chapter closing, finally, in my life. It had been closed for a long time, yes. But this felt like a final conclusion, and to tell the truth, I was glad. I hate loose ends.

Then I sat down, pulled the transcript box toward me, and opened it. But when I studied the front-page table of contents, I saw that what I was after wasn't there. With a sigh, I reached for the thick blue binder. I had never been at trial with Johnnie but I was aware of his reputation for disorganization, and when I opened the binder, I was relieved to see that Stan Simpson had ordered the material systematically. I checked the index, then leafed through the tabs until I found the section documenting the defense plan to present an alternative suspect.

And there it was: a copy of the court reporter's transcript of the closed hearing on the matter, exactly what I was looking for. This was where Johnnie had proffered evidence to support his argument that there was reason to believe that someone else —

not the defendant, Richard Bowen — had killed Christine Morris. Was it Douglas Clark, who had a very powerful motive — maybe a million of them, in fact — to do away with his wife? Or maybe the cousin, Sharyn Tillotson, who inherited nothing but seemed to be in possession of everything?

No. Neither one.

The hearing was held in the judge's chambers. Present were the court reporter with his stenography machine; the prosecutor, Henry Bell; Johnnie; Judge Sparks; and a lawyer named Larry Garcia, representing the man Johnnie intended to name as his alternative suspect in the murder of Christine Morris. Roberto Soto.

I stared at those two words, letting out my breath in an explosive rush. *Roberto Soto!* The man who Charlie Lipman said was Christine's lover. The art dealer who had helped Christine acquire her collection and — after her murder — had worked as a curator for the Morris Foundation. Johnnie was an aggressive defense lawyer, yes, and it was his job to come up with a viable alternative suspect if he could. But he wouldn't have pulled Soto out of his hat. He had to have had good reasons to offer him up to the court. What were they?

I began reading through the record. During the hearing, which seemed to have lasted a little over an hour, Johnnie had summarized the testimony of the witnesses he planned to call, in addition to Soto himself. The first was the neighbor Mr. Davidson, who lived across the street from the Morris house. Davidson would testify that about a week before the murder, while he was out in his front yard clipping his shrubs, he had seen a tall, well-built man, somebody he didn't recognize, pause in front of Bowen's open garage. Mr. Davidson thought at first he might be "casing the place," although he couldn't imagine what anybody would want to steal out of Dick Bowen's garage.

"Nothing in there but rakes and hoes and some old sports equipment," he said dismissively. But a few moments later, the man had strolled across the Morris yard and into the side door of the Morris house. Mrs. Davidson, when she was called to testify, would say that she had told her husband that the man was Ms. Morris' "arty boyfriend." She had often seen him coming and going at the house.

Johnnie's next witness would be Mrs. Adele Kern, who lived on the street behind San Jacinto and kept an inquisitive eye on the doings on that side of the neighborhood.

She would testify that the vacant lot across the alley from the Morris house and owned by Ms. Morris was used by the neighbors as an informal parking lot, especially when there was a party. Ms. Morris' guests also used it.

Around ten o'clock on the night of the murder, Mrs. Kern had noticed a dark blue Mercedes in the vacant lot across the alley behind the Morris house. She didn't actually see the driver park the car and go to the Morris house that night, but she had seen a man — the driver of that same car — do just that on previous occasions. In fact, he was a "fairly regular all-night visitor," according to Mrs. Kern, whose bedroom window overlooked the lot. Once, she had seen the Mercedes arrive and the man take a large framed painting from the rear of the car and carry it across the alley to the Morris house. She had mentioned this to her cleaning lady, who had told her that the man was Ms. Morris' "art dealer boyfriend." Asked to describe the man, the best Mrs. Kern could do was "tall and well built."

Johnnie then planned to call Sarita Ruiz, who cleaned for Ms. Morris and several other neighbors. She would identify Ms. Morris' "art dealer boyfriend" as Roberto Soto. He often brought paintings, sculpture, and other artwork to the house. When he stayed overnight, which happened three or four times a month, he and Ms. Morris slept in the same bed, the cleaning lady said. He drove a dark, late-model automobile — Ms. Ruiz wasn't up on high-end cars and couldn't identify the make — and parked it in the vacant lot on the other side of the alley.

Larry Garcia, representing Mr. Soto, responded that while it was true that Roberto Soto was a frequent visitor to the Morris house and had in fact assisted Ms. Morris to establish and expand her collection, on the night of the lady's death, he was having a late dinner in San Antonio with another client of his art gallery, a collector from New Orleans. Mr. Soto had, however, visited Ms. Morris on the previous evening — that is, the night *before* her murder — and had parked his Mercedes in the vacant lot, as usual. Mrs. Kern had simply mixed up the nights. In any event, Garcia said, the police had already questioned Mr. Soto, confirmed his alibi, and did not consider him to be a suspect. The gentleman had no motive whatever to harm Ms. Morris. The two were not only intimate and cared deeply for one another, but she was one of Mr. Soto's oldest clients. Mr.

Soto was devastated by her murder.

Johnnie replied that the investigator he had hired had spoken to Soto's alibi witness and had come away with serious questions about the validity of Soto's alibi. He planned to call both the alibi witness and Mr. Soto.

For the prosecution, Henry Bell argued that the defense had presented not one single shred of motive — and they surely would have, if they had been able to conjure one up. Furthermore, Roberto Soto could give no evidence relating to the crime itself. And finally, there was no reasonable probability that any of this testimony was worth a plugged nickel. It was a waste of the court's valuable time, it would only confuse the jury, and it would irretrievably damage the reputation of an innocent and upstanding man who had already suffered enough because of this terrible tragedy.

Johnnie's rebuttal was the usual. "The defendant has pled not guilty. He has a right to put on exculpatory evidence in his defense. The jury should hear facts that could lead it to decide that there is a reasonable doubt as to the defendant's guilt."

Well argued, Johnnie, but no dice. The Honorable Roy Lee Sparks ruled against the defense, saying that without any compelling evidence as to motive, there was no "nexus" between Soto and the murder. His Honor concluded that the other-suspect evidence was "too speculative, too distant in nature to be of relevance" and "could not create reasonable doubt in this case."

And that was that. It was true that Johnnie had not offered any evidence as to motive, which substantially weakened his theory. Still, if the jury had found Bowen guilty, he would undoubtedly have appealed; Sparks' ruling might have been overturned and another trial ordered. But it hadn't and he didn't and it wasn't.

Fortunately, Bowen was acquitted and Johnnie had no reason to appeal. And Roberto Soto's possible connection to the crime had never been reported in the media — which was a little surprising, I thought. Closed hearings in chambers aren't necessarily leakproof, and Pecan Springs has a gossip-transmission system that rivals Twitter. But a tight lid would have been kept on during the trial in order to avoid jury contamination and the threat of a mistrial. And after the verdict, the big news would have been the acquittal. After that, nobody seemed to have any interest in finding out who *really* killed Christine Morris — not even the police, who acted as if they were so embarrassed by their procedural mistakes that they just wanted to forget the whole thing.

I leaned back in my chair, the notebook open on the table in front of me, and thought dark thoughts about the American justice system. If you have ever served on a jury, you may have come away with the reassuring idea that you heard everything there was to hear about the case: all the evidence, all the witnesses, all the arguments for and against the defendant.

But you could very likely be wrong. In pretrial hearings held months before your jury was empaneled, the judge might have excluded, as Sparks did, certain crucial pieces of evidence he thought could "mislead" you or "confuse" you, or at least (and of course, this is the point) cause you to entertain a few doubts. Occasionally this system of closed hearings works in favor of the defense; more often, the rulings benefit the prosecution. Judges and prosecutors both work for the state and stand on the side of the angels. Defense attorneys, on the other hand, are seen as fierce obstructers of justice. They do the devil's work, and the bar is higher for them than for the prosecution.

But in either case, it's the jurors who are the losers. The justice system may take great pride in its reliance on the "common-sense wisdom of the jury," but the court routinely ignores the jury by keeping information — often relevant and significant information — from entering the public proceedings. And the jurors never even know what vital pieces of evidence they might have missed.

I leaned forward and began leafing through the notebook, looking for the notes Johnnie's investigator had made when he spoke to Soto's alibi witness about the "private dinner" they had in San Antonio on the night of the murder. But I couldn't find them — although I did find the name and phone number of the investigator, a San Antonio private detective named Randy Olan. I pulled a small notebook out of my purse and jotted the information down. It might be worth a phone conversation with Olan, if he was still around, and if he remembered the investigation and his reasons for doubting the alibi witness. He might have come up with something related to motive.

I thought some more, then took out my phone and called Ruby. "I'm here in Houston," I said. "I've been looking at the Bowen trial notebook and —"

"I thought you said you were going to see Lucia," Ruby said. "Sheila won't be happy to hear that you're messing around in her —"

"I am not messing around in Sheila's investigation," I replied patiently. "I'm messing around in the Morris murder case, which as far as Sheila is concerned, is a very old, very cold case. But there is something you can do for me, if you have the time. At the time of the trial, Bowen's defense attorney wanted to put on a witness to testify that —"

I told her the rest of it, then told her what I wanted. "Do you think you could do that, Ruby? Today, maybe? I'm sorry, but I can't tell you whether the person has moved or is even still alive or —"

"I'll do it, China," Ruby interrupted. "I'll be glad to. But Amy has a job interview and Kate is working, so I'm babysitting with Baby Grace today. Is it okay if I take her along?"

I had to roll my eyes at the idea of Kay Scarpetta or Anna Pigeon taking a baby on an investigation. But if I wanted this done, Ruby was the best one to do it, with or without Baby Grace. She has a knack for getting people to open up and say things they wouldn't say to anyone else.

"No problem," I said. "Sure. Take Baby Grace along if you want to."

I clicked off the phone, dropped it back in my purse, and went back to paging through the notebook. By this time, I had found what I had come to find and wasn't looking for anything in particular. Which is probably why I stared for a few moments at what was in front of me without actually seeing what it was — a white business-size envelope with a note clipped to it, stuck in the inside pocket at the back of the binder.

The note was dated and said, *Unopened envelope placed in Bowen file, at Mr. Richard Bowen's request — JD.*

The envelope was dated, too, and said, *To be opened ONLY in the event of my death — RB.*

I pulled the envelope out of the pocket and turned it over. It was sealed. I held it up to the light and saw that it contained at least one sheet of folded paper and, in the corner, a small key.

I felt a brief ethical twinge, but only a *very* brief one and nothing like the twinges I've felt when I have trespassed on someone's private property without permission. Richard Bowen was in fact dead and so was his attorney. And since no one had cared enough when Bowen died to open this envelope, I doubted that anyone would be angry at me for exercising the privilege. And anyway, who would know that I was the one who had opened it? Bowen had been dead for some years. Anybody might have found it in the file and opened it, at any time — right?

Right. I looked around and spotted a pencil holder on a shelf, filled with pencils and pens, a pair of scissors, and yes, a letter opener. It was the work of a moment to slit the envelope and slide the contents out. What I read was brief, to the point — and astonishing.

Dear Mr. Carlson:
In the event that I am found dead in circumstances that suggest suicide, I hereby attest that I do not and never will contemplate killing myself.

I have, however, made an enemy of Douglas Clark — you'll recall that we talked about him. I believe that he is planning to kill me. Some years back, we were engaged in a series of illegal activities (violations of building codes) that were never found out. He has been paying me not to reveal what we did, but I am afraid he no longer trusts me to keep our secret. I have documented everything we did and put the list into a safe-deposit box at the Chase bank on

Richmond. In the event of my death, please turn the contents of the box over to the proper authorities and ask them to carefully investigate the circumstances of my death. Doug Clark ought to be their prime suspect.

The letter was signed and dated by Richard Bowen.

Well, my goodness gracious. So Florabelle Gibson had been right in her claims about the bribery — and her skepticism about the suicide. If this letter had been opened, read, and turned over to the police after Bowen's death, the cops would have conducted a homicide investigation. As it was, whatever evidence the killer might have left behind was almost certainly irretrievable. Still, if the investigator had been careful, or even a little bit suspicious . . .

I sat for a moment, thinking about what I had found, what it implied, and what I should do. Then I copied the text into my notebook, refolded the letter, and put it and the safe-deposit key back into the envelope. On the outside of the envelope, I wrote the words *Opened and read by China Bayles* and today's date, then returned the envelope to the pocket inside the back of the binder. I gathered up my things, picked up the binder, and carried it down the hall to the reception area.

Tiffany looked up at me and said brightly, "Oh, hi, Ms. Bayles. You're finished? Do you want anything? Copies, anything like that?"

"Actually, I do," I said. I opened the binder to the section documenting the defense plan to present an alternative suspect. "Could you copy these pages for me? And the hearing transcript?"

"Of course," she said. "I'll do it right now, if you don't mind waiting. It'll take a few minutes." She hurried out of the room, only a little hobbled by the outrageously short, tight skirt she was wearing. A crack shot, competent, and sexy, too, I thought — there ought to be a law.

She was back inside of ten, with a thick folder full of copies, hot off the press. "Is this all you need?" she asked.

I tucked the folder into my bag. "I'm curious, Tiff. Who is J. D.?"

"J. D.? Oh, that's Jerri Delaney. She's a paralegal who works here part-time. Why?"

"Just curious," I said. "Listen. There's some information in that binder that I especially want Mr. Brooks to review. Please put it on his desk with a note asking him to call my cell phone, and I'll tell him where to find it. Oh, and tell him it's important, so I'd appreciate a call as soon as possible. Okay?"

"Absolutely." She was already scribbling on a sticky pad. "Are you driving back this afternoon?"

I looked at my watch. "Actually, I'm dropping in to see a friend — then I'm heading home."

"Drive carefully," she said.

I nodded. "I really have to watch out for those Hummers. And the garbage trucks. They're fiendish."

"I know. Devil drivers." She gave me a sympathetic look. "Do be careful. And come back and see us soon."

The gray clouds lidded the city, trapping the heat and humidity, and stepping out of Aaron's air-conditioned office was like stepping into a sauna. Out in the car, I rolled down the window, turned on the AC, and phoned Lucia to let her know that I'd be over in a half hour. Then I called McQuaid. It wasn't going to be easy to explain just how I had happened to discover Richard Bowen's nonsuicide note in a sealed envelope in a binder in the Houston office of my former lover Aaron Brooks. But I had to try. McQuaid was working an investigation for Charlie Lipman that involved Douglas

Clark. He needed to know about this new development.

I caught him on his way to the Travis County Courthouse to look at some property records. I made my confession as brief and concise as possible, followed it up with a quick reprise of the transcript of the court hearing, a reading of my copy of Bowen's letter, and a quick summary of what Florabelle Gibson had told me about the Bowen-Clark bribery business.

"It sounds like Clark might have gotten tired of paying Bowen to keep his mouth shut," I said, "and somehow managed to lock him in his car with the garage door shut and the motor running."

There was a long, long silence. "China," McQuaid said at last, "is there no limit to the messes you stumble into?"

I frowned. "I am sorry I didn't tell you that I was going to Aaron's office. But this isn't a mess. The letter Bowen wrote is a perfectly straight-forward confession of —"

"I know what it is," he said quietly. "And it's a damn good thing you found it. But it's still pretty messy — unless Houston Homicide picked something up, some piece of evidence that can tie Clark to the scene. Otherwise —" He stopped, but I knew what he was thinking. Bowen's letter would be enough to reopen a closed investigation, but it wouldn't nail Clark. For that, the investigators would need something concrete.

After a moment, McQuaid went on. "On this other business, the Christine Morris murder. You mentioned a San Antonio investigator who questioned Soto's alibi witness. What was his name?"

"Randy Olan." I took out my notebook, found Olan's contact information, and gave it to McQuaid. "Maybe you could find out whether he's still around, and whether he remembers the case."

"Olan's around," McQuaid said. "I know the guy. He's a good investigator. I'll give him a call and see what he can tell us. You may have lucked into something, China."

"I didn't *luck* into it," I said huffily. "Luck was not a factor here. I knew what I needed, I went looking for it, and I found it."

"Manner of speaking," McQuaid said. "So what's next?"

"When Aaron calls, I'll tell him to read Bowen's letter. He needs to contact the police officer who investigated Bowen's death and turn the note over to him. I also plan to go over all of this with Sheila tonight, since the criminal activity — the bribes and code violations — occurred in Pecan Springs and involved a city employee.

371

She will probably want to contact the investigating officer in Houston and be on hand when they open Bowen's safe-deposit box." I paused. "Is there anything else I ought to be doing?"

"Sounds like you're covering the bases," McQuaid said. "What time are you getting home?"

I looked at my watch. It was almost one. "Lucia's expecting me, so I'm going to stop at her shop for a few minutes. I'll be home in time to get supper." I smiled to myself, picturing V. I. Warshawski hurrying to get home in time to cook for the family. "I'll give Sheila a call and make sure she's available this evening," I added, "but I doubt there'll be a problem. She's supposed to be in bed, flat on her back."

McQuaid chuckled. "Flat on her back, huh? While her best friend is out and about, nailing a murderer?"

"I haven't 'nailed' anybody," I retorted. "I came into accidental knowledge of serious criminal activity and I am in the process of notifying the proper authorities. After that, it's up to the guys with badges. Isn't that the way it's supposed to work?"

"Oh, right," McQuaid said sarcastically and chuckled again.

The answering machine was on at Sheila's, so I left a message, then began to think serious thoughts about lunch. Since Aaron had canceled, I needed to get something to eat before I headed over to Lucia's. There's a fast-food joint on every corner, but I knew of a place where I could get something reasonably healthy. I drove over to Potbelly on the Southwest Freeway service road and got a Mediterranean sandwich: hummus, feta, artichoke hearts, cukes, and roasted red peppers on thin-sliced wheat bread.

I'm sorry to report that I gobbled it down more quickly than it deserved.

CHAPTER TWELVE

Yerba buena (*Micromeria douglasii,* syn. *Satureja douglasii*) means "good herb" in Spanish. It is a low-growing, aromatic herb of the mint family that is known and used as a medicinal plant in many cultures. The minty flavor (resembling spearmint) makes it a popular addition to salads and desserts, while its lemony aroma is used for scent and fragrance. When dried, it produces a pleasant cup of mildly minty tea. Yerba buena is thought to bring good luck.

China Bayles
"Herbs of Good and Ill Omen"
Pecan Springs Enterprise

Lucia's Garden is located in a shopping center on West Alabama, in the Upper Kirby district of Houston, in an upscale area of high-fashion shopping, chef-heavy restaurants, high-end home furnishing shops, and high-rise condominiums. But it didn't start there. It began back in the mid-1980s as a small one-room shop, where Lucia and her husband, Michael, shared their passion for gardening, cooking, and herb crafting with the Houston community, and has evolved through several homes, always with a focus on earth-based lifestyle.

In its current incarnation, Lucia's is a substantial bookstore and gift shop stocked with herbs and herbal products, music, incense, crystals, and intriguing gift items — "tools," Lucia says, "to help each other live more mindful and fulfilling lives." Like the Crystal Cave, her shop is also a community learning center featuring bodyworkers and healers — the kind of place where Ruby would feel right at home. And Lucia herself teaches cookery, aromatherapy, and meditation to the many friends she has collected over the years. The South Texas Unit of the Herb Society of America is located in Houston. Lucia is an active member and frequent speaker.

As I got out of the car, I saw several people coming out of the shop carrying packages, and when I opened the door and went in, Lucia herself came toward me. She is dark haired and vivid, with a dramatic flair for vibrant makeup, eclectic costumes, and exotic jewelry — a lot like Ruby, except that Lucia is short and pleasantly roundish where Ruby is tall, thin, and angular. Today, Lucia was dressed in a flowing red tunic over a long-sleeved, scoop-necked black tee, garnished with a soft paisley scarf, a necklace of crimson garnet and warm amber beads.

"China!" she cried and enveloped me in a huge hug. "What a delight to see you! Did you and your friend enjoy your lunch at Tiny Boxwood's?" I had told her that Aaron and I planned to eat there.

I made a regretful face. "He had to bail a client out of trouble. I picked up a sandwich at Potbelly's on the way over here."

"Oh, too bad," she said and added ruefully, "We could have gone to Tiny's together, but I'm here by myself today." She gave a little shrug of her shoulders. "I'm sure you know how that is."

"I certainly do," I said. "I wouldn't be in Houston if Monday weren't my day off." I glanced around at the L-shaped space, the walls filled with wooden shelves, antique pine hutches laden with fragrant soaps and essential oils, and glass display cases filled with handcrafted jewelry. "Your shop looks so great," I added, taking a deep breath of the sweet, pungent fragrance that filled the air. "I always admire your creative displays."

It's true. Nobody can build a display more artistically than Lucia and her longtime manager, Joel Miles. She travels extensively, she remembers everything she sees, and she comes back brimming with wonderful ideas for the shop.

"Well, let me show you some of the gift items I've begun carrying," Lucia said enthusiastically. I spent the next few minutes admiring her displays and picking up ideas for things I might like to stock at Thyme and Seasons and new ways to display what I already have. My shop is not nearly as sophisticated and exotic as hers — it has a different character, more rustic and down-home, like the Texas Hill Country itself. Which doesn't mean that it couldn't use a little more pizzazz. Irene Cameron's paintings, or some of the lovely gift items Lucia always carries.

We were in the book section of the shop and I was making notes on some of the latest books on herbs and native Texas plants, when something caught my eye. It was a book of the paintings of Frida Kahlo, the Mexican painter, displayed on a shelf with a half-dozen painted *alebrijes* (fantastical folk figures), a pair of decorated maracas, an Aztec calendar, some lovely Mexican embroidered cuffs, and several tin sculptures.

377

The display was intriguing, but it was the book I was interested in.

It was titled *Finding Frida Kahlo.* I picked it up and began leafing through the pages. It was a collection of photographs documenting a treasure trove of twelve hundred recently discovered paintings, letters, diaries, recipes, jottings, notebooks, and an enormous variety of memorabilia. A small yellow-haired doll. A roll of cherry-printed shelf paper that the artist had used as a journal. A love letter to her husband, Diego Rivera, which she ends with, *I ask my heart, why you and not someone else? Toad of my soul. Frida K.* Twelve hundred bits and pieces of an enormously gifted and creative life, which had apparently been stowed away in five dusty wooden boxes in a dark corner of a converted textile factory in the Mexican village of San Miguel de Allende, discovered recently, decades after her death.

"Wow." I whistled between my teeth. "What a remarkable treasure! I'll bet the art world is dancing a jig." After another few moments of looking, I put the book back on the display and asked the question that was nudging itself into my mind, like an impatient stranger, wanting an introduction. "Lucia, have you ever heard of María Izquierdo? There's a private museum in Pecan

Springs that has one of her pieces."

Lucia brightened. "Izquierdo? Oh, yes!" she exclaimed. "Everyone who knows anything about Mexican artists knows her work." She sighed. "Used to be, Izquierdo was one of the painters whose work was affordable, but not anymore. If you want to see it, you have to go to museums."

I thought again of Irene Cameron, who had studied Mexican art but said that she didn't know anything about Izquierdo. That still made me uneasy, although I wasn't sure why.

Pulling her dark eyebrows together, Lucia picked up *Finding Frida Kahlo* and began turning the pages. "And as far as the art world dancing a jig about this discovery — well, that's not exactly what's happened. There's an enormous controversy over this collection of Kahlo's work, China. Some people are saying that it's all a big fake."

"A fake?" I asked, startled. "The paintings, you mean?"

"The paintings, the diaries, the letters — the entire archive. The experts can't seem to bring themselves to believe that *any* of it is real. It's all been denounced as a forgery by lots of big-time art critics, most of whom haven't actually examined the stuff." She rolled her eyes. "They're saying that Princeton Architectural Press, which published this book, is the victim of a gigantic hoax. And that the author, Barbara Levine, and the antique dealers who claim to have found the material have practiced a gigantic con."

I stared at Lucia. "A *fake*?" I repeated. My skin was prickling.

Nodding, she put the book back on the display. "Right. But personally, I don't agree. I think it's real, every bit of it. The big problem, in my view, is that the so-called experts seem to believe that they have the authority to say what's authentic. In this case, they don't want to admit that somebody, anybody — other than themselves, of course — can know a Kahlo when they see one." Her chuckle was sarcastic. "In fact, these experts didn't even need to inspect the archive, up close and personal, I mean. They knew what they wanted to see. They didn't need to use their eyes."

Know one when they see one. The phrase echoed in my mind.

"They didn't discover it," Lucia added, "so they knew without looking that it was fake."

Didn't need to use their eyes.

"But while this Kahlo collection is probably real," Lucia went on, "there's plenty of forged artwork out there. The galleries and auction houses are flooded with it, and some of the forgeries are so good that they go undetected." She sighed. "Would you believe?"

"I'm no expert," I said quietly. "I really don't know." But that wasn't quite true. I was beginning to think that I could make an educated guess.

"Well, we will never solve all the problems of the art world, China," Lucia said. "I have some new yerba buena tea. Let's brew a cup and have a chat. I need to catch up on your life. How's everything in Pecan Springs? How's business? Have you had much of a summer slump? Are you still doing that farmers' market? Oh, and do you think you could maybe talk Ruby into coming over and taking part in our psychic fair next month? She could teach whatever she wanted — astrology, runes, the tarot, the I Ching. She could do readings, too. I'm sure she'd be a huge hit."

"I'll be talking to her this afternoon," I said. "I'll ask her if she's interested."

By the time I got back to my car, the sky had turned an ominous, metallic gray with thunderheads piling up in purple-black billows against the western horizon, an occasional lightning bolt darting from one bruised-looking cloud to another. It promised to be a rainy drive home, on slick roads. But I had left early enough to get ahead of the outbound commuting traffic, which was a relief. I kept a close eye on the rearview mirror for Hummers and garbage trucks, but so far, so good.

Nobody was answering at Sheila's house, but when I finally got Ruby on the phone, she had just put Baby Grace down for a nap. They had spent the last hour visiting with Mrs. Kern, she said. Mrs. Adele Kern, the lady who lived on the street behind Christine Morris' house and who (according to the hearing transcript) had been prepared to testify for the defense that she had seen Roberto Soto's late-model blue Mercedes parked in the vacant lot on the night of the murder. It was testimony that the Bowen jury should have heard — *would* have heard, if His Honor hadn't ruled it out.

"I'm surprised to hear that Mrs. Kern still lives in that house," I said. "It's been quite a while." But maybe I shouldn't have been. In that pretty neighborhood, people tend to settle in and stay for a while, especially if their families are grown.

"Not only does Mrs. Kern still live in that house," Ruby said, "but she remembers the whole episode very clearly. She was terribly disappointed that she wasn't called to testify in Bowen's trial, and the thought still rankles. She didn't much like Christine Morris, you see. Mrs. Kern has a very strong judgmental streak and she disapproved of her entertaining a male guest overnight. She's still convinced that Christine Morris' 'arty boyfriend' had something to do with her death." She paused, reflecting. "No, it's stronger than that, China. She thinks the boyfriend put on Bowen's shoes and beat her to death with Bowen's golf club."

The "arty boyfriend," Roberto Soto. Yes, I thought. It was a damn good thing that Johnnie was able to get an acquittal without Mrs. Kern's testimony. But the judge's error in excluding the evidence — for it *was* an error, in my opinion, and would have been overturned had there been an appeal — had let a possible murderer go free.

I sucked in my breath. Free. Free to kill again? *Had* he killed again? Was there any connection between Soto and Karen Prior? If so, what was it? The image of *Muerte llega pronto* came into my mind and stayed there.

The rain was beginning to splat down on the windshield, fat, heavy drops that sprayed out and washed in muddy rivulets on my dusty windshield. I flicked the windshield washer and turned on the wipers.

"Mrs. Kern loved Baby Grace, of course!" Ruby went on happily. "And she completely understood why I brought her with me. Before we got around to discussing the murder, we had a very nice talk about grandchildren and how important it is for them to grow up with their grandmamas living close by. She showed me photos of her own family. She has great-grandchildren!"

That's what I mean about Ruby having a knack with people. By the time she got to the difficult questions about the night of the murder, she and Mrs. Kern were old and dear friends, just two baby-besotted grandmothers cooing together over their grandbabies.

"But that's not all, China," Ruby added. "That blue Mercedes Mrs. Kern saw on the night of the murder? She has seen the car parked in that vacant lot lately, driven by that same 'arty' guy. Once or twice, it's been parked there all night — which of course gets Mrs. Kern's attention, since she knows that Sharyn Tillotson lives in that place all alone." She chuckled wryly. "To tell the truth, Mrs. Kern is a bit of a Mrs. Grundy. She suspects that Sharyn is having an affair with the guy, and she thoroughly disapproves."

"The very same blue Mercedes?" I asked doubtfully.

"She doesn't think it's the identical car," Ruby replied. "Just a later model. Lots of people stay with the same *kind* of car, you know, year after year." She laughed. "My crazy uncle Dave had this thing about Saabs, for instance. He bought a new car every three or four years, always a Saab, and always a gray one. Dave's new gray Saab got to be a family joke."

Well, now. Sharyn Tillotson had told us that Roberto Soto had continued to do curatorial work for the foundation — but she had definitely left the impression that this had taken place sometime in the past. And she certainly had not mentioned that Soto had been a recent guest. Was Mrs. Kern right? Was Sharyn having an affair with her dead cousin's lover, who might also have been her cousin's *murderer*? Just how much did Sharyn know about Christine's death?

The rain was coming down harder now, and the windshield was beginning to fog. I turned up the air conditioner and swiped at the windshield with my hand, clearing a space. There was something else I needed to know. "Ruby," I said, "have you figured

out why you weren't able to see the painting at the Morris house yesterday?"

"Not really," Ruby said with a sigh. "I'm
still trying to puzzle out the hexagram the I
Ching gave me. Hexagram 20 — Kuan. Seeing and being seen. Or maybe setting an
example for others to look at and follow.
But if the painting is supposed to be an
example for others to follow, why couldn't I
see it? Or maybe it means that my not seeing the painting is an example for others to
follow. Or maybe —" She broke off with a
sigh. "The I Ching can sometimes be *very*
frustrating. It can mean too many contradictory things."

"Plug this into your thinking," I said. I
told her what I had learned in my conversation with Lucia and what was going through
my head. That took a while, and when I was
finished, there was a whispered "Wow," followed by a long, long silence. It was raining
harder now, and I turned up the windshield
wipers. *Whap whap whap.* I peered into the
stormy distance, hands on the wheel at two
and ten. If the rain kept up like this for very
long, it was not going to be a pleasant drive
back to Pecan Springs.

After a moment, I asked, "Are you still
there, Ruby? What do you think? Does that
help at all? Does it —"

A pickup truck passed me, going too fast, spraying sheets of water that flooded my windshield and curtained my view of the road. The woman driver was hunched over the steering wheel as if she were Danica Patrick and this were the Daytona 500.

"Does it *help*?" Ruby cried with great excitement. "Of course it helps! China, that's the answer! Why didn't I figure it out for myself?" She paused, and I could almost see her frowning, turning matters over in her mind. "There was that painting, hanging on the wall right in front of my eyes, and I didn't *see* it. Why? Because it isn't the real thing, that's why. It isn't the original. It's a *copy*. That's what I think."

That's what I thought, too, and I didn't need the I Ching to prompt me. The real *Muerte llega pronto* had been sold at auction for a cool quarter of a million dollars. The painting that was hanging on the wall at the Morris house was a forgery, a fake. If that was true, who else knew? Had Christine known it — was that why she died? I thought of the Sotheby's catalog in Karen's briefcase and remembered that Karen herself had produced a documentary on art forgeries. Had *she* known it? Was that why she was killed?

But wait just a minute. I had Ruby's

intuition — her inability to "see" the painting — to thank for the notion that the Morris' *Muerte* was a forgery. How did I know that Sotheby's *Muerte* was the real thing?

Maybe it, too, was a forgery, and the real *Muerte* was on someone else's wall.

Come to that, how many copies of *Muerte* might there be, each one seeming to be the real one, the original?

And what about the other paintings in the Morris collection? Were they forgeries? How many? Who put them there? Did Sharyn know? Who had painted —

I reined myself in. I was speculating, guessing, getting too far out front of the available facts. And it was all too confusing, a series of images dancing in my head, combining and recombining like a Cubist painting, or a hall of mirrors, each one reflecting the image in all the others. It was making my head hurt.

"Listen, China," Ruby said. "There's something else. I'm really sorry to tell you this, but Blackie called a little while ago. Sheila is back in the hospital."

"Uh-oh," I said. "She's still carrying the baby? She hasn't miscarried?"

"Bad news," Ruby said. "I'm sorry to tell you, but —"

The Danica Patrick wannabe was now

about fifteen car lengths in front of me, still in the left lane, passing another car. Her pickup truck looked like it was hydroplaning, and I tapped the brake, slowing down.

"But what?" I asked.

"But it's an ectopic pregnancy." Ruby's voice changed. "You know — where the baby grows in your Fallopian tube, instead of your uterus, where it's supposed to."

"Jeez," I exclaimed fervently, as the pickup ahead of me fishtailed, slammed into the car it was passing, and knocked both of them off the road and down a steep slope. The pickup rolled twice, bounced, and settled on its roof. I clutched the wheel. "Oh, God, I hope she makes it!" I cried.

"I really don't think it's *that's* bad," Ruby said in a comforting tone.

"Yes, it is," I said. "It's a killer."

I was pulling onto the shoulder to see what I could do to help, when behind me, I saw the rotating blue light of a police car and heard the wail of the siren. Ahead of me, in the eastbound lanes, another cop car materialized and bounced across the grass median. Help was already arriving. I would just be in the way, and it was dangerous to stop along here, especially in this rainstorm. I pulled back onto the road.

"But she's not going to die, of course,"

Ruby said comfortingly. "I read somewhere that one out of every hundred pregnancies is ectopic. It used to be terribly dangerous, but not these days."

"Sorry," I muttered. "There was a wreck, a bad one, right in front of me. Some woman driving too fast for the road conditions. She sideswiped a car and rolled her pickup. Twice. But the cops are on the scene, so I'm going on. There's nothing I can do to help."

Of course, I could stop and tell one of the cops that she was driving too fast, but they would figure that out for themselves pretty quick, if they hadn't already.

"Gosh," Ruby said. "Sounds bad. I'm glad *you* weren't involved."

"Me, too." I went back to the subject. "What do the doctors say about Sheila? What are they going to do?"

"They've already done it," Ruby said. "A laparoscopy. It's a ninety-minute procedure, and when Blackie called, she was already in the recovery room. Everything went just fine and there's no reason to think she can't get pregnant again. Blackie said she'd be going home early in the evening." She sighed. "I'm so sorry about the baby, but —"

She didn't finish her sentence but I knew what she was thinking. Sheila and Blackie could have another baby. And maybe the next time, things would be a little more comfortable for both of them.

"Yeah. It's too bad," I said. "But it could have been worse." I took a deep breath. "Listen, Ruby, it's raining pretty hard and I can't see the highway very far ahead. I'd better pay attention to my driving. We can talk about all this later, when I get back to Pecan Springs."

And the way it was raining — the clouds had opened and it was pouring buckets now — that might be a while. The traffic had slowed from its usual seventy-plus miles an hour to a more reasonable sixty, and then to fifty-five, which was a very good thing, and I was staying in the right lane. But the rain was coming in such heavy sheets that the wipers were barely coping, and I was worried about somebody smashing into my rear end. I turned on my hazard lights, clenched my teeth, and focused on the road ahead, trying not to think about anything important — about Christine Morris' murder, about Johnnie's alternative suspect, about Richard Bowen's possible homicide, about Karen Prior's mugging, about the Izquierdo forgery (if that was what it was), about Sheila's ectopic pregnancy. I cleared my mind as best I could and simply concentrated on driving.

Until Justine Wyzinski called. At which point I had to pull off the road and into a convenience store parking lot. I find it a challenge to talk to Justine under the best circumstances. Driving in a torrential rainstorm, on a busy highway, it would be suicide.

When Justine and I were in law school, everybody called her the Whiz because she was so smart. She knew the answer to our professors' questions long before the rest of us, and could come up with a more or less comprehensible theory while we were still sorting out the facts. I was out-of-my-mind jealous of her and worked like crazy to keep her from getting more than a half mile ahead of me, which earned me the nickname of Hot Shot. This competitive insanity went on until we both made it to the relative security of Law Review and could relax a little and grow into a wary mutual respect. When I left the law and bought Thyme and Seasons, the Whiz publicly expressed the conviction that I had lost all my marbles and ought to be committed forthwith, while I privately thought she was nuts to keep on doing what she was doing, at the speed at which she was doing it. But aside from that small difference of opinion, we've remained friends, and every now and then, we even manage to be useful to one another.

"So," Justine said, without preamble, "you're interested in Roberto Soto. What's up with that?" Without stopping for breath, she added, "Make it quick, though, China. I'm in the parking garage on my way to a deposition, and I'm already twenty minutes late."

I was not surprised. The Whiz is a multitasking speed demon who constantly operates on warp drive, which is one reason I find it so hard to talk to her. She is always on her way somewhere, with at least three things to do when she gets there, and she is always running late. (Maybe I find this depressing because she reminds me of the person I used to be.)

I told her the story as succinctly as I could, beginning with Christine Morris' art collection and her subsequent murder, going on to Mrs. Kern's excluded testimony and Bowen's acquittal, and concluding with Bowen's supposed suicide, Karen Prior's mugging, and the Sotheby's catalog I had found in her briefcase with the marked photograph of *Muerte llega pronto,* which had sold for a quarter million dollars while a possible forgery of that painting hung in the Morris Museum. Quite a lot of facts to tuck into a three-minute summary statement. But I'm pretty good at that.

"Why can't you bring me something simple?" the Whiz complained when I was finished. I could hear her huffing and puffing — climbing the parking garage stairs, I guessed. The Whiz is five foot two, shaped like a fireplug, and twenty-five pounds over her law school weight. Her usual working costume is a baggy khaki jacket with a missing button and a stain on the lapel, a blouse that won't stay tucked, and a dark skirt that won't stay straight. Every day is a bad hair day and her plastic-rimmed glasses are always crooked because she jerks them off and uses them to punctuate her sentences. The Whiz does not dress for success. But that's because she doesn't have to. In fact, dressing down is a good thing for her. It gives other people something to feel superior about.

"I know it's complicated," I replied. "But that's why I need your help. If it were a simple matter, I could handle it myself."

The Whiz raised her voice over the screech of tires and the sound of a car peeling out. A valet, no doubt, returning a parked automobile to its owner, minus several ounces of wheel rubber. "Yeah, but this is even more complicated than the usual tangle of stuff you drag me into, China. And anyway, it's your turn. You owe *me,* remember? Not the other way around."

It was true. The last time I called Justine, I needed her help with Sally, McQuaid's ex-wife and Brian's mother, who was a person of interest in her sister's homicide. Justine isn't crazy about Sally, but she had rolled up her sleeves and jumped right in, and I was grateful. But I needed her again, regardless of whose turn it was.

"I know I owe you," I said. "And I'll make it up to you. But could you —"

"Could I help you collar Soto?" she asked. In the background, a car alarm began whooping and she raised her voice. "I sincerely doubt it. He's one slick buckaroo, and art fraud is a hard thing to prove. Expensive, too. Expert witnesses don't come cheap. But what did you have in mind?"

"For starters," I said, "what's he up to these days?" I heard a distant car horn, echoing, the way it does in a parking garage.

"He's still in the gallery business," Justine said. "Roberto Soto, Fine Art. In fact, he just made headlines, artistically speaking, with a big exhibit — three well-known Latin American painters. The San Antonio art aficionados were over the moon. Google his gallery name and you'll find the newspaper story."

"Any indication that he's back in the art fraud business?"

"He never admitted to that, you know," Justine replied. I heard the ding of a bell and the whishing of a heavy door. She was getting on an elevator. "He maintained that he had no idea that the painting he sold was a fake. He pled to a lesser charge, paid a fine, and that was it. Period. Paragraph. End of story."

"You got court costs and restitution for your client," I reminded her. "It was a forged work said to be by Dr. Atl?" I paused, thinking of something I had wanted to ask her. "Any idea who painted the forgery?" If I had the answer to that question —

"Yeah, that's right, it was supposed to be a painting by Gerardo Murillo," Justine said. "A.k.a. Dr. Atl. But people don't remember that ancient stuff, China. As far as Soto's art business is concerned, it's water over the dam. His clients either don't know that he once sold a forgery — or they don't give a flying fig."

Three *dings* and the sound of the elevator door opening. Justine was getting off at the third floor. "And as far as Soto himself was concerned," she added, "what he paid my client was simply the cost of doing business. He didn't admit guilt there, either. He just ponied up."

"There's an Atl in the Morris collection," I said. "Christine Morris acquired almost all her paintings through Soto. He continued to do curatorial work for the foundation after she was dead." I paused. "And one of the neighbors thinks he's doing sleepovers with the current head of the foundation, Christine Morris' cousin."

I could hear Justine's heels clicking. She was moving fast. "An Atl painting? A real one, Hot Shot?"

"How should I know?" I replied. "If the Izquierdo painting is a fake, who's to say that the Atl is real? Both of them likely came through Soto."

More *click-click*s. "So what are you looking for?"

"Motive." I drummed my fingers on the steering wheel. "A motive for murder." Motive was what had stopped Johnnie. If he'd had motive, he might have gotten Soto in as an alternative suspect, which would have forced the police to take another look at him. "If I'm right," I added, "there are *two* dead women — Christine and Karen — and one murderer." I thought of Sharyn Tillotson, who was either an accomplice or a potential victim, or both. "And if he's not stopped, there could be a third." This one would be an accident, probably. A fatal fall down those glass stairs. They looked like the perfect setting to stage an accident.

Justine's footsteps slowed. "Can't promise," she said cautiously. "But I know somebody I can talk to — an insider in the business. Somebody who owes me a lot more than she can ever repay. I'll call her when I get a minute. Maybe she'll give us something we can use."

"Good." I liked the sound of that *we*. "Oh, and what about the artist who painted that forged Atl? Any idea who did it?"

"No, but I'll ask my insider. She keeps her ear to the ground." The sound of a door opening and the murmur of voices. "Listen, Hot Shot, I gotta go now. There's a roomful of people waiting for me."

"Big thanks," I said, to a broken connection.

I had gotten as far as Brenham when Aaron called. Brenham is the home of Blue Bell Creameries' contented cows, who produce the best ice cream in the country — at least according to its advertising campaign. Our family likes the ice cream, although we suspect those cows aren't any more contented than cows attached to automatic milking machines everywhere in the country.

I had driven out of the rain, the highway was dry, the sun was shining, and I was in a better mood, halfway to Pecan Springs and making good time, when my cell dinged.

"Yo, China," Aaron said on the speakerphone. "Tiff left the Bowen binder on my desk, with a note to call you. What's up? Are you still in town? If you are, how about supper? It'll just be me, and it'll have to be late. Paula is working tonight, and I have to finish a brief."

Ah, life in the two-party fast lane. "Thanks for the invitation, but I'm already halfway home," I said. "Listen, Aaron, what's up is a little bit sticky. If you'll open that binder to the back, you'll find an envelope in the inside pocket. You need to read the letter that's in it."

"How about if I do that in the morning? As I say, I have a client —"

"Right now, Aaron, please. You'll see why."

I heard an exaggerated sigh, followed by the rustle of paper and, a moment later, a muttered "What the hell —" A longer silence, and then a low whistle. "Jeez," he said.

"Yeah," I said. "Please see that the letter

— you might want to copy it first — gets to the lead investigator in Bowen's death. He may have turned up something suspicious in the course of his investigation, and what's in that letter might take him where he needs to go. Give him my name and phone number. I've been doing some research into that business about the building code violations. I'll be glad to answer his questions and put him in touch with one of Bowen's former coworkers. She can testify to the details." Florabelle would be delighted to tell her story, especially if she thought it would help to nail Bowen's killer.

"Okay," Aaron said. "I'll get on it right now. I think I'll give Paula a call, too. The DA's office might have an interest in this. There was a pause, and his voice grew softer, regretful. "Sorry about the lunch we missed, China. Rain check, next time you're in town?"

"Rain check," I said briskly, although by now the sun was shining.

I was just making the turn off the highway and into Pecan Springs when my cell dinged again.

"Hot Shot," Justine said, "there's a bit of good luck — maybe — to report. That artist you were asking about? The one who painted the copy of the Atl painting? I've got a possibility for you."

"Tell me," I said eagerly. "Who?"

She told me, and I was astonished. And then the pieces fell into place and I wasn't astonished, just surprised and chagrined that I hadn't guessed. The clues had been right in front of me all the time. I just hadn't put them together.

"Well, duh," I said.

"It's not confirmed," Justine warned me. "My informant is only reporting what she heard. The case didn't go to trial, and the painter was never charged. Don't forget: it's not illegal to make a copy of a painting — as long as it's to be sold as a copy. The state has to prove that the painter intended to defraud, and the evidentiary burden is high. And afterward, Soto seems to have scrubbed everything. He has a whole new client list, other artists, and the whole thing has been forgotten."

Until Karen Prior — who had filmed a documentary on art fraud and had interviewed several experts on the subject — saw *Muerte llega pronto* in the Sotheby's catalog and began asking questions.

CHAPTER THIRTEEN

The daisy (*Bellis perennis*) is not just a pretty plant, but a useful medicinal herb. Roman military surgeons soaked bandages in the juice of pressed daisies to treat soldiers' wounds. The English herbalist John Gerard (1545–1612) calls the daisy "Bruisewort" and describes it as an unfailing remedy in "all kinds of paines and aches" and a cure for fevers and inflammations of "alle the inwarde parts."

In Germany, daisies that were picked for drying between noon and one o'clock were thought to bring good luck. And in Celtic legend, the spirits of stillborn children were reborn as daisies.

China Bayles
"Herbs of Good and Ill Omen"
Pecan Springs Enterprise

I wasn't going to make it in time for supper, so I phoned Brian (McQuaid wasn't home yet, either) and told him to take a taco casserole out of the freezer and put it into the microwave. Gretchen volunteered to throw a salad together, and there were various veggies in the freezer, as well as cookies and ice cream. Nobody was going to die of starvation before I got home.

I didn't have a plan for what was coming next, exactly. But I knew what I had to do, and it couldn't wait. I wasn't risking a charge of obstruction of justice, since justice hadn't started turning its wheels just yet. And under the circumstances, I didn't feel there was any particular danger. I wasn't trolling for a member of the Mafia.

Still, I thought it might be smart to let somebody know where I was headed. Mc-Quaid would raise a fuss about what I had in mind, so I tactfully didn't bother him. Instead, I left a message on Ruby's voice mail — and smiled when I thought it was sort of like leaving a trail of bread crumbs behind when you go into the forest in search of . . . whatever. You might stumble over a dragon. Or two.

I parked the car a couple of doors down from my destination, went up the walk, took a very deep breath, and knocked on the front door.

I was surprised when Paul Cameron opened it, looking very much himself in khaki slacks and a blue polo shirt that set off his white hair. But the blankness in his gray eyes gave him away. He knew he should know me, and he didn't.

"Hello, Paul." I held out my hand. "China Bayles — Mike McQuaid's wife. We came to your retirement party."

Some of the confusion cleared, but not all. "Of course." He shook my hand, then held on to it. "Haven't seen you in a long while, Dr. Bayles. I'm afraid I've forgotten what department you're in — biology, maybe? You do research in plants? Are you teaching this summer?"

"I'm not on the faculty," I said, extricating my hand. "But I do work with plants. It's Mike McQuaid, my husband, who's the faculty member. He teaches in the criminal justice department. But not this summer. He's doing some private investigative work." At one time, Paul had known all this, and he seemed embarrassed at having forgotten.

"Oh, now I remember," he said, attempting a laugh. "Pecan Springs' very own James Bond. Guns and car chases and wild women. Must be an exciting job." He leaned forward, his eyes glinting. "Tell me, Mrs. Double-Oh-Seven. Would your husband do some investigating for me? I have a little mystery I'd like to solve. Nothing important or monumental, just a small personal puzzle that has been annoying me lately. I wish I could find out . . ." His voice trailed off. The blankness came into his eyes again and he frowned. "Find out . . . what?" he murmured. "Now, what was it I wanted to find out?"

"I'm sure it'll come to you," I said awkwardly. I paused. "Is Irene here? I'd like to talk to her for a few moments."

"Irene? Irene?"

For a moment, I wondered if he remembered who she was. Then he nodded. "Oh, yes, Irene — ever the industrious one, painting all hours of the day and night. She's in her studio over the garage." He put his finger to his lips and made a shushing noise. "But don't tell her you talked to me. She thinks I'm having a nap, and she thought she locked the bedroom door so I couldn't get out. She wouldn't like it if she knew what I . . ." He stopped, and a sly, cagey look crossed his face. "If she knew about the little surprise I'm cooking up for her."

"I won't tell her," I said with a smile. "It'll be just our secret."

"Just our secret," he said and laughed heartily. "That's good, Mrs. Bond. You go right on back there and see her, then. I'm not allowed, of course. She's says she's working on something for me and she doesn't want me to see it, so her studio's off-limits. When she's not there, she keeps the studio door locked so I won't forget and wander in." He paused uncertainly. "Tell me — am I supposed to know what you wanted to see her about?"

"I don't think so," I said carelessly. "I wanted to ask her about some flower paintings she was thinking of doing for my shop."

He lowered his voice to a conspiratorial whisper. "When you go up there, see if you can get a look at what she's painting and tell me. I would really like to know. It's one of the mysteries I've been pondering. Now, if I could only remember the other . . ."

From inside the house, I heard a sharp popping sound. Paul heard it, too, and made a sour face.

"Uh-oh," he said, in a childlike voice. "Sounds like I forgot to turn something off. I'd better go see what it is. Irene will be so annoyed with me." And he shut the door in my face.

It was sad to see Paul Cameron in such a state, but there wasn't time to think of that now. I took special care to climb the wooden garage stairs as quietly as I could, and when

I reached the door at the top I didn't bother to knock. Instead, I simply turned the knob. Lucky for me, it wasn't locked. I pushed it open, stepped inside, and silently closed the door behind me.

"Hello, Irene," I said in a casual, conversational tone.

Her easel faced the door where I stood, the afternoon light from the north windows falling over her shoulder and onto the large canvas that was hidden from my view. She stepped out from behind the easel, staring wide-eyed at me, her mouth falling open. She was wearing her smock, and there was a smear of paint on her cheek.

"China!" she exclaimed uneasily. "You . . . you startled me. I thought the door was locked. I didn't hear you knock." She turned quickly to whip a paint-stained cloth off a chair and throw it over the canvas.

"I didn't," I said and stepped forward. "I just barged right in. I'm curious, Irene. I'd love to see what you're working on. Paul says I should try to get a look and tell him what it is — although of course I won't. Let me have a look. I can keep a secret." Although if this was what I thought it was, it wouldn't be a secret for long.

"Oh, no, no, please!" she cried. She stepped forward, trying to block me. "It's not ready for anybody to see yet. I've just been fooling around. It's not —"

I pulled the cloth off the easel, and there it was. A dramatic painting of an erupting volcano against a purple-black sky, fiery lava spilling over the peaks of a forbidding mountain range and pouring in bloodred rivulets through a field of volcanic rock. Propped on a table off to one side was a large photograph of the painting she was copying. The signature was conspicuous in the lower left corner: Dr. Atl.

I stood for a moment, studying the painting, which looked like it belonged in the same series as the one I had seen in the museum. Behind me, I could hear Irene's ragged breathing and something like a low whimper. I turned to her and said, very quietly, "It was you, wasn't it, Irene? You copied *Death Come Quickly* for Roberto Soto, didn't you?"

Now, if I had been a fictional sleuth in a mystery entitled *F Is for Forgery* and if Irene had been the villain, we would have had a little excitement here. Her eyes would have narrowed and she would have picked up something heavy — the big burnished copper pot on the floor a couple of feet away, or the stainless steel bucket that held her brushes — and swung it at my head. I would have been hit hard enough to see a cascade of stars, but in spite of the blood running down my face from the deep cut on my forehead, I would have ducked and rushed her, tackling her in the middle and knocking her onto the floor, where she would have used her training as a champion college wrestler to pin me in a cobra clutch until I passed out.

At which point she would have made good her escape down the stairs, taking her forged painting with her. She would have dashed for her car, with the idea of driving down to San Antonio to join her business associate, Roberto Soto. She wouldn't have gotten there, though, because as she sped through the red light at the corner of Nueces and the I-35 frontage road, she would have T-boned a squad car. Her car would have careened off a utility pole, exploded, and burned, and the forged painting would have been reduced to a cinder, while she would have been toted off to the hospital, where the police would have charged her with . . . well, something. As the Whiz says, when it comes to art forgery, it's difficult to make a criminal fraud charge stick, especially when there was nothing left of the evidence but a handful of ash. Maybe they just charged her with running a red light, assault on a cop car, and assault on me.

But we weren't going to have that kind of excitement, at least, not today. I was just me and Irene wasn't a villain, let alone a champion college wrestler. She was just an ordinary woman with a gift for creating art. She had made a bad choice, got trapped in a horrible situation, and was deeply conscious of her guilt and terrified that she might be involved in something much worse than forgery.

She stared at me for a moment, tears welling in her eyes and spilling down her cheeks. Then her hands went to her face and she sank into a chair, sobbing desperately. I put my hand on her shoulder, then knelt beside her and let her cry.

"Tell me, Irene," I said softly, after a few minutes. "This can all be worked out, I'm sure."

"I . . . I can't," she said. "It's too complicated. It's —"

"Yes, you can," I said. "I can't help you unless you tell me the whole story. The whole *true* story. And you can't think of the others right now — Roberto Soto, Sharyn Tillotson, and whoever else is involved. You don't want to get dragged into whatever else they've done. You have to look out for yourself. And Paul. If you're not around to

410

take care of him, he'll be completely lost."

"Whatever else they've done?" She lifted her head and looked at me fearfully, trying to judge how much I knew.

"Yes. Criminal acts that are worse than forgery. *Much* worse." I let her chew on that for a moment, then added, very quietly, "Do you know who killed Christine Morris and Karen Prior?"

Her face blanched. "No!" she cried. "No, I swear I don't! At least, not for sure. All I know is —" She bent double, her hands clasped over her head, and dissolved into a flood of tears.

"What?" I asked urgently. I put my hand on her arm. "*What* do you know?"

"That Roberto . . ." Her voice was muffled. "That Roberto killed Karen Prior."

"How do you know that?"

She was wrenched with a bitter sobbing.

"*How* do you know that, Irene?" I persisted. "I can't help you — and Paul — unless you tell me."

At the mention of Paul's name, the sobs slowed. After a moment, she straightened her shoulders, took a deep breath, and sat up.

"I . . . I went over to the museum to hang my florals in the lounge one afternoon a week or so ago. Roberto and Sharyn were in the office and the door was open. They didn't know I was there." She wrapped her arms around herself, shivering. "Roberto said that Karen had somehow found out about the Izquierdo painting. He was . . . very upset. He said she was going to ruin everything and he would have to —" She swallowed hard.

"Have to what, Irene?"

"Have to make sure she didn't tell what she knew to the others."

"What others?"

"The members of the museum board. And the . . ." She gulped. "And the police."

"What did Sharyn say?"

She shuddered. "She said, 'I hope you don't have to kill her.' And he said, 'I will if that's the only way.'"

"Did he say how he was going to do this? Or, afterward, did you hear him say what he had done?"

A head shake, hard. "No! That was all I heard, just that. I didn't want to hear any more. I stopped what I was doing and left. I was . . . I was scared."

"No wonder," I said. "I would have been petrified. But afterward — after Karen was attacked — you guessed that he had done it, didn't you? You must have been afraid." Leading questions, yes. But then, I wasn't her defense attorney, and she wasn't on the stand.

"Oh, yes!" she cried. "Yes, yes! When I heard that Karen had been attacked in that parking lot, I knew that it had to have been Roberto. I was scared to death, but I couldn't let on that I knew anything. If I did, he might kill *me*. I told him that I needed to stop painting and take care of Paul. But he said he couldn't let me . . . let me quit." She pressed her fist against her mouth, trying to control the sobs that threatened to break out again.

"He offered you more money?"

She nodded tearfully. "He promised me more, a lot more, if I would keep on. And I need it! I have to have it for Paul. Dear, dear Paul." She sat up straight, suddenly remembering, and knuckled the tears from her eyes. "Paul! Oh, my gosh! I've left him alone too long, China. He's probably up from his nap by now. I locked the bedroom door, but —" She jumped up. "I need to go back to the house. If I'm gone too long, he could start another fire. He could —"

"One more thing," I persisted. "Are you willing to tell what you know to the police?" This was tricky for me. I couldn't represent her, but she needed a lawyer with her when she was answering questions. Maybe I could get the Whiz to —

"Yes," she said. "I'll tell. I . . . I have to do *something.* I can't live with this any longer."

"Okay, then," I said comfortingly. "You go, Irene. Do what you need to do for Paul. I'll take care of the rest." I went to the easel and took down the painting. If I left it there, she might decide to destroy it, and it was essential evidence. "I'm taking this with me," I added, "for safekeeping. I'll be in touch, very soon, so we can do whatever it takes to get this straightened out."

She wiped her nose with the back of her hand. "You're . . . willing to help me?"

"Yes," I said. "As long as you'll help the police."

And that's when we heard the first fire siren.

Within five minutes, there were two Pecan Springs fire trucks and a half-dozen firefighters on the scene, hauling hoses around the back of the house. The kitchen was in flames and there was plenty of greasy black smoke, but it didn't look as if the fire had spread very far. The neighbors were gathering out front, watching sympathetically. Irene was hysterical, crying out for Paul. But a few moments later, she found him standing under a tree in the backyard, his face streaked with soot and tears.

"I didn't mean to do it, Irene," he said sheepishly. "I was making supper to surprise you, and I didn't know the grease would —" He began to cry.

"Hush, dear," she said in a comforting, motherly tone. "It's all right, really it is." She put her arm around him and led him toward the backyard swing.

"You weren't there, so I called 9-1-1," Paul said, sounding like a little child. "Did I do the right thing?"

"You did exactly the right thing," Irene said. "I'm proud of you. And just look, Paul — the firemen are taking care of everything. They've already got the fire put out. And the insurance will cover the damage."

"It will?" Paul brightened. "You mean, it's not going to cost any money?" He became crestfallen. "I don't think we have any money, Irene. I lost it all in that stock deal. It's all gone."

"Not to worry, dear," Irene said and held him close to her. "As long as we have each other, we'll be fine." She turned to look at me. "We'll be fine," she repeated consolingly, but I heard the uncertainty in her voice.

"You might not be able to sleep here tonight," I said. "Why don't you give me your cell number, so I'll know where you are."

I was jotting down the number when a heavyset woman came over to us. "Irene," she said, "Jerry and I have a guest room, and we're right across the street. Why don't you and Paul come and stay with us until you get the damage cleaned up? That way, you'll be close to home and everything you need."

"Oh, thank you, Dolores!" Irene exclaimed gratefully. "I don't want to impose, but that would be wonderful."

"You won't be imposing. And Jerry will be good company for Paul while you do what you have to do about repairs." She nodded at me and turned to leave. "Just come when you can."

"Neighbors," Irene said, shaking her head. "They're wonderful."

I nodded. "I'll call you as soon as I've figured out what's next," I said. There was nothing more I could do right now. I left her and Paul on the swing, their arms around each other.

Back in the car, I made a call to Justine, catching her as she was finishing up her work for the day.

"Let's make it snappy, Hot Shot," she

said. "I'm about ready to head home for a nice, long soak in a hot bath and a slug or two of bourbon to take the edge off, before I do something about supper." Justine may be a whiz before the bench, but cooking is not on her list of lifetime achievements. Put her in front of a stove and she's clueless.

"I thought maybe I could lure you up to Pecan Springs for supper," I said. The family was already managing without me.

There was a brief hesitation, and I knew I had her. The Whiz hates to go home to an empty apartment. She hates eating her own cooking even worse. "Got a good restaurant up there?" she asked. "How about that cowboy place?"

"Beans' Bar and Grill," I said. "I'll treat you to one of Bob Godwin's chicken-fried steaks."

Bob's chicken-fried is famous across the Hill Country, smothered in cream gravy, with French fries, fried onion rings, and Texas toast on the side. Down-home comfort food, loaded with carbs, fat, and salt, swaddled in country music, and basted with the unforgettable eau de Beans' blend of mesquite-stoked barbecue fire, tobacco smoke, and beer.

"Chicken-fried," she mused. I could see

her frowning. "What's the catch?" she asked warily.

"A consultation," I said. "With a potential client." Under the circumstances, we might have to hold the consultation in my car, parked in Dolores and Jerry's driveway.

"What client?" She was suspicious. "It's not Sally again, I hope."

"Nuh-uh. Remember that artist we were talking about? The one whose name you got from your informant there in San Antonio?"

"The art forger?"

"That client."

"Aha! You've been working the case, Hot Shot." This was said triumphantly. Justine likes it when she thinks I'm throwing my lawyer's hat back in the ring.

"A little," I acknowledged. "Come on up and I'll tell you about it. If you enjoy stories about art fraud, conspiracy, and murder, this will light your fire." When I'm talking to the Whiz, I tend to adopt her vocabulary, which is not necessarily a good thing.

"Murder, huh? I get Beans' chicken-fried, along with the art fraud and murder?"

"And conspiracy. And then you can meet the client and hear her side of it."

"Has she talked to the police?"

"The police don't know anything about her." Yet. Sheila was next on my to-do list.

"But of course, she needs a smart lawyer with her when she's prepped and ready to talk." I paused. "Of course, if you're too busy, there's always Charlie Lipman —"

"Ha!" The Whiz snorted derisively. "That hick."

"Excellent," I said. "How soon can you get here?"

"Maybe an hour, hour and twenty," the Whiz said. "I've got a couple of things to wrap up here first."

"See you at Beans' in an hour and twenty," I said and flipped the phone closed. It was time to talk to Sheila.

Blackie's big gray Dodge pickup was parked behind the chief's black Chevy Impala in the driveway of their two-story frame house on Hickory. I parked at the curb, tucked Irene's painting under my arm, and went up the walk to knock on the front door. Blackie opened it, his car keys in his hand.

"Hey, China," he said. "I guess you got the word, huh?"

Ex-sheriff Blackie Blackwell is proof of the old adage that you can take the guy out of the force, but you can't take the force out of the guy. He's quintessentially cop and as square as they come — square shoulders, square chin, square jaw. He's let his sandy hair grow a little longer now that he's out of uniform and he's working on a beard and a mustache. But when I see him, I almost expect us to snap our heels and trade salutes.

"Ruby told me," I said. "I'm sorry, Blackie. Very sorry."

"I know." His face softened. "But we can make another baby. Sheila's okay, and that's the most important thing."

"Where is she?" I asked. "I need to talk to her — tonight, I'm afraid. It's a police matter."

Blackie frowned at me. "She's upstairs in bed, asleep. Are you sure it can't wait until tomorrow?"

"I'm awake," came a voice down the stairs. A strong, clear voice. An impatient voice. "Is that China? Tell her to come on up."

Blackie and I looked at each other and shook our heads. He grinned helplessly and shrugged.

"You can't keep a good woman down," I said and headed for the stairs, carrying the painting.

Blackie raised his voice. "She's on her way, Sheila. And I'm headed out for the pizza. If you think of anything else you want while I'm gone, phone me." He whistled and a burly Rottweiler with a wolfish grin skidded out of the kitchen. "Rambo, you want to go for a ride?"

Rambo and I are old friends. I paused to give him a hug and he gave me a slurpy kiss in return. A PSPD K-9 officer, he works the day shift sniffing for drugs — nights, too, when he's called out. He added another slurp, this one to my nose, then went barreling after Blackie. Rambo sees it as his sacred duty to ride shotgun every time one of his people gets into a vehicle. And when Rambo decides to take on an assignment, it's not wise to interfere. Stubborn is his middle name.

Sheila was lying against the pillows with her iPad on her lap, wearing a sexy red nightgown, her blond hair hanging loose around her shoulders. Her knees were bent and propped up with pillows. The bedroom television set was tuned to the *PBS News-Hour.* She flicked the remote to turn it off and Gwen Ifill disappeared. On the table beside the bed was a crystal vase filled with perky daisies and a glass of water, a flexible straw stuck in it.

"So this is what an off-duty police chief looks like." I propped the painting against the wall and pulled up a chair beside the bed. "How are you feeling, Smart Cookie?"

She made a face. "Like somebody's been

digging around in my belly with a blunt instrument. Sore. Bloated, too. But the doc tells me I can go back to the office in three or four days, as long as I promise not to chase any crooks." She gestured toward her laptop, on a desk on the other side of the room, beside a carton of papers and files. "Connie brought me some of the paperwork from my in-box." Connie Paige is Sheila's assistant.

"Yikes," I said. "That looks like a month's supply."

"One day," Sheila said with a groan. "Just one friggin' day. The paperwork in this job is a killer."

I cleared my throat. "I'm sorry, Sheila," I said quietly. "About the baby. I know how excited you were."

"Yeah." She sighed. "We're sorry, too. We would have done whatever we could to keep this from happening, but we couldn't." She gave a little shrug. "Anyway, it'll give me a chance to get the department's pregnancy policy in shape. I'm making that a high priority."

"Pretty daisies," I said, glancing at the vase. "From Blackie?"

"From Ruby. She picked them in her garden." She squinted at the painting. "I don't mean to look a gift horse in the mouth, China, but if that's for me, I'm afraid it doesn't fit my décor. I don't think Blackie would be crazy about it, either."

"Would it change your mind," I said, "if I told you that the last time Sotheby's sold a painting with this signature on it, it went for a million six?"

"You're kidding," she said incredulously. "A million six?" She looked at me, frowning. "You're not kidding."

"I'm not kidding," I said. "A million six is a pretty hefty motive for a murder, don't you think? Two murders, even."

It took almost a half hour to tell the whole story, start to finish. I omitted the part about Ruby's not being able to see the painting. Sheila is one of Ruby's dearest friends, but she's even more skeptical of her psychic abilities than I am.

When I got to the end of the tale, Sheila simply shook her head. "So what you're telling me is that this art dealer from San Antonio murdered Christine Morris, then looted her art collection by selling the real paintings and substituting forgeries."

"Something like that," I said. "Although he may have been selling forgeries as well. The artist — Irene Cameron — should be able to tell you how many paintings she produced for him and what the subjects were. She might be of help in tracking them down." I doubted that the Pecan Springs Police Department had the resources for an art fraud investigation, though. They'd probably have to use the feds for that. "And you'll want to take a look at the transcript of the hearing that excluded the alternative suspect," I added. "Johnnie Carlson, Bowen's defense lawyer, had testimony that put Soto on the scene on the night of the murder and information that disputed Soto's alibi. I can get you a copy of his notes on that. But unless there's some forensic evidence that isn't referenced in the case files, there's not going to be enough to take Soto to trial on that one. In my opinion," I added. "You might think differently, once you get into the investigation."

Sheila nodded. "What about Tillotson? Was she involved in the Morris murder? Or the forgery scheme?"

"She's certainly in a position to have known about the murder," I said, "and to have had a hand in it, as well. What's more, she has profited handsomely. She's living in the house, she's managing the collection, and she appears to be sleeping with her cousin's lover."

"Hang on a minute." Sheila started to reach down to adjust the pillows under her knees, then winced.

"Want me to do that?" I got up and pushed the pillows around until Sheila said, "That's good, thanks." I sat back down again. "In my opinion," I added, "if Tillotson doesn't know what's been going on, she must be blind as a bat in a blizzard."

"Okay, murder number two." Sheila frowned. "You think Soto killed Karen Prior when she began to suspect that the paintings in the collection weren't the real thing. Is that it?"

"Yeah. Karen had done a documentary on art fraud, which might have alerted her to what was going on — and then she saw the painting in the Sotheby's auction catalog and the same, or a similar painting in the Morris collection. Irene Cameron can testify to the exchange she heard — Soto telling Tillotson that he thought he might have to kill Karen to keep her quiet. With a little luck, you can use Irene Cameron to get to Tillotson and Tillotson to get to Soto." It's the standard strategy that DAs use in conspiracy cases. On the basis of Cameron's information, Tillotson could be charged as a coconspirator, then offered a plea in return for testimony against Soto. She might be in love with the guy, but she'd struck me as a practical woman. She would no doubt rat him out in return for a lighter sentence.

"You make it sound so easy." Grimacing, Sheila moved her hips, shifting her position. "We might win a few more convictions, Counselor, if you would stop fooling around with that shop of yours and come to work in the DA's office."

"Not on your life," I said fervently. "And I didn't mean to make it sound easy. It would be more of a sure thing if there were some way to link Soto to the attack on Karen."

"There just might be," Sheila said.

I raised both eyebrows. "Oh, yeah?"

"There's a partial palm print on the top of Prior's car, on the driver's side, and a partial thumbprint on the driver's-side door. It doesn't belong to the victim or to her daughter. Now that we have a suspect —"

"Great!" I said. "After you've talked to Irene Cameron, you'll have enough to pick him up and get his prints. Let's hope for a match."

"Let's hope." Sheila shifted again. "I hate to ask you, but would you mind helping me get to the bathroom? I have to pee and I'm not sure I trust myself to get there under my own steam."

"What? Superwoman can't pee by herself?" I grinned down at her sheer red nightie. "I see the problem, girl. You've traded your cape and tights for a Victoria's Secret. How do you expect to save a dying universe dressed like Barbie?"

Sheila gritted her teeth. "You wait until you're in this situation, China Bayles," she growled. "Just see if I come and help you."

"I'm helping, I'm helping," I protested and pulled the coverlet back. "Come on, sweetie, swing your legs over the edge of the bed."

I put an arm around her and she pushed herself off the bed slowly, with a low moan. "And they call this 'Band-Aid surgery,'" she muttered, leaning dizzily on my arm as we made our way slowly to the bathroom. "Hurts like hell."

"Must've been a guy who invented that term," I said sympathetically.

She made a low sound. "If it hurts like this *not* to have a baby, I wonder how it feels to have one."

"One little challenge at a time," I said. "First, we pee. Later, babies."

In the bathroom, she sat down on the toilet. "I have to but I can't," she said after a minute, screwing up her face.

"Warm water." I filled a glass at the tap and handed it to her. "Try this. Works every time."

She poured, then gave a sigh of relief. "Yes. Oh, yes," she said happily, handing me the glass. "Oh, *yes.*"

I began to laugh. "If the guys at the station house could see you now, Smart Cookie, they would pee *their* pants."

She giggled, laughed, then gasped. "Oh, stop, China," she moaned. "I can't laugh! It hurts!"

Back in bed again, she lay down and let me adjust the pillows under her knees. "Want some water?" I asked and got a fresh glass from the bathroom for her.

Sipping through the straw, she said, "That letter from Richard Bowen. It sounds as if there was no suicide. Douglas Clark killed him — or had him killed."

"That's where I'd put my money," I said and sat down again. "But we'll have to wait for Houston Homicide to take a look at that letter and move to reopen the case. Which they probably won't do unless their initial investigation turned up some forensic evidence. Fingerprints, hair, DNA, fiber — something that would tie Clark to the scene, once they can attempt to get matches." I glanced at the clock on the bedside table and saw what time it was. "One more thing, Sheila, friend to friend. Justine Wyzinski is interviewing Irene Cameron tonight. I think she'll take her on as a client."

Sheila wrinkled her nose. She's encountered Justine before. "You couldn't get Cameron a date with the local talent?"

I laughed. "Justine has had dealings with Soto and is aware of the art fraud background in this case. She'll be up to speed before Charlie can find a clean white shirt."

"Speed is Wyzinski's middle name," Sheila said dryly.

"Actually, it's the Whiz," I said. "Same idea. Of course, it depends on how Justine sees the situation. But I'm hoping she'll bring Irene to the station tomorrow, as a cooperating witness. It would be good if someone there was prepared to talk to her. I'll be glad to brief him — or her — on what I know."

"Jack Bartlett," Sheila said. "I'll talk to him first thing in the morning. You can be reached?"

I know and like Bartlett, who is head of the detective unit. "Have Jack try my cell. I'll be at the shop." I stood up, then bent over and kissed Sheila lightly on top of her head. "I'm sorry about the baby," I said again, "but glad you're okay."

"I'll be a lot better," she said, "once we get this investigation cooking." She reached for her cell phone on the bedside table. "I'll call Jack right now. Let him know what's going on, what to expect."

"Like I said," I replied with a grin, "you can't keep a good woman down. Even if she can't pee by herself."

The door banged downstairs and I heard the clickety-clatter of Rottie toenails on the bare wood of the stairs.

"Woof!" Rambo announced joyfully. He trotted to the bed, put his stubby muzzle on the covers, and regarded Sheila with concern. *"Woof?"* he inquired.

"I'm home," Blackie yelled. "Anybody up there want pizza?"

"Woof-woof!" Rambo said.

CHAPTER FOURTEEN

If you've found a four-leaved clover, you're in luck, for these are scarce. It has been estimated that there is just one four-leaved clover for every 10,000 three-leaved clovers (*Trifolium*). According to traditional lore, a four-leaved clover brings good luck, especially if you find it accidentally. According to legend, each leaf represents an important quality, something we all need in our lives. The first is for faith, the second is for hope, the third is for love, and the fourth is for good luck. And if you find a five-leaved clover? Bushels of good luck!

China Bayles
"Herbs of Good and Ill Omen"
Pecan Springs Enterprise

"I can't believe it," McQuaid said as we stood on the front porch, our arms around each other, watching as Brian's old green Ford disappeared around a curve in the lane. "I just flat can't believe it."

A couple of days before, we had moved Brian into his room at one of the off-campus co-op houses west of the university. McQuaid had wanted him to stay in Jester, the coed residence hall in the center of campus. But I sided with Brian. He was mature enough to handle the independence. He would learn more life lessons in co-op housing, I thought, where the students had responsibility for governing the house. With luck, he might even learn to do his own laundry.

"I believe it," I said softly. "It's what we've raised him for. His own life in a new world, to prove to himself who he is and what he can be." I took a deep breath, thinking of the years that the boy and his father had been at the center of my life. "He doesn't have to prove anything to us, though," I added. "For us, he will always be just . . . Brian. Our Brian."

McQuaid shook his head. "Well, I wish him luck. And he's going to need it. The world is a different place than it was when I left for college. He won't be able to coast, the way I did my first couple of years. He'll have to be smarter, work harder, do more. *And* get lucky."

I couldn't disagree with that. That's why,

as a little going-away present, I gave him a four-leaved clover I had found in the yard, encased in a medallion for his key chain. That way, I told him, he'd always have a little luck on his side, and a small, green reminder of home.

When we went back inside, the house felt empty — especially since Caitlin was spending the weekend, the last of the summer, with my mother and her husband, Sam, at their ranch near Kerrville.

"Maybe it's time we got another dog," McQuaid said. He looked at me with an amused glint in his eye. "Unless you're sure you don't want a baby?"

"I am positive," I said firmly. "If you want to hear the patter of little feet around the house, we can borrow Baby Grace." I reached for his hand. "It's time for lunch. Come in the kitchen and I'll fix you an egg sandwich."

Caitlin's new rooster, a handsome red-feathered fellow with an iridescent ruff and a sweep of colorful tail, had arrived a few weeks before to take charge of his six-hen harem. We had a family discussion about his name. After much deliberation, Caitie rejected my Corn Colonel, McQuaid's Big Red, and Brian's Crockpot. She decided, instead, on Rooster Boy. Clearly delighted to have his very own hens, Rooster Boy is doing his lusty best to ensure that his girls are laying fertile eggs, and Caitie is hoping that one of the hens might demonstrate a maternal instinct. But so far, in spite of Rooster Boy's solicitous and persistent attentions, none have shown any sign of "going broody."

This desirable state of affairs, as Caitie solemnly explained to me, is when a lady chicken decides she wants to be a mother. "When she's broody, she'll cluck and fluff out her feathers and won't get off her eggs until they've hatched."

"And this takes how many days?" I asked. "Hatching, I mean."

"Twenty-one," she said confidently. "Three whole weeks."

"*That,*" I remarked, "is dedication." I frowned. "Twenty-one days? How do you know? You're not a chicken." I peered at her. "You're not a chicken, are you?"

She giggled and said she'd been doing research on the Internet. Ah, life lessons, learned in cyberspace.

In the kitchen, I got out the small skillet. "An egg sandwich?" McQuaid was querulous. "But we had an omelet for breakfast."

"We have *lots* of eggs," I reminded him. "How about if I add a few slices of avocado and onion and some alfalfa sprouts?" I keep a quart jar of alfalfa sprouts growing on the sunny kitchen windowsill, so they're always available for sandwiches.

"That's more like it," he said, making a detour into his study. "While you're at it, you can pile on a couple of slices of Swiss. And maybe a slice of ham." At the doorway, he turned. "Did I hear somebody say something about going out for supper with Sheila and Blackie tonight?"

"Yes, you heard somebody say something," I said. "Somebody said Beans'. Six-ish."

"Works for me," he said and disappeared.

I was getting the makings out of the refrigerator when my cell phone rang. "Yo, China," Aaron said. "You got a minute?"

"Anything for you," I replied. "How's Paula?"

"Not so good. Morning sickness."

Same song, I thought, second verse. "Tell her to try ginger tea." I took out a couple of Caitlin's eggs. "And peppermint. I'll email you a link and you can forward it to her."

He was wary. "She doesn't do folk remedies. I think her doctor's prescribing something."

"Whatever." I closed the fridge. "So what's up?"

"The homicide investigator just called with an update. He's got a warrant for Douglas Clark's arrest for the murder of Richard Bowen. They're expecting to pick him up today."

"Ah," I said, with great satisfaction. I put the skillet on the stove. "They got a DNA match, then."

As I'd learned when the lead Houston homicide detective interviewed me, Richard Bowen had not gone gently into that good night. On his way out of this world, he had managed to scratch his killer, catching DNA under one fingernail on his right hand. DNA, but no match — until Bowen's letter came to light and Douglas Clark suddenly became a person of interest. And then a suspect, on the basis of the documents in Bowen's Chase Bank safe-deposit box and Florabelle Gibson's statement, taken by the Houston detective. Now it was time for his arrest and arraignment. Sometimes these things work the way they're supposed to.

"Yeah," Aaron said. "Good thing you found that letter and read it. You get points for solving a cold case, Counselor."

"Points?" I asked, turning on the burner under the skillet and plopping in a scoop of butter. "No reward?"

"Virtue is its own reward," Aaron said piously.

"Not so much," I replied. "In this dog-eat-dog world, reward is its own virtue. Listen, I'm making an egg sandwich for McQuaid, and I can't fry an egg and talk on the phone to you at the same time."

"Paula has never made me an egg sandwich," Aaron said, aggrieved. "In fact, I wanted an egg for breakfast this morning and we didn't have any."

"That's because you don't have Rooster Boy and his six-hen harem," I said.

He sighed. "I don't think so. I think it's because Paula doesn't like to cook." Another sigh. "Don't forget that rain check, China."

"I won't," I said. But I thought I probably would.

I broke the egg into the skillet. It had two yolks. Hadn't I read somewhere that two yolks was good luck — maybe a financial windfall or a wedding in the family? The first I could handle. The second, not so much. At least, not yet.

Beans' Bar and Grill is located in a stone building between Purley's Tire Company and the Missouri Pacific Railroad, across the street from the old firehouse, which was recently converted into a dance hall. It's a down-home Texas eating and drinking hangout with a pool hall in the back, so the general conversation is frequently punctuated by the sharp crack of a cue and a jubilant "Boy, howdy! Looka that — right in the ol' pocket!" There's a mirrored wooden bar down one side for serious drinkers, of whom there are always several. The diners occupy unmatched kitchen chairs around scarred wooden tables. Wagon wheels wound with rusty barbed wire threaded with lights shaped like red and green jalapeño peppers hang like chandeliers from the ceiling, and a cigar-store Indian stands in the corner with a politically correct sign in one hand, requesting that people refer to him as a Native American. The restroom doors are labeled *Bulls* and *Heifers,* and favorites on the jukebox (judging by the number of times you'll hear them during the evening) are Willie's "Always on My Mind" and Dolly's "Here You Come Again." Down-home to the max.

When we were seated at our favorite back-corner table, Bob Godwin hustled up with two red plastic baskets of warm tortilla chips, a couple of crockery cups of hair-raising salsa, a pitcher of icy draft beer, and four mugs. Bob has tattoos on both muscular arms, thinning auburn hair, and fuzzy ginger eyebrows that meet in the middle. A proud vet, he was wearing a black T-shirt with a skull and crossbones over the words *Recon Marines*. His golden retriever, Budweiser (Bud, for short), came to the table with him to say hello. Bud wears a leather saddlebag and totes beer bottles and wrapped snacks from the bar to the tables, and cash and tips from the tables to the bar. He gets a pat from everybody, but there's a hand-lettered sign around his neck that says, *Don't feed me!* People were being too generous with their French fries and fried onions.

Bob posts the menu on the chalkboard behind the bar, under a hand-lettered sign that says, *7-Course Texas Dinner: A Six-Pack & a Possum.* I had treated the Whiz to a chicken-fried steak several weeks before, but tonight all four of us agreed on the house special, the Way Too Much Plate: a beef enchilada, two chicken flautas, a pork fajita taco, chile con queso, guacamole, rice, and refried beans.

"I've got news," Sheila said to me, propping her elbows on the table. She was in civvies tonight, a red plaid cotton shirt, jeans, and red boots, with her ash-blond hair in a single braid down her back. She was beautiful, even if she was no longer pregnant.

"Me, too," I said. "News, I mean."

"Why don't you two arm wrestle to see who goes first," McQuaid suggested. "Now, that would be something to see."

"Spin a fork," Blackie said, and he did it. "China, you won. Go."

I related the details of Aaron's phone call, although not the part about the egg sandwich.

Blackie sat back in his chair and whistled. "Doug Clark arrested for the murder of Dick Bowen? That'll make headlines in the *Enterprise*."

"I hope they can make it stick," McQuaid said. "He's a slick customer." Charlie Lipman had dropped his investigation into Clark's hidden assets shenanigans. I hadn't been surprised. Charlie is tight with his money, and on this case, he'd been his own client.

"DNA is pretty sticky," Sheila remarked. "Sounds like a solid case." She grinned at me. "My news is along the same lines. We arrested Roberto Soto this morning, China, at his gallery in San Antonio. He's been charged with the murder of Karen Prior. The feds are still working on the art fraud case. There'll be charges on that, as well — eventually."

"So the palm print and the partial thumb-print matched," I said.

"Yep," Sheila replied with satisfaction. "And after consultations with her lawyer and the DA's office, Sharyn Tillotson saw the light. She's going to plead guilty to a lesser charge and has made a full statement incriminating Soto in Prior's murder and the art fraud scheme."

I suppose I should have been elated, but I wasn't. I was thinking of Felicity and Karen's mother. Knowing that an arrest had been made might make their loss a little easier to bear. But for the victims of crime, justice is a long, painful journey, full of starts, stops, and setbacks. Today's arrest was just the beginning. If the family was lucky, the case would go to trial next year. If they were lucky again and there was a conviction, the appeal could take another couple of years — and there could be more appeals after that. And none of that would bring Karen back. For her family and friends, there would be no end to the pain.

McQuaid hoisted his beer. "Here's to good, solid police work. Congratulations, Smart Cookie."

Sheila shrugged. "Well, maybe. But we wouldn't have gotten to Tillotson without Irene Cameron. Her statement was crucial.

It gave us the key to open the other doors." She reached for a tortilla chip and dipped it into the salsa. "Irene had the courage to tell the truth. I hope the deal works out for her."

Justine had already brought me up-to-date on that part of the case. After she and Irene Cameron sat down together and talked, Irene agreed to tell the full story of the art forgeries she had painted for Roberto Soto and to testify to the conversation she had overheard between Soto and Sharyn Tillotson. Her voluntary statement led to Tillotson's questioning and to *her* statement — and that led to Soto's arrest.

The feds were involved in the art fraud part of the case, so the process would likely go on for some time. But Justine thought that the prosecutor would recommend probation in return for Irene's continuing role as a cooperating witness. A deal isn't done until the judge signs off on it, however, and there's never any guarantee. As I said, sometimes these things work the way they're supposed to. But sometimes there's a catch. Sometimes —

McQuaid lifted his beer again, in a different salute. "Well, then, here's to justice," he said. "Long may it wave."

Sitting next to him, Blackie hoisted his. "Or words to that effect."

Sheila frowned. "Remember what Margaret Atwood said about justice?" she said.

"No, what?" Blackie asked.

"Who's Margaret Atwood?" McQuaid wanted to know.

"Famous Canadian author and activist," Sheila replied. "She's quoted as saying, 'Never pray for justice, because you might get some.' "

"True words," McQuaid said approvingly. "Here's to not getting everything we deserve." The three of them clinked their mugs and drank.

But not me. "Wait just a darn minute," I said. "Speaking of justice, what about Christine Morris' murder? What's going to happen with that?"

Sheila lifted her shoulders and dropped them. "We have testimony that puts Soto at the scene the night of the murder, but that's the best we've got — so far, anyway. The original police work —"

"The original police work sucks," Blackie said succinctly. "If that had been my case, Bowen would never have been charged."

"That was Barry Rogers' fault," McQuaid said, leaning toward Blackie. "Did I tell you why I fired that son of a buck? He —" The two of them put their heads together and began to talk.

Sheila and I exchanged glances. "Well, you can't win 'em all, Counselor," she said.

"I learned that a long time ago," I said. "And if we're still talking about justice, I read that Orson Welles said something once that makes a lot of sense to me."

Bob Godwin came up to the table with two big plates and put them down in front of Sheila and me. "Ladies first," he said. "But those are hot. Don't touch, or you'll burn your fingers. Gents, I'll be back with yours in a minute." McQuaid and Blackie were so deep in conversation that they didn't hear him.

Sheila picked up her fork. "Orson Welles?" she asked with a frown.

"Yeah. Famous movie director."

"And what did he say?"

I picked up my fork. " 'Nobody gets justice,' is how I remember it. 'People only get good luck or bad luck.' "

RECIPES

CHINA'S PURSLANE AND SPINACH SALAD WITH BALSAMIC VINAIGRETTE

Malabar spinach (*Basella alba*) is a climbing vine that thrives in hot weather, long after spinach has bolted. It is high in vitamin A, vitamin C, iron, and calcium, and may be eaten raw or cooked. However, it is mucilaginous, so if you don't like that texture, use spinach instead. You can always plant it just to enjoy: it's an energetic vine with pretty red stems, white flowers, and red berries.

1/2 cup chopped purslane, thick stems removed

2 cups fresh spinach or Malabar spinach, torn into bite-size pieces

2 cucumbers, peeled, quartered lengthwise, seeded, and chopped

6 cherry tomatoes, halved

2 green onions, both green and white parts, chopped

Combine all ingredients in a large bowl. Serve with Balsamic Vinaigrette. Serves four.

Balsamic Vinaigrette
3/4 cup extra-virgin olive oil
2 tablespoons balsamic vinegar
2 tablespoons red wine vinegar
1/4 teaspoon Dijon mustard
1 teaspoon minced fresh herbs (e.g., parsley, chives, tarragon)
Salt and pepper to taste

CASS' SHRIMP, PASTA, AND ROSE PETALS

Use only unsprayed roses from a home garden (florist roses have likely been sprayed). Fragrant roses have the best flavor. Snip the bitter white heel from each petal.

1 package capellini (angel-hair) pasta (12–14 ounces)
1 tablespoon extra-virgin olive oil
2 cloves garlic, finely chopped
1/4 red or orange bell pepper, diced
1 green onion top, chopped

16 ounces medium raw shrimp, peeled and deveined

1/2 cup dry white wine

2 tablespoons unsalted butter

3 tablespoons grated Parmesan cheese

Salt to taste

1/2 to 3/4 cup red or orange rose petals, divided in half

Garnish (optional): tiny bouquet of rosemary, parsley, and a single pink rosebud

Cook pasta according to package directions. Drain, reserving 1/2 cup of cooking liquid.

While the pasta cooks, heat oil in a large skillet over medium heat. Sauté garlic, red bell pepper, and green onion top just until soft and fragrant (a minute or so). Add shrimp and wine and lower heat. Simmer until the shrimp begins to turn pink, about 3–4 minutes. Stir in butter and Parmesan. If the sauce seems too thick, add some of the reserved pasta cooking liquid, a tablespoon at a time.

Toss pasta in the skillet with the shrimp and sauce. Add half of the rose petals and toss lightly. Distribute onto four plates and sprinkle the rest of the petals over each portion. Serves four. Garnish the plates, if desired.

CASS' ROSE PETAL SALAD

Endive (*Cichorium endivia*) is a flavorful leaf vegetable in the daisy family, related to chicory. To prepare Belgian endive, slice off about one-eighth inch from the stem end. With a paring knife, cut out a cone shape about one-half inch deep from the same end, to remove the slightly bitter core. Separate into leaves. To prepare rose petals, see the recipe for Cass' Shrimp, Pasta, and Rose Petals, above.

Leaves of 2 small Belgian endives
Leaves of 1 small head of Boston lettuce, washed, patted dry, and torn into bite-size pieces
1/4 cup slivered almonds
3/4–1 cup prepared rose petals
1/4 cup extra-virgin olive oil
6 tablespoons raspberry vinegar
1 teaspoon finely minced rosemary
1/8 teaspoon ground cardamom
Salt to taste

Arrange the endive leaves on four salad plates, and add the torn lettuce. Top with almonds and rose petals.

In a small bowl, whisk the olive oil, vinegar, rosemary, and cardamom. Add salt to taste. Drizzle over salads and serve immediately.

CASS' CHILLED ROSE AND STRAWBERRY SOUP

A perfectly delicious dessert soup with the delicate fragrance of roses. To prepare rose petals, see the recipe for Cass' Shrimp, Pasta, and Rose Petals, above.

2 pints fresh or frozen (slightly thawed) strawberries
1 cup prepared rose petals
1 teaspoon rose water
1 teaspoon vanilla extract
2 cups plain yogurt
1/2 cup orange juice
1/2 cup sugar
1/8 teaspoon ground cardamom
Whole fresh strawberries and sprigs of mint for garnish

In a blender, combine all ingredients. Chill. Pour into dessert cups or bowls, garnish with strawberries and mint.

MUHALLABIYEH

Muhallabiyeh is a refreshing Middle Eastern dessert, delightfully creamy, slightly surprising. It is usually made with ground rice;

you can substitute a cream of rice cereal, which is easily available.

4 cups milk
4 heaping tablespoons cream of rice cereal
3/4 cup granulated sugar
1 teaspoon orange blossom water
1 teaspoon rose water
1/3 cup blanched slivered almonds
4–6 mint sprigs for garnish

Combine milk and cereal in a saucepan over high heat. Stirring constantly, bring to a boil. Reduce heat to low and add sugar. Continue stirring until the mixture thickens, about 7 minutes. Add orange blossom and rose water. Simmer, continuing to stir, for 2 more minutes. Remove from heat. Pour into four to six dessert cups. Cool and garnish with almonds and a sprig of mint. Chill.

ROSE PETAL SANDWICHES
Pretty tea sandwiches. To prepare rose petals, see the recipe for Cass' Shrimp, Pasta, and Rose Petals, above.

4 ounces cream cheese
1 tablespoon rose water
1 1/2 cups prepared rose petals, divided in half

Salt to taste
8 thinly cut slices of bread, crusts removed

In a small bowl, combine cream cheese, rose water, and half of the rose petals. Add salt to taste. Cover and chill overnight.

Bring cheese mixture to room temperature. Spread on 4 slices of bread and layer on remaining rose petals. Place second slice of bread on top of each and cut into quarters diagonally. Makes sixteen small sandwiches.

ROSEMARY AND THYME BREAD STICKS

You can substitute your own favorite savory herb blend for the rosemary and thyme. Basil and chives are nice, or sage and savory. Experiment — and enjoy.

2 1/2 teaspoons active dry yeast
3 tablespoons brown sugar
1 cup warm water
1 teaspoon salt
1/4 cup vegetable oil
3 cups bread flour
2 tablespoons butter
1 tablespoon extra-virgin olive oil
3 tablespoons Parmesan cheese
1/2 teaspoon salt

2 teaspoons garlic powder

1/2 teaspoon onion powder

1 teaspoon finely chopped fresh rosemary (1/2 teaspoon, if you're using dry)

1 teaspoon finely chopped fresh thyme (1/2 teaspoon, if you're using dry)

To make the dough, stir yeast and brown sugar together in a large mixing bowl, then add warm water and allow to sit until foamy on top (about 5 minutes). Add the 1 tea-spoonful of salt, the oil, and the flour, mixing vigorously. Knead until dough is smooth and elastic, about 5 minutes. On a floured surface, roll dough into a 10-by-15-inch rectangle.

Melt butter in the microwave or in a small pan over low heat. Stir in olive oil and brush evenly over dough. Mix Parmesan, 1/2 teaspoon salt, garlic powder, onion powder, and herbs and distribute evenly over dough.

Spray a 9-by-13-inch baking dish with nonstick spray. With the long side toward you, fold the rectangle of dough in half lengthwise. Cut into 12 even strips, lengthwise. Remove one, stretch it gently, twist three times, and place in the baking dish. Repeat with remaining 11 strips. Cover with damp towel and let rise for 20–30 minutes.

Preheat oven to 375 degrees F. Bake until golden brown, 10–15 minutes.

McQuaid's Secret Barbecue Sauce

2 cups ketchup
1 can beer or dark ale
1/2 cup apple cider vinegar
1/4 cup molasses
2 teaspoons cayenne (more, if you can get away with it)
1/2 tablespoon freshly ground black pepper
1/2 tablespoon onion powder
1/2 tablespoon garlic powder
1/2 tablespoon ground mustard
2 tablespoons Worcestershire sauce
1 tablespoon lemon juice

In a medium saucepan, combine all ingredients. Bring mixture to a boil, reduce heat to simmer. Cook uncovered, stirring frequently, for 1 hour 20 minutes.

China's Ginger Syrup

1 1/2 cups sugar
1 1/2 cups water
4 tablespoons peeled and chopped fresh ginger (about 2 ounces)
2 teaspoons finely grated lemon peel

Combine all ingredients in a small saucepan; stir over medium heat until sugar dissolves. Boil until reduced to about 1 1/2 cups, about 5 minutes. Store unused portion in refrigerator for up to two weeks.

CHINA'S TACO CASSEROLE

4 or 5 crumbled taco shells or corn chips
1 1/2 pounds ground beef
1 medium onion, finely chopped
1 tablespoon chili powder
1 teaspoon ground cumin
1 teaspoon garlic powder
1 4-ounce can chopped green chilies
1 cup milk
2 eggs
1/2 cup baking mix
1 cup shredded cheddar cheese
2 large tomatoes, chopped, divided in half
Shredded lettuce
Sour cream
Salsa

Preheat oven to 400 degrees F. Coat an 8-by-12-inch casserole dish with nonstick spray.

Spread crumbled taco shells in dish. Crumble beef and brown it with the onion in a large frying pan. Drain. Stir in the chili powder, cumin, and garlic powder. Evenly spread seasoned meat on top of the taco shells in dish and top with the green chilies.

Beat milk, eggs, and baking mix until smooth. Pour evenly over the meat. Bake for 25 minutes.

If serving immediately, top with cheese and half of the chopped tomatoes. Bake another 8–10 minutes, until firm in the center.

If freezing, cool and wrap (without tomatoes and cheese). To serve, thaw and reheat in 400-degree oven for about 15 minutes. Add cheese and half of the chopped tomatoes and bake 8–10 minutes.

To serve, garnish with remaining chopped tomatoes, lettuce, sour cream, and salsa. Serves six to eight.

ABOUT THE AUTHOR

Susan Wittig Albert is the author of *An Extraordinary Year of Ordinary Days*, released by the University of Texas Press, and *Together, Alone: A Memoir of Marriage and Place*. Her fiction, which has appeared on the *New York Times* bestseller list, includes mysteries in the China Bayles and Darling Dahlias series, the Cottage Tales of Beatrix Potter, and a series of Victorian–Edwardian mysteries she has written with her husband, Bill Albert, under the pseudonym of Robin Paige. Previous nonfiction includes *What Wildness is This: Women Write About the Southwest* (winner of the 2009 Willa Award for Creative Nonfiction); *With Courage and Common Sense*; *Writing from Life: Telling the Soul's Story*; and *Work of Her Own: A Woman's Guide to Success Off the Career Track*. She is founder and past president of the

Story Circle Network and a member of the Texas Institute of Letters.